Murder at Royal William Yard

By CHARLES BECKER

Murder at Royal William Yard

Published by Createspace Independent Publishing Platform, 2017.

ISBN-13: 978-1975738006
ISBN-10: 1975738004

Cover photographs: Jenny Strang.
Book design: Jim Bruce, www.ebooklover.co.uk

Contents

Dedication

For my sister, Vicky

He that has light within his own clear breast
May sit i' the centre and enjoy bright day,
But he that hides a dark soul and foul thoughts
Benighted walks under the mid-day sun;
Himself is his own dungeon.

(John Milton, *A Mask ls* 380-4)

Prologue
The Mongrel

My name is Lou, Lou Beradino. You could call me a mongrel, if you wanted. It wouldn't bother me. I like mongrels, prefer them to pedigrees. Fewer vets' bills to pay and smarter, too. Certainly, I don't get ill much and I put jigsaws together pretty well – human jigsaws, that is.

My grandfather, Fabio, was Italian and my grandmother, Maggie, was Irish. She was a lively woman with a wealth of rich coppery hair and a big smile. I take after Fabio, who was short, dark and well muscled. Not the body builder kind of muscles, all rippling definition, but cords of steel through his frame, particularly his upper body, his arms and chest, his hands. He was a carpenter and everyone called him 'Spoza', but I'll tell you about that later and maybe about how they met in a crowd in Liverpool at the opening of the Queensway Tunnel back in 1937.

My mother, Pru – her full name is Prudenza, but I never heard anyone call her that – was their only child. And I was conceived one summer's night in July 1968 at a music festival at Woburn, while Jimi Hendrix was also performing. When my mother woke up the next morning, my father, Louis Lanui, was gone. Louis was a French student she had met there.

She never stopped loving him, never stopped looking for him. She even took me to Arcachon, south of Bordeaux, when I was 10, to try to track him down. But that's another story I'll come back to, as well. I've certainly wondered about him a lot and maybe he's the reason I'm a detective with the Devon and Cornwall Constabulary here in Plymouth. I've inherited his name and, according to my mother, his love of surfing. There's a conversation I need to have with him and I don't think I'll feel at rest inside myself until I do.

Part One

Thursday 15th – Wednesday 21st January, 2015

Chapter 1
A cry for help

"H E'S going to kill me!" It was a woman's voice. *Foreign. Eastern European? Whispering. Frightened.*

Detective Sergeant Fran Bannerman was scribbling on her pad, as she listened to the recording of the 999 call.

"Who's going to kill you?"

Young. 18-25?

"Help me!" She wasn't whispering any more.

"Where are you?"

"Coaker, no!"

The line went dead.

* * * * *

Later that morning, Detective Inspector Louis Beradino stood looking out of the window of his second-floor office, from where he could see the midday traffic snarled up at Charles Cross roundabout, with the roofless ruin of the bombed-out church in its centre and the curious wafer-coloured frieze fanning out behind it, marking the southern end of the Drake Circus shopping mall. Within a five- to ten-minute stroll, he could be in the heart of the city, or down in the Barbican by the waterfront. He liked Plymouth; he liked living close to the sea better than being in landlocked Leicester, where he had spent most of his forty-five years.

"What do you make of it, Fran?" he asked, without turning.

"Not sure," she said, standing halfway in from the door, dressed in jeans and soft, black leather jacket. With her slim frame, short, dark hair and quick eyes, she carried with her an air of imminent action. "The woman, whoever she was,

was scared and trying to keep her voice down, but the call was untraceable." Fran glanced down at her notebook. "There are seven listed Coakers and one ex-directory. We've run a preliminary check on them all and there are only two likely leads: Dominic Coaker in St Budeaux, a self-employed builder with a record of domestic violence; and Eddie Coaker, a local fisherman. I caught Dominic at home, work's dried up apparently. He was surly, I'd call it, but not shifty."

"No prickles, then?"

Fran's 'prickles', a physical sensation she experienced sometimes along her arms when being lied to, was a secret between them.

She grinned. "No, no prickles. He said he'd been home all morning, fitting new kitchen units; and judging by the state of him and the kitchen, it looked like he had."

"Any witnesses?"

"Yes, his wife and a..."

"She might be intimidated by him," Lou interrupted her; "if he's been violent in the past?"

"Maybe; but I spoke to their neighbour, Jan Talbot, who said the banging and sawing had started soon after seven-thirty and had been going on ever since." Fran looked up from her notebook. "She sounded pretty fed-up."

"What about the other one?"

"Right. Eddie Coaker went out on the tide first thing this morning, two hours or so before the call. So, unless the young woman's on the boat with him, he can't be the Coaker we're looking for either."

"You've been busy," Lou said, turning round. He wasn't a tall man, five-foot eight or nine, but he moved with easy muscular co-ordination, comfortable in his own skin. He gestured towards the chair opposite and sat down behind the utilitarian, gun-metal desk. The surface was neatly organised and, as she sat down, Fran wondered what exactly he did do with his paperwork.

"Find out when he's due back," Lou said, "and what he's been up to for the past twenty-four hours."

She nodded. "According to Alan Mason, the manager at the fish market, Coaker's expected in again early this afternoon." She glanced down at her notebook. "Morning Star, his boat's called."

Lou gave a ghost of a smile. She was a step ahead. "Good," he said. "I've got a meeting with Fraud in Exeter before lunch, but I'll be back by four, so we can catch up then."

"Right," she said, standing up.

"And no young woman reported missing, I suppose?" he asked. She shook her head. "Not yet."

* * * * *

Due to a shortage of official cars, Lou had arranged to use his own blue VW Golf. As he followed the curving roll of the A38 through the Devonshire countryside, he tried to focus his thoughts on DI Bentley from the City of London Police. He'd never come across him before, but he'd sounded straightforward enough on the phone. The surprise was the subject of their proposed meeting, Councillor Ron Jellop. Jellop wasn't only a high-profile Plymouth City Councillor; he was also the owner of Jellop's Builders Merchants, started by his late father, John Jellop. There wasn't much major construction work or development in Plymouth that Jellop's wasn't involved in.

Bentley had given Lou the name and told him the French police were involved, but that was all. "Too many ears," he had said. "Let's keep this confidential." He was catching the fast train from Paddington and would be in Exeter just after midday. Lou had offered to pick him up at the station.

As he overtook a line of traffic losing speed on the hill near Buckfastleigh, a black Mercedes saloon coming up fast behind him flashed its headlights. He pulled over and it swept by, with a mud-spattered Ford Focus hot on its heels. "Leave it to Traffic," he told himself. It wasn't his business.

Every time he checked his rear-view mirror, with the rear seats folded down, the fin of his surfboard took a slice out of the road behind. There were days he felt tired of his job and this was one of them. It wasn't just the daily submersion in the intrinsic nastiness of crime and criminals, but also in the devious internal politics of the force itself. After twenty years, he was losing the will to kick against the pricks. Maybe Connie had something to do with it. Maybe he just wanted to have nights and weekends with her that they could count on, plan for.

As the A38 started to merge with the M5 going north, he eased into the inside lane and took the slip road for the city. The traffic was backed up and crawling past Sainsbury's along the Abingdon Road. He opened his window and rested his elbow there, holding the steering wheel lightly between two fingers and a thumb. Was Ron Jellop going to turn out to be corrupt? He thought back to the two or three times he'd met him. He had seemed okay: a bit full of himself, perhaps, but he had put that down to his being a local lad made good. Jellop was always spouting ambitious plans for the city, but his pride in Plymouth had felt genuine.

The thought of investigating him increased the sense of unease Lou was feeling, but there was something else playing into that. He wondered if it was the call for help from the unknown young woman. Yet, as concerned as he was for her safety, Fran was following it up. No, there was something murkier than that lurking in the shadows – and he just couldn't get hold of it.

He crossed the river. Exeter St David's was two minutes away. He checked his watch: 12.11. He was late. Hopefully, DI Bentley's train was on time and he'd be waiting outside. "Do you want to have children, Lou?" Connie's question danced into the light. That was it. No time now, he thought, pulling into the station forecourt. He scanned the figures behind the queuing taxis. That was Bentley, for sure. He flashed his lights and raised a hand out of the window, as the bull-headed man in a hoodie looked his way. Children? A shark in the water couldn't have disturbed him more.

Chapter 2
Fraud and the city councillor

By the time Lou got back to the police station, it was gone 4pm and already dark. He was due at Connie's for a meal later on. What was he going to say to her? This whole question of children and fatherhood scared the hell out of him. His own father had abandoned him...and his mother...just a few hours after he'd been conceived. It wasn't something he had ever talked about. Maybe it was time to. He trusted her, didn't he? He could talk to her tonight. No use holding all this stuff in. He had to be open with her from the start, or what kind of future would they have? His decision brought immediate relief from the worry of it, and his head started to clear. First, though, he needed to update Fran on Ron Jellop and find out what had happened with Coaker.

He found her half-way up the stairs talking to DS Macklin Thomas. They paused as he reached them and half-turned in his direction.

"Not good news, I don't suppose," Macklin said, eyeing him shrewdly.

Nobody had been at Charles Cross Police Station longer or was better informed. Despite his pockmarked face and grizzled head, Macklin often seemed to be the first person people chose to confide in. Lou had, when he'd first arrived as a newly appointed DI. He had needed someone to show him the ropes and there was something in Macklin's air of friendly gravitas that had inspired confidence. He had placed his trust in him and had not regretted it.

"No," Lou said, keeping his voice low. "We have a city councillor to investigate. I'll go through it with you after I've had a word with Fran."

"Right," said Macklin and turned down the stairs.

"Are things sorted?" Lou asked, as Fran followed him up to his office. "With Harris and the others, I mean?"

She'd told Lou about the taunts she'd been getting from a few of the junior officers. Even though she had returned from leave with her new identity officially acknowledged, the jibes continued, crudely disguised as jokes. "Hi, Franny, how's your fanny?" and "Not Fran the man, but Fran the tran!" DC Peter Harris didn't surprise him, he was a nasty piece of work and the kind of bully he'd like to have screened out of the force. But young Jason Kincaid was harder to understand and he'd thought better of him. Maybe accepting him as a Detective Constable had been a mistake. He'd have to wait and see.

"Yeah, Macklin seems to have got his message through."

"Good." He knew Fran had talked to Macklin about the abuse hurled at her.

Switching on the lights as they entered his room, he hooked his jacket on a peg inside the door and crossed to the window. He jiggled the strings on the venetian blind and, as he eased it down, the room's reflection in the glass disappeared.

"We'll send Harris on a few courses," he added, moving to his desk.

Fran nodded, taking the chair opposite, and changed the subject. "This councillor, what's our involvement?"

She wasn't any different now from how she'd always been. It wasn't just her appearance: the jeans, tee and leather jacket, the short, layered hair, or even the way she sat. It was the whole focused, alert air of her, as if she was weighing every word you said, poised and ready for action. His thoughts went back to Harris. She was still deceptively slight; but he'd seen her in action, both on and off the mat. She'd represented Britain in men's international judo competitions since she was 14 and, if Harris crossed her while off-duty, she'd tackle him head-on and she wouldn't back off.

"Wolf ring," she said, following his eyes and holding up her fingers. "Navajo." The silver and turquoise band was new – the only thing.

"Sorry." He gave her a rueful nod. "I was staring."

"You were."

"Okay. Councillor Ron Jellop."

"Jellop?" Her surprise was evident. "I thought he was in line for mayor."

"I know. But it seems he may be caught up in some questionable activities and Fraud wants us to look into it for them."

"What kind of activities."

"There seem to be two strands to it. The first one is linked to the French police, who've asked Fraud for their help. Apparently, our local wine merchant, Oliver Drew, and Jellop bought a chateau together in the south of France, in Bergerac, a grand place with vineyards and full of valuable antiques. You know; paintings, ornaments, furniture, tapestries, that kind of stuff."

Fran nodded. "And?"

"Just before Christmas, Jellop entered a load of these for auction at Christie's in London. They went for a lot of money; over seven hundred grand, according to DI Bentley."

"Asset stripping," Fran said. "It's not a crime, is it?"

"It is when those assets are classed as 'French antiquities' and you haven't obtained the necessary authorisation from the French Ministry of Culture for their removal from France."

"Right. And what's the second strand?"

"Checking on Jellop's financial affairs, Fraud discovered he has a secret bank account in the Cayman Islands, layered through various companies. They're looking into it."

Lou paused and stood up. He'd been sitting most of the day, one way or another, and he felt stiff and uncomfortable. He rolled his shoulders and neck, shook out each leg in turn and then paced up and down the room several times, before coming to a halt behind his chair and resting his hands on the back of it, as he faced her again.

"And they want us to do their leg work for them," Fran said. "That it?"

"More or less. They've asked if we can look into Ron Jellop's business relationship with Oliver Drew and how he came to have these antiques in his possession over here; and also to find out, if we can, where the money going to the Cayman Islands is coming from."

"Bit of a cheek, isn't it? I mean, tracking money's their bag." Fran was bouncing her heels on the carpet, jiggling her knees up and down. "They have the resources for it; we don't." Lou registered her irritation and sat down.

"Bentley says one of the companies up the chain has an income stream they can't identify. They don't want him to know yet that they're investigating him; and they want us to try to get some hard evidence this end, before they approach him directly."

"We're stretched as it is," she said, "and now we may have a murder enquiry on our hands as well."

"You mean Coaker. Okay. You better tell me what happened."

"Mixed bag," she said, opening her notebook. "I was on the quay when he came in. Not very forthcoming. He says he went out first thing this morning, alone. He let me check the cabin, although he wasn't happy about it."

"Find anything?"

"Nothing; but he'd had plenty of time to clean up."

"And the young woman, if there was one?"

"Who's going to notice a body tipped into the sea, miles from anywhere?"

Lou watched her carefully. She was thorough and had good instincts. He trusted her.

"So, why the mixed bag?" he said.

"Hardly any fish. Just a couple of crates half-filled."

"Fishermen have bad days; fish don't always bite."

"Mason showed me the landings register. Coaker normally brings in four or five times more than he did today. Maybe he wasn't fishing all the time; maybe he was busy doing something else."

Lou leant forward, resting his arms on the desk. "Okay, let's suppose your caller was on Coaker's boat and that he got rid of her, while out at sea. What evidence have we got?"

Fran shifted her weight in the chair, looked down at her notebook again and then back at him. "Apart from the name, none. But, if we get a forensics team on board the Morning Star, they're going to come up with blood or hair or prints or something. She'd have put up some kind of a struggle. And he may have washed everything down, but he'll have missed something. Guaranteed."

Lou shook his head. "On what grounds, Fran? There's no missing person alert, no body. We have no name for the possible victim and Coaker being at sea at the same time as her call could just be a coincidence."

"The caller said 'Coaker, no!' and then the line went dead. I've checked all the local Coakers and Eddie's the only one who had no-one with him at the time of the call." She paused. "Whether she's dead or he's done something else with her, we need to follow this up quickly. She may still be alive." Lou saw she wasn't going to let go. "Doesn't that add up to reasonable grounds?"

"We need a witness, someone who saw a woman board the Morning Star with Coaker this morning. Then we can get a warrant. At the moment, we don't even know a crime's been committed."

Fran looked away from him, bent forward and stared at the floor. She was frowning, chewing on the inside of her lower lip. He waited. Like a dog with a bone, it was what she did with a problem: took it off to a corner and gnawed on it.

"Okay," she said, sitting back, her dark eyes once more trained on him. "I spoke to people at the fish market. Coaker has a mooring over towards the China House, uses a dinghy to get out to it. Those who saw him this morning all say the same thing; he arrived alone and boarded the Morning Star alone. If she called us from his boat, she must already have been on board from the day or night before."

"Go on."

"If he went fishing the day before, I'll check what time he got back. Then I'll ask around again, see if anyone saw him taking a woman on to the boat later that day... or night."

She stood up to go.

"Okay, look for CCTV footage as well. There'll be cameras on the quay and probably on the other side too, along from the China House." As she reached the door, he added: "And see me first thing. I want you to pay Oliver Drew a visit, while I talk to Ron Jellop."

Chapter 3
Supper with Connie

As Lou turned into Rowden Street, the feeling of nausea from earlier in the day was back and clawing at his stomach; a whole tangled ball of feelings and thoughts he had tried to unpick on his way over. In the end, it seemed to come down to fear. Fear at the thought of having to talk to Connie about having children? It didn't make sense.

"For God's sake," he said, hitting the rim of the steering wheel with the heel of his hand. "You're a 45-year-old Detective Inspector! What's the matter with you?"

He pulled in short of her house, killed the lights and sat in the shadows, trying to collect himself. It wasn't the kind of physical fear he'd known at work, or even while surfing in mountainous seas. He thought of the time he'd come face-to-face with an armed robber pointing a sawn-off shotgun at him. He'd been scared then; thought he was going to die. And he'd felt a similar slide of his guts, sitting balanced on his board in a swell off Fistral Beach, watching a twenty-foot wave racing in behind him. At those times, adrenaline had kicked in like a supercharger, channelling the fear into action. But this was different. This wasn't about the preservation of his body; this was about something else, something that felt sickened and liquefied at the core of him.

He looked up the row of red-brick terraced houses to the one at the end. Connie was a pharmacist. She worked in a small chemist's, less than a fifteen-minute walk away. Although self-possessed and competent, there was a vulnerability about her he had responded to. She had been sent from Hong Kong by her parents to get a British degree and had ended up living on her own at the end of this cul-de-sac, thousands of miles from home. The thought of her aloneness calmed the panic in him. His palms were sweating and he rubbed them against his trousers before driving on to the end of the street.

As he parked, Connie opened the front door and came out to greet him. He felt a sudden tug of affection at the sight of her slender silhouette and skipping gait. She had a kind of music in her walk was how he thought of it; a rhythmical lightness of movement, like a dance. She liked to sing and was in two choirs: one at her local Baptist church, and the other, The Big Noise Chorus, not far away in Peverell.

"You just in time," she said, offering her hand to help him out. "Good thing you ring me, food ready now." Even her Cantonese intonation was sing-song.

She kissed him on the lips with a tenderness that roused him and yet dissolved him further. He didn't want to lose her, but what was she going to do when he told her he didn't want children? Inside the house, the central heating was turned up high; it was warm, but the tension didn't go out of him and his muscles stayed tight. He knew to get any relief he needed to tell her straight away, get it out in the open. Problems were best tackled head-on and without delay. He'd found that out the hard way.

"I hope you like roast pork Chinese-style," she said, leading him into a small living-room, with a bay window at one end and an archway at the other. Through it, he could see the dark wood table and chairs, the table already laid.

"If it tastes as good as it smells, I'm sure I will." His mouth was dry, but the spicy aroma spiked juices in the back of his throat. "What is that? It smells delicious."

"Five spice! You must know that."

When he was with Connie, he didn't feel like a police inspector. With most people, he experienced either a kind of reserved respect or a veiled hostility, as if they only saw his badge, not his person. But with her, he felt like he had with his mother and school friends before he'd moved south. He could relax and enjoy her teasing. It made things easier.

"You'd be amazed how much I don't know," he said. "Italian cooking, yes. Indian cooking, a bit. But Chinese cooking, not at all."

"I'll teach you. Good for you. Chinese stir fry very quick, very healthy."

While she disappeared to the kitchen, he settled back in the two-seater sofa, pushing a soft cushion behind his head, and looked at the three oriental porcelain figures watching him from a shelf opposite. He had seen them before countless times, but had never asked her about them. Three bearded men dressed in ancient Chinese robes, with one holding a child. It was the child that had caught his eye. It's funny, he was thinking, how you only see on the outside what you've already registered on the inside.

Did he really want to get involved again with someone from a different culture? These three men must represent something significant, but he had no idea what. It had been like that with Priya and her Hindu family, back in Leicester. He had been interested in a tradition so different from the lapsed Catholicism and practical atheism of both his mother's parents, Fabio from Umbria and Maggie from Cork, the only grandparents he'd ever known. The alcove shrine Priya had created in their flat had seemed so alien to him, at the start. Their first row had followed his referring to her prayers to Lord Ganesh as 'mumbo jumbo'. The memory embarrassed him. He had been so arrogant then, so cocksure of his 'Western' rightness.

Yet, even though Priya's mother had never accepted him as a suitable husband for her daughter, he had found in Priya and her faith a spiritual depth and integrity that anchored him. It was not that she converted him to Hinduism, she never tried to; but rather that her example somehow allowed him to hold on more firmly to his own deeper self and convictions. She would not marry him without her family's blessing and she would not have children without being married. She had wanted children, while he didn't, but he had never admitted that to her.

It was a problem he hadn't faced. He'd hidden it out of sight, like an unwanted bill stuffed in a drawer. But, in the end, the emotional dishonesty of it had caused them both far more pain than if he'd been straight with her from the start. After twelve years together, her family's intransigence and her longing for children of her own broke them apart. Ten or eleven years earlier, the hurt would have been so much less; and the guilt, too. He never had told her the truth and she had blamed her parents, instead of him. But he had deceived her because he loved and wanted her.

"What kind of love is that?" he growled at himself. "You weren't thinking of her at all." The memory shamed him, as it always did. It wouldn't come right until he owned up to her and apologised. Although they hadn't been in touch since he moved away, he knew he should do it, not just for his sake, but for hers too. If she despised him for it, fair enough; at least, she would know the truth. It might help her relationship with her family.

He certainly wasn't going to go down that path again. He'd tell Connie tonight. He stood up and grasped the figure carrying the young child. He wore a pale green robe with wide hanging sleeves and was holding something in his other hand, like a bowl, that Lou couldn't make out.

"Fu, Lu, Shou," Connie said, appearing next to him. "This is Lu." She pointed to the figure in his hand. "In Chinese tradition, he represents good position in society; own family, good job." She picked up the tallest of the three, the one with the thick belt and long dark beard. "Fu. He is wealth and..."

"He looks prosperous," Lou interjected. "A merchant, maybe?"

"Yes. Prosperity, that what he stands for. Middle age, he established now." She put the figure back on the shelf.

"And this one?" Lou pointed to the smiling one in yellow, with a white beard and holding a staff.

"Long life, you can see. They are three stars: Luxing, Fuxing and Shouxing. Three stages in your life, I think so. Lu is still one for you now; but Fu soon."

Lou's eyes rested on the child. "Maybe too late," he said. He pointed to the venerable elder. "Next stop," he said and grinned at her. But her expression stayed serious.

"Why you say that? You are in the strongest time of your life now. You have achieved your life. Now you can say what you will do with it."

As he followed her through to the table, he felt the challenge in her words. As he settled down to eat, he began searching for the right way to start and couldn't find it. Should he jump straight in and say he didn't want to be a father and then explain why? Or would it be better to lead up to it gradually, telling her about his own father first? Perhaps he should just tell her about the demands of his job and what it would mean to be a policeman's wife; after all, she had already experienced broken arrangements and sudden call-outs. He could go on from there about wanting to be an available dad, not like his own father; the father he'd never known.

He took another forkful of duck in its crispy skin and chewed it slowly. It was strange how present an absent parent could be, even now. He'd spent his childhood imagining him, conjuring a picture from his mother's story of him; a young man, tall and suntanned, with sharp blue eyes, strong aquiline nose and light wavy hair. French, his mother said. That was more than forty-five years ago; he'd be very different now.

"What you thinking about?" Connie asked, startling him. "You look far away."

He rested his knife and fork either side of his plate and looked at her. Whether it was the concerned attention of her steady gaze or the still beauty of her pale face, like a Modigliani almond-eyed portrait, he didn't know. All he was sure of was that he had to bite down hard to hold back the sudden tears that threatened to overwhelm him. He coughed and drank from the water glass in front of him.

"Fathers," he said. "Fathers and children."

"You want to tell me about your father?" she asked. "Is this right time now, maybe?"

He stared at his glass, trying to control the urge to get up and leave. He didn't want to talk about his father. He didn't want to think about him. She was being too pushy, too intrusive. She should know some questions you just don't ask till ... he didn't know till when. Till he decided to talk about it, that's when. He was angry. He wanted to bang the table hard. He gripped his hands tightly together in his lap. The silence was becoming unbearable, making it harder and harder for him to speak.

"What's the matter, Louis?" she asked quietly.

His head jerked up. Only his mother called him Louis, and the unfamiliar sound of his full name, spoken with such tenderness, broke the wall of anger inside him and brought him back to himself.

"I don't know, Connie." He paused, breathing hard, wanting to reach her, wanting her to understand. "It's a whole jumble of things I can't get straight. All I know is..." He hesitated, as his fear broke clear at last. "I don't want to lose you."

"You not going to lose me. How you going..." she started, when the opening riff of Hendrix's 'Voodoo Child' crashed through the stillness, cutting her off.

He slid the mobile from his pocket. "Beradino," he said, turning away from her.

"Sorry to trouble you at home, Lou." The Welsh lilt of Macklin's intonation always seemed more noticeable on the phone.

"That's okay. What's up?"

"Roz on the switchboard took a call from a woman wanting to report a missing person. When Roz asked her for her name, she rang off. I thought you should know."

"Thanks, Macklin. I'll come straight down. Ten minutes max."

He ended the call and turned back to find Connie still watching him.

"Sorry, I've got to go," he said. He pointed to his plate. "But keep this for me and I'll have it later."

Standing up, he bent to kiss her cheek, his hand on her shoulder; and, as he did so, she covered it with her own, holding it against her. "We talk about this later, Lou, when you come back," she said, lifting her face to him. There was an insistence in her tone he recognised. "You tell me everything, help me understand."

He nodded, irritated at her claim on him and the justice of it. He wanted to be gone. "Sure," he said.

Chapter 4
Truth and evasion

It was turning into a long day and by the time Lou got to the station, he was wishing he was back in his own house, having a quiet evening alone. Wembury was a coastal village five miles east of Plymouth, with a good enough surfing beach, a comfortable pub and a broad curve of bungalows, of which he had one. The summer was best, when the days were long and he was able to take his surfboard out more often than not. But even in mid-winter, like now, he could light a fire, put on some blues, lie on the sofa with a drink and forget about work for an hour or two.

"Evening, Inspector." A matronly blonde woman stood up as he approached the counter. He had mixed feelings about civilian support staff, believing they were another of the Government's cost-cutting measures designed to disguise the underfunding of public services. But Roz Lewis was efficient and he liked her.

"Hello, Roz," he smiled back. "Have you got five minutes? I hear you had a mystery caller."

Their voices echoed through the night-time cheerlessness of the station, ringing round the bare walls under the harsh fluorescent lighting.

"Of course," she said. Lowering her voice, she repeated the details of the call she'd received earlier, showing him her entry in the log. The call at 7.37pm had lasted less than twenty seconds.

"Can you replay it for me?" he asked. She retrieved the call and passed him the headphones.

"Are you police?" The voice was tense but controlled, and the speaker's accent was heavy, Russian possibly.

"Yes. This is Charles Cross Police Station, Plymouth, and I am Police Support Officer Roz Lewis. How may I help you?"

"I want to report missing person. Young woman."

"What is your name, please?"

There was a brief pause and then nothing, as the line went dead.

Lou played it through again. A young woman, Eastern European, just like Fran's desperate caller. Could both calls be a hoax by the same person? He decided not. This voice sounded deeper and the accent was different, more pronounced. He took the headphones off and handed them back.

"We couldn't trace her," Roz said.

Lou nodded. They could always trace the call, but when people didn't want to be linked to them, they simply used an unlocked, prepaid mobile and SIM card and then threw them away and got another.

"That's okay, Roz. Thanks."

Macklin was coming down the stairs, as Lou went up to find him. The collar of his heavy overcoat was turned up, with the knot of his scarf bunched and tucked in under his chin. He was running late for choir practice at the Baptist Church in St Budeaux, where he lived.

"Can it wait for the morning briefing?" he said.

Lou nodded, turning back beside him. "Yes. Not much more we can do tonight." And, giving Roz a wave on their way out, they left the building together.

Back in his car, Lou sat in the dark and scrolled down to Fran's number. She knew about the second anonymous call already. Macklin had rung her earlier, as well. But she didn't know about the East European accent or the age of the caller.

"Bit more than a coincidence, isn't it?" she said, after he'd finished. "Something's going on. Smuggling immigrants? Human trafficking? What do you think?"

27

"See what you can find out in the morning. I'm going to pay Jellop a visit on my way home, ask him about the auction. He won't be expecting me."

* * * * *

People often seemed more vulnerable in their homes than at work, as if they left their shields at the front door. Catching Ron Jellop relaxing in an armchair after supper would be very different from being shown into his office by appointment. Besides, Lou's own evening had been disrupted, so why not Jellop's?

Connie was far from happy when he called her to let her know he had to work and would then be going back home to Wembury.

"I'll be late," he said, "and you've got work in the morning. We both have. And, anyway, I need to pick up a change of clothes." It was his standard excuse when he wanted time out, and the reason he didn't keep any at her house.

"You want be on your own sometimes, that's all right. But you must tell me this. Then, I not cook for you, waste food."

"It's not like that," he started, but she cut him off.

"You said you come back and tell me about your father. Maybe, you don't want to; too difficult for you. I understand if you say that. You must be honest with me or I don't know what to think; don't know where I am with you."

She was right. Talking to Roz had some legitimacy, because she was working a late shift and wouldn't be there in the morning; but surprising Jellop was a way out of going back to Connie's and confronting the difficulty between them. He may have fooled himself, but she wasn't taken in by it, not even for a moment.

"You're right, Connie. I'm sorry." He paused, feeling blocked as to how to go on. "What am I trying to say?" He sighed, searching for the truth behind his contesting thoughts. "I'm in a panic about your wanting children and I don't know how to talk to you about it."

When she spoke again, her voice was warmer, free of the doubting edge it had had to it only moments earlier.

"We can do that," she said. "Children are big responsibility; big pleasure, too. Good thing you tell me. We can work it out, you see."

He stretched his legs out past the pedals and felt his shoulders loosen. When it always proved to be so much easier than trying to avoid it, why did telling the truth often seem so hard, he wondered.

"Look, why don't you come over to Wembury tomorrow after work and stay? I'll cook and we can have all weekend to talk."

"Okay, I come," she said. "But you tell me what you really feeling; no pretending, it only make me confused."

"I will, Connie, I will."

* * * * *

Light rain was slating through the pools of light from the streetlamps as Lou drove into the cobbled roundabout in front of the grand, arched entrance to Royal William Yard. Formerly a Royal Navy victualling yard, it was now a development of expensive waterside apartments and fashionable restaurants. He circled past the entrance and pulled up by the pavement on the far side. The lane to Jellop's fine house, Firestone Hall, was directly opposite and he could see its lighted windows flickering behind the dark branches of a screen of trees.

Twisting round, he grabbed his parka off the back seat and, with its hood up, he made his way on foot. Jellop's house stood on a promontory overlooking Plymouth Sound to the south and the Tamar River to the north-west. Lengthening his stride against the gradient, he left the lane and walked up the drive. Deep shadow bounded the garden's perimeter and an enclosed stillness enveloped him. As he approached the house, porch lights lit up its attractive slate frontage and reflected off the bonnets and bumpers of several cars parked to one side.

He paused to collect his thoughts. A brilliant flame of light suddenly flared from the side of the house across the path and grass beyond. A man stepped out from the open doorway, his face floodlit for a moment, before the door closed behind him and he disappeared across the lawn into the darkness.

A woman in an apron answered Lou's rap of the knocker. Her sharp features were thrown into relief by the brightness of the hall behind her and the still of the night was ruptured by the swell of chatter and laughter from within.

"Detective Inspector Lou Beradino," he said, holding out his warrant card. "Please let Mr Jellop know I'd like to speak to him."

If Jellop was in the middle of a dinner party, so much the better, he thought, as she ushered him in and closed the door. Eating and drinking with friends in the comfort of his own home, he'd be relaxed and unprepared. If there was any truth in Bentley's allegations, now was as good a time as any to test the man's honesty.

Chapter 5
The missing woman

Lou arrived at Charles Cross early the following morning. The day was clear, crisp and cold, and the watery sun was just showing above the rooftops as he parked and made for his office. The heaviness of the previous day had left him and he walked quickly, his thoughts focused. The sense of purpose was familiar; one he often experienced when a new case was breaking and the hunt was starting. It didn't mean he wasn't worried about the missing woman or that he felt sanguine about the corruption of a public official. On the contrary, it was his determination to resolve both issues that was galvanising his concerns into action.

He typed up reports on his meetings with DI Bentley and Ron Jellop, wanting to clear as much of his paperwork as possible before the weekend. For the same reason, he then devoted his attention to reading through the evidence to be submitted to the Crown Prosecution Service concerning the campus rape at the university last autumn. It was notoriously difficult to get a conviction when essentially it was the complainant's word against the defendant's. Since this defendant was the son of a Cabinet Minister and the account of the young woman concerned, a medical student, was hazy – she thought she had been drugged – the chances of a successful prosecution seemed slim.

A second female student had come forward, however, to say that she'd had an identical experience while out on a date with the same young man. Lou checked the details carefully, looking for flaws in her statement that would allow a defence barrister to sew doubts in the mind of a jury, or that might deter the CPS from mounting a prosecution in the first place, on the grounds of a conviction being unlikely. She hadn't reported the alleged rape initially out of shame and a fear of not being believed. Also, she did not know the complainant, being in a different year and on a different degree course. And it was only after watching a recent television documentary on 'date rape', which featured the use of the 'predator' drug, Rohypnol, that she decided to report her rape after all, "so no other girls get treated the way I was".

Lou thought the case stood up and that the CPS might well decide to prosecute. He hoped so. The Minister's son deserved to be confronted over his alleged violation of these young women in a court of law. But it was more than that. He wanted him held to account and punished. He was ruining the lives of these young women for his own gratification, with utter disregard for their well-being and future happiness. They might recover, but at what cost to their sense of trust in other people and in their own judgement? He closed the vanilla folder and slapped it down on top of the pile of papers ready for processing.

Why was he feeling so angry? He knew why. Hadn't he spent most of his childhood worrying about his mother's unhappiness and wanting to find the man responsible, his own father? He hadn't raped her; she'd been willing enough. She was bewitched by him. But he'd used her and dumped her, disappeared without a word, leaving her pregnant. It was a rape of trust, anyway! And it left life-long scars. Part of Lou's reason for joining the police was to track him down. He didn't want him as a father, far from it. His grandfather had been more than enough to fill that role. But he did want to be in a room on his own with him and make sure he fully understood the consequences of what he'd done.

Lou stretched for the carafe on the corner of the desk and poured himself a glass of water. He took a mouthful and pushed it away. He didn't like the taste of it. Pulling open the top drawer to his right, he took out a metal-framed photograph of his grandfather, his mother's father, Fabio Beradino. He placed it on the desk in front of him, then pushed back his chair and stretched out his legs. The unflinching eyes locked into his and centred him. "Ciao, Spoza," he murmured. It was a nickname that had stuck with family and friends. It had affection in it, probably because his grandmother had coined it when they first went out. She was second generation Irish from Cork and liked to laugh. "Spoza we go for an ice-cream?" "Spoza we get married?" She would mimic his inflections and touch his cheek with her palm. "Spoza we do," she would reply.

Lou observed him now, standing in the road, looking through chicken wire fencing, with sepia terraced housing stretching back on either side. A few similar figures, unshaven and wearing baggy suits and flat caps, were standing near him, watching. 'Huyton University', as Fabio liked to call it when asked about his education, was the internment camp outside Liverpool, where he, fellow Italians and other 'potential enemy aliens' were incarcerated in 1940.

No matter he had lived and worked in Liverpool for six years by then, ever since he had met and married Maggie O'Neil in '34, or that he was a skilled carpenter, who went about his business peaceably and paid his taxes. No, after the failure of the Allies' campaign to free Norway from German occupation had led to spy fever and suspicion of foreigners, Winston Churchill said, "Collar the lot!", and they had. They had come for Fabio in the night without warning. But he was one of the lucky ones. Lou thought of the cousins he had never met, Dino and Federico, who drowned in the cold Atlantic, after the unescorted Arandora Star, packed with Italian and German internees being sent from Liverpool to Canada, was torpedoed by a Nazi U-boat.

Fabio's steadfastness was the complete opposite of his own father's shallowness, or the Minister's son's duplicity.

Although Spoza wasn't tall, there was a physical confidence apparent in his stance: legs evenly apart, hands resting against his belt buckle, thumbs loosely hooked behind. He was a stocky figure, with broad, sloping shoulders and tight curly black hair. Lou knew he was like him. Their colouring might be different – his own eyes were blue and his hair dark brown – but his build was the same and he had his grandfather's quiet strength, a physical tenacity born out of inner conviction and personal dignity. If he was ever to become a father, he thought, he'd try to be as dependable and warm-hearted as Spoza.

A loud double-knock interrupted his reverie and before he had time to respond, Fran entered and approached the desk. She nodded at the frame, now in his hand. "Nonno! Things must be getting serious." She pulled up a chair and sat down. Lou slid the photo back in the drawer and closed it.

Her excitement was palpable.

"What've you got?"

She flipped open her notebook and leant forward, and he was aware of the scent of her, like rose and bay, or scented tea, something astringent, with a hint of sweetness..

"You were right. There's CCTV footage from near the China House, and from Fisherman's Quay opposite, and I've been up half the night going through it. It shows Coaker boarding the Morning Star the night before last, Wednesday, with a young woman. But, guess what?"

"Later on, he leaves and she doesn't?"

Fran frowned and clicked her tongue. "Exactly!"

"Get a clear picture of her?"

"No. It's dark and raining. She's wearing a coat with a hood. You can't see her face at all."

"Pity."

"But there's a clear shot of Coaker and I've asked for a blow-up."

"Good. Anything else?"

"Yes." The spark was back in her eyes. "I followed them backwards, checking the footage of the cameras from where they'd just been."

As she went on, his thoughts drifted. Hard evidence of a woman having been on Coaker's boat and his having denied it gave substance to the call for help they'd received. They couldn't wait for Monday. This would have to be followed up urgently, weekend or not. How the hell was he going to square that with Connie?

"...coming out of the Ship Inn." The name drew him back to the sound of her voice. "It shows them leaving together shortly before nine-thirty."

"Can you see if they arrived together?"

"I haven't looked yet, but I will."

"Right. And find out who was serving in the bar that night. See if they can give you any information about this woman, whoever she is. We need to identify her."

"Rod Sherman," Fran said. "I already checked. He's on duty again at twelve today." She looked at her watch. "I'll try to catch him before it gets busy."

She was often a step ahead of him, thinking for herself, using her own initiative. And more importantly, she had integrity. She'd be a good DI. He needed to do something about it.

"Don't suppose you've already talked to Coaker again, have you?"

A smile flickered at the corners of her mouth. "Not yet, no. And, before you ask, before I do, I'll nip up to Yelverton and see if I can have a word with Mr Drew."

"Great. And I've got some interesting news from my trip to Ron Jellop last night."

But before he could continue the phone on his desk started its demanding bleeping.

"Lou, can you pop up, soon as?" Superintendent Andrew Maynard's cheery request of command boomed in his ear.

"Give me five minutes and I'll be there."

He replaced the receiver. "The Roses at five, and I'll tell you then."

Chapter 6

Lou visits Ron Jellop again

After Fran left his office, Lou took the stairs to Superintendent Maynard's office two at a time and knocked on his door before entering, even though it was slightly open.

"Come!"

A shaft of sunlight streamed through the window on to a desk laden with files and paperwork, behind which sat the jovial, thick-eared, florid-faced superior officer, beaming at him.

"Good man. Have a seat. Tricky business this." He glanced down at the file open in front of him.

Lou pulled the familiar stacking chair further round to face him and sat down.

"Tricky business?" he said.

"Yes. Awkward, this sort of thing. Kid gloves."

Lou was used to Maynard's oblique approach. "It sounds political, sir," he said and waited.

The superintendent looked up at him sharply, shrewd eyes alert behind the genial mask.

"Local politics, certainly," he said. "It has come down to me," his eyes flicked upwards, "that Councillor Ron Jellop feels he is the subject of unwarranted police harassment."

Lou suppressed the spurt of anger he felt. "Is this the brotherhood protecting their own?"

"Have a care, Lou." Maynard's voice was lower, harder. "Jellop has friends in high places. He has done a lot for this city."

Their eyes clashed. Lou thought of his grandfather and would not give way.

"He may not be all that he seems," Lou said. "Fraud and the French police are on his trail."

Maynard stood up. He was a tall man, in his fifties, with a full head of dark brown hair turning silver around the ears. He strode to the window and paused, looking out, his hands clasped behind him. When he finally turned round, his expression was stern.

"It would be wise to go cautiously. No interviews without hard evidence. No visits to his home without an appointment. In fact, Lou," Maynard walked back and resumed his seat, "no visits to his home at all. He has an office."

"I understand," Lou said. He felt a low-level swell of satisfaction that his visit to Firestone Hall the previous evening had got under Ron Jellop's skin.

"What on earth were you doing, man?" Maynard's face was puce with exasperation. "Do you know who was having dinner there when you barged in?"

"I don't. He kept me in the hall."

"Just as well for you! Or you would've had to explain yourself to DCC Townsend."

Deputy Chief Constable Martin Townsend. That explained everything. No wonder Maynard was talking about kid gloves. Lou saw the links in the chain and rubbed his chin.

"Sir, there's a stench coming off Ron Jellop like rotten fish. Do you want me to pretend I can't smell it?"

Maynard sat back in his chair and folded his hands across his stomach, his air of bonhomie apparently restored.

"Just use a fly, Lou, not a harpoon."

As Lou left the room and headed for the fresh air, he pulled out his mobile and tapped the screen several times.

"Good morning. Detective Inspector Lou Beradino, Charles Cross Police Station. I'd like to make an appointment to see Mr Jellop, this afternoon."

* * * * *

It was overcast, and the January afternoon was already dying, as Lou made his way up North Hill on foot. He crossed by St Andrew's University and, a little way past the ornamental reservoir, turned left into a cul-de-sac with half-a-dozen terraced houses on either side. Largely unnoticed by the constant flow of traffic in and out of the city, Skardon Place immediately absorbed him into its quiet repose.

Halfway along, he found the house he was looking for. The dark blue front door had a broad letterbox and a heavy knocker in the shape of an anchor, both of them brass. He rapped it twice and waited. The neighbouring houses were well-maintained and the atmosphere was of a discreet mews. University or Church owned, he guessed.

A young woman answered the door, her fair hair coiled back tightly across the tops of her ears into a bun. She led him through to a comfortably furnished sitting-room at the rear of the house. Through French windows at the far end, Lou saw the shadowy outlines of a small, walled garden beyond.

"Mr Jellop will be with you in a moment, Inspector," she said, with a trace of an accent that he thought might be Polish. "Would you like a cup of tea?"

"No thank you," he said. As she turned to leave, he added: "Have you worked for Mr Jellop long?"

Appearing not to hear him, she continued out of the room, closing the door quietly behind her.

Lou looked around the room carefully. He was surprised to find himself in this tastefully decorated drawing-room, rather than the managerial office he had anticipated. There was a feminine elegance to the pale salmon walls and sage green carpet and to the way the colours were picked out again in the covers and cushions of the sofa and armchairs and the chaise longue against the wall by the fireplace.

For all its elegance, the room's anonymity bothered him. He looked from the tall shades of the table-lamps to the gilt-framed mirrors on the walls. There were no pictures, no family photos, no books, no personal possessions of any sort.

The door opened and Ron Jellop entered. He was a heavy-set man, with a broad chest and a large, balding head.

"Good afternoon, Inspector," he said, holding out his hand, his deep Devon burr warm and pleasant.

Lou felt the latent power in the firm handshake.

"Please." He gestured Lou towards an armchair and they sat facing each other across a marble-topped coffee table. "We have half-an-hour. How can I help you?" As he spoke, he undid the inner button of his double-breasted jacket and settled his arms easily along those of the chair.

Despite the affable tone, there was an authority in his voice and steady gaze that Lou had to steel himself to resist.

"You were less ready to talk to me last night, Mr Jellop. What has changed?"

"I have boundaries, Inspector, and I believe in old-fashioned courtesies. My home and family are separate from my business and council affairs. And you crossed that boundary last night by coming to my house unannounced and disturbing me in the middle of dinner with friends. Whereas today," he lifted his hand momentarily and let it fall back, "you have behaved differently."

Lou wondered how DCC Townsend's presence at dinner fitted in with this analysis, but decided to hold on to that card for the time being.

"As I mentioned last night, the Bordeaux police have been in touch with us through Interpol, concerning certain valuable items that you entered for sale through Christie's London auction rooms last October. Such works of art are classed as "cultural goods" and cannot be removed from French territory without an accompanying authorisation from the Ministry of Culture, either in the form of a movement certificate or an export licence, neither of which you appear to have had."

Jellop nodded impassively and said nothing.

Lou continued, choosing his words carefully: "To help us with this investigation, can you tell me how these works of art came to be in your possession?" He already knew the answer, but wondered how truthful or otherwise Councillor Jellop would be.

"Certainly. It couldn't be more straightforward. You know, I am sure, of my family's company, Jellop Builders Merchants, and its subsidiary, Jellop Developments." Lou nodded. "Mainly, we operate in and around Plymouth. Last year, however, we became involved in a venture to restore a French chateau in the Dordogne. Some of its antiquities were surplus to requirements and, at the request of the owner, we brought them back and put them up for auction."

"Who is the owner?"

"Currently, Oliver Drew, although I understand the property is now up for sale."

Lou knew that Oliver Drew and Ron Jellop were both directors of Maple Investments Ltd, the company that the Fraud Squad was investigating; but he chose a different card to play.

"Let me see if I have followed you accurately. Mr Drew acquired a chateau in the Dordogne and asked you to become involved in its restoration. As a result of this connection, he asked you to transport various antiquities from the chateau to Plymouth and to put them up for sale by auction in London, which you did, although no authorisation from the French Ministry of Culture had been obtained." He raised his eyebrows. "Is that correct?"

"Hindsight is a wonderful thing, Inspector," said Jellop, smiling broadly. "I'm a local lad. I grew up in the building trade. I don't know much about antiques or French law. We did maintenance work in the chateau: repaired the roof and window frames where necessary, and some of the flooring; replastered the walls; refitted the kitchen and bathrooms; and did some restoration work to dilapidated masonry in the grounds. As far as I knew, we were just taking away unwanted furniture and knick-knacks, as we often do at the end of a job."

"You don't often..." Lou began, but was interrupted.

"One moment, Inspector. There's something you should know. As soon as I became aware that we had inadvertently breached these French regulations, I instructed our solicitors, Merrybell and Carpenter, to contact the relevant authorities to ask what reparation we can make. And, while I know ignorance is no justification before the law, I am hopeful that they will accept that we are acting in good faith and will not wish to punish us too harshly for a genuine mistake."

"Some of these knick-knacks..."

Jellop cut him off again. "Excuse me," he said, standing up, "let's throw some more light on these proceedings." He moved around the room, switching on the table lamps, and drew closed the full-length velvet curtains, also sage green, across the French windows.

As he returned to his armchair, he straightened his shirt sleeves, pulling down on the cuffs from where they had ridden up. As he did so, Lou noted the lustre and roll of the folded cream cotton and the gold links holding them together, flat ovals with looped initials engraved on them.

"You were saying, Inspector..." Jellop glanced at the jade-cased clock on the mantelpiece. "We have just over ten minutes, if there is anything else."

"Knick-knacks don't often sell for thousands of pounds," Lou said. "Over seven hundred thousand in this case. As a city councillor, Mr Jellop, do you approve of asset stripping, in principle?"

"We follow the market, Inspector. There is nothing untoward in what we do, except, I admit, in this particular instance, which we are doing our best to rectify. And there, I'm afraid, we must leave it."

Jellop stood up, but Lou remained seated. "One more question before I go." Lou flicked through the cards at his disposal. He wanted to ruffle Jellop. "I believe you know Alastair Shingle, senior planning officer for the city."

"Yes, I've known Alastair professionally for a long time. Our paths often cross during the course of council business."

"And your building firm is often chosen for council projects. I'm thinking of certain housing and refuse developments recently, for example."

"Jellop's goes through the usual tendering process, Inspector, and the council know from past experience that we can be trusted to do a good job for a fair price, and, more importantly, that we can be relied upon to do so on time and within budget, which is not always the case in our trade."

Far from looking ruffled, Jellop was beaming down at him.

"And now, if you don't mind, I'm afraid I must be going." He moved to the door and opened it.

Lou stood up. "Do you have other involvements with Mr Shingle?" He watched Jellop's face carefully as he crossed the room to him.

"Alastair and I founded the local charity for the homeless, Topcoat, as I'm sure you know." He held his hand out and Lou took it. Their shake was as it had been at the start, firm and brisk. "Good day, Inspector."

Lou turned in the doorway: "In 1983, the former wine cellars of John Grenville & Company, a listed building, for which a planning application to build a block of flats had been turned down, mysteriously burnt down." For the first time, the muscles in Jellop's face tightened, as his jaws clenched, and his smile faded.

"As a result," Lou continued, "a second planning application was approved. The coincidence is that the young planning officer involved in that application was Alastair

Shingle and the developer, who then built those flats, was Jellop's."

Jellop stiffened and squared his shoulders. "That will do, Inspector. The fire was investigated thoroughly at the time and declared accidental. The night watchman had carelessly left his newspaper on top of a paraffin heater."

The young woman who had let Lou in reappeared in the corridor. Jellop's smile returned. "Life is full of coincidences, Inspector," he said, placing a hand on Lou's shoulder. "Sophie, Inspector Beradino is leaving. Please show him the way out."

Chapter 7
DS Bannerman meets the Drews

Rachael Drew hurried out of the kitchen, grabbing a neat grey rucksack from the table as she crossed the hallway, and took her car keys from the bowl on the ledge by the front door. She didn't want to argue any more, she wanted to be gone. As she paused by the mirror, pushing the chestnut strands of hair back from her forehead, her husband, Oliver, came after her and caught hold of her wrist.

"Didn't you hear me? I said I don't want you going back to the college."

His breath was hot on her cheek and its reek of salami disgusted her. She turned her face away, looking down at where he had hold of her.

"Let go of me!" She tried to pull her arm free. Years of horse riding had developed and strengthened her muscles, but he was stronger. He tightened his grip and with studied deliberation lifted the rucksack from her shoulder.

Their eyes met; his pale blue and cold, hers amber-flecked and wary.

"You're not going," he said. "P-p-people, important people like the J-Jellops, are already starting to gossip. You'll thank me later."

"You're hurting me." He let go of her wrist and she massaged the livid skin gently, her mind racing. How did the Jellops know? Surely, Polly wouldn't gossip. No, he was making it up. He always stammered when he was lying; looking her in the eyes and nodding like this, as if to affirm the truth of what he was saying. After fourteen years together, she knew the signs.

He just wanted to control her. But it was no use going without the essay and her books. Panic flared in her as she saw herself imprisoned in a life and role of his determining.

"Give me my bag!" She made a grab for it, but he spun clear of her, lifting it high above him, out of her reach.

He grinned at her. "What are you going to do now?"

She stared at him, fury at her impotence flushing her cheeks, her throat. She saw the businessman facade, the dark suit and tie, the polished leather shoes and the carefully combed hair. He was heavy boned and powerful. One of his party tricks was tearing telephone directories in half. She knew she had no hope of recovering her rucksack unless he chose to give to her.

"You're a bully," she said quietly. "That's all you are." She saw his eyes go blank and his smile fade. Her words had caught him by surprise, confounded him for the moment. She took her chance and was out of the door before he could stop her. She ran towards the yellow Volvo estate next to his Rolls, stabbing at the button on her key pad, yanking at the door handle, missing her grip, finding it again, pulling the door open wildly and jumping in, hot tears streaming down her face.

She could hear the crunch of his feet on the gravel and she fumbled getting the key into the ignition.

"You're not going," she heard him say, as his shadow closed over her window.

She pressed the locking switch just in time to prevent him opening her door and started the engine. The side of his fist thumped against the glass, and she whipped her head away instinctively, as if his blow would strike her.

"Get out!" he yelled, his face suddenly next to hers at the window.

She wrenched the gear stick into reverse, her foot slipping on the clutch and the cogs grinding in revolt. The car jumped backwards and she spun the steering wheel round and jammed the lever into first. But as she did so, he stepped in front of the car. She stamped on the brakes.

"Turn off the engine," he commanded loudly, "and get out of the car." He was standing with his legs astride, the palms of his hand resting flat on the bonnet.

She hit the horn with the heel of her hand and kept it there. He raised his arm and brought the clenched side of his fist crashing down on the bonnet. The front of the car lurched down, and the muscles in her pelvis tightened in fear. She saw the refracted light from the dent in the metal and took her hand off the horn. A sinking weariness pulled the energy downwards through her. She felt her arms grow heavy and let her hands slide off the wheel into her lap.

She was aware of him standing up straight and walking round to her door. "What's the use?" she thought and pressed the switch. There was a click and he pulled it open. He stood waiting, as she turned off the engine, extracted the key and pulled up the handbrake, letting every ratchet do its job.

As she stepped out, her eyes were on the ringed finger of his free hand. She thought she was going to be sick and icy beads of sweat glistened across her forehead. In the road beyond their hedge, the sound of an approaching car grew louder, then changed note as it slowed. As the police car nosed between the gates, they both seemed to freeze: Oliver, holding the door open while looking over his shoulder, and Rachael, one foot on the gravel, head tilting to see past him.

The patrol car rolled to a stop in front of them and a young woman in jeans and a leather jacket got out.

"Good afternoon. Mr Oliver Drew?"

Oliver turned. "Yes," he said and walked towards her, hand outstretched. "Good afternoon." They shook hands. "And this is my wife, Rachael." As he gestured towards her, Rachael closed the car door and made towards them.

"How can we help you?" He smiled, half-turning to include her. "Not been speeding again, have you, darling?"

She wondered at this self-possession in him, that he could turn so seamlessly from hostile intimidation to smooth good humour. If she were to ask this policewoman to help her, to explain what had just happened, she'd never believe her.

"Detective Sergeant Fran Bannerman," the woman said, holding out her warrant card. "There are a few questions I would like to ask you, Mr Drew, in connection with a recent sale of French antiquities at Christie's auction house."

"Of c-course." Rachael caught the discomfort behind his small stammer and was glad. "Let's go inside." He held his arm out towards the house. "And Rachael will bring us some tea, won't you, darling?"

"I'm afraid I can't," she said, leading them towards the door, where she paused to let them enter ahead of her. "I'm late for my course already." She followed them in, picked up her rucksack and put her hand out to the detective. "Please excuse me."

As she pulled out on to the Yelverton road and turned left at the roundabout towards the city, an exultant sense of anticipation began to surge through her. She would do this, she would get this qualification and then she could apply for university. The road across the moor uncurled before her and she pressed her foot down.

Chapter 8
The Roses

Lou was sitting alone with a pint of bitter, Butcombe Gold. The draught beers at The Roses changed all the time. This one was amber, with an edge of sweetness that curiously left a dry taste. He took another mouthful, thinking of Fran, wondering about gender change and the mixed reactions hers had provoked. No-one in this place would look twice, he thought, but a pub wasn't a police station. Well, not this sort, anyway. No bouncers on the door, no large-screen football, and no wary locals barricading the bar. He liked The Roses. It was friendly and comfortable; a sort of social centre, as far as he could see, used by all ages and backgrounds, and only a three-minute walk from his office.

Bright and colourful itself, with tall arched windows and green-going-on-turquoise walls, it didn't matter if you were from Warsaw, Saltash or the Cameroons; if you were interested in art or music, or just chatting, you were welcome.

He saw Fran come in and watched her at the bar. She was the same as she'd always been and yet she was different. She'd been a man and now she was a woman, but she remained the person he'd always known. It was other people's perceptions that were the problem, or could be. He frowned. It wasn't simple. He could see the difficulty of it for sporting bodies, like her International Judo Federation. After all, physiologically, wouldn't she still be stronger than a female opponent, at her weight? Would it be fair to let her compete as a woman? But the World Championships! He knew how much that meant to her.

She brought her drink to the table and sat down. Ginger beer, he guessed. She wasn't against alcohol, he knew that, but she seldom drank any. She said it slowed her reflexes.

"I was just wondering about Astana," he said. "Are you going?"

She raised an eyebrow. It wasn't the topic she'd been expecting.

"Kazakhstan doesn't appeal much." She took a drink and stood her glass back on the table. "But, if they let me, I will."

"Haven't they decided yet? It's been months."

"It's *'under consideration'*."

"Surely they know you have legal recognition, don't they?" He felt the injustice of her being left stranded in a kind of athletic limbo.

She shrugged and looked down, pushing at a cuticle with her thumb nail. "Sports bodies can exclude trannies, if they want to. The IJF's no different. It's meant to depend on the level of testosterone in your body, but who knows?"

Lou was caught in two minds: he could see she was uncomfortable and he respected her right to privacy, but they didn't have no-go areas between them. They worked well together, because they trusted each other; and it cut both ways. She knew all about his missing father and about the failed relationship that had brought him to Plymouth from Leicester, personal things he had spoken of to no-one else, apart from Connie – and even she didn't know as much as Fran did. Not yet, anyway.

"It's okay, Lou. This gender mix-up isn't common enough yet. People don't get it." She looked up at him, her eyes clear, ready for business. "But they will."

"Okay," he nodded. "So, tell me, how did you get on at Yelverton?"

She pulled out her notebook.

"No need for a court recital," he said. "The bones will do."

She grinned at him. It was an infectious smile that flooded her solemn face with warmth and good humour and then was gone again.

Lou listened patiently as she recounted her conversation with Oliver Drew, whose story was much the same as the one he'd already heard from Jellop.

"He said he'd restored a dilapidated chateau in the Dordogne, with Ron Jellop as his partner in the project, and that various pieces from the chateau were considered out of keeping with the renovations and sent for sale at auction."

"How did he react when you mentioned the French police had contacted us?"

"He kept good eye contact. Told me he thought the items involved were his property to do with as he pleased. And he said what's really valuable about Chateau..." she glanced at her notes, "...La Fleur, from his point of view, are its vineyards, which have been neglected. Apparently, no wine has been produced there for years, even though it carries a high 'appellation', Cotes de Bergerac. Restoring the vineyards and producing wine again was his main interest, he said."

Was it? Why sell it on so quickly then, Lou wondered, assuming what Jellop had told him was true. Asset-stripping seemed more likely. He kept the thought to himself. "Did you believe him?"

"As I said, his eyes didn't waver and people don't often look you in the eye when they're lying or, at least, they soon look away again. But he did stutter a bit, which he hadn't before." She paused. "No, I didn't believe him. I think he's an operator. Too smooth for me."

Apart from the bit about the vineyards, the rest of her account tallied with Jellop's, and Lou imagined they had worked on their story together. In any case, he would let DI Bentley know and then it was up to the French Police to decide what they wanted to do about it. As things were, he wasn't so much interested in the missing antiquities as in the Cayman Island account and where Ron Jellop's unattributed stream of cash was coming from. Maybe Drew and Jellop had other business interests together.

"What's he like?" he said. "Oliver Drew, I mean, apart from being an operator."

She took a drink and held on to the glass, "A lot of front. You know, big house, Roller out front, immaculately tailored suit. Very charming and polite..."

"But?" She hadn't been impressed and she didn't like him, it was clear.

"When I got there, something was going on between him and his wife. They were in the drive and the body language was...I'm not sure how to put it exactly...false. He was very...well...smooth." She shrugged her shoulders. "It's the only word I can think of, sort of oily urbane and sure of himself, if you know what I mean." Lou nodded. "But she'd been crying; it was obvious. There were red rings round her eyes and she left the first chance she had, some college course she was going to. It felt uncomfortable, tense."

"When you can, do a bit of digging, or maybe get Debbie on to it." Fran had a lot of loose ends to chase down and DC Debbie Denton was the best at getting relevant information out of a computer. "Let's see what we can find out about Mr Drew's background and his business activities."

Fran drained her glass and stood up. "Like another?"

"No, thanks. I need a clear head." He watched her edge her way to the bar. The place had filled up and he hadn't even noticed.

"Are you using this?" He looked back. A middle-aged woman with hooped earrings and a cowl-neck sweater had her hands on the back of the chair next to Fran's and was staring at him defiantly.

"No, that's fine. Take it." The tension went out of her and she smiled. "Thanks."

As she carried it away, he checked his watch. It was past six already and Connie was expecting him in half-an-hour.

"Right," he said, when Fran returned. "What happened with EC and the guy from The Ship?" Initials were an easy form of confidentiality to use in public places. Eddie Coaker might not be as well-known as Ron Jellop, but you never knew who was listening, or what connections there might be.

"He was on his boat, though he wasn't going out." She lowered her voice and drew her chair in closer to the table, resting her forearms on it. She leant forwards, her pad open in front of her. "Gale-force winds forecast for later on, he said. I checked; they were. When I told him about the CCTV footage from last Wednesday night, showing him taking a young woman aboard the small skiff he uses to get to his boat and back, and none showing her landing again, he said...," Fran flicked over a page; "he said, 'Sex, love. We all need it, don't we? Even your lot'. He said he didn't know the woman's name, as he'd picked her up in The Ship earlier on. Thought it might be Sarah or Sophie."

"What about there being no sign of her coming back from the boat?"

"He said he went to deliver some fish to a customer in Stonehouse..."

"Have you had the blow-up back yet?" Lou interrupted, remembering his visit to Firestone Hall the previous night. "You know, the one of him and the young woman leaving the pub."

"Yes, but it's back at the station, although, hang on a moment." Fran pulled her mobile from inside her jacket and thumbed the screen, scrolling. "Here it is." She passed it to him. "Easiest way to carry photos for possible IDs."

Enlargement had softened the contrast in the picture, losing sharpness and definition, so that the face caught in the street lights seemed smudged. Even so, Lou recognised it at once.

"Well, he wasn't lying about that, anyway!" he said, glancing up. He tapped the screen. "I saw him in Stonehouse last night, at RJ's. As I got there, he was leaving by a side door and acting like he didn't want to be seen."

"Bit of a coincidence, isn't it?" Fran's eyes narrowed. "And did you speak to RJ?"

"I did and he wasn't very happy about it." He grinned at the memory of Jellop's discomfort and pushed the smartphone back to her. "But this means RJ and EC know each other. And talking of coincidences, the young woman who showed me into his office this afternoon was also Eastern European, I'd say. With the two mystery callers, that makes three." He paused. "Just what is going on? And what did EC say about the one left on his boat?"

"He said that when he got back, she was gone. He hasn't heard from her since and doesn't expect to."

"Convenient. And how come there's no footage of her coming ashore again?"

"He just laughed. Said if you land further along, there are no cameras, and that maybe she'd probably got a lift with someone else."

"What about meeting her in The Ship? Does his story check out?"

"RS, the barman at The Ship, knows EC and remembers him talking to a woman in the bar late that afternoon. He says she was already there when EC came in and that they left together."

"Get a description?"

"Yes," She glanced down again. "'Attractive; medium build; fair hair cut short; smartly dressed under her coat; dark skirt and lighter sweater, both brown; mid-late twenties. He said she had a slight accent, thought she might be Polish or Scandinavian. He said he hadn't seen her before."

"Fits your caller, and there's no evidence of her having left his boat. Next morning, he goes out fishing, we get a call for help and he comes back alone." Lou drained his glass.

"Feels like we're getting close to *reasonable grounds*," Fran said.

Lou knew where she was going. "Except no missing person matching that description has been reported yet, and there's no body."

"What about the call Roz took last night? That was about a missing person; a missing young woman."

"There were no details, Fran."

"There's another thing," she said. "RS said she had a bag with her." She flicked through her notebook again. "Yes, a canvas holdall, like a weekend bag." She looked at him. "Was she going somewhere?"

"EC could have just picked her up, like he says," Lou said, drumming his finger-tips on the edge of the table. "Or it could have been a pre-arranged meeting and he was going to take her somewhere in his boat."

"You don't go fishing in a skirt."

"A rendezvous at sea? What for?"

Ron Jellop's smiling face popped into his thoughts: "Life is full of coincidences, Inspector". He stopped drumming.

"EC meets young woman and takes her to his boat. Next day, he goes fishing and comes back alone. That evening, he visits RJ at home, at night, using a side door, ostensibly selling him fish. Another coincidence?"

Fran frowned. "You're losing me."

"Something RJ said." Lou looked at his watch. He was going to be late. He reached for his mobile.

"Hi...Yes, I'm fine, just running a bit late...About half-an-hour...Okay...Yes, yes, I will."

He slipped it back in his pocket. "I've got to go. Let's pick this up again first thing Monday. See what's come in by then."

He pushed his chair back and started to get up, but Fran stayed where she was.

"If she hasn't been killed, she may be being trafficked. Another two days and it'll be too late to help her. We need everyone on this now, Lou."

He sat back down again, his anger at her challenge to him checked by her seriousness.

"Maynard will want more than we've got. He won't authorise a full-scale investigation, if EC could've been dropping her off somewhere. I can hear him saying it." He mimicked the superintendent's cheery delivery. "Had a lovers' tiff, most likely, and dumped her on a beach somewhere to find her own way home. Probably been there since yesterday."

"Then why the second call?"

Lou continued the impersonation: "Sharpen up, Bannerman. Panicking friend, sister even; happens all the time. Two minutes after she puts the phone down, the other one walks in, right as rain."

"What do you think?" She was watching him intently, still, like a cat waiting to pounce.

"It doesn't matter what I think. We need something concrete." He knew she wanted more from him than that. "Get Kincaid and Webb on to it. Check hotels, boarding houses, hostels, staff agencies. See if anyone's missing. Check the hospitals, too; any unidentified patients or casualties."

As he spoke, he saw the outward focus of her eyes change.

"Okay," she said. She was still looking at him, only she wasn't seeing him any more. The same concentration was there, but it had turned inward.

"What is it?" he asked.

"Nothing yet; just an idea."

He stood up. "Monday then. I'll be in Wembury, if you want me before that."

Fran slid out, nodding to the couple hovering, waiting for their table. She picked up the glasses, left them on the bar and followed him out.

Chapter 9
Rachael connects

Once inside the Tamar College of Further Education, Rachael felt safe again, for the time being. The English Literature A Level class was full and she was relieved to see Polly waving from near the front, where she'd kept a place for her. There were twenty-four in the class, when they were all there, sitting at tables for two organised in three rows four deep. Their lecturer, Roger Millman, was already on the podium, bending over the console, controlling projections on to the walled screen behind him.

"Thought you weren't coming, lovely," Polly said, scooping some books back on to her side of the table, her smile wide and welcoming. They had only known each other since the start of the course in the autumn, when they had first sat together, but Rachael felt a surge of affection roll through her. It was like having Barbara, her best friend from school, back again.

Dumping her bag on the table, she bent down and kissed Polly on the cheek, resting her hand on her shoulder. "I nearly wasn't," she said.

She slipped off her coat, hung it across the back of the seat and sat down, glad to feel the warmth of Polly's shoulder against hers. She took a deep, calming breath and realised that these afternoon classes had become 'home' to her; sitting next to Polly and listening to Roger sharing his knowledge with them, opening windows she had never looked through before or even knew existed. This was where she liked to be: this was where she felt safest and most herself.

"Right, welcome everyone." Roger moved in front of his table and leant against it. She watched him scanning the faces in front of him, until he found hers. She smiled back at him and saw the softening in his eyes, as if something relaxed in him knowing she was there.

"Have you time for a coffee afterwards?" Polly whispered, leaning in towards her.

"Yes, that would be lovely." She felt excited; they were crossing a boundary. Occasionally, they had lingered to chat after the class was over but they had never met outside the college before. She thought of Barbara again. Theirs had been a school-bound friendship, because her parents wouldn't let her invite Barbara home. "She's not a friend who will be of benefit to you," her father had said, which had left her puzzled, whereas her mother's objection had been much clearer. "She's not one of us, is she, darling? It never works, you know; oil and water don't mix."

Barbara had won a scholarship to St Catherine's and her fees and uniform were paid for her. Otherwise, her working-class parents couldn't have afforded to send her there. Her father was a painter and decorator and her mother worked part-time at Woolworths. They just weren't good enough for Rachael's architect father and church-committee mother.

Roger Millman's voice slid into her reverie. "Patriarchy seeks to subordinate women to men in multiple ways. As we have already seen in Willy Russell's play, Educating Rita, Rita's husband, Denny, is against her going to university and bettering herself. He wants her to stay at home and have children. When he finds out she's secretly 'on the pill again', he burns all her books. Similarly, here..."

"No." Her father's voice came back to her. "Three decent A-levels will be perfect. No need for more academia. Your mother's found an excellent course for you in Paris. It kills two birds with one stone: cordon bleu cookery and fluency in a second language. Then you can have your pick. Young men will be falling over themselves."

How could she have been so feeble? She hadn't got 'three decent A-levels' anyway, just a C and a D; that's why she was here now. In frustration, she stretched her legs out above the floor and brought both feet down together with a thump. Heads turned her way and she looked down. How could she have sacrificed herself so willingly? Barbara got Oxford, while she got Olly. She wondered what had happened to Barbara after that. Maybe she could search for her on Facebook.

* * * * *

At the end of the lesson, Roger asked them to leave their essays on his table. "I'm looking forward to going through them over the weekend," he said, grimacing and provoking a chorus of jeers and rejoinders: "I bet!", "Poor you!", "Better than football!" He grinned at them and added: "I'll let you have them back next time."

"Let's go to Pezzittino's," Polly said, pushing her books into a duffel bag. "It's quiet there."

"Good idea. Shall we go in..." Rachael was going to suggest they went in Polly's car. She liked the idea of walking back to get hers afterwards and delaying going home. But Roger's urgent voice cut across her.

"Rachael, have you got a moment?"

Polly touched her arm. "I'll wait for you outside."

Rachael watched him come across to her, loose-limbed and boyish in his movements, pushing his dark hair back off his forehead. A lock of it fell back almost instantly.

"I was worried," he said, with a quick smile as he reached her. But there was anxiety in his voice and eyes. "No call earlier and then you were late. I thought something had happened to you."

"I'm okay." She felt the need to reassure him. She glanced round, noting two older women at the back still at their desk, chatting. "Can we meet later and I'll tell you all about it then? I'm going for a coffee with Polly now..." She paused to look at her watch. Ten past four. She made a quick calculation.

"If I come round at about five-thirty, quarter to six, will you be back by then?"

"Yes, that'll be fine." His face relaxed and he grinned at her. "That'll be much more than fine." His sudden, playful happiness was puppyish; as if he'd spied a treat she was holding and was looking at her with expectant, tail-wagging eyes.

As she went in search of Polly, she became aware that, instead of the usual excitement she felt at a rendezvous with Roger, the prospect of seeing him later on felt like a burden. Normally, the thought of seeing him energised her and left her feeling lighter in spirit and body, whereas, now she was feeling heavy, weary even, as if the earth was dragging at her bones.

Chapter 10
Rachael's dilemma

They found a table in the corner, by the window, and Rachael sat down with her back to the wall. The room was small, but cosy: half delicatessen, half tables and chairs. But it was the soft background music and the smell of freshly-ground coffee that brought her a sense of warmth and welcome.

"So, come on now, tell me all about it. You looked ashen when you...thank you..." Polly leaned back as the waitress – Rachael thought she might be the owner but wasn't sure – put two large cappuccinos in front of them. "...when you came in," she continued. "What's your Oliver been up to? He's always...well, what's the word? He always seems such a charmer, when he comes to see my Ron."

"Oh yes, he can be very charming all right. He's good at that, when he wants to be." Polly's large, clear eyes were listening to her intently. That was what it felt like. There was something so open and trusting in her regard that, for a moment, Rachael was swept back to childhood teas with her grandmother and the sense of warmth and safety she had felt then.

"But there's a very different side to him, believe me, and I'm only just beginning to see it," she added.

Polly nodded and waited.

"He tried to stop me coming today; that's why I was late." Rachael hesitated. Polly's husband knew Oliver. Could she trust her? She didn't know her that well.

Polly was looking at her over the rim of her cup, as she took a sip. Lowering it, she licked the smudge of foam from her top lip and said, as if reading her mind: "I don't know if you want to tell me about it. But if you do, it'll go no further."

Rachael's eyes blurred and tears began to slide down her cheeks. She brushed them away with the back of her hand. "Sorry!" she said, shaking her head angrily to clear her thoughts, her hair flying one way then the other, before falling back across her shoulders. A shudder went through her and she fumbled with her cup.

"It's all right, lovely. Take your time." Polly's voice was low and soothing and as she spoke, her warm fingers curled gently round Rachael's wrist.

Rachael started to sob and pulled her arm away, searching in her pocket for a tissue to wipe her eyes and blow her nose. She looked back at the older woman through abject eyes. "Oh God, Polly, I'm sorry. I don't know what's the matter with me."

"What happened with Oliver?"

Her question came like a whisper and Rachael saw again Olly's maddened face, his fist smashing down on the car bonnet, and she couldn't control the trembling that started in her legs and rattled her cup in its saucer, as she tried to lift it.

"He wouldn't let me leave. I was in the car but he jumped in front of it. I'd have had to run him over." She stared hard at Polly, as if hanging on to her with her eyes, wanting her to understand, wanting to see in her face that she understood.

"Tell me."

"He frightened me. I couldn't get past him, I knew that. I gave up. I turned off the engine, unlocked the door, waited for him as he walked round, wondering what he was going to do to me."

She lowered her head, her shoulders shaking. The woman from behind the counter emerged with a glass of water, set it down on the table beside Rachael's cup, exchanged glances with Polly, who mouthed 'thank you', and went back again.

"No wonder you're upset," Polly said, taking a pack of tissues from her bag and pushing them across to her.

Rachael took one and made a cushion of it to wipe her eyes, then took another. She blew her nose and tried breathing deeply and slowly to calm herself. Finally, dabbing each nostril one more time, she folded her hands back in her lap.

She looked up and smiled. "That's better." She took a sip of the water and then a longer drink of it.

"You came, nevertheless. So, what happened?"

"The cavalry arrived!" Rachael gave a short laugh, remembering Olly's shock. "The police came. A young woman. She wanted to ask Olly some questions. There wasn't anything he could do to stop me, with her there."

Polly was studying her, her expression serious, as if weighing up the cost of something. Rachael stood up. "Back in a minute," she said and crossed to the counter. The woman pointed the way. "Thanks for the water," she said over her shoulder and saw the woman nod.

By the time she got back to their table, she was feeling more collected. Even so, as she sat down, she felt awkward and looked away from Polly out of the window.

"Do you think he's jealous of Roger? Is that it?"

Rachael's head snapped back. "What?"

"I'm just wondering why he's so against you coming to the classes."

She realised at once there was no accusation in Polly's question, only her own guilty conscience, and the sudden surge of panic and anger in her subsided as instantly as it had erupted.

"Yes, maybe. He did say something before about gossip. Mentioned you and Ron, actually."

"Us?"

"Yes. But don't worry; I knew he was making it up. He stammers when he lies. I always know."

"Why would he make things up about us and you?"

"Oh, you know, divide and rule. He probably sees you as more of a threat than Roger."

"That's ridiculous!"

"No, think about it, Polly." Rachael leaned forward, getting a glimpse of something for the first time and trying to catch hold of it. "It's what we've been learning about."

Polly tilted her head, looking puzzled.

"It's what he was saying about Educating Rita just now. You know, about Rita's husband not wanting her to study, feeling threatened by it."

"You think Oliver's feeling like Denny?"

"Exactly. It's nothing to do with Roger. Olly doesn't want me getting A-levels and going to university. He left school at 16. He doesn't want me going past him, as it were." What had been abstract before, with their lessons on 'patriarchy' and 'male hegemony', was suddenly utterly vivid and concrete. "That's it, isn't it? He wants to keep me dependent on him. I'm a possession, aren't I? And possessions don't have legs of their own, do they?"

She sat back and half-laughed, half-snorted.

* * * * *

Stoke Damerel, although an inner suburb of Plymouth, always seemed to her like a village, with its own charm and integrity. She wandered through it and on down the hill towards the college, so buried in her thoughts that she barely noticed the chill in the air or the smoke streaming from the last of the rush-hour traffic. As she had said goodbye to Polly, she had been clear inside herself that her marriage was over and that she would leave Oliver. An overwhelming sense of exhilaration had burned through her: the same feeling of joyous release she used to feel on the journey home from boarding school, with two months of summer holiday stretching ahead and no-one's wishes to please but her own.

As she approached a junction, two youths in hoodies came hurtling round the corner on skateboards and almost collided with her. "Sorry," said one, flashing her a smile. She thought of Nick and Sam; and the imagined faces of her two sons shattered her elation, plunging her into gloomy reflection on the impossibility of it all. What would a broken home do to them? Who would they live with? What would she have to offer them compared to Olly? What would she do for money? Nothing was more important than their happiness. She would have to wait, at least until they were ready to find their own way. Nick was already fifteen, but Sam was two years younger. He wouldn't be eighteen for another five years. Five years! She'd be forty by then. That was so old. How could she begin again then?

"Easily!" she snapped out loud, trying to cut across the trajectory of her plummeting spirits. "Another year of A-levels, three more at university. That's almost five years. You'll be as good as there." And once she was at university, her life would be very different anyway.

"University! Who are you kidding?" A mocking voice filled her head and she felt again the futility of all her hopes and plans. "Looks and no brains," Mr Falkner, her form teacher, had told her. But Roger believed in her. He was full of enthusiasm for her work. He was predicting an A-grade, if she kept going. "Just wanted to get into your knickers!" the mocking voice said. Her cheeks burned. "And he has, hasn't he?"

Back in the college car park, she stood in front of her car, fingering the dent, the key in her other hand. She wanted time on her own and wished she hadn't arranged to meet Roger. The car park was emptier now, although a few cars were still arriving. She pressed the fob, saw the orange flash and got in. As she closed her door, a pale coloured people-carrier pulled into the space beside her. Its lights died and she watched the bearded driver get out and walk across to the glass doors, pushing them open, before disappearing inside.

"I can't," she said and rummaged in her bag for her mobile. She tapped in the number.

"Hi, Rachael!" He always sounded so glad to hear from her. She closed her eyes.

"Roger, look I'm sorry to do this, but I've got a dreadful headache. I just want to go home and go to bed."

"Why not come here? I'll turn the lights out and you can be as peaceful as you like. I'll make you some peppermint tea. Never fails."

"That's kind, but I need to sleep."

There was a pause. "Come on, Roger," she pleaded silently, "make this easy for me." But when he spoke again, his voice was lower, tighter.

"So, I won't see you for another week then?"

"No, but it soon goes."

"Not for me, Rachael. I see so little of you."

"I know. I'm sorry."

"Can you find some time over the weekend? Any time? It doesn't have to be in the evening."

His words were hemming her in and her head was throbbing. She began massaging her forehead with her fingertips.

"Roger, I can't think straight right now. Let me call you later."

"I wish you'd come."

"I'll call you. Bye."

She closed her eyes and tipped her head back against the headrest. "One's bad enough," she murmured. "Why on earth get involved with two? How stupid can you be?"

Chapter 11
Lou's disappearing father

By the time Lou had picked up Connie and driven out to his bungalow in Wembury, he was feeling too much in his 'police-head' to tell her about his childhood. Whether he was just making excuses to avoid the subject again or not, he was too preoccupied to care, and he decided he would let it happen in its own time over the weekend. At some point, there would be a right moment, he was sure of that.

He cooked pasta with prawns for supper and as they ate, without mentioning any names, he told her about the missing woman and what had happened. He wanted her to know, so that if he got called in before Monday, she'd understand.

"Exciting life, but not easy life," she said. "Better in the summer, no mobile on your surfboard."

He smiled, glad at the lightness of her words and the ease with which he had paved the way, but later she came back to it. She was curled up on the sofa next to him with a mug of tea, watching him bending forward over the coffee table, using thin-nosed pliers to squeeze together a silver link that had come apart near the clasp of her necklace.

"What they need you for, maybe? What can't wait till Monday?"

It was a simple silver necklace, with small rectangular links near the clasp, growing larger and circular towards the front. He had given it to her for Christmas, knowing she wore little jewellery, but wanting to give her something personal and hoping it might be something she'd like. He held it out to her, accepting her mug, as she took hold of it and raised both hands behind her neck to fasten it.

The beaten links, reaching an inch or two below her throat, lay flat under the fall of her black hair and across the dark wool of her sweater. She smoothed it into place and, taking back her cup, waited for his answer.

Sealed in by the night, with the room cast in shadows, such light as there was caught against the pale planes of her cheeks, giving her face a visionary radiance.

"You're beautiful," he said, and he gazed at her, some vulnerability in him both pierced and reassured at the same time.

"Lou," she remonstrated softly, dropping her eyes away. "Beautiful like old bucket, I think."

Her words broke the stillness, like a pebble in a lake, and the little chopping waves of worry began to ripple through him again.

* * * * *

The following morning was clear and blustery, with the tide halfway out, and he and Connie walked the muddy coastal path out to Wembury Head, returning along the stony beach, clambering over rocks where the retreating waves still rushed in to cover emerging curves of sand.

As they stood on the mat just inside his front door, hands against the wall for balance, wrestling their boots off, they heard the shrill cries of the phone. Her eyes caught his in a momentary plea, before he turned away to answer it.

"Buongiorno, carissimo." His mother's voice rang cheerfully in his ear and he felt the relief of it not being Fran or Macklin.

"Ciao, Mamma, come stai?"

Greeting each other in Italian was their way of connecting through the life they had shared with her parents, Maggie and Fabio, her 'Spoza'. Lou had loved his grandmother, but she had died first, and the memory of his grandfather was more vivid in him. Fabio had been both grandfather and father to him. It was something he would need to explain to Connie, he realised, as he watched her disappear into the kitchen.

"How's Connie?" his mother asked.

"She's here now. She's fine." He knew she was fishing for more than that. She didn't know yet that they were talking about getting married, and he felt a sudden urge to confide in her. But she had been as distraught as him when Priya had left, and he didn't want to inflict that on her again, especially as he knew she would blame herself if his unwillingness to become a father sabotaged this latest relationship. He didn't want that.

"We've just been for a walk. Quite wild out there today." He tried to steer their conversation on to safer ground. "So, good timing on your part. How's Don?"

"That's partly why I'm ringing. He's had a chest infection and I think a break from the university would do him good. You've no idea how much pressure lecturers are under these days, but I better not get started on that." Lou heard her anger flare and die. "The point is, we're thinking of driving down next weekend, if that's okay with you. Just a couple of nights. Give us a chance to see you and to meet Connie, hopefully."

Lou sat down in the armchair near the window and looked out over the rooftops to the choppy grey and white sea beyond. He'd put off their last visit just before Christmas because of a fatal stabbing. He couldn't do the same thing again. He knew his reluctance wasn't about the pressure of work, even though that was real enough. The truth was that, if they came, his relationship with Connie would be formalised in a way it hadn't been so far. That was the pressure; he would have to sort things out with Connie about not having children before they came.

"Louis? Are you still there?"

"Sorry, Mum. I was just thinking." He missed having her nearby and he liked Don. He was grateful to him for the happiness he had brought his mother and also for his own release from a sense of responsibility for her. It would be good to see them, and he wanted his mother to get to know Connie. "That'll be great," he said.

* * * * *

The *right moment* came the following day, a dark, windy one, with heavy clouds bellying overhead as they strolled to the village local, The Odd Wheel, for lunch and a drink. They were holding hands, still bound together by the tenderness of their earlier love-making.

"Now your mother is coming," Connie said, her voice dipping and rising in its distinctive way. "Maybe you tell me about your father, so I don't say the wrong thing." As she spoke, her hand squeezed his for a moment before relaxing again.

A jet of anger flared in the pit of his stomach and spread, burning, across his chest. "Louis Lanui," he said, shaking his head; and then he repeated it more thoughtfully, bringing his emotions under control. "Louis Lanui."

For a while he was silent and Connie waited as they followed the bend in the road past the general store and lengthened their stride up the slope.

"When my mother was twenty, she went to a music festival at Woburn Abbey. It was 1968 and the height of the hippy movement. You know, protests against the Vietnam War, free love, all that. She was camping there with friends and it was the kind of atmosphere where they were all very trusting and loving, as well as stoned out of their heads, and everyone talked to everyone else as if they'd been friends for years." His mother's words came back to him, as he told Connie about it. "They were in love with love."

"Yes, I have seen this," she said. "On television. Very muddy, taking their clothes off and jumping in the water."

Lou smiled and nodded. "Anyway, Mum got talking to this French student, Louis Lanui. She says she just fell in love with him straightaway, knew he was the one for her. He seemed to feel the same way, she thought; and they became lovers." He gave a short laugh, almost a snort. "While Jimi Hendrix was giving a performance of his own, apparently. Anyway, the next morning she woke to find he was gone and she never saw or heard from him again."

"It's a problem with drugs, I think," she said. "Plenty feeling, not much thinking. Poor your mother! Now she pregnant, not know it yet."

"Yes," he started, but she cut across him.

"Poor you, too. No father to welcome you. Did your mother look for him?"

"Yes, she did, especially once she knew she was pregnant. She tried the French police, but they weren't interested. Not surprising. I mean, no crime had been committed and, if they got involved in looking for every runaway lover, that's all they'd be doing."

"She don't know where he comes from?"

"No. not at first, but she knew he was at university in Bordeaux. He'd told her that." Lou took a deep breath and blew it out noisily through pursed lips, wanting to find a way to condense the details. "It's a long story. Anyway, we're here now."

He went to turn down in front of the gabled, grey stone pub, with its large wooden wheel bracketed to the wall, but Connie came to a halt, hanging on to his hand, so that he had to break his stride and take a pace back to her. "I want to hear this long story, Louis," she said. "This is the story of your life. You go on telling me this inside, yes?"

Her seriousness caught him by surprise and deepened his.

"Hey, Lou!" He turned to find a surfing couple he knew from the beach, gesturing to him from the doorway. "You coming in?"

"In a bit," he called back, raising his free hand. He watched them disappear into a sudden golden blaze of bodies and voices, before the closing door extinguished it and the peace outside returned. He knew he didn't want to go in. If they did, it wouldn't be possible to go on with what he was telling her or to stay connected with it in himself.

"Can we keep walking?" he asked her. "It's too crowded in there."

"Yes, better you go on telling me now, Lou. I want to know about your father. I want to understand what happened to you."

They turned, crossed the road at a T-junction and began to walk in the same general direction as they had just come from, but along the higher road that curved round and then down towards the beach, bypassing the heart of the village.

"So," Lou said. "Where was I?"

"Mmm...your mother, you say she knows this man, your father. He goes to university in Bordeaux."

"Yes, that's right." He paused, picking up the threads of the story again. "Okay, so she tried contacting the university, rang them, but they wouldn't tell her anything, said it was confidential. But by the time she was five or six months' pregnant, she decided to go to there in person. Anyway, same deal, they still wouldn't tell her anything, until someone, I don't remember who...it might even have been another student, maybe, took pity on her and gave her Louis Lanui's home address in Arcachon, which is just south of Bordeaux on the coast."

"And she go there? Find his family?"

"Yes, she did...go there, I mean...but only on a day trip, because she didn't have much money." An angry pity wrenched at him as he pictured her, and he gritted his teeth for a moment before continuing. "It turned out to be a rented flat. Other people were living there and they had no forwarding address for him. She looked in the local phone directory and found several Lanuis listed. She wrote the details down on a piece of paper, so that she could try to contact them when she got home."

"Why not while she there? Why..."

"She didn't have the time or the money or the language, Connie." The words came out clipped and impatient. "She was on her own in a strange place, pregnant and exhausted, I imagine, after all the travelling."

"I'm only wanting to understand," she said, freeing her hand from his. "No need to be angry with me."

He touched her arm lightly, hoping she would stop, as he did, but she carried on for several paces, before she turned and waited for him. "I'm sorry," he said, coming up to her. "It's just that when I think of what Mum must have gone through then, I get mad with Lanui for deserting her. She was twenty years old, that's all. It's not you I'm angry with, it's him."

"I know that. He desert you, too, though he not know it. But I don't like you shouting at me."

He was going to say he hadn't shouted at her, but swallowed the words. Instead, he nodded and offered his hand. "I'm sorry. My fault. I shouldn't have been cross with you."

She took it and they walked on in silence, bending their heads against the wind. After a while she said: "What happened after she went to the flat?"

"Well, she tried the local police station, but it was too difficult. She couldn't make herself understood and they weren't interested, so she went home. Only by the time she got there, she'd lost the piece of paper with the addresses on, and she gave..."

"Oh, no! What she going to do now?"

Lou laughed in spite of himself, surprised by the immediacy of her shock.

"At first, she gave up. But after I was born she tried again. She hired a private detective to find him. She said she thought if Lanui knew he had a son, he would want to be with her. But in the end he wasn't getting anywhere and it was costing too much. She couldn't afford him."

As they reached the junction with the lower road, he paused to blow his nose. "Wind's making my nose run," he said, stuffing the hanky back in his pocket. "Which way? Beach or home again?"

"Home again." She gave a little shiver. "Good to get warm."

He put his arm round her shoulders and they turned up the hill.

"There was a note, you see," he went on. "I haven't told you about that, have I?"

"No. What this note say?"

The words in his mind were as clear as if the scrap of paper was in front of him. "It said, *Forgive me, I must go. It is too much to explain, I am not what you think. Je ne t'oublierai jamais – Louis.*" He saw she did not understand. "It means *I'll never forget you.*"

"He can't say that!" she said fiercely. "That not tell your mother anything. Better he say nothing. Better she think he not care at all, just one-night stand."

Lou squeezed her. "Thank you," he said. "And you're right. She kept that note in her purse all the time I was growing up. When I was 10 she decided the two of us should go to Arcachon and have another go at finding him. She never gave up hope that if she could find him everything would be all right, that she would convince him that whatever he felt was too much to explain, whether he was ill or a criminal or whatever, it didn't matter, because she loved him."

"But you couldn't find him, I know."

"No. We were there almost a week and tried everything." He remembered the heat, the brilliant sunlight shattering like glass on the sea, and that wide expanse of sparkling blue he'd never seen before. The water was warm off the beach and he remembered arguing, pleading with his mother that they spend the day there and not go off trudging through the hot streets again. "But if we find him, Louis," she had coaxed him, "maybe we can live here, or at least spend time here." And the desire to have that was stronger than anything he had experienced before. She towelled him dry, dressed him and took him back to the town by her side, looking at the map, finding addresses, knocking on doors.

His mother's mantra came back to him and he spoke the words aloud: "Nous cherchons Louis Lanui. Pouvez-vous nous aider, s'il vous plait?"

"What that mean?"

"*We're looking for Louis Lanui. Please can you help us?* It's what my mother said at every door we knocked on."

"But you never found him." Her voice was low, almost a murmur.

"We found an uncle. His English was better than our French, which was lucky because Mum couldn't understand most of what people said to us."

They reached the bungalow and he paused to hold the gate for her. Once inside, with their coats off and sitting in the kitchen while the kettle boiled, he continued the story.

"The trouble was this uncle said Lanui's parents were both dead and that after his mother had died he'd moved to San Francisco. Worse still, the last time he'd heard from him, Lanui was moving south. Big Sur, I think, or maybe Carmel. Not sure. Anyway, guess what?"

Lou watched the confusion in her eyes as she tried to come up with something and failed.

"I don't know. What?"

He grinned at her. "His uncle said Lanui was a keen surfer and that's why he'd gone to California. It must be in the genes!"

"Maybe," she said, touching his arm. "Or maybe it gave you the idea then."

He hadn't thought of that before. But either way he felt glad to have a connection of sorts.

"His uncle give you an address for your father?"

"No, he didn't have one. He said they'd lost touch after Lanui moved. We left our details with him, asked him to contact us if Lanui got in touch again. But he never did, and a few years later Mum told me the uncle had died." He lifted his hands and let them fall back on the table with a dull clonk. "So we ran out of leads."

He got up and went across to the kettle.

"And you never found your father, Lou, not even when you became a policeman?"

He filled the cafetiere with boiling water and carried it back to the table with a couple of mugs.

"No. I tried, but there's no record of a Louis Lanui living in California, or even of having a current visa for the US. He has disappeared. He may even be dead, for all I know."

"That's very sad for your mother, but very terrible for you having no father." She went to reach out to him, but he dropped his hands in his lap, resisting her pity, resisting her closeness.

"The point is," he said, ignoring her look of hurt. "I don't want us to have children. I don't want to be an absent father, and I would be."

"That what this long story all about then?

"Yes."

"We have to talk about this." Her gaze was unwavering, but he looked away, ashamed, knowing he didn't want to. What was the point? "We will find a way, you see. You be very good father, I think."

He'd expected her to be angry or to cry. What he wasn't prepared for was her calmness – no remonstration, no threats, just reassurance. No 'I', just 'we'. It left him unsure of what he'd felt so sure about only moments before. How could he be a 'good father' if the job always had to come first?

She was still watching him, waiting. The Hendrix riff of his phone exploded in his pocket, startling them both and releasing the tension in him. He carried it into the other room.

It was Fran. "Sorry to disturb you, Lou, but Jellop rang, asking for you. Thought you'd want to know."

"Go on."

"He wants to talk to you, wants you to have breakfast with him tomorrow at the Holiday Inn, 8am. I said I'd let you know."

"Does he?" He thought about the location. "Neutral territory. What do you think?"

"Maybe he wants to own up to one or two things, make a deal."

Lou didn't think so, but he wondered what else Jellop might have to say. "Okay, tell him I'll be there."

"You see," he said, walking back into the kitchen. "Any time, night or day."

Connie walked across to him and linked her arms round his neck, tipping her face up to his. He could smell the coffee on her breath as she said: "Maybe being a father more important for you than being a policeman."

Chapter 12

The bribe, the threat & a breakthrough

Next morning, Lou left his car at the police station and walked across town to the Holiday Inn. It was another cold, dark January morning, with street-lamps lighting his way up Royal Parade. The boulevard was largely empty, although small groups of early workers were beginning to emerge from a string of golden-windowed buses, their freezing breath caught briefly in the flare of the doorway as they stepped down and off into the gloom.

Turning left across the plaza by the Guildhall, he checked his watch and lengthened his stride. It was four minutes to eight and punctuality was important to him, a form of good manners. As he followed Armada Way towards the ridge of the Hoe, the ground started to rise and the Holiday Inn came into sight. Ahead of him, the eastern sky was growing lighter over the sea, becoming opaque.

He took the lift up to the restaurant on the penthouse floor. Ron Jellop was sitting alone at a corner table, with a murky view across the bay to Cornwall and Mount Edgcumbe to his right and a clearer one across the restaurant in front of him. He spotted Lou half-way across the room and raised a hand in greeting.

"Good morning, Inspector," he said, rising to shake Lou's hand. "Good of you to come. Please, have a seat." He gestured to the chair on his left, facing the window, but Lou preferred the one opposite, with an easy view into the room.

As Jellop resumed his seat, a young waiter appeared beside him. "Ah, George, impeccable timing! This is Detective Inspector Lou Beradino and I'm sure he must be ready for some breakfast." He turned to Lou. "It's a self-service system here, but George will be happy to get us anything we need."

Lou ordered scrambled eggs on toast and coffee, then turned his attention to Jellop. "Now, Mr Jellop, I..."

"Ron! Call me Ron, Inspector; everybody does."

Lou continued, as if there had been no interruption. "I am wondering what it is you want to talk to me about."

"The direct approach." Jellop put his cup down, dabbed the corners of his mouth with his napkin and leaned back, linking his hands across the club tie and dark blue edges of the blazer covering his stomach. "Good. I like that. It's my way, too. One knows where one is."

Lou waited. The level of hubbub in the restaurant was gradually increasing, as a steady stream of guests flowed in from their rooms for breakfast.

"Plymouth's on the way up, Inspector. Despite austerity and the cutbacks, investment capital is pouring into the city and the council has ambitious plans, as you no doubt know: the regeneration of the west end, including Union Street, the development of Millbay, the Bretonside Leisure Complex and so on. The 'Ocean City' is suddenly on the radar of financiers and entrepreneurs, not just nationally, but internationally."

Jellop spread his arms wide, as if embracing the world, and Lou noted the tone of ownership in his voice.

"This is my home town, Inspector. I feel proud of what is being accomplished here and at playing a constructive part in it. Well, that's my line, of course, construction!" He smiled broadly, enjoying his own joke.

Again, Lou watched and waited.

"The point is..." Jellop began, but was interrupted by the arrival of George with Lou's breakfast.

Lou poured himself some coffee and twisted the pepper grinder over his eggs. "Please go on," he said. "I can listen while I'm eating."

"The point is that prosperity is coming to Plymouth and it's only fitting that those who have been instrumental in securing it should be duly rewarded."

Lou's pulse quickened and he registered the new alertness in his body. With deliberate calm, he cut off another mouthful of egg and toast and chewed it slowly.

At a nearby table, a little girl in dungarees stretched for the ketchup bottle, knocked over her mother's glass of orange juice in the process and started to wail. Lou watched the ensuing melee around her, as staff mopped up the juice and her parents wiped her tears.

"The whole community will benefit, I imagine," he said.

"Indeed it will. However...how shall I put this? You are a man of the world, Inspector. I dare say you have seen things I will never have to. You and your colleagues keep us safe and, so too, the streets of this city. I respect you for that and I thank you for that."

There was an hypnotic rhythm developing in Jellop's speech. The public orator in action, Lou thought.

"And it is only fair and just that the guardians of our well-being should be made aware of our deep appreciation of the job they do, and that such appreciation should not consist only of words, even though these contain the full measure of our gratitude, but should also embrace tangible evidence of this. For service over and above the call of duty..." Jellop leaned towards him, nodding his head in confirmation. "And we know of your personal bravery and successes, not least, of course, in uncovering and exposing the gang bringing in slave labour on the Roscoff ferry. You took a bullet yourself that time, I understand."

The memory of it manifested in a twinge in Lou's left upper arm, close to his shoulder. "Fortunately, it just winged me," he said.

"Even so, as I was saying, for service of that kind, where you put your life on the line for the protection of other people, you deserve due recompense. Do you follow me?"

Lou had had enough. "Mr Jellop, before you say something you may regret, let me make something clear to you. I already receive 'due recompense' for the job I do, to use your phrase. I had hoped that, when you asked to see me this morning, you might have reconsidered our last two meetings and had new information of substance to give me, either about the French police enquiry or about your association with Mr Shingle. If this isn't the case, what else is there to discuss?"

Lou saw the genial expression on Jellop's face undergo a subtle change. The half-smile stayed, but the eyes narrowed and their focus became more concentrated. When he spoke, his voice was lower and his delivery slower.

"Are you a sportsman, Inspector?"

"You haven't answered my question."

"I played prop forward for Plymouth Albion. It can get rough in the scrum and you rely on your team-mates to bind close with you, so you become a single unit of power and purpose. From time to time, we had a player who wasn't up to it and we had to get rid of him. You can't afford a weak link."

Lou was looking at Jellop's bull neck and the pack of muscle rising from his shoulders under his jacket. The physical power of the man was evident. He imagined seventeen stone or so of Ron Jellop in full flight coming at you, the ball clutched tightly to his chest, head lowered like a battering ram.

"Can I get you some fresh coffee, sir?" George's voice preceded his shadow across the table, as he addressed himself to Jellop.

"No, thank you, George. The Inspector and I must be on our way."

The waiter nodded to them both and took Lou's plate with him as he left.

81

"The point is, Inspector," Jellop resumed, "you are not a local man and either you are with us or against us, part of the team or off the pitch."

Jellop's hands were resting against the table's edge, his fingers linked together. There was no trace of a smile on his face now and there was something granite-like in his demeanour and his words, something hard and unyielding. He was waiting for Lou's response.

"From what you've just said, Mr Jellop, I take it that you have no new information for me, which is disappointing. To use your analogy, the team I play for is the Devon & Cornwall Constabulary and I have no intention of becoming their weak link." Lou took his wallet from his hip pocket and placed a ten and a five pound note together under the edge of his side plate. He stood up and held out his hand.

Jellop rose, took Lou's hand in his own powerful grip and said: "The disappointment is mutual, Inspector. You'll find your chain is already broken. And, trust me, you get injured in the scrum when you're not properly supported." He gave Lou's hand a final shake and released him.

* * * * *

Lou went for his six-monthly dental check-up on the way back to the station, and it was almost ten o'clock by the time he got there. Fran was waiting for him. His office door was open and, as he approached, he saw her sitting in front of the desk tapping at her iPad, her heels bouncing up and down. She was humming. Catching sight of him, she jumped up. "So, what did Councillor Jellop have to say that was so urgent?"

"Good morning, Fran," he said, taking off his jacket and hanging it across the back of his chair. "You're busting to tell me something, I can see. So, you go first and we'll get back to Jellop later."

She frowned, grinned and, when he did, sat down again. When she was excited, her chin would jut forward and the words would fly out. She was excited now.

"I was at a Pride meeting yesterday with Kate and Molly, you know, and the others, and there were some new faces there, students from the University. It suddenly dawned on me: what if the missing woman is an international student here at St Andrew's? If she hasn't shown up, people may just think she hasn't come back from wherever she's from and assume she's dropped out or is ill. I mean, it's probably normal not to see someone over the Christmas break, particularly if they live abroad, isn't it?" Lou nodded. "So, I went to Registry first thing and asked if any students are missing. They said they'd check and get back to me. They rang about ten minutes ago with a list of names."

Fran took her notebook from her inside pocket and flipped it open, then turned it round and laid it in front of him.

"One name stands out: Nina Lapinski." She pointed to it and Lou noticed the bitten fingernail. "The others are male mainly or have British-sounding surnames. Of course, the women there might have a British husband. I'm following them all up, but I've already had Registry fax me a photo of Nina. She took an A4 sheet from under her iPad and handed it to him. "Look, she matches the barman's description." She waited, watching him expectantly. "Attractive. Short fair hair. Mid to late 20s. Eastern European."

Lou studied the head and shoulders photograph.

"Looks like a mug shot," he said. "At least it's in colour. The cheekbones have a Slavic look." He clicked his tongue. "But it's too easy to read what you want into it. Check with the barman. If he confirms it's her, I'll request resources for a full enquiry." He handed it back to her. "Nice work, Fran."

"And you?" Fran said, folding the sheet into her pocket. "How was breakfast?"

Lou sat back and reflected for moment, letting his gaze wander to the window and the pall of clouds beyond. "Councillor Ron Jellop tried to bribe me." He looked back at her. "And, when I didn't bite, he shifted smoothly into intimidation."

"He threatened you?"

"He wrapped the cudgel in a rugby scarf but, yes, he threatened me."

Fran looked puzzled. Lou took a compact recorder from his jacket pocket and played her the end of his recent conversation. The background din of the restaurant was surprisingly loud, but Jellop's words were firm and clear.

"Your chain is broken and you'll get injured!" she said. "Somebody here is on his payroll. Do you believe that?"

"I believe...no, I know...he has influence here, yes."

"And what about getting injured? Shouldn't you organise a tail, someone to watch your back?"

"It was a warning, Fran. He won't do anything yet." Lou smiled at her, one of his wolfish grins. Like a hound on a scent, she recognised the quiver in him. "But don't you think it's a bit of an over-reaction to questions about his property dealings? There must be something else he doesn't want us to find out about."

"Nina and Coaker?" Fran said.

Lou nodded. "I'm beginning to think so."

Chapter 13
Rachael's decision

"Well, dear, I am sorry to hear things are so difficult for you. But life isn't always a bed of roses, you know. If you want my advice, lose yourself in a good book. That's what I used to do, when your father was playing up."

Rachael held the receiver away from her face and snarled at it. She was as frustrated with herself, as with her mother. Why did she always think things were going to be different between them, when they were always relentlessly the same? She checked her watch; she wanted to be out before Oliver got back. Any time after seven, he'd said, and it was almost that now. She put the handset back to her ear.

"...and, besides, you have so much to be thankful for, with your lovely house and the boys. When I think..."

"The boys are back at school," Rachael interrupted her. "I hardly see them. Anyway, look, sorry, but I've got to go before Olly gets back. I'll speak to you later."

She put the phone down on her mother's offended goodbye, seized her bag off the sofa beside her and hurried out into the hall. Grabbing her hooded parka and keys, she slammed the front door behind her so that the Yale lock caught and ran to the car, struggling into her jacket as she went.

Once out on the road to Plymouth, she realised from the oncoming headlights that she was just as invisible as these early evening drivers Even if she passed Olly coming the other way, all he would see would be her lights, not the car, not her. She let go of the breath she didn't even know she was holding, relaxed her grip on the wheel and settled back against the seat.

"Playing up!" She spat out her mother's words. "Fucking around, you mean!" Why the hell had she stayed with him? Why had she put up with it? Her father had treated her mother like his skivvy for years. Where was her self-respect? And then he'd left her, anyway, as soon as she hit the menopause. Traded her in, like an old car, for that piano-legged gold-digger, Nancy Miller!

"Well, you're bloody well not doing that to me, Oliver Drew!" she yelled and banged the steering wheel with the edge of her hand.

* * * * *

When she reached the city, she turned away from the noisy lights and buildings of the centre and drove west towards Stonehouse, where she could walk close to the sea. Normally, when she felt lost, she would walk up on the moors, drawing inspiration from the raw beauty there. But, in the dark, among the ruts and shadows, it would be too treacherous, and she felt drawn to the undulating expanse of the ocean instead.

She passed the Marine barracks and took the narrow spur towards Devil's Point, where the River Tamar pours into Plymouth Sound. As she rounded the bend, her headlights lit up a low stone wall separating the road from the rocks and the darkness beyond. Switching them off, she eased to a halt and sat, waiting for her eyes to adjust.

Gradually, the denser shapes of Drake Island and the breakwater further out began to solidify against the black cloth of the sea, and every now and then moon-silvered crests glittered under the shuffling clouds.

Her phone rang. It was Roger and she ignored it, not wanting to be disturbed. But the moment was broken. She turned on the car's lights again and followed the road round to the car park at the end.

She was surprised how full it was and she couldn't find a space. Finally, she pulled into a disabled bay facing the sea, feeling guilty, and sat for a while with the motor running, unwilling to lose the warmth of the heater. If challenged, she would move.

She looked in her mirror at the rows of cars and felt irritated, knowing most of them belonged to diners at the growing crop of restaurants in Royal William Yard, which had been the Navy's principal depot for provisioning its warships for over a hundred years. She understood the attraction of its splendid, magisterial buildings and setting, facing up the Tamar towards the Devonport Dockyards. Nevertheless, this was a free car park, where people could come for a stroll or to walk their dogs or go fishing off the rocks. It wasn't meant for those wanting to avoid paying the Yard's parking charges. Eventually, the council would see what was going on and turn it into a 'Pay and Display', and another free amenity would be lost. It wouldn't matter to the diners, in the end; but, to the hard-up, it would.

She wished they had never built the steel staircase that now breached the Yard's massive walls and joined its previously impenetrable western end to the southwest coastal path. It made it so easy to park here and walk down. Increasingly, despite her privileged background, Rachael felt herself identifying with the poor and oppressed. It was the course's doing. It was Roger's doing! His talks on 'The Feminist Critique of Patriarchy'. The books he had recommended they study: D.H. Lawrence's 'Lady Chatterley's Lover' and its 'Preface'; Kate Millett's 'Sexual Politics'; Alice Walker's 'The Colour Purple'; and, of course, Willy Russell's play 'Educating Rita'. Not least had been his outrage at Olly's treatment of her. He had thrown open the curtains in her head and let the light flood in, when she hadn't even realised she was in the dark.

She watched the shadow of a yacht slipping past Drake Island, its lights appearing and disappearing. "I didn't know what I didn't know," she told herself, aloud. "Why don't I want to see you, now? I used to long to see you, be with you." She couldn't explain it. Something had changed. She pictured Roger, his lean body, the soft haze of hair across his chest, dark and silky, the warm flood of him inside her. He was such a tender lover, so sensuous and generous. With Oliver, it was always as if she was being raided, a sort of smash and grab. But, with Roger, it had felt like she was receiving, that he was giving himself to her, that they were sharing. And it had liberated some deep joy in her, some appreciation of herself.

"You felt so exciting then," she whispered. "I felt so alive! But, now..." She stared at her hands clenched round the steering-wheel. "Now, you feel like a burden." The acknowledgement of the feeling shifted something. For the moment she felt lighter, as if she had been relieved of a heavy bag she was carrying. Her fingers relaxed their grip, and she ran them through her hair, holding the weight of it away from her neck, enjoying the coolness of it.

Had she swapped one oppressor for another? Had she been freed from one prison only to be led into another? Was her liberator now her jailer? The thoughts tumbled over each other. She let go of her hair, opened the door and got out. How could the love she was so sure of have so suddenly turned to doubt? The night air was chill. She pulled up her hood, drew the zip tight to her chin and started to walk to keep pace with her mind's restlessness. She walked back the way she had driven in, keeping close to the wall. Occasional slithers of moonlight sliced Jennycliff beach on the far side of the bay. At the bend, she turned off, passing a small, castellated artillery tower, and followed the path along the coast. She paused by steps leading down to a small cove and listened to the washing in of the waves and the light rattle of shingle, as they sucked back again.

She didn't want to be with either Oliver or Roger, she realised. She wanted to be on her own with Sam and Nick. The thought of them made her eyes swim and she longed to see them, have them with her. But, when she thought of holding them, hugging them close to her, it was their younger selves she was imagining. She couldn't picture them letting her cuddle them now. Sam, maybe sometimes, when he was homesick, when he was saying goodbye; but not Nick, he had become self-contained, independent of her. "Bloody school!" she shouted at the sea. "Sam, I love you!" She was calling to them now. "Nick, I love you! I'm thinking of you! I want you here with me!" She trailed off, talking to herself. "I want you here with me. This sending you away is wrong; it's all wrong."

She pulled a tissue from her pocket and blew her nose. Tears were sliding in at the corners of her mouth and she scooped at them with her tongue, comforted by the salty taste of them. Turning, she continued on almost to the end of the path, where it widened with some benches overlooking Millbay and the dock where the Brittany ferries came in from Roscoff and Bilbao. A tall figure in a beanie, carrying a fishing rod and bag, loomed close to her, taking her by surprise. "Evenin'," he said, striding on, before cutting right at the path's end and disappearing.

As she retraced her steps, her thoughts became caught up in a whirl of hopes and impossibilities. One minute her mood was dark, with sinking feelings of despair, and the next minute her spirits soared, lit up by flashes of elation, like firework rockets, momentarily brilliant and then extinguished.

She would not stay with Oliver. He didn't love her; she was just another asset to impress people with, using their admiration and their money to fuel his schemes. Like the photograph of the boys he carried in his wallet to show what a good family man he was when, in reality, he never spent much time with them at all. His attentiveness and danger-ousness were what had attracted her to him in the first place. He had made her feel beautiful, special, with the risks he took for her. On the eve of his wedding to his wife-to-be, he had climbed two storeys to her bedroom window and made love to her, while her parents slept on below; and then, after less than a month, he had left his bride in order to be with her. He had dazzled her, played on her adolescent vanity, taking grainy black and white shots of her, developing the photographs himself, cropping and editing them into a portfolio for her to take to a modelling agency.

He had seduced her into believing in him, in just the same way as he now seduced backers into financing his schemes and other women into sleeping with him. And the black-souled beauty of it was that he counted on people being captivated by his audacity, his outlaw-like spirit that chal-lenged convention, and by his ability to make them feel that, in tying their fortunes to his, their lives would be more exciting, their pockets fuller and their own aspirations more readily realised. "Lucifer," she said and shuddered, seeing so starkly the route of her own undoing.

She walked on past the car park along the path that curled back from the bay to follow the river. She could see the illuminated rise of it further on, where it sloped up to meet the walled entry to the Yard's staircase. She paused, not wanting the lights and bustle of it, and an elderly couple walking their dog nodded as they passed, causing her to veer away on to the grass and down towards the rocks, where it was darker and more solitary. She would change her life. She would take responsibility for herself and for Nick and Sam; not be passive like her mother, but active in her own right. And, as she thought of what that might mean, a vivid image came to her of a manageable terraced house with bay windows and views out over the sea. It was decorated in the bold colours and fabrics she liked, with airy bedrooms for the boys upstairs. She would work, while they went to school locally, and she would be financially independent, for the first time in her life. "Captain of my own ship," she whispered, glancing at the swaying lights of a ghostly shape anchored out by the breakwater.

But the image and the hope of it dissolved in the arc of Oliver's arm bringing his fist crashing down on her car bonnet. He would do everything to prevent her going; and she knew from experience that there were no lengths to which he would not go to have his way. He would fight for custody of the boys, with some high-powered barrister on his side. What could she afford? He controlled their money. She didn't even have a bank account of her own. And he would have so much more to offer materially. Maintaining the boys at a prestigious public school would be seen as a good thing, wouldn't it? Her wish to take them away from there would be derided as selfish and against their best interests. She could hear the judge's words already, dismissing her as a suitable custodian for them, "when it is clear that the father has done everything reasonable to keep the family together and is in the best possible position to make suitable provision for the well-being and future prospects of these two young men".

She shivered and stamped her feet against the numbness in her toes, wishing she'd brought her boots. Something soft brushed her leg and she jumped, twisting round to see a pair of glinting eyes beside her. "Scotty! Come away!" commanded an invisible voice from above her. The eyes vanished and the smudged shape bounded away from her.

She curled her fingers more tightly in her pockets, her nails pressing sharply into her palms. Surely she could persuade Olly to let her go. Why would he want to keep her against her will? What possible pleasure could there be in that for him? Besides, he would be free then to have affairs whenever he wanted, with no need for secrecy and duplicity.

No, after the first shock, he would see the sense of it. She wouldn't ask for much, just enough to buy a house and to help with the boys' upkeep, until she finished her studies and started working. She would make him see the sense of it. She'd go home and do it now; face it and get it over with. The thought both thrilled and terrified her and, as she made her way back to the car, her father's words from her childhood came back to her: "Fear knocked on the door, Faith answered and there was no-one there."

Repeating them aloud to herself, she drove slowly out of Plymouth and home across the moors to Yelverton. She would free herself from Oliver and end her affair with Roger. She could do this, she told herself; she could take control of her life, one step at a time. But, as she turned into their drive, a cold fear balled in her stomach and ran up the fine hairs at the back of her neck. The Rolls was there and the lights in the house were on.

Chapter 14
Rachael gathers courage

When Rachael entered the house, the door to the living room was ajar, and from the hall she could see Oliver sitting on the sofa, surrounded by a spread of papers. A bottle of red wine was open on the coffee table and, in front of it, were a glass a third full and a heavy onyx ashtray, with a thick cigar resting in it. A steady plume of smoke wavered upwards, permeating the house with its familiar spicy, cedary aroma. He was leaning back against the cushions, writing on a notepad on his lap.

Her plan had been to go straight to bed and face him in the morning, but as she crossed the hall to the stairs something instinctive carried her, almost propelled her, through the open doorway.

"Oliver," she said, stopping on the other side of the coffee table, facing him. "I don't want to go on like this. What happened earlier isn't okay." He went on writing, not looking up at her. "It's not good for either of us and, if Sam and Nick had been here, they'd have been..." She paused, searching for the right word. "They would have been frightened."

He underlined the figures he had just written with two thick bars of black ink and stared at them, slowly recapping his fountain pen. "The police are investigating the sale of the antiques from the Chateau," he said quietly, still looking at the pad in front of him. "It's a misunderstanding, of course, but you know what the boys in blue are like. So, I want you to be very careful about what you say if that CID woman or anyone else starts asking you questions." He leaned forward, picked up the wine glass, swirled it, took a mouthful, seemed to chew on it before swallowing and set it down again, lifting his cigar from the ashtray. He settled back against the cushions, looked at her finally and blew a smoke ring. "As far as you are concerned, you know nothing about these business matters and you simply refer anyone who asks about them to me."

She felt like slapping his self-satisfied face and ramming his foul cigar down his throat. "Did you hear what I said?" she asked. "I'm talking about us, our marriage, the boys. I want a divorce. I don't want to go on with this." Her words surprised her or, at least, the ready way they came out did. She felt strong and in a strange way, even though her heart was hammering, she felt resolved and self-possessed.

"You're not yourself today, are you?" He smiled. "Got the rags on?"

His vulgarity, so often delivered with an impish grin, caught people by surprise and jolted them into defensive laughter. He had a reputation for being 'naughty' and 'unconventional' and even 'a bit dangerous'. Women seemed to be tempted by him, while men rather admired him, wishing they had his nerve, his cheek. But tonight Rachael saw only the drive in him to have his way, and his contempt for others, his deep unkindness. She turned to go, impatient to be free of him.

"There's no question of your leaving, Rachael, or of divorce. You and the boys are my family; we stay together. If you try, the courts will take the boys off you. But it wouldn't come to that because...," he paused. "Well, accidents happen, don't they?"

His stillness and the calm of his words froze her. Glancing over her shoulder in disbelief, she saw him nod at her. "I mean it," he said. "Now go to bed like a good little wifey, I won't be long, and tomorrow we'll go on as if nothing has happened, and you will let the college know you're leaving." He laid his cigar down and picked up his notepad.

His violence and his implacable belief in his own ability to outwit all and any authority frightened her. She felt him capable of murder – her murder. It would be another challenge, another risk. He would sit as now, with wine, cigar and notepad, and work out a plan, an accident.

As she went upstairs, she couldn't stop her hand from shaking on the banister. With rising panic, she grabbed her night things from their bedroom and locked herself in the guestroom. Long after she heard him go to bed, she lay awake, listening, waiting, convinced he would come to take her, to claim ownership of her, to rape her. And it would be rape, because she never wanted him to touch her again, ever.

* * * * *

She woke to hear the crunch of the Rolls' tyres on the gravel outside her window. Light January sunshine was spreading across the carpet and up over the duvet, slicing her in half. She listened to the fading growl of the car leaving the driveway and felt a surge of relief at his going. Turning on her back, she watched the bare branches of the beech tree gently scratching at the pale sky. She was glad to have the house to herself and glad she had left the curtains open to the moon and the stars, so that she could lie here now in the warmth, with the day's brightness gathering around her.

Gradually, the events of the previous night came back to her, playing like a film across the transparent screen of the window pane. Crushed hope pressed heavily across her chest and shoulders, forcing her to lean up on her elbows, just to prove to herself that she could. She might be caged, but she was not yet flattened. There had to be a way to get away from him safely and to have Nick and Sam with her. She slumped back again, pushing her arms under the duvet and pulling it up to her chin. It was hopeless: she had no money to live off, nowhere to go, no way of providing for the boys, let alone getting custody of them.

Maybe Roger could help her. He would gladly let her stay with him and feed her at least, until she sorted things out. And he'd protect her. For a moment, her spirits lifted again and the determination to fight Oliver and not be cowed by him energised her into kicking off the cover and swinging her feet off the bed on to the rug. As soon as she was dressed, she would try to ring him. He'd be a good person to talk to. She couldn't think of anyone else she could turn to. He'd know about practical things. She would be entitled to alimony, and half the house must be hers.

She went down the landing to their bedroom and through into the bathroom. As she stood against the basin in her nightdress, cleaning her teeth and watching her reflection in the mirror, the electric brush pulsing in her hand, her thoughts started to race. Maybe she could even keep the house, if the boys were to live with her, and Oliver would have to move out. She'd get an order from the court to keep him away, because of his threats; and he would have to pay her enough to live on.

"There's no question of you leaving!" Oliver's voice dissolved the mirage. She hunched over the basin to rinse out her mouth. Roger wouldn't be able to protect her twenty-four hours a day. And he wasn't the answer, anyway. She was going to break with him, too. The memory of her decision to do so from the previous night reared up in front of her. She wasn't going to go from one cage to another.

"I can't think straight," she yelled, glaring at herself. Tears bubbled in her eyes and, rocking back, she turned away and went to lie face down across the double bed, with her arms outstretched and her face turned sideways. Why was there only Roger? What had happened to her friends? She thought of Lyn and Mary. As far as she knew, they still lived near Beaconsfield in Buckinghamshire, where they'd all grown up and gone to school together. Mary had been the first to get married. Rachael had always liked going round to their flat for meals, when she was still single and living at home. But Oliver didn't want to mix with them, called Graham a 'loser', because he was content with his job, programming computers. And he didn't like Lyn either. She was a 'dyke' or a 'ball-breaker' – only because she'd resisted his advances and seen through him from the start. It was so clear now. He'd cut her off from her past and isolated her, moving to Devon and binding her to him with children and the life he'd chosen.

Dear Lyn and Mary. She was half-laughing now, remembering the boys pulling on Mary's ponytail in the schoolyard, her and Lyn pushing them away, and Barbara helping, too. She'd trusted Barbara the most, but Lyn and Mary had been such fun. There was that field by the river, or was it the garden of the house across the road? Grass, anyway, and a white marquee, with a band playing and everyone in fancy dress. Mary had a low-cut blouse and a basket of oranges. Lyn was standing beside her, an Apache squaw with scarlet headband holding a feather in place against her long back hair. A young man in a purple toga and golden laurel wreath crown took the feather and slid it into Nell Gwynne's cleavage; then he turned from them and held out his hand to her. "Oliver," he said. "Shall we dance?" And he took her and whirled her and...

"...you get this, give me a ring. We must talk. I've no classes this afternoon, so..." She woke with a start at the sound of a voice in the hall below and was half-way to the stairs before she realised it was Roger leaving a message on the answerphone. What was he thinking of! She raced down the stairs and seized the receiver. "Roger? Hello? Hello?" She'd missed him. She jabbed at the buttons, deleting the message without playing it. For God's sake, what if Oliver had been at home! What was he thinking of! Pure anger and frustration drove her back upstairs. She grabbed her mobile from the bedside table in the guestroom, turned it on, saw the missed calls, Sam's too, and rang him back.

"Rachael! At last! How are you? I was worried. I kept..."

"What the hell are you thinking of? What are you doing calling the landline? Are you mad?" She was so furious with him she could hardly get the words out fast enough.

"You sound angry. Are you all right?"

"Of course I'm fucking angry! And, no, I'm not all right. Not at all."

"Look, Rachael, I can't really talk now. I've got a class waiting. But I'm free after lunch. Why don't you come over?"

"Good. I will." She ended the call abruptly and went to get dressed. She'd see him all right and she'd end it.

Chapter 15
Fran on the trail

Fran sat at one of Cap'n Jasper's bench tables, fondling a mug of tea to keep her hands warm. The cafe was at the end of the Barbican, overlooking Sutton Harbour, with the Fish Market opposite. Protected from the tide by lock gates, Sutton Pool, as it was also known, was indeed an area of still water. Yachts and small craft barely moved against their pontoon moorings, row upon row, constantly reducing the space of open water available and crowding up around North Quay, with its string of tall apartment blocks. But the protected Pool also meant the working boats could come and go, irrespective of the tides, and unload their catch easily.

Rod Sherman, barman at The Ship, had just confirmed that the woman in the photo, Nina Lapinski, was the same person who had been waiting for Eddie Coaker and who had left the pub with him that day. He had agreed to call in at the station after his shift and make a formal statement. For the first time since that desperate phone call, Fran felt something firm under her feet. They might not have a body yet – It might be out in the depths somewhere with the fishes – but they had a name. And they had CCTV footage to go with Rod's testimony, showing Nina boarding the Morning Star with Coaker, but none of her leaving again. And no-one had seen her since, not her friends in Plymouth anyway. The Polish police were checking with her family, but she would be very surprised if Nina turned out to be there. There was no record of her having booked or caught any flight home over the Christmas period. She knew because she had contacted the airlines herself.

An open fishing boat, with a solitary man in a woolly hat at the tiller, passed in front of her, heading out. She drained her mug and stood up. She needed to talk to Lou, see if they could pull Coaker in for questioning, but she had one more call to make on her way back to the station.

She walked up Buckwell Street towards the city centre and turned off right through a pedestrian archway into a cobbled street, following it round to the Plymouth Arts Centre. It was a narrow, long building at the top end of a short terrace. It had gallery space, a small cinema for arthouse films, a bar on the ground floor and a restaurant area upstairs. She nodded at Tom, the manager, a lean man with thinning hair, who was bending over a seated woman in a shawl she hadn't seen before. More often than not, when she went in these days, he would be in the middle of instructing some new volunteer in the computerised niceties of issuing advance tickets, while customers waited patiently on the nearside of the counter with tightening smiles, their two minute 'pop-in' turning into ten.

Fran walked on, past a coloured glass installation, into the bar area, with tables and chairs on either side. She saw Kate, Molly and Sean sitting at one, their coats, scarves and bags spread across another. Otherwise, the place was empty, apart from Val behind the bar, restocking the fridge. Friends like them, from the local Pride group, often got together in between the monthly meetings held here. If you were lesbian, gay, bisexual, transgender or questioning, this was a safe and comfortable place to be.

"Uh-oh!" grinned Kate, catching sight of her. "Here comes trouble."

"Hi Molly, hi Sean." Fran kissed them both and pulled up a chair next to Kate, without looking at her. "Who's your friend?"

Kate wrapped an arm round her neck, pulling Fran towards her and kissed the top of her head.

"Wasn't she outside with all those bags, freezing to death?" Sean said, indicating several carriers half-covered under the pile of discarded clothing. "We took pity on her, brought her in for a warm drink."

"Bag ladies are always welcome here!" Molly chided him, her chins wobbling with delight.

Even though a boy then, it was Kate and Molly who had become her best friends at secondary school, when first arrived there aged eleven, and had remained so ever since. She and Kate were the same age, with only a month between them; but Molly had started school late and was a year older. Even so, it was more her nature than the age difference that had made her feel like a protective elder sister to them. Form monitor, head girl, senior girl guide, Molly was seen as sensible and responsible from the beginning; and they had sheltered in authority's affirmation of her, their own antics going largely unnoticed.

Indeed, it wasn't until Molly declared herself a lesbian at sixteen and became a founder member of Pride locally the year after that her radical politics became apparent. And it was typical of her motherly inclusiveness that she had been the one to befriend Sean, when he had turned up at an LGBTQ meeting about six years earlier, after taking a one-way flight from Cork to Plymouth to escape his family's wedding plans for him. But Kate was her closest friend. She was married, had two girls and was happy with her husband, Doug. Fran valued the support of the Pride group and the friends she'd made there, but Kate had been her mainstay while she was transitioning.

"Want a drink?" Kate asked her.

"Just had one, thanks."

"What about lunch, then? We're thinking of going to Monty's for a sandwich, in a bit."

"'Fraid not. I'm on duty, got to get back. I just came by to see if any of you might have heard anything." She lowered her voice, looking quickly at each of them. "In confidence, a Polish student from the uni has gone missing: a young woman, twenty-three, Nina Lapinski." Fran fished out the photocopy and stroked it out straight on the table.

Kate looked at it first. "No, I don't recognise her," she said and twirled the picture around for the others to look at.

Molly and Sean both shook their heads.

"We think she may have been abducted by a man called Eddie Coaker," Fran said, "who seems to be involved with a well-known local city councillor."

"Coaker?" Molly said, looking at Kate. "Wasn't it him who got in a fight with one of Jay's boys? Brian or Keith, don't remember which. Ended up in hospital, anyway."

Kate pursed her lips and slowly shook her head. "Not ringing any bells."

Fran went to pick up the photocopy, but Sean put his hand on it. "This councillor," he said, "wouldn't be Ron Jellop by any chance, would it?" She felt a prickle at the nape of her neck. "Could be," she said. "Why?"

"There's a whisper going round," he said, looking up at her, "about a ring of prostitutes operating out of the university." He tapped Nina Kapinski's picture. "Foreign girls."

"And Jellop?"

"Ah, you're a dreadful woman, DS Bannerman!" he said, scooping back his thick, reddish-brown hair and glancing over his shoulder. "This is gossip I heard at Nexus and I don't believe everything I hear there." It was a gay bar on Union Street with a mixed reputation, although, in Fran's experience, any trouble was usually down to straights going there looking for it.

"It's okay, Sean. I'm not asking for a sworn statement. Rumours are fine." She wanted him to get on with it.

"There's a banjo player, Damien, does some busking. You probably know him." Fran nodded quickly. "He sees things out on the streets. He said a lot of young women were coming and going from a house in some cul-de-sac near the university."

"Student digs, most like," Molly said.

"Well, it could be that, Molly, sure enough. But the thing he noticed was the number of well-heeled men going there too, including Ron Jellop and..." He looked back at Fran, hesitating. "...your boss, DI Beradino."

"Now that does sound odd," Kate said. "How did he know who he was? I mean Jellop's well-known, face in the paper all the time; but that's not..."

"Ah, there you are. Beradino's a personal hero. Plucked Damien out of a rip off Whitsand Bay...last summer, I think."

Fran's mind was racing. Damien must be talking about the house where Lou had met Jellop. But a high-class brothel? There had been no word of that at the station. And why would Jellop risk inviting him there? Is that what Nina was involved in? If so, why did she have to be got rid of? And what was Coaker's part in all of this?

The others were watching her, waiting to see what her reaction would be. She picked up the photocopy, seeing the face there differently now.

"You think she may be one of them?" Kate said.

Fran ignored the question. She felt concerned for their safety. Making eye contact with each of them in turn, she said: "What you've told me is helpful and I'll certainly follow it up. But what you know may be dangerous." She held up the photocopy. "This stays between us, right? Not a word to anyone. Really, not a word." She paused and waited for each of them to respond.

Molly nodded with a shrug. "Sure," said Sean. Kate nodded too. "We won't."

"Good," said Fran, standing up. "I owe you."

* * * * *

"So, what do you think?" asked Fran. Lou was grinning at her. The afternoon was already dying through his office windows and light from a desk lamp was pooling across the pad in front of him.

"If it swells, ride it!" he said, putting his pen down, his eyes gleaming. "And I think maybe we've just caught one, thanks to you."

"This is wave talk, right?"

"Right. And I have a sense this one's going to carry us a long way. We need to put Jellop's house in Skardon Place under surveillance. Get Carol and Martin on to it right away, but check with Macklin first." Detective Constables Carol Barker and Martin Webb were officers he'd picked. They were thorough and kept cool heads. He trusted them. "Let's see who these young women and well-heeled men are; how many and how often."

Fran frowned, even as she nodded agreement. He recognised the expression. Something was bugging her. She hadn't finished yet.

"What about Coaker? If Jellop is running prostitutes and Nina was one of them..." She was speaking low and fast and hesitated. "...or still is, Coaker's got to know what's happened to her, one way or the other. I want to pull him in, search his boat, search his house, while there's still time to find her, save her maybe."

"Get corroboration of Damien's story and I'll clear it with Maynard."

Fran paused in the doorway on her way out, turned and took a step back into the room. "Lou," she said, "I want to thank you for your support over Harris and Kincaid. I've been meaning to say it."

Lou saw her discomfort. Talking about her feelings didn't come easily. "That's okay," he said. She had managed her transition so well that, sometimes, he forgot how much she'd been through. He stood up and walked over to her. "This must've been a rough time. If you need any slack, let me know."

She flashed a quick smile. "Yeah, well, I'm in my right skin now." Lou raised his hand in acknowledgement and her expression settled back into its usual concentrated seriousness as she added: "But I'll feel better once we've pulled Coaker in. He's dangerous, Lou. I can feel it."

Chapter 16

Roger's joy undone

Roger lived ten minutes' walk from the college in a terraced house his mother had left him. Albany Road was short and narrow, and all the parking was taken when Rachael got there. She pulled round the corner at the end, found a space and sat with her hands on the steering wheel, rehearsing what she wanted to say. Her anger at his phone call to the house had subsided and, in its place, had come guilt. She wasn't afraid of Roger, of him becoming violent, not like Oliver. But she didn't want to hurt him. He'd been kind and loving towards her in a way she hadn't known before. Of course he'd be upset; there was no way round that. Even so, she wanted him to see that she hadn't just been using him and that she had to establish herself, find out her own way of being, before going back into another relationship. He must understand that.

Number 11 was half-way down the row of two-storey houses, each with a front door and ground-floor window giving directly on to the pavement. His was pale blue with a navy door. She raised her hand to the bell, but before she could press it, the door swung back and there was Roger, dark hair and stubble, his eyes shining. "Come in! Come in!" Seizing her hand and pulling her into the narrow hallway, he wrapped his arms around her and buried his face in her hair. "Oh..." he groaned; "my beautiful Rachael! I've missed you! I've missed you! You've no idea!"

Resting her palm against his chest, she extricated herself as gently as she could, before taking off her coat and scarf and finding space for them on the hooks inside the door.

"Let's go into the den," she said, taking his hand. "It's freezing out here."

But he held back. "Why don't we go upstairs? It's much warmer in bed." His grin was boyish and she saw the hopefulness in his eyes. "And much more fun!"

"I know it is, but I need to talk to you, things I want to explain." She led the way towards the room at the back and as she opened the door its smoky heat enveloped her like a blanket. Bright flames were dancing and curling around a log in the small, black grate, crackling and sending out little sparks. An unexpected grief rose up in her, clawing at her throat, so that she stood stricken, looking about her at the cosy shambles of his life, her heart softening and her intended words draining away. Her life had changed here. She had come alive here, as if waking from a dream. And he had done it. He had woken her up. She wasn't sleep-walking through her life any longer, because of him.

"What's up?" he asked, sliding his arm round her waist.

"Do you remember the first time you asked me here?" she said, resting against him. "I was so in awe of you."

He laughed and his voice was full of surprise. "In awe of me?"

"Yes."

"Why?"

"Because of who you were."

"Who was I?"

"A college lecturer. An intellectual. A man of culture. And because of all of this." She stepped away from him, half-turning with a sweep of her arm. "The oil paintings. The essays on your desk. All these books." She pointed to the shelves in the alcoves either side of the fireplace, crammed from floor to ceiling. "And the carpet."

"The carpet?"

"Yes, the carpet! I'd never seen a room with a red carpet before. Or should I say vermilion?" She gave a little laugh and tried to mimic his voice, lower and more pedagogic. "Pigment from the powdered mineral cinnabar."

"You're mocking me." He grabbed at her, but she swayed away from him, moving towards the grand sofa between the door and the garden window.

"And this," she said, sitting down, rearranging the scatter cushions and rubbing her palm over the bottle-green velvet. "Old and faded, but so comfortable. I felt I was in a new world – richer, softer, kinder."

"That's Mum." He plonked himself down and ran his arm along the cushions behind her. "It was hers." He paused and when he spoke again his voice was tender. He reached to cup her breast in his hand. "It's been our bower, hasn't it?"

"Don't," she said, lifting his hand away from her, her sadness turning to resolve once more. But she kept hold of it in her lap and looked earnestly up at him. "I've given this a lot of thought, Roger, and I know I'm going to hurt you, even though I don't want to." He went to move his hand, but she tightened her grip. "I've told Oliver I want a divorce."

"But that's great," he said, as the log flared and crackled, before falling deeper into the grate. "We don't have to wait any longer. You can come here." He jumped up. "I can't believe it." He started twirling with his arms outstretched, his eyes half-closed and his mouth half-open in a triumphant smile. "She's mine! She's mine!" he chanted, spinning faster and faster. "She's all mine, for ever and ever!" But he lost his balance and toppled over on to her, catching her jaw painfully with his elbow. He rolled off to the side, clasping on to the tops of her arms and pulling her with him in a tangle of limbs, so she found herself lying face-down on top of him, his body shaking with panting and laughing and his cheeks flushed beyond the midnight shadow of his jaw.

Awkwardly, she heaved herself up and away from him. Her sweater was rucked up and the front of her shirt underneath was untucked from her skirt. She stood straightening them, shoehorning the shirt back into place with the curve of her fingers. "Roger, I need you to listen to me." She stopped, waiting for his attention. Their eyes met and he smiled, but she did not, nor did she look away.

"All right," he said, drawing his legs in and pushing his back upright against the cushions. "I'm listening."

She sat down again, leaving a space between them. "I want to try to explain something and it's not easy, because I'm only just working it out myself." She leant back and looked across at the flickering of the fire. "I've never lived on my own. When I married Oliver, I left home and moved in with him." She paused, her thoughts drifting back to the townhouse he'd had then. How excited she had been, leaving the restrictions of her parents and having a place of her own. Except it hadn't been hers at all; she could see that now. "And that's the point," she said aloud. "I've never looked after myself, I've never..."

"But you don't need to," he interrupted her. "I'll look after you." He made to move closer to her, but she put out her hand and held him away.

"No, Roger. You're not listening to me." She glanced at him. "Just let me finish. Please."

He shrugged. "Go on then." But before she could, he added: "Seems like loving you isn't good enough."

She heard the petulant little boy in him and felt frustrated. "After all you've taught us...taught me, I thought you would understand...yes, you of all people." She paused, collecting her thoughts. "It's nothing to do with your loving being good enough or not. I've got to find my own strength. I've got to prove to myself that I can take care of Nick and Sam, whatever happens." She turned back to him. "Surely you can see that?"

"I've been teaching you to believe in yourself and determine the kind of life you want. And you've done it." He sprang up and walked restlessly to the window and back.

"You're amazing. You've called the bully's bluff." He stopped in front of her, his leg touching hers. "You had that courage. I knew you had it in you. I always knew that...from the first time I met you." He was waving his arms wildly in the air as he spoke and showering her with spittle.

"Roger," she remonstrated, trying to stem the flood of his reaction. But he seemed not to hear her. His arms dropped by his side, concern sweeping the excitement from his face. "But how did he take it?" His eyes raked over her. "Did he hurt you?" She shook her head. "Thank God!" He sat down again and tried to put his arm round her. "But he may. You can't trust a bastard like that. You must come here." He was nodding at her. "In fact, don't go home. Stay here. We can fetch your things..."

"Stop it!" Rachael shouted, struggling to get free and standing up. She glared down at him. "Just listen to me!" The force of her anger stilled him. "We shouldn't have started this. It was wrong. Only..."

"It wasn't wrong!" he interjected, his voice caught high in his throat and he coughed to clear it. "It was beautiful. It is beautiful! And now..."

She cut across him. "Let me finish!"

He clenched his teeth and she saw the muscles tighten at the hinges of his jaw. "I was using you to escape from Oliver, and it was exciting. I needed your attention, your love...no, that's not it. I needed your loving, the physical reality of it, to wake me up, to feel alive again. But I have to do this on my own. If I simply jump from Oliver to you, I'll have just..." She couldn't think how to express it. "Well, I'll just have swapped one cage for another." Her tone was pleading now and she stopped, waiting for some sign of acknowledgement from him that he understood.

"That's ridiculous!" he snorted. "Setting you free is the whole point; and I'm the one holding the cage door open, for heaven's sake!" He got up and moved towards her, stretching out his arms, his expression changing from anger to indulgence. "Come here. This is silly."

"No," she said, stepping quickly past him. "You're still not listening to me, are you?" He followed her, as she circled the coffee table, keeping it between them. "You want me for yourself. That's not setting me free. But even that's not the point."

"What is the point?" he said, standing still and spitting out the last word.

"I'm married. I have two sons. You were my teacher. It was…"

"AM your teacher!"

"It was not right for us to get involved. And I blame myself for that, as much as you. But now…"

"Blame? That's…"

"LISTEN to me!" she shouted, losing her temper. "Stop interrupting me all the time and just try to understand what I'm telling you!"

"Oh, fine!" he said, flouncing down on the sofa. "Go ahead. Don't worry about me. Let's hear all about your bourgeois moral angst. Didn't seem to bother you too much when you were sucking my dick, did it?"

Although his coarseness and self-pity jarred in her, what she saw in his eyes was a furious, impotent hurt, which both alarmed her and touched the compassion in her. She had loved him desperately and she didn't want to cause him pain. He was watching her, breathing fast, almost panting.

"Roger," she said, her voice calmer, softer. "I have to end with Oliver and find a home for me and the boys. I told you, I've got to find my own independence, prove I can look after myself and them. Once I've done that…well, we'll see what happens. I don't want to hurt you, I owe you so much."

His mouth was a hard straight line. "I lost my mother to a bully. I'm not losing you." He sat rigid, his eyes dark and frozen. She resisted the urge to go to him and comfort him.

"I never knew my dad. Mum said he was a gambler and a loser; better off without him. And we were all right...for years...just the two of us...we were."

Rachael knew what was coming next. He had told her about his brutal, ex-army stepfather. The 'fascist dictator', as he called him, who had laid down the law and thrashed him regularly. She didn't want to get side-tracked. She wanted things to be clear between them before she left. "Look. Roger," she began. "I've got to go in a minute. So, I..."

"And then he came along," he said, as if unaware she was speaking. "Brave Mike Walters. Six-foot-four. And what was she? Five-foot, maybe? And me? Even less. At the start, anyway." His head dropped. "Big man!" He stopped talking, staring at the carpet.

Rachel shifted her weight to her other foot. She wanted to sit down, but knew that would make it harder to leave. She wanted to be gone, wanted to be free of the mounting heaviness in the room that was dragging at her.

"I'm sorry," she said; "I've really..." She petered out, watching him, as he lowered his head again and started rocking, his hands between his knees. She didn't know what to do and a kind of panic rose up in her. She wanted to flee but her legs wouldn't move.

He was mumbling, talking to himself, and she could only make out snatches of it: "...happy together we......why...do that......an act everyone......family man...sadistic bastard......shouldn't...let him in...I...you...that enough." He shuddered and slumped back, his face pale drawn. "Wasn't that enough?"

Rachael went over to him, touched his shoulder lightly. "I'm sorry," she said. "I have to go now."

She went out into the hall and pulled on her coat. Taking her bag from the hook, she went back into the doorway. He hadn't moved.

"I still want to come to your classes," she said, trying to soften her guilt at leaving him. "I'll see you there."

She hesitated, waiting for some response from him, for some sign that he would be all right. When he spoke, his voice was low and oddly neutral. "We're going to be together, Rachael. Always. You can count on that."

His words echoed uncomfortably as she closed the front door behind her. It was already dark outside and the ice in the air bit at her cheeks and fingers. Even so, as she walked away, fumbling for the gloves in her pocket, her body seemed to unclench and her breathing deepened. She was glad to be escaping these houses, these witnesses to her visits. She wouldn't be coming back and her spirits bobbed up at having a weight lifted from them.

As she rounded the corner, she remembered Sam's missed call. Back in the car, the digital clock showed 15.57. Another hour and he'd be out of class. She'd ring him then. She sat, with the engine running, wondering how she was going to tell him and Nick what was happening and how they would react. Not over the phone, anyway: she'd have to go to see them. Or should she wait until they came home for half-term? But that was still five or so weeks away. She shivered and tried the fan, but the air from the heater was cold and she switched it off again.

Chapter 17
Rachael rings Sam

When Rachael got home, the drive was empty and the house was in darkness. Inside, she left the lights off, glad of its stillness. Slipping quickly out of her coat and shoes, she went noiselessly up the stairs and along the corridor into Sam's room. It was the smallest of the five bedrooms and the furthest from the stairs. Closing the door, she was startled by the black bulk of the wardrobe looming behind it. She moved quickly to the bed and switched on the lamp beside it, igniting the room into colour and blackening the window.

She sat down and closed her eyes. She often chose to sit here, when the boys were away. Alone in the peace and quiet and surrounded by his things, she felt closer to Sam, more in touch with him inside herself. Nick's room was much larger. It had been their nursery when they were younger. But now it had its own ensuite shower and, with its varnished wood floor, pinball machine and sporting posters, it was a louder, noisier room than Sam's.

She looked around; everything felt snug and comfortable and Sam-like. He'd pushed the divan into the corner and asked her for cushions to make it like a sofa in the daytime, with an L-shaped shelf above it for his books and collection of Hobbit figures – Bilbo Baggins and Gandalf and Smaug the dragon. How she had loved the warmth and fresh-bathed scent of him then, as he snuggled against her, lost in Tolkein's world, while she read, peering over her arm at the illustrations, until sleep finally crept over him and sealed him away.

"Funny boy," she thought. "So vulnerable and yet so full of his own ideas." She smiled, rubbing her palm over the rust-coloured duvet and looking down at the airforce blue carpet. She'd suggested sea greens and blues, but these were the colours he'd wanted.

Easing the mobile from her pocket, she pushed a cushion behind her and straightened her back against the wall. After only a couple of rings, Sam answered: "Mum!"

"Hi, Sam. I'm sorry I missed your call. Are you okay?"

"Well, no..." She heard the familiar quaver in his voice and knew he was struggling not to cry. "...not really."

She waited, wanting to give him time to compose himself and to deal with her own desire to rescue him, to drive there immediately and bring him home.

"It's just...the thing is...what I mean is...oh, Mum..." She heard the misery in his voice and held her breath. "Can't I come home? I hate it here. I can't get anything right and I'm trying so hard." He was sobbing and the words were tumbling out. "I got punished over my German homework and I spent hours on it, I really tried. Now I've got to do it again and a whole other lot, which will take me hours and hours. And, if I do that, I won't get my history essay done and then I'll be in more trouble. And Hooper's making me do extra cross-country runs because..." She heard him choking, caught between ranting and crying. "...he says I need to toughen up, but it's not...."

"Come on, Sammy," she broke in. "Try to calm down a bit. Let's talk this through."

"I can't." She heard him sucking in great gasps of air, trying to stop the flood of his own sobbing. "Please let me come home. Please! I won't be any trouble and I'll work as hard as anything, I promise."

"Look, sweetheart, I can't do anything immediately, but I'll come down on Saturday and take you both out for the day and we can talk about it properly then."

"It's no good. I've got all this work to do and the run, and Nick's got a rugby match with the colts." He started wailing again. "I can't bear this."

Rachael heard the front door open and close again. She folded her free arm across her chest and held herself tightly.

"Sam, it'll be all right. I'll ring Mr Johnson and arrange everything. Don't worry. He's your housemaster and he can sort this all out; that's his job. The main thing is I'll pick you up at 11am, and Nick too. We'll have an early lunch, get Nick back in time for the match, and then you and I can go off somewhere and work out what we're going to do. Okay?"

"Okay. You won't be late, will you?" His sobbing was coming to a shuddering stop. "And you will ring Mr Johnson, won't you? Today."

"Rachael?" Oliver must be on the stairs, coming up looking for her.

"Is that Dad?"

"Yes. I've got to go. Be good and do your best, and I'll see you on Saturday."

"Rachael?" His voice was much closer now. He was opening every door, checking every room.

"'Bye, sweetheart." She blew two kisses into the phone.

"'Bye, Mum. I love you."

She saw the door handle turning.

"I love you, too."

She slipped the phone back in her pocket as he came in.

"Ah, there you are." He was smiling. She watched his hands as he came towards her. She always thought of them as butcher's hands, heavy and meaty. He often used them to amuse and intimidate new friends with his party tricks: not just tearing phone directories in half, but also placing three short planks of wood on top of each other, supported by bricks at either end, and driving the edge of his hand down, chopping them in half, karate-style.

He stopped short of her, his arms by his side. An inch of Mediterranean blue shirt cuff showed beneath the sleeves of his double-breasted, dark-blue herringbone suit.

"Ron and Polly have invited us out to dinner on Thursday. Their place first for drinks and then on to the Cantina."

"Canteen," she said. "River Cottage Canteen." It was Hugh Fearnley-Whittingstall's restaurant in the Old Brewhouse at Royal William Yard. She liked it, but she didn't want to go. Not with Oliver, anyway. Not any more.

"Yes, the Canteen, that's right. It should be fun."

Legally they were still a couple but, inside her, she had already separated from him. Her future was no longer linked to his. His needs were no longer her concern.

The realisation left her less afraid of him. "You go. I..."

"I what?" she wondered. "I'll have a headache on Thursday." She couldn't very well say that. "I don't want to. You'll just be talking business. You don't need me there."

He squatted down in front of her, so that their faces were level.

"The invitation is to both of us. P-Polly will feel snubbed if you don't go."

He's getting jowly, she thought. Too many business lunches and dinners. God, she wanted to be free of his world! She hadn't realised just how much. As for Polly, he didn't know anything about her. Polly wouldn't mind at all, she'd understand perfectly and, besides, they'd be seeing each other the day after anyway, at the college. Oh, God, and Roger too! What would that be like? Maybe she should stop going. But she had to get that A-level, now more than ever.

Oliver stood up, wincing as his knees straightened. She struggled to collect her thoughts to answer him, but he pre-empted her.

"I've been thinking about Sam," he said. "He's not settling in well, is he?" He was giving her one of the 'honest and true' looks he deployed whenever he was being particularly devious; eyes steady, slightly wider open than usual. "It'll be best if we d-don't visit him for a while. Let him get used to the life there. Only upsets him, when he has to say goodbye to you each time. In fact, let's not have them home this half-term. A lot of the overseas children stay on, so Sam and Nick can too."

She felt winded. His unerring instinct for landing a blow to the solar plexus never failed to take her by surprise. She hadn't seen it coming and he knew it. His look was concentrated, like a fisherman with a bite, waiting to see how she'd react.

"Be good for him," he added. "Time to let go of your apron strings and stand up for himself."

It's what he always did, upped the ante. He just kept raising the stakes until she or whoever found the risk too great and gave in to him.

"All right," she said. "I'll come on Thursday. But I've already arranged to see the boys on Saturday and, of course, they'll come home at half-term."

She moved to get up and he bent down, taking hold of her arm to help her. "That's my girl," he said, and kissed her on the cheek. "What's for dinner?"

Any residual sense of responsibility towards him dissolved in her at that moment. He had got his way and that was all he cared about. It didn't matter whose feelings he trampled on in the process, not hers, not even his sons'. They were all there to be used and manipulated for his own ends.

"Lamb," she said, her voice low with contempt.

"Perfect. I'll open the '98 Cheval Blanc." He ran his finger down her back, until it reached the base of her spine, where she felt his hand turning to cup her bottom.

"I've got to call Jeremy Johnson," she said, moving away from him.

She scrolled for the number as she walked down into the hall, aware he was close behind her.

As the phone was answered, she turned to face him. "Hello, Mr Johnson, it's Rachael Drew." He smiled and she watched him head into the living room.

She made the necessary arrangements for Saturday and also secured an assurance that Sam's extra work and run could be rescheduled. Afterwards, she rang Nick to make sure he knew what time they were meeting and to pass on a message to Sam that she'd fixed everything with 'JJ', as they called him.

"Okay, Mother, see you soon," he said at the end, using the term teasingly, knowing she didn't like it. "I won't have lunch though."

"Why not, cheeky? We can eat early." She usually took them to The King's Arms nearby and they served food from midday. There was time; the match wouldn't start until 2.30pm.

"We're playing Tolmore. I want to feel l-e-a-n and m-e-a-n." He dragged out the two words for emphasis.

"Worried they'll beat you?" she said and wished she hadn't. Somehow, he always managed to provoke her into retaliation, even when she was determined not to let him.

"We'll slaughter them," he laughed.

She went through to the kitchen, wondering how they could be so different; Nick so invincible somehow and Sam so easily wounded. She wouldn't tell them her plans yet. She'd wait until they were home for half-term. She would tell them then, she resolved, although she dreaded the thought of it. Nick would react angrily and attack her, whereas Sam would go quiet and disappear to his room or become her shadow.

She uncovered the lamb and switched on the oven. Nick would demand to live with Oliver and Sam would never cope with going back to school, once he knew his home was breaking up. She took the kitchen scissors off the hook by the sink and went out into the garden for some rosemary.

Chapter 18
Team meeting

Lou had his way. Superintendent Maynard argued that Sean's uncorroborated and off-the–record statement to Fran was no more than 'hearsay', which, if acted upon, could give Councillor Jellop further cause for complaint of unjustified police harassment. Lou pointed out that, after less than twenty-four hours since Skardon House had been placed under surveillance, seven young women, later identified as foreign students at the University, had been observed entering and leaving the premises, which had coincided with the visits to the house of certain well-dressed men, all now identified, including the superintendent himself.

"I meet Councillor Jellop there, from time to time, on official business, as you have done yourself," was Maynard's calm reply. "And the other visitors are just as likely to be business and professional people connected to Councillor Jellop's building firm. As for the young women, there could be any number of reasons for them being there. Part-time work as office assistants or cleaners, perhaps. Research even, if they're from the Business School. A lot of foreign students are here doing MBAs these days. Some of them may be on work experience placements or looking for holiday jobs, come to that. You need more concrete evidence than you're giving me, so far."

"We will talk to these students and the men..."

"You will not! I will not have officers of mine hounding an eminent local benefactor and questioning his business associates on a hunch. What are you thinking of, man? Councillor Jellop could sue us on any number of counts."

'Eminent public benefactor' was not how Lou thought of Ron Jellop, and a small smile rippled across his otherwise impassive face, like a breeze on a lake.

"There's nothing funny about it," said Maynard. "Men and women are piling in and out of here all day long – and this is not a knocking shop! Skardon House is his place of business. Of course people will come and go there. For heaven's sake!"

Fighting the laughter fizzing in his throat and eyes, Lou said: "Skardon House is listed as being for 'residential use'." Maynard dismissed the remark with a backward sweep of his hand. "And he parks on yellow lines no doubt."

What he could not so easily dismiss, however, was the mounting evidence linking the disappearance of Nina Lapinski both to Eddie Coaker and to the abruptly-ended 999 call for help. With deeply ridged lines of concern furrowing his forehead, Maynard agreed that Coaker should be questioned under caution and a warrant obtained to search the Morning Star. He also appointed Lou as senior investigating officer and allocated him a team of six: Detective Sergeants Fran Bannerman and Macklin Thomas and Detective Constables Martin Webb, Carol Barker, Debbie Denton and Jason Kincaid.

"Resources are scarce, Lou," Maynard said. "We need quick results. Concentrate on Coaker – and leave Jellop alone."

* * * * *

Later, when Lou walked into the allocated, first-floor incident room, the team was already gathered and waiting for him. It was an open-plan office, with light bouncing off the light wood, metal-legged worktops from a run of windows on the far side. Behind a table at the near end, Fran was handing photos and printed details to Macklin, which he was pinning to a large wall-mounted board, while the four DCs looked on.

It reminded him of classrooms at Judge Meadows, the comprehensive he'd gone to in Leicester, and he had the same urge now as he'd had then to bunk off to the park with his basketball. Only now it would be the beach with his surfboard. Same difference. Outside, the day was bright and crisp and he felt stifled by the room's stale, overheated air, as if someone had thrown a rug over his head.

"Open a couple of windows will you, Jason?" he said to the young detective leaning against the wall just by them. "Can't think clearly in a fug-up." Walking over to the table, he took in the blow-ups of Nina Lapinski, Eddie Coaker and the Morning Star.

"Right," he said, standing to one side so as not to block anyone's view. "Glad to have you here. This is a suspected murder enquiry but, as we don't have a body yet, we need to act quickly in case Nina Lapinski, a missing Polish student from the University," he pointed to her photo, "is still alive. We have CCTV footage that shows local fisherman," he moved his finger across, "Eddie Coaker almost certainly left with her aboard his boat, the Morning Star, last Thursday morning." He tapped the third photo. "She didn't come back with him and she hasn't been seen since. After I've finished, Fran will fill you in on the details and give you your assignments. Meanwhile, Macklin will run this room and you report back to him. Any questions so far?"

"What's the connection between this and the house me and Carol have been watching in Skardon Place?" said Martin Webb. His knees didn't fit easily under the table and he sat hunched forward, his feet tucked back under his chair.

Despite his size, Martin's straightforward manner made him a reassuring presence rather than a threatening one. He might lack leadership qualities but people trusted him and often ended up telling him more than they'd planned to. He was better on the streets than in the office, and Lou valued his thoroughness.

"Okay, Martin, this is sensitive." Lou looked around at the others. "This goes for all of you. There's a possibility that Councillor Ron Jellop is running a prostitution ring from Skardon House, involving Eastern European graduate students at the University." He looked back at Martin. "It may be Nina Lapinski was one of them."

"Lou…" Debbie Denton began, only her rimless glasses and neatly brushed hair visible above the computer monitor in front of her.

"Just a moment, Debbie," said Lou, holding up his palm. "One thing I need to stress. If, during your enquiries, any other information surfaces involving Ron Jellop or Skardon House, you are not, I repeat 'not', to act on it without first consulting Fran or Macklin. No exceptions. Understood?"

He looked at each face in turn until they had all nodded their assent, including Jason Kincaid.

"Good. Now Debbie, what is it?"

"I've been checking the records and Edward Coaker has no previous convictions. However, Fraud officers from the Met are investigating Ron Jellop's financial affairs, with particular reference to an undisclosed bank account in the Cayman Islands. Also, at the request of the French police in Bordeaux, they are looking into his sale of French antiquities without a licence at Christie's Auction Rooms in London, last October. I understand we may be assisting them in that enquiry already."

She spoke slowly and precisely. As the well-educated daughter of a second-generation West Indian family from Swansea, Lou knew there were people who were prejudiced against her. They took against the colour of her skin and then they resented her self-possession and clear articulation. But he also knew how skilled and efficient she was behind a computer and how loyal a colleague. No-one had been more supportive of Fran than she had been.

Her precision and clarity were invaluable assets to the team, qualities she must have inherited from her mother, a barrister and QC in London, a city 'silk'. He had a lot of time for her, respected her. It wasn't easy being black in the South-West. First thing that had struck him when he arrived from multicultural Leicester was all those white faces. Priya in her green and gold sari jumped into his mind and out again as Macklin cleared his throat, bringing him back into the moment.

"Thanks, Debbie. And, yes, we are liaising with the Met in an unofficial capacity over Jellop's financial affairs. But our focus is purely on the disappearance of Nina Lapinski and her possible involvement in prostitution at Skardon House. Eddie Coaker is our primary suspect and we will be arresting and interviewing him later today. Okay, that's it from me. Fran and Macklin will take you through the rest."

Turning, he moved closer to the table. "See you both upstairs afterwards." They nodded.

Climbing the stairs, he thanked providence — he didn't believe in God — for the two sergeants he had available to him, remembering others he'd worked with who had been...he searched for the right word...*untrustworthy*, even though for different reasons. But Fran and Macklin were rock-solid.

As for the DCs, Jason's attitude towards Fran's change of gender had taken him by surprise. Maybe it was just the immaturity of youth and he'd have learnt from it. In any case, he'd keep an eye on him. But Carol, Debbie and Martin were entirely reliable; he knew that from experience. Debbie would soon make DS and Carol wouldn't be far behind her, particularly once Fran got the promotion she deserved. Pity she wasn't ready yet to replace him.

The thought caught him unawares. He pushed his way into his room and closed the door. Who said he was leaving? He'd been remembering Connie's words ever since their talk at the weekend. They kept echoing in his head, like bars of a song he couldn't stop humming: "You be very good father, I think...Maybe being a father more important than being a policeman."

But he hadn't decided anything. There'd hardly been any time to give it serious consideration. He crossed to his desk and sat down. And yet, at some deeper level than thought, the decision had already been taken. He knew it now. He was going to give up the police force for family life with Connie and be a father. There would be children, his children. All the givens, all the certainties in his life, were dissolving and something unformed, unknown was opening in their place. He felt winded and excited and suddenly vulnerable, a sort of nakedness.

And what would happen when..if..he left? They'd probably appoint an external candidate, as they had done in his case. He or she better be worthy of them. A surge of protective anger swept through him. There were so many ambitious officers out there, scheming and trampling their way to the top; the sort who would use a good team to propel their own star, without acknowledgement and careless of the well-being of those under them – or worse, actively sabotaging the careers of potential challengers to propel their own meteoric rise. Fran would need to look out.

"Coaker first!" he said aloud, pulling a pile of papers towards him, forcing himself back into the present. "And then I'm coming after you, Councillor Jellop." He knew now what the fishy smell was: forget the crooked property deals, Jellop was running a prostitution ring right under their noses. He felt incensed at the man's arrogance, the arrogance of power. Jellop had agreed to see him at the very place he was using as a brothel. "He must think he's untouchable," he muttered, and thought of Maynard's instructions to leave Jellop alone. "Maybe he is."

He opened the top drawer, took out the photo of his grandfather and felt the warm centring Spoza's steady gaze provoked in him. He had always thought of Maynard as limited, good at dealing with top brass and getting resources, if not much good at detection. But he'd had him down as straight. Maybe Maynard was just seduced by Jellop and the circles he moved in. Or did it go higher than that? It was DCC Townsend having dinner with Jellop, not Maynard. One thing Lou was sure of was that Coaker was involved in this prostitution racket with Jellop and Nina Lapinski was the key to unlocking that particular box of tricks. "We'll get him, Nonno." He replaced the photo and slid the drawer shut.

As he scanned an internal memo about the proposed 'strategic alliance' between Devon & Cornwall Police and Dorset Police 'to realise a number of efficiency savings' through 'shared leadership' and 'outsourcing', he followed two differing trains of thought.

The first concerned the content of the memo, which was, in his view, part of a government-driven campaign to get 'more for less', dressed up in the jargon of 'challenge' and 'flexibility', where workers in all public services, not just the police, were being cast as inadequate when they objected to, or broke under, the overload they were being saddled with.

The second was chewing on the mechanics of Jellop's operation and how it could be possible for young women from Eastern Europe to be registered as graduate students for higher degree courses at the University, while working as prostitutes at the same time; and doing so, virtually on campus, without a whisper having reached police ears before now. How did Jellop recruit them? How did they hear of him, without any of the police 'sources' in the University picking up on it? And what was Nina's story? Why had she been 'disappeared'?

He looked back at the memo. Half his days now were being used up reading through ever-increasing piles of ideological claptrap like this. If the time it took to write it and the time it took to read it were used in the prevention and investigation of crime, there would be no need for any more bloody 'targets'. He tossed the memo into the filing tray, shoved it into the bottom drawer and closed it. As soon as he'd run through procedures with Fran and Macklin, he'd take Fran and go to arrest Eddie Coaker. If he was out on the high seas, they'd bring him in later. One way or another, he was going to interrogate Coaker before the day was out.

Chapter 19
Ron & the girls

"Good morning, everyone, and welcome!" Ron Jellop beamed. He was standing at the head of an oval conference table, an imposing figure; over six-feet tall, with a broad, sun-tanned face and the powerful build of the former flanker he had been for Plymouth Albion, the city's Championship rugby team. The club's cherry-coloured tie covered the swell of his belly under the open blazer.

At the other end, facing him, was a spare, weather-beaten man in jeans and a thick roll-neck sweater, with salt and pepper stubble and short-cropped hair. He wasn't smiling and the lines at the corners of his dark eyes were drawn tight, as he squinted at the row of young women either side of him. There were nine in all, five down one side and four on the other. "Nina won't be joining us today," the man said, moving the spare chair away from the table to the wall by the door. "She sends her apologies." He noted the fleeting exchange of glances between some of 'the girls', as he called them.

"Thank you, Mr Coaker," Jellop said. "Please, sit down everyone." He gestured towards the chairs with an expansive sweep of his arm. Generally, he enjoyed these monthly meetings but on this occasion he was aware of the need to manage the matter of Nina's sudden disappearance with care. "They'll bring us some refreshments in a little while." He looked with satisfaction from one attractive young face to the next as he spoke, holding each expectant gaze just long enough to register a personal contact before moving on to the next.

It was a habit of easy command he had developed over thirty-five years in charge of Jellop's Building Contractors, a company founded by his father, and also, in more recent years, as a city councillor. He was aware of the tension Eddie Coaker's pronouncement had provoked and he sought to allay it. "We are sorry to see Nina go and I know you will all miss her. However, we must respect the confidentiality of her reasons for deciding to return home, and I trust you will feel reassured to know that any similar decisions on your part will be treated with the same respect. This is, after all, an enterprise for our own mutual benefit. And I am very glad to be able to tell you that our sales for last month have beaten all previous records."

As he saw interest beginning to replace anxiety in the faces turned towards him, he paused and picked up a slim sheaf of papers from the table. He looked at the figures typed there, then raised his head and nodded at them. "It's true. The figures don't lie. In December, due to your hard work, with just two more sessions a week, our turnover was up ten per cent, which means an extra two hundred and twelve pounds in your pay-packet." Seeing their smiles, he grinned back at them and held up a hand, as if to pre-empt any interruption. "And, at Mr Coaker's suggestion and as a belated New Year present from us in appreciation of your contribution to this joint enterprise of ours, we have rounded this up to two hundred and fifty pounds extra each."

There was a frisson of excitement in the flurry of exclamations around the table.

"This brings my sister piano lessons now!" said an elfin young woman to his right, with short black hair and a stud in her nose. "I can't believe it."

"I'm glad, Olga." Jellop caught Coaker's eye. A closed-lipped smile flickered across the crust of Coaker's face and was gone. Jellop relaxed, feeling they had successfully cleared the rapids and were back in calm water.

The door opened and a waiter wheeled in a trolley, which led to an interlude as the girls rose to help themselves to the selection of drinks and biscuits he laid out on the trestle table under the windows. The last to return and take her seat was a striking figure, with a wealth of rich dark hair framing high cheek bones, from between which sprang a prominent roman nose. It curved from a broad bridge, between her fierce eyes.

"Mr Jellop," she said, sitting down, "do you know why Nina went home? She was my friend, but she never told me she was going. She never said goodbye to me and I do not understand this."

"Well, Raluca, as I've already explained, her reasons are confidential and I would need her permission to say more." Jellop sat back, folding his hands over his stomach. "However, I know you are her friend and I can see you are worried about her, so I will say this much: there was a need for haste and secrecy in her return to her family, and my guess is that she felt it would be unsafe to involve you." He paused, looking carefully at the faces all turned to him, like flowers to the sun, before finally returning to Raluca.

She didn't believe him; he could see it in her eyes. She stared back at him, holding his gaze, as he smiled pleasantly at her. Raluca broke contact first, looking down at the notepad in front of her and picking up her pen.

"Please give me her address in Poland and I will write to her." She looked up at him. "I want to know that she is all right."

"That, most of all, is confidential, for obvious reasons. I'm sorry, Raluca, but without Nina's say-so, my hands are tied." Once more, he saw the anger flaring in her eyes. This time she did not look away.

"Back to business!" Coaker's rough voice sliced through the silence. "I've got fish to catch." He was sitting erect, his arms spread wide, hands gripping either edge of the table. "And some of us have appointments to keep." He looked up and down either side of the table and then at the open diary in front of him. "Including you, Raluca."

"Quite so, Mr Coaker," Jellop said, relieved at the interruption. "Thank you. Now, first of all, as always, are there any issues..."

"I will ask at the University," Raluca said; but her words were lost in the shifting of bodies and rustle of papers, as Jellop continued.

"...you would like to bring to the meeting's attention?"

Maria, a freckled-faced Latvian and the youngest in the group at 21, said the radiator in her room wasn't working properly and clients had complained of the cold. "Needs bleeding probably," Coaker said; "I'll sort it." Next, Sophie, smartly dressed in a twin-set, her fair hair coiled tightly in a bun, asked whether medical appointments would have to be paid for and, if so, whose responsibility that was. Ron assured her that it was in their contacts that they were all entitled to free medical care through the University.

"This was explained to you all when you first arrived," he said. Then, wondering if some uncomfortable problem might be lurking behind her question, he added: "I realise there was a lot to take in that day, particularly in another language. So let me just remind you of a couple of points that sometimes crop up." He hesitated for a moment, before deciding upon plain speaking. "If any of you have any problems to do with contraception or sexual diseases, ask to see Dr Alexander at the medical centre. She is our friend and she will help you." He paused again, this time for effect to underline what he was going to say next. "Similarly, if any of you misses your period, do not hesitate. Go to see Dr Alexander at once. She will take care of everything."

Most of their faces turned away from him as he was speaking and looked down at the table in front of them. And when he finished the air was heavy with their concentrated silence.

"Are there any other matters you want to ask about?" Several heads shook without looking up.

"Good," he said, adopting his earlier tone of bonhomie. "I'm very glad that you feel able to bring your problems here and I hope you know that both Mr Coaker and I will always do our very best to resolve them to your satisfaction." He noticed one or two heads lift up and turn to him again. Now, if you look at the first sheet in your folders, you will see we have much to celebrate." Like a fresh breeze stirring becalmed sails in the doldrums, new animation spread through the expressions and movements of the young women, as they stretched out their hands and shifted in their seats.

"Our estimate is that by the time you leave us at the end of July..." Seeing some puzzled expressions, he qualified what he had just said. "Let me explain. Our contract is for one year from 15th September, including twelve weeks' holiday, with six to be taken from the end of July, which brings us back to mid-September. This means you are free, contractually, to leave at the end of July."

There were smiles on several faces and he beamed back at them. "It's a good arrangement, isn't it? Effectively, you will have worked for forty weeks, and our estimate is that you will leave here with your Masters degree and total earnings of £12,200 tax-free, once university, management and accommodation fees have been deducted."

While one or two of the 'girls', as he called them, discussed the figures with each other, Jellop read through his own exclusive set with satisfaction.

Each girl: 4 x £50 = £200 a day x 5 days = £1,000 a week x 40 weeks = £40,000 pa gross

less: University Tuition Fees –£9,000
Management + Accom –£18,800
Total deductions: –£27,800
Net income = £12,200 p/a

Management:
Fees: 9 girls x £18,800 = £169,200
Less net loss NL = £500
Total = £168,700

Expenses:
Rents, Energy etc = £30,000
Coaker's Fees = £37,400
Total = £67,400

Net Profit (Cash) = £101,300

"Well," he thought, "nothing ever does go quite according to plan. They certainly don't in the building trade. And look at Nina." He shook his head. "Silly, silly girl." Then he grinned, "But a hundred thousand smackeroos, tax-free!"

He stood up and retrieved two magnums of Krug champagne he had ordered from the fridge in the corner, while Coaker collected the tray of tall flute glasses from the counter next to it.

"Time to celebrate!" he announced, as he walked back to the table, raising both bottles in the air, one in either hand, while Coaker put the tray down in front of his chair. Twisting off their wire cages and easing the corks out with his thumbs till they popped, he filled the glasses a little at a time, leaving the rush of froth to die back, before completing the transformation of clear glass into fizzing gold.

Coaker resumed his seat and Olga took it upon herself to hand round the elegant glasses, with their effervescent columns of bubbles like small tornadoes spiralling upwards, until everyone had one.

"To a successful 2015!" said Jellop, holding up his glass. Coaker and the nine young women raised their glasses towards him and took a sip. As they put their glasses down again, Irina, the only Russian student in the group, raised hers again, "S novym godom!" she said. "Happy New Year everyone!" She clinked her glass against her neighbour's and then all of them were leaning and stretching across each other, bumping glasses and muttering toasts. "Nowego Roku!", "Okrzyki!", "Pricka!", "An Nou Fericit!"

At the end of the table, Coaker caught Jellop's eye and tapped his watch. Jellop nodded and, as the last of the toasts faded on the air, he was on the point of raising his hand to attract attention and bring the meeting to an end, when Raluca stood up and, raising her still full glass, said: "To our good friend, Nina!". Under her gaze, Jellop saw all the girls rise, and he rose too, so that only Coaker remained seated, until finally he also got to his feet, his eyes like stones. "Nina!" said a chorus of voices, in a rainbow of Eastern European accents.

Chapter 20
Nina & the truth

After Olga, Raluca and the others had left, Coaker moved into Olga's seat next to Jellop. "We have a problem," Jellop said, keeping his voice low.

"Leave Raluca to me," Coaker growled. "She's got family to worry about."

"That's not what I mean. I don't want any more violence; it attracts attention. Besides, it's not our way. The beauty of this scheme is that everyone wins, everyone's happy."

Coaker's head was bent, looking down at a scab on the palm of his left hand and kneading it with the thumb of his right. Jellop had known him since junior school. He'd been a small boy, slow at reading and writing, without much of a home life. His mother had died while he was a baby and he lived with his dad, Nathan Coaker, a fisherman. When the Fenton twins took to waiting for him after school to taunt and bully him, Jellop had been the one to step in and take them on. They'd soon backed off. After that, knowing Jellop was looking out for him, the other kids left Eddie alone.

Puberty and working on his dad's boat had made the difference. After they'd gone to separate secondary schools, Eddie had met the Fenton twins one Saturday morning down in the Barbican. One had finished up in the water and the other in A&E with a broken nose and a severed ear.

"No, Raluca's not the issue," Jellop said. "And, incidentally, if she gives you any trouble, send her to me. Money solves most difficulties." Coaker hawked up some phlegm, eyed the floor, decided against it, swallowed it and went back to the scab. "The issue is you, Eddie: you and Detective

Inspector Lou Beradino. I've had a telephone call, a tip-off, you might say."

"He's got nothing on me," Coaker said.

"Apparently he has."

Coaker's head darted up, his small eyes narrowing. "What?"

"He thinks Nina didn't go home and that you're responsible for her disappearance." He paused, watching him carefully. "Is there anything you haven't told me? Anything I ought to know about, Eddie? Like a phone call of distress to the police, for example."

Coaker's jaw clenched. His thumb stopped rubbing against the scab. A silence of stifled anger hung between them. Jellop took a folded white handkerchief from his pocket, shook it open and, making a cushion of it, dabbed away the beads of sweat gathering on his forehead.

"We may be in trouble, Eddie," he said, keeping his voice steady. "You need to tell me exactly what happened out there, so that I know what we're dealing with." He included himself deliberately, both because he knew the trail would lead back to him and also because he knew that, if Eddie felt cornered and alone, he only had one reaction: he would attack, violently and blindly, whoever was in his way.

"Stupid cunt!" Coaker hissed.

The door opened and the waiter, who had brought the refreshments earlier, pushed a trolley ahead of him into the room.

"Later, thank you!" Jellop commanded and the waiter and trolley withdrew. He waited until the door clicked shut. "Go on," he said.

"She had a second phone. Never expected it." Coacker started rotating the stem of his champagne glass between his fingers, eyes fixed on the stream of bubbles. "I heard her from the wheelhouse, so I went aft, grabbed it off her and threw it overboard. They'll never trace it."

Jellop waited but Coaker had stopped.

"What happened next?"

Coaker shot him a glance and looked back at his glass. "She knew the boat we were meeting wasn't going to help her get home."

"Come on, that can't be right. She would never have gone with you if she'd thought that."

Jellop felt agitated. Coaker wasn't making sense and if he didn't believe him, the police certainly wouldn't. As it was, he had never liked the plan. Nina thought she was getting a cheap ride across the channel to start her journey home for Christmas, when in fact the rendezvous at sea would be the start of her being trafficked to Marseilles instead. But, once she'd refused the money he'd offered her, he'd had no better idea for silencing her and stopping her from making trouble with the other girls.

"She thought she was coming to a secret meeting with you. I'd told her we wouldn't be leaving till after the weekend. Once she..."

Jellop's exasperation boiled over. "Why complicate things, Eddie? Why change what we'd agreed without asking me?"

Coaker was glaring at the table. The whole idea had been his and Jellop knew he should never have agreed to it. Only the situation had nonplussed him. He was aware some of the girls went to church but it had never crossed his mind that a sermon would cause one of them such a crisis of conscience that it would end up threatening the whole operation. Nina wanted to save her friends' mortal souls. "This path is no good," she told him. "The Devil is tricking us." She wanted him to end their contracts at Christmas, give them what they were owed and leave them to make their own way.

Coaker's tight voice cut across his thoughts. He was angry and trying to control it. He didn't like being told off or held to account. "I wanted rid of her quick. Didn't want her talking to the others, especially that bitch Raluca. I knew how close they were. And I was right." He glanced up defiantly. "You saw that just now. Besides..." He hesitated.

"Besides what?"

"Meant she didn't have any luggage with her. Less likely to be noticed."

"Street cameras notice every damn thing!" Jellop thought, but kept it to himself. What he needed to focus on was what Coaker was going to tell Beradino. First, he needed to know exactly what had happened on board that boat.

"What was her reaction when I didn't show up?"

"We had some tea while we were waiting." Coaker stopped. He was smirking.

"And?"

"Had something in it, didn't it?" His face twisted sideways looking at Jellop. "Didn't wake up till we were miles out."

Maybe it wasn't murder after all. "So, you met the other boat as planned?" Jellop tucked the hanky back in his pocket.

"She attacked me. Like a bloody cat!" Coaker wrenched down the wool neck of his sweater, revealing a livid scratch across his throat, jagged, where the skin had been torn. He let go of it and emptied his glass. "I hit her. Had to. No choice." He shook his head and belched twice, widening his mouth each time to let the gas out. "She went down...hit her head on the gunwale...caught the cleat. It split the side of her face open. Blood spurting everywhere, like a gusher!" He glared up at Jellop. "They wouldn't have taken her like that." He looked away. "I tipped her over."

Jellop shut his eyes. "That's murder, Eddie." The enormity of the word stunned him and blotted out his usual clear overview of events. 'Polly mustn't find out!' was the only thought revolving through his head. He was thirteen again. In the wing mirror, he could see his father walking across the builder's yard towards the entrance, where he'd just stalled the lorry after scraping its side all along the stone pillar. It wasn't his father's anger he feared; it was his mother's disappointment in him he dreaded far more. "Whatever possessed you, Ronnie?" she had said, looking at him as if she no longer knew who he was. That bewildered look in her eye had hurt him so much more than his father's heavy hand. He didn't want Polly looking at him like that.

Coaker broke the silence. "Anything else? I need to get back."

Jellop opened his eyes. "You're going to be arrested, Eddie, and the Morning Star is going to be subjected to forensic investigation. I think that probably counts as something else." He bit off the end of each word, fixing Coaker with a chilly smile. "Yes, indeed."

"I sluiced her down. They won't find a fucking fish scale. The Star's clean. Those bastards..."

"Listen to me, Eddie," Jellop said, "and listen carefully. We're going to have to be very focused to smuggle this ball over the line." Even as he was speaking, a plan was forming. "First of all, when they arrest you, say nothing and ask for a solicitor. That's your right. Okay?"

"I'm not stupid."

Jellop ignored him. "When it comes to it, if it ever does, say you met Nina in the Barbican, when it was raining, and she slipped over on the cobbles. Say you helped her pick up the things she'd dropped...her shopping, whatever, nothing they can check... and that you'd offered her a coffee in Monty's or..."

"Why?" Coaker broke in. "What do they know?"

"They know enough to arrest you! They must have some evidence...CCTV footage, a witness, something...that places Nina on your boat."

"This DI..." Coaker's voice was so low, Jellop had to strain to hear him. "Why don't you take care of him?"

Jellop sat back, stroking the edge of the table with his fingertips, his hands moving lightly away and back again, soothing himself as he recalled his breakfast with the detective.

"He doesn't understand how things work here, I'm afraid. I offered to help him and he refused."

"Did he?" Coaker scowled and his eyes become more hooded. "He'll have a soft spot, don't you worry. Everybody does, and I'll find it."

Jellop registered the ominous calm of the threat and shook his head. "No, Eddie; that'll only cause us more trouble. We have to be cleverer than that." He paused. Maybe it was time to find something else for Eddie to do, somewhere far away. He'd have to give it some thought. But, before that, Eddie needed a story that would hold up.

"Where were we?" he continued, wanting to recover his earlier train of thought. "Ah yes, you're both at Monty's. So, let's see...Right, one thing led to another and you arranged a date at The Ship. From there, you went back to the boat, had a few more drinks and chatted for a bit. After a while, she told you she was meeting a girlfriend in the Barbican. Say you don't remember the name, but it sounded foreign; and that you rowed her across to the steps by Jasper's to save her the walk round. After that, you left the dinghy in your usual place and went home."

Coaker grunted. Jellop stood up; he wanted to stretch his legs. He refilled his glass and tilted the bottle towards Coaker's, but he put his hand across it.

Ron smiled. "It's a hard story for them to disprove. And if she wasn't on the boat when you went fishing the next day, you have a solid alibi for where you were when she rang the police."

"Doesn't exactly tie in with what I told them before?" Coaker said.

"You were confused then. This'll do, as long as there's no trace of blood on Morning Star. Finger prints won't matter, because you've said she was there. Remember, they have to prove you're guilty and they haven't even got a body to say she's dead."

Ron looked at his watch. It was past midday. He was going to be late for the planning hearing. "I've got to go." He placed his hand on Coaker's shoulder. "If we keep our wits about us, we'll be fine. We just need to hold our nerve." He gave a gentle squeeze. "And our temper."

Chapter 21
Coaker in custody

Fran put the phone down and looked across the desk. "The Morning Star's moored at Fish Quay with the engine running."

"Right, let's go," Lou said.

With blue lights flashing and siren shrieking, the drive to the quay by the fish market took just three minutes. They passed the National Marine Aquarium car park and sped through the entrance gates to the quay, slicing between a long, one-storey building with a corrugated metal roof on their left and a row of trawlers moored on their right. Cars and white vans were parked at the edge facing the trawlers, while stacked along the walls of the building's commercial units were orange fish crates and buoys, dark pots and traps, and green nets in small mounds.

As they neared the fish market at the far end, they saw the Morning Star roped to the quay. They slid into a parking bay and walked 20 yards back to the boat. Lou noticed white jets spitting intermittently out of the stern, white slashes against the steely water. The boat looked well cared for, not what he'd expected. The sky blue hull was freshly painted, so too the wheelhouse and cabin to the front, white with a mint green roof, the boat's name spelled out across it in a single line. He could see the dark shape of a man moving inside. The deck was clear from the wheelhouse back to the raised rack in the stern, where the crab and lobster pots, buoys and fishing nets were stowed. It was a working boat, less than ten metres long, he guessed, and a good size for one person to manage on their own.

Fran hung back to let him step on board first, then followed him down. The man, already aware of them, was half-way out of the wheelhouse and moving towards them.

"Mr Edward Coaker?" Lou said.

"Yes, I'm Eddie Coaker. You're on my boat." He stood in front of them, legs less than shoulder-width apart, his arms loose beside him. Fran could feel the throb of the engine through the soles of her trainers.

"I'm Detective Inspector Beradino and this is Detective Sergeant Bannerman, Charles Cross Police Station. We are here to arrest you in connection with the disappearance and suspected death of Nina Lapinski." Lou saw no change in the close scrutiny Coaker was giving him. "You are the last known person to have seen her alive and we're taking you into custody to help us with..."

"I can't leave the boat here," Coaker growled. "I need to moor her back on the pontoon." He pointed across the inlet.

"We have a warrant to search the Morning Star and a forensic team will be here shortly." Lou noted the start of anger in Coaker's eyes, the instinctive curl of his fists and the quick look away, as he absorbed the news and struggled to regain his self-control. "We've already informed the harbour master. And I must caution you that you do not have to say anything..." Coaker hawked up a mouthful of phlegm and spat it out like a projectile over the side of the boat. "...but it may harm your defence if you do not mention when questioned something you later rely on in court. Anything you do say, however, may be given in evidence."

Lou kept his tone neutral and did not prolong eye contact unnaturally. He had no wish to provoke Coaker or to have to resort to handcuffs. Coaker shifted his gaze to Fran, who was standing with notebook open, but with a physical alertness Lou recognised. For a moment, Lou thought Coaker was going to try his luck, but the shoulders relaxed, the fists uncurled.

"Let's get this done," Coaker said, stepping forward. "I've work to do."

* * * * *

Back at Charles Cross Police Station, Lou and Fran left Coaker with Bel Thompson, the duty sergeant. He would be informed of his rights to a phone call and legal advice. After that, she would organise for his fingerprints, photographs and DNA samples to be taken. There were a couple of hours to wait before they could begin their interrogation.

They found Macklin Thomas and Debbie Denton in the incident room.

"I need an update," Lou said. "We've just brought Eddie Coaker in and we're going to question him once Bel's done the necessary."

"Any luck with the boat, Debbie?" Fran asked, walking over to the computer table.

"No," Debbie said, peeling her eyes from the screen to look at her. "Nothing so far. The Morning Star's certificates are up-to-date and the harbour master's log confirms what Coaker told you about his sailing times on the day of Nina Lapinski's disappearance."

"What about his personal situation?" Fran said. "Have you checked his mortgage, bank account?"

"He has no mortgage. The house was his parents. Father died first and his mother left it to him. The electoral roll shows he's lived there all his life."

"Sounds good to me," Fran said. "Secure base, know where you're coming from."

"Yeah," Debbie said, exchanging a knowing look with her. Cardiff or Jamaica? Male or female? Identity issues were something they'd taken into the small hours.

"One thing, though," Debbie said as Lou joined them. "Well, two, really. The Fish Market's records show that, on the day Nina went missing, the Morning Star's catch was minimal."

"Yeah, we talked about that at the time," Fran said, and Lou nodded.

"What's the second thing?" he said.

Debbie's fingers flicked across the keys while she eyed the monitor. "I checked his bank account. He has two with the Co-op, current and savings. He's got..."

"Bank living up to its name and being co-operative, that's unusual," Fran said.

"Not exactly," Debbie said, getting there first. Lou caught her glance to Macklin, who was grinning but instantly busied himself with something he was writing.

"So, exactly how have we come by this information, Debbie?" Lou asked.

"It's a suspected murder case, right?" Debbie sat up tall, pushing her shoulders back, and looked him squarely in the eyes. She was backing her call.

"Yes," he said. "So?"

"Getting around obstacles to catch crooks is what we do. The computer's my way of helping with that. That's why you put me on it."

"Do we have a warrant?"

"No."

"It's applied for." Macklin's baritone rolled across the room.

"Go on," Lou said.

Debbie looked back at the screen. "He has savings of £77,500."

"Money in crab pots then!" Fran said.

"What's interesting," Debbie went on, "is that the last deposit into the savings account was for £35,000 last September, on the same day that the same amount was credited to his current account from Babbage Holdings Ltd."

"And they are?"

"Who are?" Lou and Fran's voices chimed together.

Debbie smiled, revealing pink gums and salt white teeth. She looked from one to the other, pausing for effect.

"It's a Cayman Island account and, although there's a dummy board of directors and a barrage of subsidiary companies, guess who's the principal shareholder, when you get to the end of the chain."

"Ron Jellop!" Lou said.

"Not quite." She raised an eyebrow. "Polly Jellop."

"Very interesting," Fran said. "Now why is Ron Jellop paying Coaker a large sum of money that he wants to be untraceable?"

"It's not the only payment," Debbie said, holding their attention again. "He's received similar amounts from Babbage Holdings for the previous two years as well. Both in September."

"Like an annual salary," Lou said.

"What type of employment?" Fran asked, then added: "It's to do with the prostitutes, isn't it? He's Jellop's enforcer." The connection hit her. "Jellop knows about Nina."

Lou locked eyes with her, but didn't say anything.

"Lou," Macklin began, getting up and walking over to them. "There's someone who wants to talk to you about this. She rang through this morning, asking to speak to the detective in charge of the case. She wouldn't talk to me. Her name's Raluca. She wouldn't give me her surname either, but she left a number." He handed Lou a slip of paper with a mobile number written large and clear in black ink. "She wants to speak to you urgently."

"Raluca," Fran said, testing the name aloud. "Wonder where she comes from?" She paused before continuing, looking at each of them in turn. "Eastern European maybe? Another student at the university maybe? Another Jellop protégé on the game maybe?" Like tumblers on a safe lock, pieces started slotting into place.

"One way to find out," Lou said, raising his hand with the piece of paper in it. Good work, Debbie. Keep digging and let me know if you find anything else. The more we know when we question Coaker, the easier it'll be to spot the lies."

"Assuming he says anything," Fran added under her breath.

Macklin went back to the table by the boards. Lou followed him. "Macklin, any news from the others?"

"Martin's talking to staff at the University. Carol and Jason are door-stepping known contacts and friends of Nina Lapinski. They haven't called anything in so far."

"Okay, keep me posted."

Macklin nodded and Lou headed for the door.

"Come on, Fran. Let's call this number and see where we are with Coaker."

Chapter 22
Coaker interviewed

B ack in Lou's room, they sat either side of the desk, while he punched in the number and lent back as the calling burr began to repeat itself. He let it ring until the voicemail cut in and asked him to leave a message.

"This is Detective Inspector Beradino," he said and gave his number. "Please call me. If I'm unavailable, ask for Detective Sergeant Macklin Thomas and leave a message with him."

While he was talking, Fran walked over to the radiator. It was lukewarm on top, but hotter as she slid her hand lower. Lou put the receiver down, opened the wide middle drawer of his desk and tossed a stubby brass key at her. She caught it one-handed and turned it in the bleed valve. Air hissed out, followed by a jet of water. Closing it off quickly, she wiped her fingers against her jeans and gave it back to him. "Thought it was cold in here."

He had no sooner put the key back in the drawer and started to close it than the phone rang. "Beradino," he said, picking it up. "Yes, put her through." He caught Fran's eye and nodded once. "Yes, Raluca, I'm DI Beradino and I'm leading the inquiry into the disappearance of Nina Lapinski."

"Nina is my friend. I am afraid something terrible has happened to her." The woman's voice was clear and firm, although strongly accented. Polish? Russian? He wasn't sure.

"What is your connection with Miss Lapinski?" he asked, scribbling on a pad, tearing off the page and handing it to Fran.

"I cannot tell you this. It is not safe for me speaking to you."

Fran read the message, nodded and hurried out.

"Why have you asked to speak to me then?"

"There is a man you must talk to about Nina, but you must not mention my name." She paused and he waited. "You will not mention my name?"

"We will protect your identity, Miss.." he offered, but she didn't bite.

"He is Coaker."

"Is that his first or last name?"

"Mr Coaker. We don't know his first name."

"We, Raluca? Who is 'we'?"

"Does not matter. You must listen to me. Mr Coaker is very bad man. I know it. He has done something with Nina. You must find him and then maybe you find Nina."

"I would like to talk to you in person, Raluca. If you give me your address, I'll come to see you."

"No. This is not possible. You do not understand. You must not contact me." The line went dead.

Lou stared at the granite sky through the rain-smudged window, nodding to himself. Not only were they going to be able to tie Nina's disappearance directly to Coaker, but they were also going to establish his links to Councillor Jellop and the prostitution ring he was running. There was still a lot of work to be done to nail the evidence for the CPS but, in essence, he knew the shape of it now. The puzzle was solved. The first domino piece to fall would knock over Jellop's other scams. Oliver Drew and Chateau La Fleur, Alastair Shingle and the planning applications, he already knew about; but there would be more, he was sure of that.

"No luck," Fran said, re-entering the room, her voice dissolving the swirling colours back into quilted greyness. "Prepaid mobile, no GPS."

"See if Martin's still at the University and ask him to check for students with first name Raluca, however that's spelt."

"R. A. L. U. C. A. I just googled it, it's Romanian."

A smile flickered at the corners of his mouth as he watched her use her mobile.

"He was about to have lunch," she said, slipping it back in her pocket; "but he'll go by Registry first."

Lou looked at his watch and stood up. "We haven't got long. Let's grab a sandwich in the canteen and go over our approach to Coaker at the same time."

* * * * *

After lunch they met the duty solicitor, John Palmer, and briefly disclosed the allegations against Eddie Coaker: that Nina Lapinski had last been seen in his company, boarding his boat; that she had not been since; and that they suspected him of murder and of disposing of the body at sea.

John Palmer was a mild man in his forties, with thinning, wispy hair the colour of faded autumn leaves and a boyish grin. "What evidence do you have, Inspector?" he asked. Lou mentioned the desperate phone call, the witness at the pub in the Barbican and the CCTV footage. "Somewhat inconclusive, wouldn't you say?" he smiled. Lou had no intention of revealing any more than was necessary at this stage. The less Coaker knew of the accumulating evidence they had against him, the better their chances of catching him unawares later on and tripping him up.

"Any forensic evidence, for example?" Palmer continued. "I understand you are searching my client's boat."

"It's too early to say yet."

"In which case, I would like to talk to Mr Coaker before you question him."

They left the solicitor with Bel Thomas. "What do you reckon?" Lou asked Fran as they went back upstairs.

"Palmer's advice will be 'no comment'. It's his best option. We'll be struggling to get anything out of Coaker."

"The circumstantial's building. If the forensic team come up with something concrete, depending on what that is, we might well have enough to charge him."

"Not by tomorrow though." Fran led the way into Lou's office and waited to close the door. As she sat down, he started to pace slowly between the desk and the window.

"The magistrate will give us four more days if we need it. Meanwhile, we'll get a warrant to search his house. But right now, let's go through what we know already and think about his blind spots." Fran pursed her lips and looked doubtful. He shrugged his shoulders. "He might blurt something out. You never know."

* * * * *

When Lou and Fran entered Interview Room 2, almost two hours later, Eddie Coaker and his solicitor were sitting side by side on the far side of a metal-legged table close to the wall, facing two empty chairs. Despite a row of narrow windows higher up, two long strip lights bathed the room in the harsh glare of neon. Lou took the chair opposite Coaker, while Fran slipped into the other, facing John Palmer. They placed their notebooks on the white laminate table top and Fran pressed the button on the square black PaceNet unit next to her. Whatever was said, there would be audio-visual evidence.

Lou recorded the date, time and names of those present and then repeated the caution in full, while Coaker sat impassively, looking at the table top.

When Fran asked him to confirm his full name, permanent address and date of birth, he didn't look up, but rattled off the information in a monotone: "Eddie Coaker. 15 Victoria Place, Plymouth, PL2 3RY. 12.11.1974."

That was the last time he spoke. To every question they asked him, he kept his head bowed and stayed silent. Eventually Lou said: "If you are an innocent man, Mr Coaker, the court may find it strange that you have been unwilling to answer even the simplest and most straightforward of our questions." Coaker took a hanky from his trouser pocket, blew his nose, stuffed it back and resumed his inspection of the table top.

"My client has nothing to say at this stage," said Palmer, "which is his right, Inspector. Unless you intend to charge him, he would like to be released to return home. And, in view of his long established and settled life here in Plymouth and his clean record, I would suggest there is little point in continuing to hold him under arrest."

"This is a suspected murder enquiry, Mr Palmer," Lou said, "and Mr Coaker is the person most able to assist us, if he chooses to do so. We shall not be releasing him therefore, before we have had time to complete our search of his boat and home and assess the evidence we find there." He shifted his gaze to Coaker. "This will include the removal for inspection of all computerised and paper records, as well as a thorough investigation of telephone calls and banking transactions for the past five years."

Coaker raised his head and looked at him for the first time. "You'll regret this, Beradino," he said, his voice so low Lou bent closer to hear.

"Please repeat that more loudly, Mr Coaker," Fran said. "It was too soft for the recorder."

Coaker glanced at her, blew her a tight, rasping kiss and looked back at the table top.

"For the record," Fran said slowly and clearly, "Mr Coaker is refusing to repeat the threat he just made to Detective Inspector Beradino, which was: "You'll regret this, Beradino.""

Palmer cleared his throat and looked anxiously at Coaker. "As an innocent man," he said, "my client's remark was an observation, not a threat."

Lou smiled at him, he couldn't help himself. "First interview concluded," he said, eyeing the wall clock, "at 15.48, Wednesday, 21st January, 2015."

Part Two

Thursday, 22nd – Saturday, 24th January, 2015

Chapter 23
Roger stalks Rachael

Roger couldn't get Rachael out of his mind. But it was more than thinking about her, his whole body ached for her. It was Thursday and already two days since she'd walked out on him. He was going through the motions at the college but he felt nauseous and hollow, and he couldn't concentrate. When he got home, he paced the house, not knowing what to do, but wanting to do something. He looked at the mess in the kitchen and went back upstairs to his bedroom. The landing was dark and cold. He didn't want light. He didn't want warmth. He stripped out of his work clothes, tossing them on to the unmade bed. Pulling a crumpled pair of black jeans out of the laundry basket, he stepped into them and grabbed the shirt and sweater he'd worn the day before from the back of the chair by the window. He hadn't separated them and he pulled them on over his head as one, khaki under navy.

Finally, not bothering with socks, he pushed his feet into old trainers with their laces still tied. As he straightened up, he caught sight of himself in the mirror over the chest of drawers. He looked dreadful, his eyes dark hollows, his hair sticking up in clumps, black stubble sprouting from the blue-black cowl of his jaw. He stared at the desolation of himself, as if at another. He felt far back, far down in a pit, detached from the person he was looking at. He went downstairs again and sat in an armchair, one leg swung over the arm, staring at the window and the overcast day outside. He'd left early; soon it would be dark again. He stayed there motionless for a long time, almost invisible in the shadows of the unlit room.

He heard footsteps outside and the rasp of the letterbox as something was shoved through. A little later the phone rang but he didn't answer it. He didn't want to see anyone; he didn't want to speak to anyone; he didn't want to move. He wanted to wallow in the glue of his misery, to give himself over to it and drown his pain in it.

But underneath it all, he longed to hold her again, to feel the softness of her and bury his face in her hair, in the musky smell of her. He wanted to curl round her under the covers, circling his arms together under her breasts, and lose himself in the world of her. He loved the down of her, the gold hairs that laced her arms and belly, so fine that only light from behind caught them, revealed them. He ached for the feel of her palm on the nape of his neck as she pulled him to her. There was nothing without her, only this dark emptiness, this sense of utter abandonment and of plummeting down a well, watching the cap of light at the top shrink and disappear.

Outside the day was dying, the shapes through the window softening, losing their sharp edges, becoming smudged by the gathering gloom. He loathed himself for not being enough. If there was more of him, Rachel would have wanted him. She had once, but not any more. What would she want with him after what she'd had? This pokey little terraced house? A glorified schoolmaster for a partner? No, not a partner! A husband! He wanted to marry her. He wanted her to be his wife. Someone scornful mocked him, laughing: "You?" He knew the voice. "You're just a little twat!"

Hatred froze his self-pity. Ex-army security guard, 'handsome' Mike Walters, was standing over him, sneering, bending his six-foot-four frame downwards. "Do you hear me? A little twat!" "Come on, Michael, he's just doing his homework." It was his mother's voice. The figure wheeled away. "Mind your own business, you stupid cow!" He heard the slap, her cry. He ran at him, yelling "Stop it! Stop it!", and tried to grab his arm. Suddenly, he was dangling in mid-air, grasped under his chin by the throat, while he heard the lick of the belt being whipped out of its loops. "I'll teach you, you little twat."

Roger saw his stepfather in the armchair opposite, legs stretched out, a can of beer in his hand. The fury in him battled with the fear. He eyed the poker in the fireplace. He'd smash his head in. He seized it and rushed him, grabbing him by the throat, pinning him back in the chair and, holding the poker by its blackened tip, he brought the brass knob smashing down on his skull, again and again, until it cracked open like a boiled egg and all the yolky brains spilled out over his sneering moustache. Then, one more sidelong whack to smash all those handsome white teeth. "Now say it!"

Both his feet were on the floor, his hands gripping the arm ends, and he was breathing heavily. He'd never been able to save his mother from the brutal beatings she took. She was hardly more than five-feet tall, but she always tried to step between them, to save him from the fists and the belt. He'd never been able to save her, and Mike Walters had murdered her in the end. The coroner didn't call it murder, but what else could you call it? He was drunk, driving too fast, flew off the road at a bend and into a tree. Doing more than 90 miles an hour, the police said. Both dead. Of course he killed her!

His grip slackened and he slumped back. He was sobbing, his chest juddering. Before Walters, life had felt so good, so safe. He'd never known his dad. "He was a gambler," his mum told him. "Took off with our savings and I never heard from him again." For almost eleven years, it had just been the two them. Whenever he thought of her, she was sitting in the back room in her chair by the window, as she concentrated on her sewing, her thick auburn hair caught loosely behind by a scarf to hold it out of the way. She made patchwork quilts and cushion covers to order, in bold, jewel-like colours, and the floor and table near her were covered in the fabrics she was working with, like an artist's palette. She loved books, too; it was where he had got his passion for literature from. She may have been a farm worker's daughter, but her father had painted watercolour landscapes, and she had grown up more interested in the forms and colours of the land than in working it. On market days too, her father had stolen time and taken her to the town's museum to look at the paintings and artefacts there.

Roger's flow of thoughts drew out a different memory. He was walking beside her, holding her warm hand, looking at paintings in a gallery. It was the Penwith Gallery in St Ives; he recognised the long, whitewashed walls, the subterranean feel of it, and the scattered plinths with sculptures on them. He loved these days out with her, following her from canvas to canvas, sharing in her excitement, eating fish and chips on the beach afterwards.

Why had she spoiled that? Why had she needed someone else? For Christ's sake, hadn't he been enough, even for her? He caught sight of the small, framed photograph on the mantelpiece, indistinct in the half-light. He pushed himself out of the chair, seized it and hurled it on to the hearth, the glass shattering and one edge of the frame springing apart. He stared down where it had bounced face upwards, as it smashed, and the smiling face stared back at him from the debris. He picked it clear of the shards of glass and straightened up, looking at it still.

"That bastard stole Mum," he cried out, "but no-one's taking you!" He thought of Oliver. "Nor keeping you!" he shouted. These men who battered and violated the women who loved them, he wouldn't tolerate them. "If you lay another finger on her, I'll kill you. I'll smash your bloody head in!" He had to protect Rachael; she was in danger, he knew it. That's what these men did. When you tried to leave them, they killed you. He had to get there first.

He ran into the hall, adrenalin pumping. He grabbed his leather jacket from the hook and shrugged his way into it, stuffing the photo into the inside pocket and grabbing his car keys from the dish. He was halfway out of the door when he wheeled around and seized the baseball bat from the umbrella stand.

* * * * *

By the time he reached Yelverton, it was dark and raining, the road smeared with the gold of oncoming headlights. He had her address, but he'd never been there. The satnav led him up an unlit lane, past houses shrouded in darkness. He slowed, hunched over the steering wheel, flicking his eyes from side to side, straining for a clue, some indication. As he passed a curling driveway on his right, he thought he saw Rachael's Volvo estate in the porch light. He turned in the next entrance and came back, stopping where he could see the pool of light more clearly. It was her car, the dense shadow of another closer to him. They must both be home. He switched off his lights. Gradually, as his eyes readjusted, he began to make out two dimly glowing windows, one on the first floor at the far end and the other, fainter, on the ground floor before the porch.

The rain was easing and he switched the wipers to intermittent. What was he going to do? He slipped into reverse and the backing lights showed that the lane widened fifty yards behind him to create a passing point. He eased the car backward into the indent and switched off. Once out, he found the rain was light, more like a damp blanket hanging in the air. He took his cagoule from the boot and slipped it on, pulling up the hood. Then, retrieving the baseball bat and closing the driver's door softly, he stole back up the lane and stood under cover of some rhododendron bushes just inside the driveway entrance.

Perhaps he should knock on the door, confront Oliver and claim Rachael. She would feel differently then. Their love for one another would be out in the open, and Oliver couldn't hurt her, because he would protect her. They could leave together. She could come back with him tonight. Everything could be changed tonight, forever. The sky was lightening, as the clouds thinned, and a waxing moon peeked through. Roger pushed back his hood and was about to start up the drive when the front door opened, spreading a fleece of gold across the gravel, and Rachael stepped out. She was followed by a man in an overcoat, who paused to lock the door behind them.

Roger watched as they passed her car and reached the one beyond. When the doors clicked open and the indicator lights flashed, he turned and ran back up the lane. Once behind the wheel again, he waited as the headlights nosed out of the drive and swung away from him. As the tail lights receded, he rolled forward and followed with his lights off. The sight of the Rolls-Royce maddened him. This smug, self-assured wife-beater, clothing himself in the trappings of success and respectability, was defiling truth and beauty, the two values he prized most in art and in people. Keats was right; it was all we needed to know. As he turned out on to the main road, he switched on his lights and shadowed the Rolls towards Plymouth and the Drews' dinner date with the Jellops..

Truth and beauty illuminated Rachael with the same loving grace and warmth as his mother. They were rare. They were beacons. How dark and colourless his world had become after his mother was killed. Her love had been chopped off and everything turned grey and cold and lonely. And then, long after he'd given up any hope of finding again what he'd lost, Rachael appeared in his class, rekindling the light in him and turning the drab of his life back into colour. He'd been given a second chance — and he wasn't going to let go of her this time.

Chapter 24
On watch At Royal William Yard

"Supper as well as lunch," Polly said, looking in the mirror over the basin. "I'm going to have to double up on my zumba!" She breathed in, holding the palm of her hand against her stomach, and grinned at Rachael's reflection. Rachael was standing behind her, brushing her hair back into place, where the breeze off the river had ruffled it on the short walk from Firestone Hall into Royal William Yard.

"I'm just going to have some fish," she said. "The pollock maybe."

They were alone, although they could hear the muffled din and clatter from the restaurant quite clearly. Polly took out a small scent bottle and sprayed it in a neat circular movement around her hair and throat. Rachael closed her eyes. It was a subtle fragrance, familiar, like honeysuckle. There was always a trace of it left in the air where Polly had been.

"Okay. Ready?" Polly turned, popping the fastener of her neat black purse.

"There's something I want to ask you." Rachael hesitated.

"Go on."

"I feel a bit awkward."

Polly put out her hand and touched her on the arm. "Tell me." The concern and warmth in her voice cut straight through the defences Rachael had prepared for the evening's ordeal.

"Rachael, love, whatever is it?"

Rachael took a tissue from her sleeve, wiped her eyes and stamped her foot in frustration. "It's nothing. I'm being silly."

She tucked the tissue back under the cuff of her sweater. "It's just..." She sighed, raising her hand in the air and letting it fall back again.

"Just what?"

"Oh, it's all such a mess, Polly! I tried to end things with Roger yesterday and he didn't accept it at all, just like Ollie won't. And it looks like Ollie's being investigated by the police. A CID woman came to our house the other day...but I've already told you that, haven't I?"

"What did she want?"

"To speak to him. I don't know what about. I was leaving. That was the day I was late getting to college, remember?"

"Yes, I do. But what did Oliver say about it?"

"He just brushed me off with it being some routine thing to do with the Chateau in Bergerac, but I know there's more to it than that. And Ron's involved in that too, isn't he? That's what I wanted to ask. Do you know anything about what's going on."

Polly frowned. "Ron hasn't said anything. But then he wouldn't. He doesn't bring business home. He's always been good like that."

"But they are involved in it together, aren't they?"

Polly pursed her lips. "Look, I'll ask Ron later on and let you know. I don't think there's..." She stopped as the door swung open and two young women entered, both talking into their mobiles. Polly raised her eyebrow and held the door for Rachael.

They paused in the recessed section at the far end of the converted warehouse, their eyes adjusting to the dimmed glow of the restaurant. "I'll call you tomorrow, all right?"

Rachael nodded. "Thank you. I need to know...for the boys, that's all."

"Yes, my love, I see that." Polly dropped her voice and bent closer. "But what about Roger? What happened?"

"He just acted as if I hadn't said anything, at first; and then ended up just staring through me, saying we'd always be together. It was scary. And now I feel like I've done him some terrible kind of harm." She looked away in the direction of their table. Oliver was watching them. "Come on, we'd better go back."

As they threaded their way between the other diners, Polly whispered: "It'll be all right, my girl. And don't forget, I'm here. Any time."

Rachael reached behind, found her hand and squeezed it.

"Ah, there you are," Ron said, getting to his feet and holding Polly's chair for her. "Just going to send out a search party," he laughed.

* * * * *

Roger peered through the window, watching them, his hood shrouding his face. He kept one hand deep in his pocket, clenching and unclenching his fingers against the cold, while the other gripped the baseball bat close against his leg. Hearing voices approaching, he drifted back into the shadows of the columned archway and waited. He would wait all night if he had to.

One thing was sure, Drew wasn't going home again, wasn't going to abuse Rachael ever again. Three figures passed close to him, all in coats, one in a trilby, their voices echoing against the slabs of stone. They didn't see him and he watched as they turned in at the Canteen, the man in the trilby holding the door.

Rachael would be his. He would keep her safe and help her come into being. The feminine was rising. He believed it. He wanted it. Masculine hegemony was in decline. People couldn't see it yet, because small changes had taken so much time and effort they seemed irrelevant in the scale of things. But it was like levering a boulder on a hilltop: hard to get the lever far enough under to get any purchase; harder still to begin to rock and move it on its axis; and often, just when you thought you were winning, it would rock back again and settle exactly where it had been before. But, eventually, with enough determination, it would catch at the tipping point and begin to roll. And then you didn't have to do anything. It just gathered speed under its own momentum and flattened anything in its way.

Thousand-year Reichs, Iron Curtains, even Mighty Ozymandias – they might all seem to be immutable and everlasting, but people didn't read Shelley any more. They didn't know that two vast and trunkless legs of stone stood in an antique land, nor hear the echo as Saddam Hussein was toppled from his desert pedestal? Change would come, it always did, and would wipe away those patriarchal sneers of cold command.

Even this place, this two-hundred-year-old bastion of the Royal Navy, built to provision the battleships of the British Empire and named for a king, had changed. Roger looked up at the building's massive silhouette, imagining the days when the Brewhouse had housed the rum store and repair workshops.

Officers had overseen ratings loading the ships right here beside him, imposing their iron discipline on them. How would those sailors feel now, transported across time to find their warehouses turned into luxury apartments, restaurants, even artists' studios; or to see members of the public, families with children, lovers, friends, pensioners, all wandering about the Yard, enjoying the splendour of it. How unimaginable it would have been to them, as they loaded ships bound for the Baltic and the war in Crimea, that such people would be strolling and lazing, enjoying the views up the Tamar, eating and drinking and taking it easy – casual chatter and 'selfies' replacing barked orders and salutes.

Yes, Royal William Yard was magnificent, but he didn't believe in imperial power, in its drive for domination and self-aggrandisement. Take away the patriotic humbug and how were its values any better than those of the market place or corporate empires and the scrummaging for profit, the values of men like Oliver Drew? He was a parasite, a leech puffed up with the blood and spoils of his victims. He despised him and his kind, pigs at a trough, their guzzling snouts as greasy as their cold-souled smiles. Where were empathy and co-operation and creativity, rather than greed and violence and consumption? Yang values had obliterated the yin in the West for centuries, but the tide was turning and a rebalancing was coming. And he would do everything he could to support the Rachaels of this world, like his mother too, against the likes of Oliver Drew or Mike Walters.

He tilted the face of his watch to the lamplight. Almost 8.40pm. They'd be at least another hour, probably more – much more. It's what these men did, sat stuffing their faces in fancy restaurants, boring their bauble women with their business talk and sleazy jokes. But he'd wait all night if he had to.

Rachael's Christmas story haunted him. He had pictured it over and over to himself. She told him how after they'd become lovers, she didn't want to have sex with Drew any more, didn't even want him to touch her. So Drew had waited until their sons were home for Christmas, when he knew she wouldn't cry out or make a scene, wouldn't want to upset them, and then he forced himself on her. Raped her! Of course it was rape. She'd said she didn't think you could call it that because they were married. But he'd made her see it for what it was, a deliberate violation of her, an act of physical violence against her, no different from any other kind of rape – a contemptuous act of subjugation. *You belong to me and I will do with you as I please – what I want, when I want.* Roger freed his hand from his pocket and slammed his fist into the pillar. Pain shot through his arm like an electric shock and burnt like fire in the bones of his knuckles. He shook it wildly in the air and then clamped it tight under his arm. As the raw burning subsided into throbbing, the fingers of his good hand tightened their grip on the baseball bat.

The night air off the river was cold. He curled his toes inside his trainers and released them, trying to work some feeling into their numbness; but the shoes were insubstantial, their canvas easily penetrated by the winter chill. Finally, he moved from his cover into the lamplight, turned the corner and walked along the wharf. On one side was the Clarence building, with the ghostly shadows of its original loading derricks still protruding from the upper storey. And on the other side, even in the dark, he could make out the black mushrooms of the mooring bollards at intervals, now screened by the developer's protective barrier of strength-ened glass and railings.

He continued to the very end, where a steel cantilevered staircase descended from the dark portal recently cut into the top of the huge defensive wall at this western end of the Yard. These steps were now officially a part of the Southwest Coastal Path, connecting the naval yard to Devil's Point Park, overlooking Firestone Bay and facing out to sea across Plymouth Sound. He watched the stream of changing colours from concealed lights rippling down the staircase − purple, yellow, green, pink, blue, and purple again. They flooded the steps and spread a pale halo on the wall behind, shading off into jagged darkness at the edges.

Roger turned round and stood looking back to the corner of Brewhouse. Realising he could no longer see the entrance the Drews and Jellops had entered by, he started to hurry back, afraid they might leave in his absence, even though he knew it was too soon. He transferred the baseball bat to his aching left hand, shielding the weapon from sight, as he strode back.

Drawing level with the same window as before, he looked in. Through the other diners in between, he saw Rachael, an upturned fork halfway to her mouth, and he drew in a deep breath of relief. A bearded man at the table by the window looked up and seemed to see him. Roger recoiled instantly and retreated to his former vantage point, concealing himself once again in the shadows of the colonnade's pillars.

Chapter 25
Murder & possession

"Another Cognac, Oliver?" Jellop asked, his large face relaxed in good humour. Rachael exchanged a glance of desperation with Polly. Their waitress had cleared the table almost half-an-hour ago. All that was left were the men's brandy bowls and coffee cups and their own water glasses now almost empty. The restaurant was waiting to close. They were the last. Under the table, Polly nudged her husband's thigh with her knee.

"No, I'll wait till I'm home and tucked up with a Cuban." Oliver grinned at Jellop and then at Polly, pleased with his own joke, inviting them to laugh with him. It was his technique. Rachael could see it so plainly now, yet for years she hadn't. He used his brand of humour to lure you into a form of involuntary conspiracy with him. Not to laugh, or at least smile, when he was grinning at you, sucking his cheeks in, his mouth in an O, like a naughty boy who has just said something outrageous, would be to reject him. It would be unequivocal and people were too polite or too kind to risk hurting his feelings. But it was more than that. He inveigled people into feeling that if they weren't with him, they were against him; and that to be with him would add some exciting opportunity to their lives, whereas not to laugh with him would mean to be cast out. She saw Jellop laughing willingly and Polly's restrained smile.

Oliver stood up, saying he needed 'the little boys' room'. It was another gambit of his she knew well. On the way, he would settle the bill. It would look generous, but you would be in his debt. He never allowed himself to be paid for. And sure enough, when Jellop raised his arm towards the manager and made a scribbling motion, asking for the bill, the man came across and told him discretely it had already been paid.

Outside, Oliver took Rachael's arm. "We're going for a stroll up to the end and back. Stretch our legs and get some air. How about you two? Want to join us?"

"No thanks, Oliver," Polly said. "I'm falling asleep on my feet." She turned to Jellop and slipped her hand in his. "Come on, Ron, let's go home."

Roger watched the exchange of kisses and heard Oliver call after Jellop and his wife: "We'll drive straight off when we get back to your place. Don't wait up for us." Jellop raised his free hand without turning, as they continued on their way, hand-in-hand.

Rachael started up the quayside, wanting to get back to the warmth of the car and home as soon as possible. Oliver strode after her and coming level put his arm around her. As he did so, Roger moved out and followed them as they passed in front of the Clarence building, hugging the shadows of it walls. Almost midnight, a slow drizzle was fuzzing the orange lamplight. He saw Rachael try to pull away and Drew tighten his grip. Everything inside him went loose. He felt calm and perfectly balanced. There was no-one else about and only one apartment had its lights showing, and that was on the top floor. All he had to do was close the gap as they neared the end and strike before Oliver turned.

But as he stole nearer to them, Oliver turned sideways unexpectedly, steering Rachael to the railings, his profile suddenly revealed. They stood side by side, staring out across the river. They were arguing, trying to keep their voices low, but he heard Rachael's sharp "No!"

Roger stopped breathing; he was up to them now. The baseball bat arced through the air, his arm at full stretch, his whole weight up on his toes and flying forward behind it.

Rachael's shriek sliced the night as the rounded club caved in the back of Oliver's head. His body slumped, ready to fall; but, before it could do so, Roger, dropping the bat, grabbed Oliver with one hand on his coat collar, the other between his legs, and heaved him up and over the railings. "What are you doing?" Rachael cried, pawing at his arm, as the body went over. They heard the dull splash and peered after it, as it bobbed, sank, reappeared further away, a black shape like a seal's head, already caught in the estuary's strong currents sucking it out with the tide.

"Ollie!" she screamed, as they watched it losing definition, merging with the shadows of the river and disappearing. "Oliver!"

Roger bent down, picked up the baseball bat and hurled it far out. He turned back to her and she saw his eyes glittering within the shroud of his hood. "You're mine now," he said softly. She wanted to run, to be gone, but there was no connection with her body. She froze.

"What have you done?" she moaned. "Ollie's drowning; we've got to..."

"Come to me." He was holding her wrist, drawing her to him.

"Don't!" She twisted towards the building. "Help!" she yelled, trying to pull herself free. "Hel..."

But his grip was too strong and he reeled her in, cupping her mouth with his other hand, stifling her cry. He wrapped himself round her from behind, so she couldn't move, binding her arms with his own in front of her. "Now we'll be together," he whispered, rocking her from side to side, his breath warm in her ear.

Rachael closed her eyes, trying to block out her terror, and that was when she saw them across a room, bathed in sunlight; Sam and Nick standing together, smiling and waiting for her. As she moved towards them, the darkness at her back started to fall away. She felt lighter again, more fluid, and a warm peacefulness enveloped her. Sam's laughter was dancing though her and Nick was stretching out his arms. He was taking her hands, spinning her round.

"You and me," he was saying, as she opened her eyes and the sunny room and the boys dissolved into the horror of Roger's hood and the night. "Just the two of us." His glittering eyes bore into her. "For ever and ever, Amen."

"Let me go!" she cried, jerking her hands free. She wanted to run, but he caught hold of her again easily, grabbing her by the shoulder and using the weight of his body to pin her against the barrier. "Get off me!" she yelled, hitting out at him, until his gloved fingers closed around her throat. She tried to knee him in the crotch, but his legs were smothering hers and she couldn't. He was forcing his thumbs closer and closer together against her windpipe, choking her, as she gasped for breath and couldn't find any. "For ever and ever, my Rachael," he said again. Frantically, she tore at his wrists, ripping at his skin with her nails until, with a yelp of pain, he pulled back his head and smashed his forehead against the bridge of her nose.

"HEY!" A man's roar ballooned into the silence above them. "STOP THAT! STOP THAT NOW! I'M COMING D..."

Even though she'd gone limp, Roger pressed harder, shaking her, trying to get it over with quickly. He heard a lock turning and a door open. "GET OFF HER!" The man was coming at him, something in his hand. Roger jumped away and ran for the staircase. He took the steps two at a time, racing into the darkness at the top. The man didn't give chase, but knelt by the body, turning Rachael on to her side and gently easing her head up, away from her chest. And, as he felt for a pulse, he pulled a mobile from his dressing-gown pocket.

Chapter 26
The murder scene

The phone was ringing. Lou opened an eye. The room was black. He squinted at the green blur to his right. The numbers swam into focus: 2.07am. He stretched for the receiver, pushing himself up in the bed.

"Yes?"

"Lou, I'm outside the Clarence building, Royal William Yard." It was Fran. "We've got an attempted murder. The victim is Rachael Drew."

"The Drews!" He swung his legs out and stood up.

"I thought you'd want to know."

"How is she?"

"She was still unconscious when the ambulance left. Looks like she'd been hit in the face and strangled, but there was a faint pulse. They were giving her oxygen."

Swapping the receiver between hands, he shrugged on his shirt and grabbed a pair of trousers from the chair.

"What about her assailant?"

"Male, wearing a hoodie, dark clothes. Ran off when challenged, up the staircase to Devil's Point."

"You've got a witness?"

"Local resident. Saw what was happening from his flat and ran down."

"Okay, I'm on my way."

Even with clear roads and controlled disregard for the speed limits and traffic lights, Lou took thirteen minutes to cover the seven miles. His journey started among the dark, snaking lanes out of Wembury and ended crossing the LED lamp-lit streets of the City. On the way, he thought of Oliver

Drew and his association with Ron Jellop. Crooked businessman maybe; but wife murderer? He didn't think so. Oliver
Drew wasn't the kind of man to strangle his wife in public
and then disappear. No, he would pay for someone else to
do it and have a rock-solid alibi for himself — one of his wine
tastings, with fifty of Plymouth's finest bearing witness.

Flashing past the Marine Barracks in Stonehouse, he came
to the small, cobbled roundabout in front of Royal William
Yard, the same roundabout that gave on to the driveway of
Jellop's house.

He accelerated through the Yard's grand archway
entrance. Massive shadowy buildings of limestone and
granite on either side funnelled him past Slaughterhouse
and Mills Bakery, opening up for the Marina on his right,
then closing him in again between Cooperage and Brewhouse, before delivering him up to a mass of flashing lights
and vehicles at the back of Clarence.

He pulled into a resident's parking space, angling in
towards the apartment block. Walking round the end of it
towards the river, he noted three squad cars, a couple
unmarked, probably SOCOs, a fire engine and a second
ambulance. "Too many people," he was thinking, glad Fran
was there already to protect the site's integrity.

"Morning, Inspector," said a voice from behind a spotlight.

"That you, Kincaid?" Lou raised a hand to shield his eyes.

"Yes, sir." DC Jason Kincaid's tall, slim frame emerged
from the shadows of the steel staircase.

Lou nodded and walked on, bending under the crime
scene tape. Ahead of him, the quayside lamps and police
spotlights lit up the paved space between the building and
the glass-panelled safety fence. He saw his weekend disappearing into it. Don and his mother were coming to meet
Connie and he wouldn't be there. He couldn't do that to
them. But he already had Coaker to deal with — and now
there was a would-be killer on the loose.

A short figure detached itself from the group clustered near the river and started towards him. The zipped leather jacket, short dark hair and quick movements were reassuring. He paused, waiting for her briefing out of earshot.

"Sorry to spoil your sleep," she said, reaching him.

"E la vita!" he said, raising his palm with an upward tilt of his head, in a gesture imbibed from his grandfather. He'd think about Connie later. "SOCO here?"

"Yeah. Rain hasn't helped, but the witness says no-one else was around. So they may get lucky."

"Good witness?"

"Yes, clear and to the point." She got out her notebook and pointed her torch at it.

"Like you," Lou thought.

"Commander George Pelham. Ex-navy, retired. Around 11.45pm, he heard a scream. He was reading in bed and went to the window." She raised her arm, swinging the torch's beam on to the building. "That's his flat, top floor, this end."

"Still up," Lou grunted, seeing the glow behind curtains.

"He saw a woman and a man arguing and fighting by the barrier," Fran went on. "He called out to the man to stop and then rushed down. As soon as the assailant saw him approaching, he ran off up the steps. Commander Pelham didn't pursue him, but stayed with Mrs Drew and called 999."

Lou looked up the flood of changing lights to where the stairs turned back on themselves in a second flight up to the black cut through at the top. The attacker would be long gone by now.

"Any update on Rachael Drew's condition yet?"

Fran shook her head.

"Have we anyone at the hospital?"

"Annie Brennan went with her. She'll let us know the moment Mrs Drew comes round, if she does."

"Let's hope she does." Lou stamped his feet and rubbed his hands together. "Meanwhile, I want twenty-four hour surveillance outside her room."

"Think he'll try again?" Fran sounded doubtful.

"We don't know why she was attacked, so let's not take any chances."

She nodded. "Okay, leave it with me."

They glanced round at the two figures in white paper suits working the patch where the body had fallen.

"Have you contacted Oliver Drew yet?"

"No, he's not answering any of the numbers we've got for him. Patrol car went to the house, but couldn't get a response. Rachael Drew's car was there but not his."

"We better put out an alert."

"Already done." She grinned. It was infectious, and he smiled.

"I could've stayed in bed, couldn't I?"

They stood side by side looking towards the river, both quiet, both thoughtful. Eventually Lou said: "She wouldn't have been out here on her own late at night, would she?"

"No. He must have been with her, whoever he is."

"It's cold. Let's walk a bit." He pointed along the wharf towards Brewhouse.

"Someone she knows and knows well." Fran continued, falling into step beside him. "Like her husband. Remember I told you things seemed pretty tense between them that day I called round."

"Or, it could be a lover?" he said, playing the devil's advocate. "A lovers' quarrel, maybe?"

"Hmm?" She wasn't convinced. "Then, where's Oliver Drew? I don't trust him. Why's he not..." She stopped to answer her phone. "Hello? Yes, speaking...Where?...You're sure?...Okay, thanks." She slipped it back in her pocket.

They'd come to a halt, while she was listening.

"You're going to love this," she said. "Oliver Drew's car's been spotted." She paused.

"And?"

"It's parked two minutes from here. It's in the driveway of Firestone Hall."

"Jellop's house? That doesn't make sense. If the Drews are staying there, why haven't the Jellops reported her missing by now?" Lou strode away and Fran had to run to catch up.

* * * * *

They heard bolts being drawn back, a mortice turned and the latch lifting. The door opened and a crumple-faced Jellop, in a heavy woollen dressing-gown and leather mules, stood facing them, a stout shillelagh in his fist.

"We're sorry to disturb you at this hour, Mr Jellop," Lou began, but Jellop interrupted him.

"What the bloody hell are you doing here? You know what time it is?"

"May we come in? It's a private matter."

"No, you may not! You've been told to leave me alone. Maynard'll have you back on traffic for this." He went to close the door but Fran had her foot in the way.

"Someone attempted to murder Rachael Drew earlier tonight outside the Clarence building. If..."

"Impossible!" Jellop exclaimed, opening the door wide again. "Where's Oliver?"

"We thought he was with you." Lou pointed to the Rolls. When he looked back, he saw the belligerence in Jellop's expression had given way to bemusement. He was holding the door frame as if for support, deep lines corrugating his forehead.

"No, he went with Rachael. We had dinner together and afterwards they went for a stroll to get some air, and we came home. I don't understand. What's happened? How is she? Where is she?"

Jellop's shock at the news was clear.

"Where did you have dinner, sir?" Fran asked. Her notebook was out and she was already writing in it.

"The Canteen. You know, Hugh's place, River Cottage."

"And, at what time did Mr and Mrs Drew leave you?"

"I don't know. Half-past eleven maybe. Something like that. We were the last out. We walked back here and went to bed. They were going to collect their car and drive home, when they were ready." He shivered and took a step back. "You better come in. I'm getting cold."

The house was warm and they followed him through to a spacious farmhouse kitchen with a scrubbed butcher's table in the middle and copper pans hanging from rails above it. He indicated to the chairs. "Cup of tea?" He moved to the kettle without waiting for an answer and filled it at the sink. When he looked round at them, they both nodded.

"When you left them," Lou began, "what mood were they in? How did they seem to you?"

"Normal. Like they usually are." He put teabags in mugs as he spoke. "Oliver was on good form. Full of bright ideas about the round house he wants to build. Thinks he's found the right site for it. Picking my brains about..."

"And Mrs Drew?" Fran interjected.

"Rachael?" He seemed puzzled by the effort to recall her part in the evening's proceedings. "Well, she was quiet, I suppose." The kettle steamed and clicked. He glanced round at them. "But that's not unusual. Still waters, you know." He put a jug of milk on the table with their mugs. "Help yourselves." He sat down. "Poor Rachael. Where is she? You didn't say."

"What's happened to Rachael?" Polly Jellop entered the room and they all turned at the sound of her voice. She was dressed, her dark hair caught up in a loose coil above a roll-neck sweater and jeans. She refused the seat her husband offered her and remained standing, her face pale and strained, while Lou and Fran were introduced. Lou apologised for disturbing them and explained the reason for their visit.

"Is she safe? Can we see her?" The concern in her voice was plain. Lou had decided not to answer Jellop's questions about Rachael until he was more certain about what had happened, but Polly Jellop's eyes were waiting for an answer, not leaving his for an instant.

"She's in hospital, Mrs Jellop. Derriford. She suffered a brutal attack and her condition is critical. I'm afraid she can't be seen by anyone for now."

Polly looked away to her husband, all colour drained from her face. "Where's Oliver?" He shrugged his shoulders, and then stiffened as a new thought struck him. "Maybe he was attacked too? Maybe he was the target? That's more probable, isn't it, Inspector?" He turned to Lou, his face resuming its customary animation and self-assurance. "Who'd want to attack Rachael? No, Oliver's a much more obvious target. Rachael just had to be got rid of, that's all...you know, as a witness."

"Why do you say 'more obvious', Mr Jellop?" Fran asked.

Jellop hesitated. "He's the man; a mugger would go for him first." He looked uncomfortable. "Wouldn't he?"

"Then where is he?" Polly said, before Fran could speak again. "Muggers don't try to kill people, Ron." She looked at Fran. "Much more likely he has enemies we know nothing about." She paused and, frowning, she added: "Anyway, how do we know Oliver didn't attack Rachael?"

"Polly! For goodness' sake! What are you thinking of?" In contrast to his wife's pallor, Jellop's face flushed crimson as he protested.

"What was Mr Drew wearing?" Fran asked. "It was cold and wet outside."

"An overcoat," Polly said. "Charcoal, with a velvet collar. You know, more London than Plymouth."

Fran glanced at Lou; no hoodie then.

"Mrs Jellop," Lou started, watching her carefully. "Do you have any reason to believe Oliver Drew may have attacked his wife?"

In the silence that followed, as the other three waited for her reply, Polly sat down on the chair her husband had offered her earlier. Head bowed, she contemplated her hands folded in her lap.

"Rachael spoke to me in confidence a little while ago." She looked up at Lou. "She was planning to ask her husband for a divorce, Inspector."

Fran and Lou exchanged glances. Most murders were committed by a relative or friend of the victim, and by a spouse or partner most commonly of all.

"You never said, Poll." Jellop was bewildered. "We were all having dinner together just a few hours ago. I don't understand..." He trailed off.

"I see," Lou said. "And do you know whether she had done so and, if so, what Mr Drew's reaction had been?"

"I don't."

"Mrs Jellop," Fran said, remembering Lou's earlier suggestion of a lover's quarrel; "do you know if Mrs Drew was involved with someone-else? Could that have been the reason for her wanting a divorce?"

Polly looked at her for a long time and then slowly shook her head. "I don't," she said.

* * * * *

Later, after the detectives had left, and they were lying in bed again, neither of them sleeping, Polly's thoughts stayed with the female detective's question. It wasn't for her to gossip. If there was any justice in the world, Rachael would recover and she could decide what she wished the police to know about her private life. She had only mentioned Rachael's wish for a divorce in the heat of the moment. The fact that Oliver was missing and that they had been together when she was attacked had conjured a picture in her mind of a row between them, ending in Oliver trying to kill her. She'd never trusted him, not in spite of his charm but because of it. There was something devious about his flattery, his attention. If he had harmed Rachael, she wanted him found and held to account.

But that Detective Sergeant, Fran something, had asked about a hoodie. The police must have had a description from a witness. If Oliver hadn't tried to strangle Rachael, where was he, and who had attacked her?

Her thoughts returned to Roger and to her unsettling conversation with Rachael, after they left the Ladies. "He didn't take it well." That's what she'd said. It was almost six o'clock by the time she drifted into a dream-disturbed sleep.

Chapter 27

Roger goes home

Roger stood in his living room in the dark, waiting and listening. Imperceptibly, his breathing slowed and deepened. No-one was coming. No-one had followed him. Was Rachael dead? He raised his hands palms up, looking at fingers he couldn't see. Oliver was. The force of the blow still pulsed in his bicep. He pulled off his gloves, dropping them on the floor, then his hoodie. A moment later, he was running up the stairs naked and into the bathroom. He showered with the lights off, clenching against the sting of the scalding jet, until the chill left him and his body relaxed into the heat of the water.

Afterwards, his eyes accustomed to the dark, he dressed for college and stuffed the discarded clothes from the living room into a bin liner. No lights, no fodder for nosey neighbours. Pulling on a duffle coat, he slipped out of the back door and through the garden gate into the service lane behind. The wind funnelling down it was icy. He pulled up the hood and walked swiftly to his car, which he'd left two streets away so as not to disturb his neighbours. Pushing the bag into the passenger seat, he got in, closed the door softly and pulled away, with the lights off for the first fifty yards.

He kept to side streets until, around the back of Union Street, he saw a line of wheelie bins up an alley. No-one about, no CCTV. Killing the lights again and leaving the motor running, he took the bag. The first bin was jammed full and stank of fish. He was holding his breath, wanting to be gone. Lifting the second lid, there was space. He grabbed the top bag and stuffed his underneath, pushing down hard so the lid closed. He spun away to the car.

Once home, he eased the back-door shut and slid the bolts. Without taking his coat off, he went through to the living room, kicked off his shoes and lay down on the sofa. Almost at once, he got up again and fumbled for the wool blanket over the back of the armchair. Shaking it free of its folds and drawing it over him, he stretched out on his side, pushing a cushion into shape under his cheek. As his eyes closed, Oliver's seal head bobbed up out of the river. He tugged the cover closer to him and fought against the vision, imagining instead that he was holding Rachael, kissing her eyelids and burying his face in the almond-scented softness of her hair.

The room was full of grey, early-morning light when he woke. It bathed the shapes in shadows, leaving their colours unrevealed. He waited for his eyes to adjust and focus. He studied the clock on the mantelpiece. Eight-twenty, he thought. The night came back to him and with it a prowling fear. He strained for sounds, as if his pursuers might be inside the house. If he hadn't thrown the baseball bat in the river, he could have dealt with that man running at him. He could have made sure of Rachael.

He shoved the blanket aside and stood up, checking the clock. It was almost twenty-five past. He had time; his first class was at ten. His mouth was dry and his tongue felt swollen. He drank with cupped hands from the kitchen tap, then filled the kettle and sat down, his elbows on the table, his head resting in his hands. What if she wasn't dead? What if she was alive? She might tell the police everything, identify him. He didn't care about that. If she was alive, she'd never be his.

The kettle's roaring flooded his thoughts. He waited for the click but it didn't come. Clouds of steam were spraying out of it. The legs of his chair grated against the slate tiles as he leapt up. The lid wasn't properly shut and he banged it down, switching the plug off at the same time. She might be in hospital if she'd survived. He scooped coffee into the cafetiere and half filled it, turning back to look for his phone. He found it on the coffee table in the other room and clicked on Rachael's home number, then killed it before it had time to ring.

"Stupid! Stupid! Stupid!" he muttered, on his way upstairs to the bathroom. "Playing straight into the hands of the police."

"Do nothing!" he told his reflection, as he shaved and cleaned his teeth. "Be patient. Act normally. Get the Herald, see what the coverage is. Call the hospital from the college pay phone, perhaps." If she was there, maybe he could get to her.

"Ah, the working man!" his unemployed neighbour said, eying Roger's briefcase as he left the house.

"Someone has to keep you in cycle parts." Roger flashed him a smile.

"Cold though, ain't it?" the neighbour said, scratching his bald patch with the end of a spanner he was holding. "Brass monkey weather."

"See you later, Alan." Roger started up the pavement, stepping carefully over the wheel lying on its side.

"Where's your car then?"

"Had to leave it round the corner," Roger called over his shoulder. "Too parked-up here."

Chapter 28

Lou smells a rat

After Lou and Fran left the Jellops' house, they drove in his car as far as the Holiday Inn on Armada Way.

"Nice one," Fran said, as he parked. "A quiet room at the back'll do me."

"Breakfast," he said.

"At this time?"

He checked his watch. "We're already seven minutes late. They open at six-thirty."

She followed him in and up to the restaurant. Settling down at Jellop's corner table, he said: "Long night, Fran. This is on me. A bit of warmth and comfort, while we see where the pieces fit."

A waitress took their orders for coffee; and Fran followed her across to the self-service buffet to fetch juice and muesli for herself and a cooked breakfast for Lou.

While she was gone, Lou took in the room. It was busier than he'd expected. There were several business types in suits and ties; two older ones on their own and three younger ones together, animated, buoying each other up for the day ahead. On the far side was a family group: parents and a couple of grandparents, three children. The mother was bottle-feeding a baby, while the grandfather was trying to console a little girl in tears. But it was the eldest of the three children, a boy, who held Lou's attention. He was explaining a picture he'd just drawn to his father, who was leaning into him, an arm round his shoulders. They were laughing, sharing a joke, the father pointing at something and the boy protesting. Lou felt a familiar lurch into loss: a sadness in his gut like nausea, followed by rising anger, as he imagined finding and confronting Louis Lanui.

He looked away to a young woman sitting on her own in a red sheath dress, wearing a necklace and pendant earrings. She looked dressed for dinner rather than breakfast. Had to book in for the night unexpectedly, he wondered, but it was an idle thought and he let it go. Deeper down, he was picturing Connie and a son of their own. His gaze drifted back to the family. He wouldn't be an absent father. Someone else would have to take care of the Coakers and Jellops of this world.

"Your coffee, sir." The waitress was back, closely followed by Fran. They pirouetted around each other setting things down.

"Enjoy," the waitress said, turning away.

"Won't," Lou muttered, irritated by the platitude.

"What's up?" Fran asked.

"You ever think about quitting, doing something nine to five, weekends off?"

"Not for long," she said, stirring blueberries and grapes deeper into her muesli. "Low boredom threshold. You know me."

"Family life. Doing things together. Sharing things. Looking out for each other."

"Didn't know you were a violinist."

"I'm serious."

"Lot of misery behind closed family doors. You know that."

He did know that, but he felt irritated again by her brusqueness.

"You were unlucky," he said.

"Me and thousands like me."

They ate in silence for a while. The eggs were tasteless, the tomatoes worse and the coffee insipid. At least the bacon was lean and moist. Sometimes he felt only Italians knew how to cook properly. Maybe the Chinese too; he liked Connie's food. Her coffee wasn't up to much, but then tea was their thing.

"Fed up with bodies?" Fran said finally, draining her juice.

"Haven't got any, have we?" He pushed his plate away, angry at his own bad temper.

"Like some time on your own? I can head back." When he looked at her, she didn't look away. She met his gaze and held it. She hadn't changed; the candour in her regard was the same as the first time he'd seen her — or him, as she was then.

"Sorry, Fran." He paused, wondering how much to say, and glanced across at the family's table. They'd gone, leaving a rubbled skyline of crockery and scrunched-up napkins behind them. "I haven't had the board out since last month. I get bottled-up."

She nodded. "If I don't train, I feel like a fish on a slab, beating my tail and getting nowhere."

"Okay, so where are we?" He was about to ask her to summarise the two cases, which seemed to be meshing unexpectedly, when a thought hovering out of sight in the wings came out centre stage. "He's in the river!"

Fran caught the changed energy in his voice. "Drew, you mean?"

"Yes. Or out in the Sound by now. The tide was going out, wasn't it?"

"Not sure." She googled tide times for Plymouth on her phone. "Low water was three twenty-five this morning."

"The Drews are last seen walking away from Brewhouse along the wharf in front of Clarence. A short while later, Commander Pelham is looking out of his window and sees a hooded figure trying to strangle Rachael Drew. No sign of Oliver. So, where's he gone?"

"He could have planned the hit, picked an argument and walked off, leaving her alone."

"Putting himself at the scene of the crime? He's not stupid."

"Means a full search," Fran said. "Budget holes all round."

Lou was already gesturing to the waitress, scribbling on his palm with his finger.

"Macklin won't be in yet. You go back and get things rolling. All the agencies: Maritime and Coastguard, RNLI, MoD Police."

Fran stood up. "Poor bugger. Those currents, he wouldn't stand a chance."

"I'm going to the hospital. I'll see you and the team at ten. Depending on what more's come up, we'll decide about Coaker then."

The waitress laid the bill down beside him, as Fran hurried out. "Everything all right for you?"

* * * * *

Once Lou had identified himself at the main reception, PC Annie Brennan was located and soon appeared in the foyer. The hospital had the air of a deserted shopping mall. The shops were closed, a couple of orderlies went past, one pushing an empty trolley, and a handful of bleary relatives stood around waiting. Strip lights blared and the heels of Annie Brennan's court shoes echoed as she led him to the ICU wards on Level 4.

Brennan was a competent, middle-aged officer whom Lou respected. She gave him a quick update as they walked. "There are two intensive care wards. Mrs Drew's in Pencarrow, which deals with head injuries mainly. She's still unconscious and on a ventilator to help her breathing. I spoke briefly to one of the doctors, who was non-committal. She said Mrs Drew's condition remains critical. Obviously, she's not allowed visitors at this point, so I haven't actually seen her. It's a fourteen-bed ward and thirteen are occupied right now, but it changes all the time."

Lou was surprised to find the waiting room crowded, with all the chairs taken, and people walking up and down and others standing round a drinks machine. Taut faces turned to them as they entered, hoping for nurses or doctors with information.

"We can go in here," Brennan said, opening the door to a small interview room. "They've said we can use this for now."

He went in and she closed the door behind him. They sat across from each other at a small table. "How easy is it to enter the ward?" Lou asked. "Can you just walk in, if you want to."

"No. You have to use the intercom first or ask a member of staff."

"Good." He got up, opened the door and sat down again. He had a full view of the waiting room, but not of the ward entrance. "It's possible that whoever attacked Mrs Drew might try again, if he knows she's not dead." He checked his watch. "It's almost ten-to-eight. Who's meant to be relieving you?"

"Rob Turner. But there's been some trouble in Union Street and they're short-staffed with this flu bug going round. So I said I'd stay till midday. I think it'll still be Rob then."

"Okay. But listen, Annie, and pass this on to Rob too. I want you to be extra vigilant about who goes into Pencarrow. Keep the entrance monitored at all times."

"Visiting times will be hardest," she said. "We'll need to check everyone going in." She moved to the doorway and looked towards the ward entrance. "Difficult when your loved one may be dying," she added softly, almost to herself.

Chapter 29
Lou is summoned by Supt Maynard

Lou was leaving the hospital car park when his phone rang. It was Connie. "One moment," he said. "I'm driving, I'll pull in." A bus was moving out into the traffic and he turned in behind it. "Hi. What's up?"

"This not a good time, Lou?"

"There's a lot going on, Connie."

"I never know when is the right time to speak to you."

Lou felt cornered and irritated. He hadn't time to explain everything, but that wasn't her fault. "I'm sorry. Can we eat together this evening? We can talk then."

"I like that. What time you come?"

"I'll be there for seven, earlier if I can."

"See you then," she said. "Ngóh oi néih, Lou."

"Yeah," he said, the lightness and song in her voice breaking the night's hold on him. "I love you, too."

"See, that not so hard, is it?" she laughed. "You feel better now."

Her voice stayed with him after she rung off. He did feel better and he drove back to the station slowly.

* * * * *

"MCA is co-ordinating the search," Fran said when Lou stopped by her desk on the way to his room. She was typing on her computer and looked up briefly, before continuing while she spoke. "They've got a chopper up. Inshore Rescue dinghies are combing the Sound and the MoD launch is checking the estuary. The Navy's keeping a look out as well. If Oliver Drew's out there, we should find him."

Lou felt relieved. The coastguard guys were professional and thorough, the RNLI too. Fran was right; if Drew had been dumped in the river, they'd find him. Meanwhile, he could concentrate his energies elsewhere.

"And the Super wants to see you," Fran added, sliding into her impression of Maynard's well-modulated tones; "As soon as you please, Detective Inspector."

"I'm on my way."

Andrew Maynard's door was open. Lou gave a peremptory knock and walked straight in. There was no-one there and he was just turning to leave when the burly senior officer walked in.

"Ah, Lou. Just the man." He closed the door and gestured to the chair across the desk from his own. His face was pink from his morning shave and he seemed in good humour. "Looks like you've got the Lapinski disappearance resolved. Nasty business. Men like Coaker, well..."He raised his hand in the air and let it fall again. "Can I redeploy two of your team straight away? Tim Davey's shorthanded, several of his crew off sick."

"I can't spare anyone yet," Lou said. "There's a lot of hard evidence to nail down before we can take Coaker to the CPS and there's..." He hesitated. "There's a prostitution ring involved. Nina Lapinski was part of it and Coaker seems to be the enforcer. The young women involved are all overseas students from Eastern Europe registered at the University here." He paused again, rehearsing his words carefully. "In addition, we have documented bank evidence that Coaker is in the pay of a company, Babbage Holdings, registered in the Cayman Islands. Its principal shareholder is Polly Jellop."

Maynard stared hard at him, his smile gone, and Lou decided to press on. "Also, as you may have heard, there was an incident in the night." Maynard nodded. "Rachael and Oliver Drew had been dining with the Jellops in Royal William Yard. Oliver Drew and Ron Jellop are business associates. They have a joint venture in a chateau with a vineyard in Bergerac in France."

"I know where Bergerac is," growled Maynard.

Lou knew the irritation was about Jellop's involvement and wondered again about their relationship.

"After the meal, the Jellops returned home, while the Drews went for a walk by the water to get some air. We don't know what happened exactly. However, a witness, Commander Pelham, who has an apartment in the Clarence building, saw a man in a hoodie trying to strangle Rachael Drew. After shouting out, he ran down and the assailant fled. There was no sign of Oliver Drew and we've not been able to contact him."

"Was Drew wearing a hoodie?"

"No. An overcoat, according to Mrs Jellop."

"What about his car?"

"It was discovered in the Jellops' driveway, where Oliver Drew had left it earlier on."

"He's in the drink then, isn't he?" Maynard stood up, bending forward with his fists on the desk top supporting him. "Have you notified the MCA?"

"A full search of the Sound and Hamoaze is underway."

"Right. Well, let me know the moment they find him. And what about Mrs Drew? How is she? And have we got an officer guarding her?"

Lou answered both questions, while acknowledging to himself that, with the exception of his remark about Bergerac, Maynard's attention was fully focused.

"What about the CCTV footage from Clarence?"

Lou shook his head. How had he forgotten to check that, and Fran too? It was routine.

"For heaven's sake, man! Don't tell me you haven't done that yet!"

"DS Bannerman may already have it in hand, sir. I'll double-check." What had he been thinking of, going to the

Holiday Inn for breakfast at a time like this. If they had gone straight back to the station, he wouldn't have seen the father with his son and started thinking about his own or about what the future with Connie might bring.

Maynard was scrutinising him. "Not like you, Lou. Anything you need to tell me about?"

Lou attacked as a defence; it was safer not to reveal chinks in one's armour. "I've been thinking about the Coaker-Jellop connection and the prostitution ring. I'm thinking we might let Eddie Coaker go today and see where he leads us."

"If he is the murderer of Nina Lapinski and we release him, we may be putting other members of the public at risk." Maynard sat down again, linking his fingers across his chest.

Lou thought of Raluca. She might well be in danger if Coaker found out she'd contacted the police.

"Or he may do a runner," Maynard added. "In which case the media will have a field day at our expense."

"We'll set strict bail conditions. We'll take his passport and he'll have to report here daily. Also, we'll keep him under twenty-four-hour surveillance." Lou knew he would have to spell out the positives, if Maynard were not to play safe and veto his plan. "If Coaker is the lynchpin of the prostitution ring, as we believe, there will have been a missing link between clients and the girls while he's been in custody. Once he's free of us, he'll be active in taking control again. Martin Webb and Carol Barker will trace his every move. We'll soon have all the evidence we need to charge him." Maynard was nodding. "And Councillor Ron Jellop too," Lou added.

Maynard's hands moved to the arms of his chair. "Before you take any action against Mr Jellop, you bring whatever evidence you have to me first. Is that understood, Detective Inspector?"

"Yes, sir," said Lou. "It is."

As he rose to leave, Maynard said: "The man in the hoodie, any thoughts on who he might be?"

"Oliver Drew is the sort of man who could have made enemies along the way. If we find his body in the water, he may well have been the target and Mrs Drew an unfortunate witness, who had to be silenced. But..." Lou paused.

"But what?"

"Strangling. No professional would use that method. It's an emotional, personal way of killing someone. It's not clinical."

Maynard walked round the desk. "What are you suggesting?" There was an irritation in his voice. "You think Mrs Drew was the real target? You think there may be a third party, who wanted both Drews dead? A jilted lover, maybe?"

"Mrs Jellop told us that Rachael Drew had asked her husband for a divorce. It's possible she was involved with someone else. If and when she regains consciousness, we'll be able to ask her."

Lou was finding the room oppressive. The taller man was standing too close to him and the cloying scent of his aftershave was stealing his air. "Out there," he said, stepping aside to point to the window and to give himself some space, "we will either find Oliver Drew alive and with a lot of explaining to do, or we'll find a suspect who Commander Pelham and CCTV footage from Royal William Yard can put at the scene of the crime."

"A statement of the blindingly bloody obvious!" Maynard glowered at him. "Have you thought to ask Mrs Jellop if she knows who this possible 'other person' might be?"

"She says she doesn't."

"You don't believe her?"

"She may be protecting her friend. Once she's slept on it, perhaps she'll feel differently."

"Right," said Maynard, moving back to his desk. "Find this man in the hood before he tries again, and don't let Coaker out of your sight. I want no more murders, attempted or otherwise."

"A statement of the blindingly bloody obvious," Lou muttered as he headed for the incident room.

Chapter 30
Double trouble

Lou was on his way to the incident room when Fran came leaping up the stairs, two at a time. "Annie Brennan just called," she said, grabbing hold of the rail and stopping just below him. "Rachael Drew's regained consciousness. They think she's going to be all right, but they're not letting anyone talk to her for twenty-four hours, including us."

"Have you told the others?"

"Not yet." She turned and walked down beside him.

Just short of the incident room, Lou stopped. "We're going to let Coaker go, but I want a close tail on him. We mustn't lose him. Who would you pick?"

"Jason," she said.

Lou was surprised. He knew about the needle between the two of them, since Jason's jibe about her identity change. It must have shown in his face.

"He's a throwback, I know, but he's a good shadow. Remember the Johnson case? People just don't seem to see him. Besides, he's got no ties; he can afford to pull some overtime."

Lou smiled. "Okay. I told Maynard that Martin and Carol would pick it up between them, but maybe it's better to have them free. Anyway, let's go and see what we've got."

The atmosphere was expectant when they walked in. The talking stopped and alert eyes followed him as he crossed to Macklin Thomas's table. He turned to face them.

"Glad you're all here. We've got two suspected murders and no bodies, Nina Lapinski and Oliver Drew, as well as the attempted murder of Rachael Drew. They're separate cases, but they may be connected. So we all need bringing up to speed on where we've got to." Lou looked to his left. "Macklin, will you kick off?"

DS Thomas pushed his chair back and stood up. He held a page of notes in his hand but hardly referred to them. His voice was clear and strong, with the familiar melodious lilt to it.

"Let's start with Nina Lapinski and Eddie Coaker. We've had word from forensics that the Morning Star's clean. Nothing damming there at all."

"Have they sent us their report yet?" Lou asked. He was disappointed. He'd been hoping for traces of blood that would prove to be Nina's.

"No, not yet," Macklin said.

"What about Coaker's computer? Has that thrown up any hard evidence?"

"We've good news there, at least," Macklin said. "Haven't we, Debbie?"

"We certainly have," Debbie said, the satisfaction plain in her voice, and a warm smile transformed the habitual seriousness of her expression. From Lou's point of view, quite apart from her magic with computers, her presence infused any meeting with a sense of calm confidence. He felt his own spirits steadied by her.

"Go on, Debbie," Macklin said; "Tell us what you've found."

"The bank account details are as you already know them, with large annual payments from a Jellop-controlled company registered in the Cayman Islands." She included the whole team as she spoke, turning her head to make eye contact with each of them. "Just as interesting are some encrypted files I found, which contain lists of initials and contact numbers for specific years. Not calendar years, however, but academic years."

"NL on this year's list?" Fran asked, thinking of Nina Lapinski.

"It is." Debbie looked at her. "And so is RN." She shifted her gaze to Lou. "Raluca Nicolescu, we think. Martin has spoken to her, but he'll tell you about that in a moment. For this year, there are ten sets of initials. Carol and I have cross-checked these with the list of new postgraduate students at the University and we've come up with a further eight eastern European young women with corresponding initials."

"Any duplicated initials?" Lou said. "Of students not from those countries, I mean."

"Only one set," Debbie said. "And they matched a young man from Taunton."

Lou nodded. "Fine. Anything else?"

"Yes. In another file, I found dates and numbers for flights from corresponding airports – Bucharest, Warsaw, Moscow and so on – all scheduled for arrival at Heathrow during the second week of September. And these were cross-referenced to matching train times from Paddington to Plymouth. That's it, Lou."

Lou's eyes gleamed. "Something concrete at last! Good work, Debbie. Thank you." He looked round at the others. "So we know these are the young women who are involved in a prostitution scam involving City Councillor Ron Jellop, with Eddie Coaker acting as their pimp. But what isn't clear yet is what the tie-up is with the University and how Jellop and Coaker get these young women to go on the game for them."

"I think Martin can help you there," Macklin said. "Martin."

All eyes turned to the tall figure in heavy brogues and a tweed jacket leaning against Debbie's computer table. As Martin Webb straightened up and took a notebook from his inside pocket, Lou dropped his head and closed his eyes.

When he opened them again, he caught a ghost of a smile on Fran's face beside him. Lou respected the officer's dedication and integrity, but found him stolid. He wished he would lighten up a bit. On the other hand, he was reliable, and potential witnesses seemed to trust him; jurors too.

"Last Friday, ninth January, I intercepted Ms Raluca Nicolescu in the foyer of the University's Business School."

"Martin?" Lou said.

"Yes, chief?" He looked up.

"Could you just recap the significant points for me? I don't need the full details, for the time being."

Martin shifted uneasily, moving his weight from one foot to the other and back again. He looked down at his notes, then back at Lou.

"Right," he said, marking his place in the notebook with a finger and holding it beside him. "I found Ms Nicolescu to be a forthcoming witness, very willing to talk to me, once I had persuaded her that we would protect her."

"What did she tell you?" Lou prompted him.

"She believes Mr Jellop and Mr Coaker arranged the disappearance of Ms Lapinski and she is afraid they have killed her. When she asked them directly, Mr Jellop told her Ms Lapinski had returned home and he was not at liberty to divulge her contact details."

"Isn't she a friend of Nina's?" Fran said. "How come she doesn't know where her home is?"

"Ms Nicolescu says she and the others signed confidentiality agreements as part of their contracts not to reveal..."

"Contracts!" Lou took several steps towards him. "These young women have contracts?"

"According to Ms Nicolescu," Martin said, quickly looking in his notebook and turning pages, "contracts were arranged in their home countries in advance of their coming to the UK."

"And what is the nature of these contracts?" Lou was standing directly in front of him now. He wanted to grab the notebook and scan it for himself.

"Mr Jellop undertook to arrange for Ms Nicolescu to be accepted on to a Masters Business Administration Degree course at the University here and to provide suitable accommodation for the period of her stay, together with part-time work which would earn her not less than £12,200 tax-free, after course fees and related expenses were deducted."

"Did he indeed? And what was her end of the deal?"

"In return, Ms Nicolescu agreed to provide personal services for respectable gentlemen to be supplied by Mr Jellop's associate, Mr Coaker, at a rate of four engagements a day, five days a week, at times to fit in with her academic timetable."

"You can see the attraction," Carol Barker said. "Nine months self-sacrifice and they walk away with a quality UK degree and over £12,000 into the bargain. No wonder they don't complain!"

"In its way, it's a very clever scam," Macklin said. "Everyone gets what they want. Even the University."

"Be interesting to know how Jellop gets the Uni to play ball." Fran looked at Lou.

"Another contract, no doubt," he said, and then looked back at Martin. "Did Raluca show you her contract?"

"Better than that," Macklin interrupted, opening a folder and holding up an A4 document. "She gave him a copy."

Lou was thinking past Coaker now to Jellop. "Whose signature's on the contract?"

"It's a company stamp for West Country Educational Services Ltd."

"Some education!" Fran said.

Lou didn't smile. "What about the 'respectable gentlemen'? Have we any names?"

"Indeed we have," Macklin said, producing another sheet of paper and handing it to Lou. "Jason and Carol had Skardon House under surveillance. You'll recognise the names, and we have time-dated photographs as well."

Lou scanned the names: businessmen, councillors, solicitors, even court officials and a head teacher. He looked up. "Nice work, Carol...Jason. You too, Martin. We can go with this." He looked around. "Well done all of you. But there's more to do. Jason, we're releasing Coaker later this morning, and I want you to be his shadow. Don't lose him, whatever happens. He has a bail condition to report back here first thing Monday morning. That gives him almost two days to hang himself."

A slow smiled creased Jason's long face. "I'll stay with him."

"Check in with DS Thomas every time you change location. Meanwhile, Carol, go to Royal William Yard and get whatever CCTV footage you can find for Thursday night and Friday morning covering the quay outside River Cottage Canteen and the Clarence Building...say from 10pm to 2am."

"Will do."

"Go through it with Debbie and see if you can spot the man in the hoodie and any clues that might help us find him...and Oliver Drew come to that. You may already know we've launched a full-scale search of the Sound and estuary for his body, so proof he went into the river will be welcome."

He paused to look round the room to make sure he hadn't forgotten anything. His eyes came to rest on Martin. "Martin, I want you to stay close to Raluca. If Coaker finds out she's been talking to us, she could be in real danger." Okay, that's it for now."

The detectives started to move and talk. "Did you want to say something about Rachael Drew?" Fran asked Lou.

"One moment, everyone," he said, raising his voice. Faces turned and the murmuring and shuffling stopped. "I meant to say that we've had news that Rachael Drew has recovered consciousness. We can't talk to her until tomorrow, we've been told. However, PCs Annie Brennan and Bob Turner are keeping a twenty-four-hour watch over her, in the meantime. So let's nail her assailant as quickly as we can."

He raised a hand palm out to signal he was finished.

"I'm on my way," Carol said, heading for the door, and the meeting broke up.

"Is there anything-else, Macklin?" Lou asked.

"Two things: Commander Pelham came in and gave a statement, confirming what he'd told us already, nothing new."

Lou nodded. "The other?"

"Who's going to take over from Jason, and when?"

"I'll take the graveyard shift," Fran said.

Lou was relieved. Fran could take care of herself and, like Jason, she could fade into the background when she wanted to.

"Okay, but go home early and get some sleep."

He looked down at the table and picked up a couple of the folders. "I'll bring these back before I go." Macklin nodded. "And let me know when Eddie Coaker's ready for release. I'll be in my room."

"Be careful, Lou," Macklin said, his grey eyes steady and serious. "Men like him...Ach-y-fi!"

* * * * *

The concern behind Macklin's exclamation of disgust stayed with Lou on his way back to his office, until the Voodoo Child riff shattered it.

"Mum!" he said, closing the door.

"Ciao, caro. Sorry to disturb you. I expect you're busy."

"Just a bit! But that's okay. I was going to ring you. I wanted to check what time you'll be here."

"Ah, that's why I'm calling, Louis." There was a pause and he knew there was a problem. "Don's not well. Nothing serious, just his chest again. But we'll have to postpone for now."

The relief was instant, as if some pressure on his chest had lifted. "Actually, Mum, don't take this the wrong way, and please wish Don a speedy recovery from me, but it may be for the best. I'm in the middle of what looks like a double murder enquiry and I'm going to be up to my eyes in it. So..."

"Poor Connie!" his mother broke in. "Does she realise what she's letting herself in for?"

For a moment he considered telling her he was going to resign and all the rest of it, but he decided not to. He wanted her to meet Connie first, so she'd understand why.

"She'll be sorry you're not coming," he said, sliding around her question. "But you'll be down soon, won't you?"

"Spoza we will!" she said and the flood of affection he felt at his grandfather's nickname released it in him for her, too. He missed her playfulness and having her nearby. He wanted to see her.

"That'll be Fabio!" he replied.

Chapter 31
On the loose

Coaker pocketed his possessions, signed for them and left the police station without saying a word. The clouds were clearing from the west and weak January sunshine cast lengthening shadows across the pale lemon streets. Standing at his window, Lou watched him cross at the lights, turn left in front of the shopping mall and disappear down the steps to the underpass at the corner. A slim figure in a parka soon followed him down.

Lou moved back to his desk and opened the top folder.

* * * * *

A little over an hour later, Jason came to a halt in the shadows at the bottom of the road and watched Coaker enter a terraced house halfway up, closing the door behind him. The downstairs window beyond it flared into life, before dimming to dull orange, as curtains were pulled across it. Four-twenty and dark already. Jason walked up the unlit side of the road to the top and turned, taking a sideways step into the shadows of a tree.

Tugging off a glove, he took out his phone and used the direct line. "It's me, Sarge. He's been to Fish Quay, but he only lives round the corner and he's home now. I'm at the top of his street on the bend. I can see his front door and the mouth of the service lane behind the houses. It' a cul-de-sac. If he leaves back or front, I'll see him."

As he spoke, a couple emerged from a house several doors below Coaker's and turned down the slope, walking arm-in-arm. Near the bottom, they separated and got into a car. He watched the tail lights come on and then the indicator flashing, as it pulled out, turned towards town and disappeared.

The street was empty again. He pulled his glove back on, shoved his hands deep in his pockets and checked the entry to the service lane to his left, about fifty yards from where he was standing. All was quiet, apart from a drinks can rocking intermittently between cobbles, caught in the glare of a street lamp.

* * * * *

Meanwhile, a little earlier, on the other side of town, Roger set his last class of the day an essay question under exam conditions on one of their set texts, The Handmaid's Tale by Margaret Atwood.

"When I say 'turn over your paper', you will have fifty minutes to write your answer and I'll give you regular time checks as we go along. Meanwhile, remember three key points. First of all, read the question carefully at least twice. Make sure you understand what it's asking you. Secondly, and most importantly, answer the question!" He paused for effect and looked round at the anxious faces in rows in front of him. There were a few nervous smirks and titters. "And, last of all, allow yourself five minutes to make a rough plan, just like we've practised, *before* you start writing." He stressed the word and checked his watch. "Okay, turn over your papers now. You have until five to four."

Most did as he suggested; others started writing straight away; and a couple seemed to stare at the paper and freeze. He walked up and down the aisle between the desks a couple of times, checking no-one was cheating. As he passed the two 'freezers', he whispered, "Use panic breathing", to each of them. Back in his chair, he watched their chests rise with deep inhalation and then fall again more slowly with the protracted exhalation, as he had shown them.

As he kept an eye on them and the time, his thoughts slid away to the hospital. Finding out where Rachael was without giving himself away would be the problem. There would be a lot of people milling around at visiting time. Around half-past four would be perfect. He'd ask at Reception and say he was her brother, Geoff Drew. No, Munroe! *Her* family's name! He mustn't forget. That way he could find out where she was. After that, he'd have to trust to chance.

* * * * *

The hospital foyer was busy when he got there and he had to wait in line at the Information desk. "How can I help you?" asked a bright-eyed woman, when it was his turn. His hands started to sweat and he resisted the urge to rub them against his coat. "I'm looking for my sister, Rachael Drew." She tapped her computer. "Pencarrow Ward, Level 4," she said, handing him a leaflet and already looking past him to the person pushing in behind. "Where's Audiology, love?"

Roger took a step away and began studying the hospital layout in the leaflet, while listening carefully, a plan already forming. He waited patiently, head bowed, trying to remain as innocuous as possible. Some voices were difficult to hear, either too soft or too low for him to make out what was being said.

He checked his watch; he hadn't even been there ten minutes yet. It seemed much longer than that. He was aware of a security guard near the entrance looking at him; probably because of his knapsack. He'd have to move soon. He slid the leaflet into his inside pocket and took out a notebook and biro. He started writing in it thoughtfully, while occasionally flicking back several pages, as if to refer to something; until a woman's voice caught his attention and ended his charade.

"My grandfather's in one of the intensive care wards." Her intonation rose at the end, as if asking a question. "But I see there are two and I don't know which one he's in." From the corner of his eye, he saw a raincoat and a shoulder bag.

"What's his name and I'll have a look for you?"

"Jerry Hopkins...with a J...thanks."

There was a pause, and Roger took a step back towards the counter.

"Here we are. He's in Pencarrow Ward on Level 4." The receptionist handed her a leaflet, and she moved away before stopping to look at the diagram.

Roger passed her, walking deeper into the hospital. He followed the signs for Level 4 and queued for a lift. As the doors closed, he saw the young woman hurrying towards them; but she was too late.

As a group of people exited towards the ICU wards, Penrose and Pencarrow, he placed himself just behind a short woman in a cherry beret in the middle of a gaggle of other visitors. A police woman was standing by the entrance to Pencarrow Ward and, as she watched them, he lent forward to the woman in front of him. "Is there a drinks machine in the waiting room, do you know?" It was the first thing to come into his head. He just wanted the PC to think they were together.

She jumped and jerked round. "I don't know. Sorry." Her face was white and drawn and he was struck by the dark hollows of her eyes.

In the waiting room, he sat down next to her. She crossed her legs and turned away from him.

He sat wondering if he could use Jerry Hopkins' name to get past the police woman without being challenged; and, if so, what then? He had no doubt she was there to protect Rachael. He was tingling all over. His finger tips were prickling, as if alive with electricity. He placed them together, end to end, and a current fizzed through them, along his arms and into his chest. He closed his eyes. She was asleep, lying on her back, her hair splayed across the pillow. No more Oliver, he could lie with her forever. He lay down beside her, buried his face into the pillow next to her cheek, breathing in the scent from her neck. She opened her eyes and saw him there. She screamed. He was throttling her; he could see her terror. He moved his hand and dug his nails into his wrist. She was just through that wall.

The nail punctured his skin drawing blood. He grabbed a tissue from his jacket pocket and held it against the cut, his body calming and the room coming into focus again. He stood up and paced till he could see the police woman. She was still there. Jerry Hopkins' granddaughter was walking towards her. They spoke. The police woman disappeared into the ward, closing the door behind her. When she reappeared a few moments later, she nodded and held the door open. They younger woman went in and the door closed again.

Roger sat down and, as he did so, a nurse came out of Pencarrow and walked towards him. "Not the lift," he thought; "the stairs are faster." She stopped at the woman in the beret beside him. "Mrs Lawrence, your husband's awake and asking for you." The nurse smiled and stood aside, as the visiting wife rose with a little cry and went quickly past her. Roger's knee was jumping up and down, his heel too. A heavy man sitting opposite was watching him. He stilled his leg. He couldn't see how he could get to Rachael. Even if he posed as a relative of Jerry Hopkins or Mr Lawrence, there were nurses on duty; and, anyway, the other patients would cry out if he started anything with Rachael. He decided he would leave with the woman in the red beret, when she came out, as if he had been waiting for her; but he'd stay in the hospital, use the cafe, check back ways out, kill time, until it was late and only the night staff left. He'd find a cupboard or a loo cubicle to wait in. Two or three o'clock in the morning would be the time to move.

Chapter 32

The snatch

It was past five when Connie sealed the bag of the last of the prescriptions she had made up and carried them through to the cabinet behind the counter in the shop, where they were stored alphabetically for collection.

"Thanks for getting those done," Joy said as Connie pulled her coat on. "You go; I'll lock up."

"Okay, see you in the morning." She liked the manageress: Joy was relaxed and led from behind, so different from Mr Hawley, her predecessor. Connie knew she worked better when she was left to get on with things and not interfered with unnecessarily.

As she stepped out into the darkness, she tucked her chin inside the zipped rim of her anorak and hunched her shoulders against the cold. Headlights and tail lights were streaming to and from the T-junction with Mannamead Road, where the rush-hour traffic was heavier still.

She crossed one road and then the other, and as she headed up the hill she thought about Lou and Hong Kong. She felt sure her parents would approve of him and she smiled, knowing how happy they would be if she were to find a good husband and have children. But, then, they would want her and Lou to live in Hong Kong and be near them. She felt a familiar homesickness; a sadness like grief. She wanted to go home, speak her own language again, feel warm again and eat her mother's cooking again.

She turned left into Whiteford Road, glad to be free of the noise and fumes of the evening traffic. The street was lined with parked cars and tall trees, their roots pushing up the pavement slabs, narrowing the path and forcing her to tread carefully. She didn't like this road, the trees made it dark and oppressive, but it was the most direct way to her house. There were lights on in the houses she passed and occasional passing cars, but the path was empty. A man in a small van stopped a little ahead of her and wound down the passenger window, as she came level with him. She couldn't see him clearly.

"Can you tell me the way to..." He peered at a piece of paper in his hand. "Ford Park Lane?"

"I'm sorry," she said, moving closer to the window. "I know the name, but I can't think where it is."

"I've got a map 'ere somewhere," he said, putting the piece of paper down and picking up another. "Hang on, I'll come round and show you." He got out and came round the front of the car. He was wearing a dark beanie and he smoothed out the hand-drawn map on the bonnet, where the street light just caught it. "'Ere's where I'm trying to get to," he said leaning over it and pointing to a road on the diagram with his finger.

He straightened and moved back, so that she could bend forward for a look, still keeping his finger on the spot. There was tiny spidery writing, which she had trouble seeing. She lowered her head further to look more closely; and, as she did so, he slid his free hand round her mouth and pulled her back upright, tight against him. Instantly, his other arm came round her, holding her fast.

"Don't struggle and you won't get hurt," he said in her ear as he bundled her to the rear door, opened it and shoved her in face-down on the floor. He climbed in and sat on her back, knees either side of her. Her cry, as he pulled her head up by her hair, was quickly stifled by the tape he stuck across her mouth. Shifting his weight on to her thighs, he wrenched her arms behind her and taped her wrists together, finally getting off her altogether to bind her ankles.

All she could see was the torn back of the driver's seat, with a plume of stuffing hanging out. A hand came past her and grabbed a coil of rope from the bottom of the seat. His weight came on her again as he stretched for it. She felt his body press against her and panic leapt through her, shooting bile up into her mouth, burning her throat.

Then, he was off her again, looping the rope between her feet and arms and pulling it tight, until her ankles were trussed up against her wrists. The muscles in her thighs started to cramp and the pain was excruciating. The door banged shut behind her and, as he got in the front, a gust of air blew dust in her eyes. She tried to blink it way but it settled like grit and she longed for the free use of her hand to wipe it away.

As he drove, she rolled one way and then the other with every bend. What was he going to do with her? Who was he? Why had he picked on her? Had anybody seen her being grabbed and reported it? Did the police already have a description of the van? Would Lou come for her? At the thought of Lou, the ice of shock and terror that had locked her melted into a flood of yearning to be rescued, to be safe. Hot tears flooded her eyes, washing away the dust and coating her cheeks.

The darkness in the back of the van brightened and faded again with every street light they passed. She tried to keep track of the turns they were taking, but soon lost all sense of direction. Instead, she started to count the seconds and minutes, so as to have some idea of how far away he was taking her, until the rolling and bumping and terror froze her into despair and confusion. Eventually, it was darker and the van slowed, then stopped. Her heart raced. The lights of an oncoming vehicle flared through the windscreen as it passed. The darkness returned more complete than before and the van rolled forwards again.

Shortly afterwards, it swung suddenly to the left and stopped. The motor shuddered and died. "We're 'ere," the man said, getting out. It was a coarse voice, low with gravel in it. The rear door opened and the chill night air poured in. He untied the rope and slashed the tape round her legs. As he dragged her out on to her feet, she glimpsed lights bouncing on water, a second before he covered her eyes with a rag, knotting it behind her head.

"It's tricky 'ere," he said, "so do what I tell yer." He pushed her along in front of him, one hand on her shoulder guiding her. "Stop," he whispered and moved past her. She thought of running but knew it would be useless. She heard a lock turn and perhaps a gate being opened. The hand was back on her shoulder. "Come on. Now wait." Whatever he was doing, he was being as quiet as he could be. She heard something click and then click again. She couldn't make it out. Then he was behind her again, pushing her forward, until he said: "Wait. Six steep steps coming up. Feel for 'em." She did and at the bottom they went on again. She strained for sounds to give her a clue where they might be but everything was quiet, apart from an occasional clinking sound that she recognised but couldn't place.

"More steps," he said, stopping her. "Seventeen this time." The steps were uneven and she felt she might pitch forward. The hand on her shoulder steadied her. "Wait 'ere," he said, as they reached the bottom. He squeezed past her and she heard him straining at something and grunting. A key turned in a lock and a door scraped open. The hand was back. "In 'ere."

The stench of the place made her duck her head involuntarily to try to escape it. "Better'n roses!" he laughed, no longer whispering. The smell was vile, like cat food mixed with urine. "You'll get used to it. Stand still." She did as she was told, while he cut her wrists free, quickly retaping them in front of her. Then he grabbed her arm. "Come on, in 'ere." They went through a doorway and he led her on until she felt her foot touch something. She stopped. "It's a mattress," he said. "Sit down." He gave her a push and she stumbled over, falling down and catching the side of her head a glancing blow against the wall. Twisting on her side and using her elbow for support, she tried to prop herself up into a sitting position.

"You're safe 'ere. No-one's going to 'urt yer." He paused and then chuckled. "Well, not as long as your favourite policeman plays ball, that is. So just make yerself comfortable and I'll be back later."

She sat still, listening intently, as first the inner door and then the outer door were closed and locked. She heard his footsteps fading, going away up the steps, and after a bit the sound of an engine coughing into life and swelling. Then it, too, grew fainter until it dissolved altogether.

Chapter 33
Lou gets a call

"That you, Beradino?" The voice was distorted, broken-up and croaky. The call had come through on his personal number.

"I'm parking. Hold on." He was backing into a space just down from Connie's house on the other side of the road. The voice didn't stop.

"I've got something of yours."

Lou straightened the wheels, pulled on the handbrake and turned off the engine. Connie normally put the outside light on for him, but the house was in darkness.

"Are you listening to me?" The voice was louder, angrier, and he recognised it.

"I'm listening," he said, instantly loose and alert, as if a big wave were coming in.

"Right then. You want to see your chinky girlfriend again, you do what I tell yer."

Still talking, Lou got out and ran across the street to Connie's house. "Don't be stupid, Coaker! We'll pick you up in minutes." He banged on the door and tried the handle.

"Not in, is she?" The laugh rattled in his ear. "Told yer, I've got 'er."

How the hell had he given Kincaid the slip and got to Connie? "Go on," he said, getting back in the car and starting it up.

"It's simple." Lou manoeuvred out into the road again, while the voice went on, the rear tyres squealing as he backed to the junction. "You kill the investigation into Lapinski and all the rest of it, and Suzie Wong goes free."

Lou reversed out left, then thrust the gear stick into first and took off, foot hard down.

"I couldn't do that now, even if I wanted to. And I don't!"

"She's pretty, in't she? Sort of clean and unused, like." In the silence that followed, Lou began to think the line had gone dead, but the voice came again, low and mocking. "Yes, very desirable that, in certain quarters, if you know what I mean. Very valuable."

The picture of Connie's defencelessness and of his own powerlessness to protect her sliced through his guard.

"You touch her, Coaker, and I'll fucking tear you apart!"

Holding his phone to his ear with his shoulder, Lou slammed the flashing blue light on to the roof of his car, while screaming down Mutley Plain into North Hill.

"I already touched 'er. And you ain't going to find us." He sounded cool, cocky. "So you may as well slow down." The laugh came again, like a smoker's cough, coarse and phlegmy.

The burst of anger had cleared Lou's head.

"I don't think Ron Jellop's going to be very happy with your latest stupidity, do you?"

There was silence again and Lou waited. Cars were pulling over, out of his way, as he swept past the university and bore left towards Charles Cross.

Then the voice started again, neutral and controlled. "Stop the investigations. Maynard won't object. You get your girl back. You've got twenty-four hours."

Lou cleared the roundabout and shot through the red lights at the turn-off for the aquarium. "We'll find you, Eddie. You won't get away."

He heard a click and the line went dead.

A moment later he turned into Coaker's street and his lights picked up a dark figure running down the road towards him.

"Which house, Jason," he yelled, switching off and jumping out.

"Just here, sir. What's up?" Lou followed him to a door a few yards away and pounded the side of his fist against it five or six times. When there was no immediate response he did the same again.

"Round the back! Fast! I'll stay here."

He watched Jason run until he reached the corner at the top and disappeared.

Lou waited, knowing Coaker wasn't there and that he'd given Jason the slip. He rang the station and told the duty sergeant to put out an All Points Warning for Eddie Coaker to be arrested on sight and brought to Charles Cross Police Station. "And make sure DS Thomas knows and tell him Meilin 'Connie' Wu has been kidnapped. Then circulate her details and description to all officers out on patrol. Get them from Debbie Denton."

The door opened at the house one down and a bearded man in a cardigan stepped out. "What's going on?" he asked.

Lou flashed his badge. "Detective Inspector Lou Beradino," he said. "I'm looking for Eddie Coaker. Have you seen him this evening?"

"No, I haven't seen 'im in days. The Ship's your best bet. Or the Dolphin."

Before he could say more, Lou heard a lock being turned and the door in front of him opened.

"No-one here," Jason said, gulping air, his chest and shoulders heaving.

Lou looked at the bearded man. "Thank you, sir, that will be all for now." He stared at him until the man finally shrugged his shoulders and went back inside his house.

"Have you checked upstairs?" Lou asked Jason.

"Not yet."

"Go on, then."

While he was gone, Lou stood in the short hall and rang Fran. She only lived two minutes away. "What's up?" she said, her voice thick. He heard her cough and clear her throat.

"I'm at Coaker's with Jason. Coaker's gone."

"But Jason..." she started, before he interrupted her.

"Coaker rang me. He's got Connie. Meet me here, quick as you can."

"I'm on my way."

He pocketed the phone and closed the door as Jason came down the stairs. The heel of his boot caught on the lip of one of the treads, throwing him off-balance, and he leapt the last three stairs into the hall to save himself.

"There's no-one up there."

"Right. Somehow he managed to get past you, while you..." Lou paused. Jason's cold blue eyes were holding his without flinching. Had he let Coaker go, he wondered. Had someone got to him? Jellop maybe? And why wouldn't Maynard object, come to that? "How did you miss him, Jason?"

"I didn't. He never came out the house or up the lane." Jason's face was taut with anger and his tone insistent. "I was on the corner the whole time. I'd have seen him."

The roar of a motorbike sliced the rope of tension between them and Lou moved to open the door, just as Fran pulled up outside. She cut the engine, got off and eased the bike back on its stand. He watched her lift off her helmet and, as the familiar, concerned eyes turned towards him, he felt reconnected and less out on his own. Fran he could trust. Connie would be okay. They'd find her.

He wheeled round on Jason. "Go and talk to all the neighbours, everyone in the street. Find out whether anyone saw Coaker leaving here tonight. And find out whether they know of any other properties he owns or rents!"

Tracing the call could wait. They'd get the caller's location but nothing else – and it wouldn't be where Connie was. Coaker wasn't that stupid. No, better to search the house first and quickly.

Chapter 34
The attic

While DC Jason Kincaid went to question the neighbours, Lou charged back into the house. "There must be something here," he said as Fran caught up with him in the hall. "Something to tell us where he may have taken Connie." He led the way, following a narrow passage past the living room and the bottom of the staircase. There was a closed door to his left and an open one ahead, through which he could see a slim fridge-freezer beside a back door. He went in on the left.

"Strange room," Fran said, coming alongside him.

They stood for a moment, taking it in. It seemed to be half office, half workshop. There was a large knee-hole desk against the wall, with stack drawers either side. Its stained leather top was clear of clutter, apart from a cordless phone set at forty-five degrees on the rear right-hand corner. A wooden armchair was pushed in close to it.

"Everything ship-shape," Lou said.

A workbench ran along the wall opposite. It had two vices on its edge – one metal, one wooden – and two tool cabinets fixed to the wall above it. Its deep top was clear, apart from a box of small tins at one end, with pieces of rag stuffed in with them.

Beside the desk stood two four-drawer, grey-metal filing cabinets. Lou walked across and pulled the top drawer of each of them open.

"Not locked anyway," he said. "I'll start here."

"I'll take the upstairs," Fran said.

There was little enough paperwork in the filing cabinets, mainly old log books of the Morning Star and related documentation from the Ministry: past UK Fishing Vessel and Oil Pollution Prevention Certificates, as well as Anti-Fouling Declarations. The other drawers were filled with nautical paraphernalia, including a brass barometer, some clips and hoses, fishing net needles, an unmatched pair of rollocks and a couple of pairs of binoculars.

Coaker was tidy, well-organised, but there was no clue to where he might have gone. Lou looked through the kitchen cupboards, full of pots and pans, crockery and glassware, none of them matching but all clean and orderly. In the drawers by the sink he found bone-handled cutlery, remnants of an expensive canteen, he guessed. Maybe a wedding present of his mother's. And in the second was a bewildering array of knives: butcher's knives, paring knives, sharpening steels, knives for gutting and filleting fish and others he didn't recognise.

As he moved back down the passage towards the living-room, Fran's excited shout came from over his head. "Lou, come and look at this!"

Racing up the stairs, he turned on to the landing, only to find his way blocked by a metal loft-ladder.

"Up here," Fran said, peering down at him and as he started to climb, her face disappeared.

The floor of the loft was boarded and a naked bulb glared from the central beam. Apart from a standard lamp lying on its side and a couple of log-shaped polythene rolls, the attic space was empty. The roof beams came down sharply on either side to meet the bare brick walls, so that Lou could only straighten up by moving to the centre, next to Fran.

"That's why Jason didn't see him leave," Fran said, pointing to a gap in the brickwork of the wall to the adjoining house, leading through into its loft.

"It goes on for three more after that but be careful, there aren't any floorboards in the next two...or lights."

"And the one after that?"

"The last one's boarded and has a bulb like this one, only I couldn't find a switch."

"Come on," Lou said, starting back down the ladder. "Let's find Jason."

Out in the street, they saw him working his way up the hill. He was about to knock on another door when Lou shouted: "Jason! Hang on a minute."

As they hurried up to him, he took a step towards them. "What's up?"

"While you were watching Coaker, did you see anyone leaving one of the houses further on down?"

"Same terrace," Fran added.

"Yeah, a couple came out of one. Either the last one or the one before."

"When was that?"

Jason opened the notebook he was holding and flicked back. "4.47. A man and woman left together, walked down the road and got into a car and went off towards the centre."

"Descriptions?" Lou said.

"Make and registration?" Fran asked at the same time.

Jason looked from one to the other, narrowing his eyes and biting down, tightening the muscles in his long face. In the shadows cast by the street lights, he reminded Lou of a rodent, something rat-like, furtive and aggressive. He looked back at Lou.

"They were in coats with hoods. The woman's was darker. They were walking away from me. I didn't see them clearly. Middle-aged, I think...the way they were moving."

"Height?"

"The man was a head taller. Getting on for six-foot, I'd guess." He was looking down the road, trying to picture them. "The woman was wider. A big woman, if you know what I mean. Heavy-looking."

"And the car?" Fran asked.

"Dark saloon. Four-door. I didn't get the reg. It was shielded by other cars till it pulled out. I didn't give it much attention; I was focusing on the lane and Coaker's house. It was just a glance really."

"But it turned right at the bottom?"

"Yes. I saw the brake lights come on and the off-side indicator flashing. Then it was gone."

"Right," Lou said. "And did you see them come back again?"

He noted a change in the young detective's expression, as the set surliness gave way to something more puzzled, more animated.

"No. Not before you came anyway. But I think she may have come back. Don't know about him. I was talking to the couple next door but one." He pointed. "And I saw a figure lower down, opening a door and going in. Could've been her." He started to move. "I'll go and check."

Lou put out his hand. "No, Jason. We'll go. You carry on here."

They strode away from him down the slope.

Chapter 35
'Babs' to her friends

Fran rapped the iron knocker. It was circular, dark and pitted like the door. She was about to try again when the door opened and a burly figure obscured most of the light from the hall behind. Lou and Fran flashed their warrant cards as they introduced themselves.

"What ya want?" Her voice had the thick rasp of a heavy smoker and drinker.

"We're involved in a murder investigation," Lou said, "and we wish to talk to Eddie Coaker, a neighbour of yours."

"So?" She folded her arms.

"We have some questions we'd like to ask you, concerning his whereabouts. May we come in?" Lou took a pace forwards but she didn't move.

"No," she said.

"Obstructing the police in their enquiries is an offence," Lou said.

"Ask your questions," she said, taking a packet of cigarettes from her cardigan pocket, extracting one and lighting it with a match from a box in the other hand.

"Please confirm your full name and address," Fran said, opening her notebook.

"'Elena Bonham Carter," the woman grinned, revealing stained and missing teeth. She coughed violently and it rattled in her chest.

"One woman is dead, another has been attacked and is in hospital, and a third has been kidnapped." Lou grabbed the cigarette from the woman's mouth and threw it in the gutter, then put his face very close to hers. "We don't have time to mess around. You co-operate and answer our questions inside right now, or I'm arresting you for conspiracy to pervert the course of justice." His voice was loud and threatening. Fran glanced at him. "Do you understand me?"

"Bloody coppers!" she said, raising her eyes at Fran. She turned and walked back into the house.

They followed her through to a dimly-lit room at the back. It was hot and stuffy, with an old-fashioned sofa and two large armchairs bunched around a tiled fireplace. An electric fire stood in front of the grate, its three bars throbbing red, and a shaggy black cat was stretched out along a rug in front of it. The woman sat down in the chair with a used ashtray on one arm and a table with a glass and a bottle of whisky next to the other. She heaved herself sideways and poured herself a drink. Lou took the armchair facing her and Fran the sofa.

"Can't drink on duty, can ya?" she said, taking a mouthful and swallowing. "Shame. Anyway, I'm Barbara Anne Parker. Babs to my friends, which you're not. And this is my address."

"You were seen leaving this house earlier this evening with a man, who did not return with you. You both got into a car and drove off together towards the city centre." Lou leant forward, his forearms on his knees. "Who was that man, Mrs Parker, and where did you take him?"

"Paul Butler. Friend of mine. Took 'im back to Stoke. His place." She fumbled in her pocket for another cigarette. "Ask him, if ya like. 27 Alcester Street."

Fran jotted it down. "We will," she said.

Lou watched the match flare and the flabby cheeks suck in. "Your attic connects with Eddie Coaker's at number three. He used it this evening to evade us with your help, didn't he?"

"Don't know what ya on about."

"He got you to give him a lift in your car. Not long afterwards, a young woman was kidnapped just off Mannamead Road on her way home from work. Since then, we've had a call from Eddie threatening her safety." Her bleary eyes were following him now. He lent back. "You're at risk of becoming an accessory to murder. Mr Paul Butler, too. So, unless you want to face going to prison for a very long time, you better start telling us the truth."

She looked down at the cat and pulled hard on her cigarette. When she spoke again, her words came out wreathed in smoke. "All right, I took 'im. Dropped 'im by Toys R Us."

"Western Approach car park," Fran said, looking at Lou. She turned back to Barbara Parker. "Does Eddie Coaker own a vehicle? A car? A van?

"Seen 'im with a small grey van," the woman said. "Dunno if it's his." She was breathing quickly, her big shoulders moving up and down.

"Mrs Parker," Lou said, "you're going to come to the station in the morning and make a full statement. And we are going to find out everything there is to know about your friendship with Eddie. If you conceal any helpful information from us here and now, I'm going to put you away. Do you understand me?"

She nodded without looking up.

"Okay. So think carefully before you answer this." He paused to let the words sink in. "We know about his house. We know about his boat, the Morning Star. So where else might Eddie be hiding this young woman?"

She stubbed out her cigarette, sat back and pulled her cardigan closer about her. She looked at Lou, then at Fran and back again at Lou.

"I dunno," she said at last.

Lou's fist smashed down on the side of the armchair and the cat rocketed out of the door. He ducked his head and rubbed his hands backwards and forwards along his thighs, trying to control the violence he was feeling. The woman's thick voice started up again.

"He has a dingy. Up the river somewhere. That's all I know."

"Which river?" Fran asked.

"Tamar."

"How do you know?" Lou stood up.

"He told me."

"Why did he tell you?" He was standing over her now. "What were you talking about?"

"I don't remember. Bloody ages ago."

Lou waited. He didn't move. He watched her brushing ash off her skirt; repeated short strokes of her fleshy hand, even after all the ash was gone.

"'Ang on. I remember. Cremyll ferry was out of order. Engine...rudder...not sure exactly...something like that. Anyway, Eddie knew I used to meet my sister over at Edgcumbe on a Tuesday and said he had a dinghy, could take me across if I wanted."

She levered herself up, forcing Lou to step backwards. She was level with him now, staring at him defiantly. "'E didn't 'ave to. Ferry was working again the next day. But that's what Eddie's like. He's a mate. You can count on him. Now I've nothing more to say."

Brushing past Lou, she walked through the doorway towards the front door.

"Sort out Jason and the house," Lou said to Fran when they were outside again. "Then go back to the station and bring Macklin up to speed. And see if you can get a trace on Coaker's call."

Fran nodded, but she was watching him closely.

"You okay, Lou? You were...you know..." She hesitated.

"I was what?"

"Pretty threatening. When you grabbed her cigarette, I thought you were going to hit her. Are you too close to this?"

Anger flared in him. He wanted to lash out at Fran and tell her to "fuck off!" Instead, he stayed silent, staring back at her, struggling to contain the rage boiling in his chest. Coaker had a dinghy opposite Edgcumbe. Maybe he was holding Connie down by the water some place. When he found him... He looked down at his fists; they were half-raised and balled tight.

"Leave it, Fran," he said finally. "I need some time." And he walked away to his car.

Chapter 36
The shed

Connie woke. It was dark. She didn't know what time it was. Curled in a ball and uncovered, she was freezing. Clasping her hands together, she squeezed her arms against her body as tightly as she could. She thought she could hear water lapping and lay motionless, straining to be sure. A faint susurrus, like soft breathing. Was it or wasn't it? She stood up beside the mattress. Her eyes were growing accustomed to the darkness and she could make out the form of the door across from her. She struggled up beside the mattress and started jogging on the spot, trying to get her blood circulating, trying to get some warmth into her bones.

By the time she stopped, she was breathing hard. She wriggled her toes. She felt comforted that sensation had come back into them. But as her breaths lengthened and her heart slowed, the damp chill seeped back into her. The air was dank and the smell of it took her back to the dilapidated boathouse half falling into the Min River that scared her as a child. It was near her grandmother's house in Sichuan Province and she was forbidden to go there. But a dread fascination had lured her into it more than once, with its echoing, watery dinginess and shafts of sunlight sending rippling reflections off the water's surface across the cob-webbed roof. Tears gushed down her cheeks and she slumped on to the mattress, sitting hugging her knees, her head bowed over them, rocking backwards and forwards.

Her grandmother, small and gnarled like a vine, was vividly present in Connie's closed eyes, with her back humped and twisted from the tortures she had suffered

225

under Chairman Mao. She could hear her coarse, staccato voice: "Remember, Little Fish, your soul is free." They had beaten her, raped her, buried her husband alive, but she had survived. Connie longed for her now, much as she had feared her as a child on those spring visits with her mother.

A muffled thud made her look up. She scrambled to her feet and stood motionless, listening. Soft footsteps...coming up, not down? Something scraping. The click of a lock and a sudden draught around her ankles. Another click. She held her breath. "Stay with me, Popo," she told her grandmother. Light swept the gap at the bottom of the door and, a moment later, it opened and a powerful torch beam blinded her. She ducked her head away, raising her tied wrists to shield her eyes.

"'Ere!" The beam wobbled, as something came through the air at her. She flinched. "Blanket for yer." It fell by her feet, half-on, half-off the mattress. The beam jerked down and up again, as something smaller, faster came at her, barely missing her and hitting the wall and bouncing down near the blanket. "Bottle of water!" It was the same rough voice as before.

"I need the toilet," Connie said.

The beam moved off her face, travelling slowly down the length of her body and up again. Briefly, she saw the dark mass of the man's head and torso.

"You'll fetch a tidy sum, if it comes to it," he said and, after a pause, added: "There's a bucket in the corner." He swung the light to it and back into her eyes again. "All mod cons!" he laughed, hawking up some phlegm and spitting it out.

"I'm hungry," she said. "I need some food."

The beam swung away again as the figure turned for the door.

"Go to sleep. I'll give yer something in the morning."

The door closed and the light died. She heard the key turn in the lock. She reached for the blanket and felt for its corners. Awkwardly, she lifted her arms above her head and manoeuvred the blanket until it fell over her shoulders and she could draw it around her like a cape. She listened for the sound of the outer door, but it didn't come. Instead, a dull orange glow smeared the floor under her door and she could hear the man moving about.

She felt afraid and angry. "Untie my wrists...please!" she shouted. He didn't answer but went on doing whatever it was, shuffling and grunting. She waited and then called out again: "I can't do anything with my hands tied. I can't sleep like this."

"Say yer prayers then."

The orange glow disappeared. There was a muffled creak and rustle and then silence.

Chapter 37
Hospital night

Roger tilted his watch to catch the low light in the cubicle. 2.23am. No-one had used the loos for several hours. There had been some loud voices outside in the corridor shortly after 1am but since then all had been quiet. He moved out and stood in front of the mirror over a basin, stretching his back and arching his shoulders. He had pins and needles in his right foot and he paced up and down to get rid of them. A general wash of dull light through the mottled window cast deep shadows and outlined his reflection.

He shrugged off his knapsack and unzipped it. Pulling out a white lab coat he had taken from the college, he put it on. He hoped he might pass as a medic, if no one looked too carefully; although he'd have to leave his pack behind, he realized. As he moved towards the door, he fashioned the rubber tubing he had taken from a Bunsen burner into a loop showing above one of the side pockets like a folded stethoscope.

The corridor was empty and he slipped quickly towards Level 4. As he came round the corner by the lifts, a hospital porter with his hands on an empty trolley and a nurse beside him were standing watching one of the doors sliding open.

They hardly seemed to notice him as he walked past. When he neared the ICU wards, he saw there'd been a changing of the guard and a large policeman was now filling the chair by the entrance to Pencarrow. He paused in the shadows of a recess by reception. His college ID badge might fool from a distance, but not close up. Besides, it had his real name on it.

He looked round for a weapon, something heavy he could use as a club. All he could make out that might be suitable was a fire extinguisher. Maybe it would do. He stepped towards it, as the PC stood up and shook his legs. He was looking down the corridor, staring straight at him. Roger stopped breathing. The policeman turned and walked through the door to the visitors' toilets across from the waiting area.

Running on tiptoe, Roger reached the ward door. He pushed, but it was locked. He'd have to use the intercom to ask for admission. He knew that. Why hadn't he thought of it? He was never going to get to her undetected now. He glanced over his shoulder for signs of the PC and then back at the door. Through its glass panel, he saw two elderly figures coming towards him. Visitors? At this hour? How could that be? They paused and pressed a button by the wall. The door unclicked and they came through, holding it open for him. "Thank you," he said and slipped in, closing it softly. The short corridor bent at a right angle a little way down and, as he turned the corner, he saw two broad swing doors straight ahead of him.

Gently pushing the right-hand one open far enough to go in, he was surprised by the size of the space in front of him, with beds on either side in large individual bays. On each side of the beds were consoles of machinery, many with flickering digital screens and with connecting wires from under the covers. As he paused, a man lying on his back in the bed nearest to him stopped snoring and turned his head with his eyes open. Roger smiled in his direction and walked past, peering at the occupant of each bed in turn until he found Rachael at the end, on the far side. Behind him the snoring had started again. He stood looking at the familiar figure, suddenly warmed by a feeling of completion. Her face was turned sideways, her hair straddling her throat and shoulder and spreading out across her pillow.

"Oh, Rachael!" he murmured, moving beside her. He held a long breath in as he fought to composc himself. "I so loved you." Raising her head gently, he pulled the pillow from under her and folded it down over her face. There was a muffled moan and she stared to squirm. He climbed on top of her, pinning her, and pushed down more firmly. "I will never leave you," he whispered.

A staccato bleeper started screaming into the silence and then a buzzer. "Hey!" a voice croaked weakly from the bay opposite. "Stop! Stop! What are you doing?"

Another bleeper started to intercut with the first. Roger scrambled off the bed, taking the pillow with him and dropping it on the floor, as a nurse burst into the ward, closely followed by the policeman.

Bending over the body, Roger looked over his shoulder at them and shouted: "Quick! Over here!"

As they rushed towards him, still facing the bed, he yelled out, "Cardiac arrest!", and made as if to start the CPR chest compression moves he had learnt on the First Aid course at college, pulling back the sheet and moving his hand towards Rachael's heart. But as they reached him, he ducked backwards and made a dash for the door. He heard the policeman take off after him and saw another nurse hurrying in ahead of him. He ran at her as fast as he could go, raising his hands to push her out of the way, but she dodged to the side and stuck out the toe of her shoe as he came flying past. It caught the tip of his raised foot and sent him crashing off-balance through the doorway face down on to the floor beyond. Pushing hard against the linoleum with the heels of his hand, he snaked his foot up, ready to spring off again, when PC Bob Turner's hurtling fifteen stones landed on his back, flattening him out straight. As he choked, gasping for breath, his hands were wrenched and cuffed behind him.

"I'm arresting you for the attempted murder of Rachael Drew at Royal William Yard," Bob Turner panted in his ear.

Pulling him to his feet and facing him, he added: "You don't have to say anything. But it may harm..." Roger didn't listen to the caution. The policeman's words, 'attempted murder', were pounding too maddeningly in his head for that. What if she still wasn't dead, even now? Throwing back his head like a wounded animal, he let out a great roar of anger, full of pain, and bellowed out her name, "RACHAEL!", which ricocheted down the hospital corridor, ringing off the walls and cleaving the silence of the night.

Chapter 38
Coaker calls again

Later that morning, Lou listened impatiently, as Fran began to update him on the night's events and Roger Millman's arrest. They were sitting in his office either side of the desk, with winter sunshine slanting in through the windows out of a cloudless, pale blue sky. He was sitting upright, tapping his fingers against the arm ends of his chair.

She paused. "What's up, Lou?"

"Has there been any news about Connie? Anything about Coaker or the van?"

"No, nothing yet. Except DVLA has confirmed a grey Vauxhall Combo van is registered in Coaker's name and they've given us the number." Her voice softened, as she added: "We're on it. It's just a matter of time."

"We don't have time!" he snapped and regretted it at once. He stopped tapping and tried to focus on what she had been telling him.

"Sorry," he said; "Rachael Drew, how is she?"

"Stable, according to Bob Turner." Fran moved the angle of her chair. The sun was in her eyes and she had a headache from too little sleep. "Emotionally shaken up, but physically no worse than before. And apparently her two boys are being allowed to visit her today for the first time. Should give her a lift."

Lou wasn't sure. "Poor kids. Have we had any news about Oliver Drew?"

"Nothing so far. Word is they're giving it one more day and then they'll scale the hunt right down from search to observation."

"He has to be somewhere," Lou said. "Maybe Roger Millman will tell us. Has he made a statement yet?"

"Not yet. But Oliver Drew definitely went into the river."

Lou's thumb stopped tapping and a new alertness sharpened his eyes. Fran allowed herself a thin smile.

"We got the CCTV footage from Clarence. It shows the attack. The hooded figure, almost certainly Roger Millman, comes up behind Mr and Mrs Drew at the railings. They're facing the river. He's carrying something which, when we blew it up, is clearly a baseball bat. He smashes it down on the back of Oliver Drew's head, bundles his body over the fencing into the water and hurls the bat in too. After that, there's what looks like an argument between him and Rachael Drew, and then he headbutts her. She collapses and he starts to throttle her on the ground, until suddenly he looks up and runs off. A moment later, Commander Pelham comes into the frame."

"What do we know about Millman?" Fran scanned her notes. "Local man. Lives alone in his deceased mother's house. Teaches English at Tamar College. No previous."

Something linked to this information hovered in the back of Lou's mind but, as he struggled to get hold of it, it disappeared.

"Any connection to Ron Jellop or Eddie Coaker?" he said.

Fran shrugged. "None yet."

"Okay. Go and talk to him. See what you can find out."

"One thing," she said, standing up. "Polly Jellop wants to speak to you."

He nodded and watched her walk to the door, his thumb stroking his lips.

After she'd gone, he pushed his chair back and went across to the window. He stood for a long time staring into the burnt-out bowels of Charles Church on the roundabout, the morning traffic circling it in rhythm with the changing lights. Although a memorial to those killed by the incendiary bombs dropped on Plymouth by the Luftwaffe during the Second World War, it had a sombre beauty and acted as a balm for his fears, allowing him to think.

Where was Coaker's dinghy, he wondered. Where was he holding Connie? And what did he hope to achieve? Ron Jellop would be arrested soon, whether or not he had anything to do with Connie's kidnapping. There was nothing Maynard could do to prevent that. And the prostitution ring was already identified and would be closed down. It only left Nina Lapinski. Killing Connie couldn't do Coaker any good, except as an act of revenge. Lou remembered Coaker's threat when he had interviewed him, the snarl in his voice, the narrowed eyes. "You'll regret this, Beradino." Maybe he should let Coaker off the hook to get Connie back unharmed. He could park the circumstantial and let Nina's case fade as unexplained, unsolved. But how could Coaker be sure he wouldn't come after him again, as soon as Connie was safe?

"No deal!" Lou said aloud, breaking away from the window.

He went back to his desk and rang Polly Jellop. Her warm, Devon voice soon answered.

"Mrs Jellop, this is DI Beradino. I understand you want to speak to me."

"Good morning, Inspector. That's right, I do. Thank you for calling back."

Lou waited. When she continued, her voice was more authentic, he felt. Less sure of itself, more hesitant, more serious.

"I probably should have told you this earlier...when you were here the morning Rachael was attacked. I didn't, because...well, because I didn't want...I mean, I thought I was protecting her. I didn't want to speak out of turn. But I see now I should've said something. Only, it was something she had told me in confidence, you see."

"Yes," said Lou.

There was a pause. "Rachael and I are in the same English class at the college." Lou smiled, as the illusive thought came clearly into the light.

"And Roger Millman took that class," he said.

"Yes." She sounded surprised. "You already know then?"

"Know what, Mrs Jellop?"

Once again, there was silence from the other end of the line, although he could still hear her breathing.

"What I have to tell you, Inspector, is confidential. May I have your word on that?"

"We will be discreet, Mrs Jellop. But this is a murder enquiry and anything you tell me may be used in evidence."

It wasn't a promise of total confidentiality but it did offer discretion and, by implication, an assurance that what she told him would not become common knowledge or the subject of idle gossip.

"All right then. The point is Rachael confided in me that she was having an affair with Roger Millman. That was last term. But after Christmas she decided to end it. She was going to divorce Oliver and start a new life on her own with the boys. With Nick and Sam."

"I see," said Lou. "So had Mrs Drew told Roger Millman of her decision?"

"Yes, she had. That's why I wanted to speak to you. She said he'd been very upset. And after you and your colleague left the other day, I started worrying that maybe it was Roger who had attacked Rachael, not Oliver, which was my first thought. In fact, he may..."

"Thank you, Mrs Jellop," Lou interrupted her. "That's very helpful. It gives us a possible motive and we'll certainly follow this up."

He resisted the urge to tell her of Millman's arrest and the evidence they already had against him. Never mind, she'd learn about it soon enough. Instead, he asked if she had any further information to give him. She said she had not. He thanked her again and ended the call.

Lou liked Polly Jellop; there was something solid and honourable about her. How much did she already suspect about her husband, he wondered. How would she react when he was arrested and charged? The public humiliation and media interest would be intense. He wished he could spare her that. But it was time to address the matter with Maynard, he decided. Ron Jellop could not be saved from arrest and certain prosecution, as far as he could see, nor did he deserve to be.

He was reaching for the phone to check if his superior was free, when his mobile rang.

"That you, Beradino?" It was the same cracked, distorted voice.

Lou hurried out of his room, trying to shield the phone from the echoing stairwell by holding it close to his chest. He slowed and lifted it.

"I need to speak to Ms Wu to know she's unharmed. There can be..." Fran saw him from her desk, his finger pointing at the phone, and leapt up to start a trace. "...no deal till..."

"Too late for deals. I'm leaving. Taking your girl with me."

"Let her go, Coaker, and I won't come after you."

The chopped-up, dry rattle laugh cut through the end of Lou's offer, before he'd even finished.

"No way! This is payback. I lose, you lose."

Lou struggled to think of a hook to keep him talking.

"Maybe it wasn't murder. Maybe Nina Lapsinki struggled with you for the phone and fell overboard. Maybe it's manslaughter. Let Ms Wu go and you'll do less time."

Lou jerked his head away from the burst of raucous laughter that followed.

"I'm not doing any time. And your pretty girlfriend's going to earn my keep."

The line went dead.

Lou looked at Fran, but she shook her head.

He ran his fingertips over his palms. They were sticky and he thought he was going to be sick.

"You've gone green at the gills," Fran said, coming over to him. "What's up?"

He started to tell her and choked on his words halfway through.

"Let's go outside," she said, and led the way into the car park until they were out of earshot.

He was glad of the cold; it was like a slap. "I can't think straight, Fran," he said. "How am I going to stop him? How am I going to save Connie in time?"

"It's not just you, Lou," she said. "Leave this with me. I'll put out the alerts. No boat's leaving here without our knowing who's on it. You step away. Go and clear your head. We'll get her." She touched his arm and repeated, "We'll get her." Then she turned and ran back into the station.

Chapter 39
Breakthrough

Lou left the building and drove out to Devil's Point. His head was roiling with images of what Coaker had in store for Connie, and what Lou was going to do to him when he caught up with him. Waves of fear and anger chopped up his thoughts. He felt caught in a hurricane, with no overview of where he was or which way to go.

He pulled into a disabled space in the car park overlooking the bay and got out. He crossed the path, walked across the grass, where it sloped down towards the mouth of the river, and sat down. The sea was calm and dully reflective like pewter. Beyond Drake Island, one of the new radar-deflecting frigates was anchored out by the breakwater, with its unfamiliar superstructure, obliquely angled and encased.

Drake Island. Privately-owned now, uninhabited. His eyes travelled back to it, to the derelict buildings above the rocks, barracks from the time of the Napoleonic wars. Prisoners had been held there; died there too, many of them. It would be a perfect place to take Connie. He shook his head. It wouldn't. It was too public. Too many boats going by, too many curious binoculars focused on it from the Hoe. Best place to hide a tree is in a forest, not out on a plain.

Lou's mind was racing. There was so little time left to find her. If Coaker was planning to leave and take Connie with him, where would he go, and how? He must have contacts abroad. Why else would he have been taking Nina out to sea? Maybe he'd been planning to murder and dump her all the time. But why risk it? Ron Jellop wouldn't want to be party to murder. No, it was much more Coaker's style to want to make money out of her. Sell her as a sex worker: Marseille, Amsterdam, Stuttgart. He smashed the side of his fist down on the ground. It was cold and hard, and the jolt of it shattered the pictures multiplying inside his head, bringing his thoughts back to Coaker and the present.

Coaker would need a boat. He couldn't put to sea in a dinghy and the Morning Star was still impounded. A sudden splurge of black fur close to Lou's elbow made him flinch, as a beefy Labrador pushed past, pausing to sniff the soles of his shoes. Instinctively, he stretched out a hand but a whistle and a shout caused the dog to trot off, nose to the ground, zigzagging towards a man walking away along the path. If Coaker kept a dinghy up the river, as Barbara Parker had said, perhaps he had a boathouse or a shed or something, big enough and secluded enough for hiding Connie. "Use your bloody eyes!" he told himself, standing up. He turned and strode towards the rise leading to the steps down into Royal William Yard, lengthening his stride as he went. At the top he crossed to the chest-high wall and looked down at the estuary.

The pedestrian ferry from Stonehouse to Cremyll was half-way across. It seemed small and toy-like, with its blue superstructure and bright-red funnel lit up in the morning sunshine. On the far side was Cornwall and Mount Edgecumbe Country Park. How peaceful and inviting it looked, with its shrubs and trees rising from the foreshore and spreading out across the rising ground behind. And yet somewhere out there, maybe even in his view, Connie was a prisoner. He followed the shoreline up river, past the pub and boatyard and the moored boats beyond, to where it curved out of sight. But his instinct was that Coaker was holding her on this side, the Plymouth side.

He looked down at the water. The tide was ebbing and he could see the strong currents and disturbance traced in its surface. The tide was going out the night Oliver Drew was pushed in. Where had it taken him? Why hadn't he been found? Two black rubber, combat raiding craft travelling in tandem caught his eye. They were low in the water and moving fast, sinister-looking with their crouched marine crews, and difficult to spot among the other small craft in the estuary. They were heading home upstream towards the Devonport dockyards. He watched them until they passed out of sight beyond Mutton Cove, round beyond the colourful figurehead of 'King Billy' and the start of the dockyards.

One thing was sure; Coaker would have to be hiding on this side of the yards. Devonport was the largest naval dockyard in Western Europe. Nuclear submarines were based there, as well as frigates. If he wanted to remain undetected, he'd steer well clear of it.

Lou took the steps down and stood at the glass-panelled fencing by Clarence Gate, where the Drews had been attacked. He brought his attention back to Mutton Cove and panned slowly right along the river bank, where the low white silhouette of the walls of the swimming pool stretched out in front of Mount Wise's grassy hillside.

He followed the line of the ivy-clad path walls on round. High fencing topped with coiled barbed-wire marked the border of the MoD land beneath it. By the bank, a solid stone structure rose roofless, with four arched bays open to the river. And nearby steps led down to the water's edge. But he could see nothing hidden there. No building or boat, where Coaker could keep Connie and himself out of sight.

Scanning on right, a couple of faded buildings by Messum's boatyard surprised him: a small cottage with a pale red roof and near it, closer to the water, a flat-topped cream building. Office maybe. He'd never noticed them before. Did they belong to the boatyard? And where was the entrance? How did you get to them? He could just make out a landing stage, but no boat, no dinghy. In the yard itself, a crane was moving among the masts of the yachts stored there for the winter. Maybe the access to them was from inside the yard.

After that came a slipway and the Ocean Court Marina apartment block, with its white balconies shelving in and up in tiers, like a liner, their reflections shimmering towards him. Coaker wasn't likely to be holed-up there, too many ears and eyes. Lou looked back at the cottage and his heart quickened.

Further round from the marina's plethora of pontoons and moored boats, his view was blocked by the granite edge of Brewhouse. He moved on again and made for the corner by the Canteen, where the Drews and Jellops had eaten their last meal together. From here he could see the final stretch of the inlet, from the blue ship-building sheds of Princess Yachts to the ferry pier and waterfront buildings of Stonehouse. He took out his phone and jabbed at it.

"DS Thomas." The familiar voice steadied him.

"Macklin, I'm at Royal William Yard and I'm coming back now." Lou looked at his watch. "Can you get everyone together for a briefing?"

"I'm not sure where Fran is right now, but..."

"We're going to search the waterfront between here and Mutton Cove, every house, boat and shed. We'll need uniform support."

"Leave it with me, Lou."

Lou was halfway to the station when his phone rang. It was Fran.

"We've just heard from Jason. He's over at the Ocean Court apartments. He's found a small grey van under a tarpaulin, parked against the wall. I'm on my way and Macklin's getting Carol and Martin to meet us there."

"Two minutes!" Lou said, swinging left at the roundabout by the Brittany Ferries terminal and accelerating towards Union Street.

Chapter 40
Getaway

All Connie could hear was the slap of the water and the whine of the outboard. Her ribs were hurting from the struts she was lying on and she tried twisting more on to her back. Spray was collecting in rivulets, washing up and down with the movement of the dinghy. She was cold and damp, and the fungal smell of the salty wood was making her nauseous.

Her wrists were still tied and, as another wing of spray swept over her, she tried to pull herself up from the waist to get clear of the water, but Coaker, sitting in the stern with his hand on the tiller, stuck his boot in her chest and pushed her back.

"Keep yer fuckin' head down!" he yelled. "I already told yer."

Her head cracked back against the struts, blurring her vision, so that the dipping gunwales and rising coastline crazed and mashed into one another, only to be replaced the next instant by the opaque blankness of the sky and then, once again, by the fractured contours of boat and land. She closed her eyes and prayed to her grandmother. "Help me, Popo. Please help me."

* * * * *

Lou swung into Richmond Walk ahead of a squad car catching him from behind. Together they sped along the narrow, twisting cul-de-sac, past Jewson's timber yard on one side and the Mayflower Marina on the other, breaking at Ocean Court, where the lane bottle-necked before delivering them out into a space overlooking the river. Half-a-dozen parking spaces were partially filled either side of the lane, which ran out at the entrance to Messum's Boatyard, just past the slipway.

He pulled in by the wall, where Fran and Jason were standing next to the grey van, already cordoned off, the tarpaulin on the ground beside it.

"SOCOs are on their way," Fran said, moving towards him as he got out. Behind her he saw Carol and Martin hurry from the squad car and cross to Jason.

"We need MoD back-up to cover the river. He may have a boat."

She turned, reaching for her phone, and followed him back to the others.

"How did you trace it, Jason? How do you know this is the one?" He pointed at the van. A Vauxhall of some sort, he wasn't sure which. It was almost invisible in its dullness.

The smirk of self-congratulation died into the narrow coffin of the young DC's long face. "After you left, I spoke to Babs Parker, one of Eddie Coaker's neighbours..."

"I know who she is," Lou said. "What did she say?"

"Yes, she said she'd spoken to you and DS Bannerman. Didn't seem very..." Whatever he'd been about to say, Jason seemed to think better of it. Instead, he went on: "She said she'd told you about the dinghy but after you'd gone she'd remembered Coaker mentioning a slipway. Said she wasn't going to be accused of 'withholding information'."

"They're sending an inflatable," Fran said, pocketing her phone.

Lou gave her a quick smile and a nod before turning back to Jason, who was now looking at Carol and Martin as he spoke.

"This was the only slipway I could think of nearby. I told DS Thomas and he said to come and have a look."

"Good work," Lou said. "Okay, let's get organised." He looked from face to face as he spoke. "Connie Wu is being held near here. Her life will be in danger if Coaker sees or hears us coming. He's planning to leave Plymouth and take her with him, which means he may have a boat. The MoD are sending an inflatable to watch the shore..."

"That may be them now," Martin said, pointing upriver towards the dockyard. They watched a black smudge grow larger and more distinct as the rubber craft maintained a steady course towards them, moving at the customary patrol speed.

"Right," Lou said. "Carol, Martin, there are some buildings on the far side of the boatyard. See if you can get through to them that way. If you do, conceal yourselves and wait for a signal from me. And if you see anything, let me know."

"Okay," Carol said and turning to Martin added: "Let's go."

"Hold on." Fran looked at Lou. "Can I have a word?"

They moved away from the van towards the river.

"What is it, Fran?"

"Coaker may be armed. We need to wait for armed back-up. No-one's even wearing a vest."

"He's not going to wait while we follow procedure."

"What's he going to do? The MoD boat's covering the river and we're blocking the road. We've time to negotiate Connie's release and make sure no-one gets hurt."

"We don't know for sure that they're where I think they are." Lou was struggling to keep his temper. He knew Fran was right, the guidelines for hostage situations were clear. But if Coaker once got Connie into a boat and out to sea, the chances of getting her back safely became much slimmer. "We don't even know he hasn't already left with her."

Fran stood her ground. "Don't make this personal, Lou. Our first responsibility is for everybody's safety."

"We're going to see if they're there." Lou walked back, gesturing Carol and Martin towards the boatyard. As they walked away, he beckoned Jason to him. "Get a loud-hailer and come with me."

As Fran came up beside him, he was calm and firm. "Fran, you stay here and wait for special weapons. Let me know when they get here." He turned away. "Come on, Jason," he called and started towards the path leading up behind the boatyard.

* * * * *

Connie kept her eyes closed. Her head was pounding. Where was he taking her? What could she do to help herself? Where was Lou? Why hadn't he found her yet?

If she managed to jump into the sea before he could stop her, what could she do with tied hands except float on her back? He'd soon get her again, and then what?

The boat was rising and falling and rolling much more than before. She squinted through one half-opened eye. Clumps of spray were flying past. Another wave swept under the dinghy, tipping it landwards. Briefly, she glimpsed an unfamiliar headland, before it dipped and rolled back the other way. The sky's brilliance sent a lightning jag between her eyes and she squeezed them close again. Behind the lids, she saw an image of rocks and breaking waves, with grass and buildings rising above them.

After a long while, the movement of the boat eased, as if the sea had suddenly flattened. She squinted open again and saw a grassy cliff close by. A child in a bobble hat was waving, backed by three adults, it looked like. Could they see her? She was about to raise her tied hands and yell for help when a stinking tangle of fishing net landed on top of her.

"Lie still or I'll fillet yer!" Coaker hissed.

Through the coarse mesh, she lay watching the mosaic of sloping folds of grass and rock slipping by, until all was sky again, broken by an occasional mast. She couldn't make sense of where they were. A tiny bird darted onto the rim of the dinghy and off again. She thought of the caged sparrow in her parents' tiny apartment and a longing to see them overwhelmed her, until the jolting despair that she never would, not in this life, eclipsed their memory with returning terror.

The high-pitched whine of the outboard motor changed key and the bow of the boat seemed to settle further into the water beneath her. She felt it rub gently against something, losing momentum. She half-opened her eyes again and peered sideways through the netting at Coaker. He was standing up, reaching for the side of a yacht. Pulling with his hands, he edged the dinghy to the stern and hopped aboard. The tipping and recovery of the dinghy, as he sprang off it, lurched her one way and back again.

She watched him secure the dinghy's painter with a swift swirl of his hands before he disappeared out of sight. He was going to transfer her on to this boat. They'd be at sea. Nobody would know where they were. He could do what he wanted. She felt a flooding warmth spreading between her legs. "No!" she cried, kicking out furiously against the net, trying to get it off her. She would jump.

Almost as he landed back in the boat, his fist slammed against her jaw, cracking it sideways. Flipping her over, he knelt on her back and forced an oily rag between her teeth and knotted it tightly at the back of her head. He yanked her up and, grabbing the tie of her wrists, hauled her after him on to the yacht. Not waiting for her to stand up, he dragged her to the opening to the galley, swivelled her round and posted her feet first down the short flight of wooden steps. Her legs buckled as she hit the floor and she fell forwards, saving her face with stretched arms.

What little light there was disappeared as the hatch was clamped shut and she lay moaning in the darkness, her head pounding, the whole side of her face swollen with pain where he'd punched her.

Chapter 41
Empty nest

"We're in position. We can see the buildings and the landing stage below them." Carol's voice was low but clear. "There's no sign of movement inside and no boat by the landing stage."

"Stay as you are. Jason and I are at the gate above them. Once we've found a way in and down, I'm going to use the megaphone. Fran and armed back-up should be with you shortly."

"Who are you calling shorty?" came Carol's murmured reply.

Lou smiled, in spite of himself, as he slipped the phone back in his pocket. Her occasional silly jokes were as disarming as they were unexpected. The gate was padlocked and the coils of barbed-wire across its top made climbing the fencing hazardous. A teenage boy with a ginger pup of unguessable antecedents came round the bend from Mutton Cove. Lou saw him stop and stare at them.

"Jason, go and talk to that lad. See what he knows, then send him back out of harm's way."

Lou watched Jason walk away. Maybe he'd been wrong about him. He'd got more out of Babs Parker than he and Fran had. Whether it was his youth or his rebellious air, the public didn't seem to mind talking to him. There was something casual and unthreatening about his manner. The dog jumped up at him and he saw Jason bend down to play with it before even talking to the teenager, and when he did it was still from the crouched position, looking up. The boy smiled and became more animated, pointing towards the cottage and the water. His face was serious now, talking quickly, checking his watch, nodding. Lou saw Jason stand up and touch the boy's shoulder. The boy grinned, turned away down the path, clicking his fingers for the puppy to follow him. Lou couldn't hear the click but the gesture was clear.

"We're too late," Jason said, running up to him. "Ben's been playing with his dog down near the swimming pool. He says he saw two people come out of the cottage earlier on and he stopped to watch them because he thought the buildings were deserted, or at least..."

"What time was this?" Lou interrupted.

"He wasn't sure, thought about thirty or forty minutes ago."

Lou started striding back towards the boatyard, with Jason partly jogging to keep up. "Where did they go?"

"Down to the landing stage. Pulled a dinghy out from under it. Ben hadn't noticed it before. He said it had an outboard."

"Was it a man and a woman?"

"Two figures was all he could remember, one taller than the other and wearing a beanie, he thought."

"Which way did they go?"

"Towards Devil's Point."

Lou called Carol. "The birds have flown. You two go and have a look and meet me back at the slipway."

As they neared the boatyard, Fran saw them and came to meet them. While he updated her, Lou saw the concern in her eyes deepening under the frown of concentration. It added weight to the fear he was trying to keep at bay.

"We've got to move fast," he said. "Ring MCA and MoD and tell them what we're looking for. He's not going to put to sea in a dinghy, he must be hugging the coast."

Fran walked away towards the river, her phone in front of her and then up to her ear.

"Jason, get through to Macklin. Tell him what's happened and ask him to recall the back-up, wherever the hell they've got to," said Lou.

As Jason peeled away, Lou went to the railings near Fran and looked downstream to the mouth of the estuary. If Coaker had another boat ready...what more could they do? He pressed the contact number on his mobile.

"Debbie, can you get down to Sutton lock as fast as possible? You're looking for Coaker. He's taken Connie with him. They were in a dinghy, but'll need something bigger. MoD and MCA are on the look-out, but another pair of eyes, you know. If he gets out to sea..."

"I'm leaving now, Lou." He heard her add something; "Macklin" he thought, but it was muffled, her mouth away from the mic, and then the line went dead. He hadn't realised Fran had come up beside him and was waiting for him to finish.

"I was just talking to MCA. They may have something." The urgency in her voice sent a wave of adrenalin through his chest and arms. His fingertips were tingling. "While we were talking, they got a call from the Yealm Yacht Club at Newton Ferrers."

Lou was already moving towards his car and Fran went with him, still talking: "Someone rang them to say they'd seen a man boarding one of the yachts moored there. Some sort of neighbourhood watch against boat thieves. Thought he looked sus..."

"Let's go," he said as the car's indicators flashed and the locks clicked. "We can talk to Carol and Martin on the way."

As he reversed, Jason's face appeared at his window. He pressed the switch and it slid down. "Jason, stay here till they come for the van, then report back to Macklin." He didn't wait for a reply and was already past the Ocean Court flats by the time the window closed again.

Chapter 42
Ariel

It was early afternoon and the winter sun was already sinking towards the skyline, dragging a dark cloak over the slopes to the west. The day was dying and as the light started fading from the Yealm estuary, Coaker felt a new chill lifting off the water.

It was just a button; no need even to hotwire it. The engine caught with a couple of watery farts and a belch of oily smoke, then settled into a low chugging. He smiled as he checked the fuel tank. It was less than a quarter full, but that was more than enough. He wasn't coming back.

As he freed the rope from the mooring buoy, he felt the waste of her. She was a sound sloop, single-masted and fifty years old at least, but easy to sail single-handed. He looked around. The varnished mahogany was in good order and the rigging on the mast cased and tight. She was obviously well cared for. He hoped she'd be spotted and saved before she foundered. Boat thieves were scum but he had no choice. Once they'd cleared the estuary, with the sails up and the engine running, the three miles to international waters would take less than half-an-hour. Another hour or so after that and Laurent, or his brother Pascal, would be waiting. They just needed a time to be there.

Coaker checked his watch and texted Laurent: 15.45. As he raised the anchor, he thought of their previous rendez-vous. A vivid close-up of Nina's head hitting the cleat as she fell took him by surprise. Her panicked eyes and screaming mouth. He gave his head an angry shake to clear it, but the image hovered. "Stupid bitch!" he said, moving to the stern. He'd meant to knock her out, not kill her.

Standing to see over the cabin, he guided the sloop out into the main channel. He'd rig the sails once they were in open water. He ignored Connie's muffled shout from below and her short-lived banging on the hatch. He'd never imagined leaving Plymouth, living somewhere-else. A dark toad of anxiety squatted in his gut. What was he going to do in the long run? The chink would tide him over for now, but after that, what then? Ron Jellop had a place in the Caymans; maybe he could find something there. Ron owed him. Ahead he could see the lights of a yacht coming home. His own lights were not on; he wanted Invisibility. He kept to starboard and saw a man's face in a cap slide past in the gathering shadows, staring at him. Coaker raised his hand in greeting and, once past, opened the throttle a little wider.

Even if the man was suspicious and called the coastguard now, they'd be pushed to catch him, but he'd probably wait until he was moored before taking a decision, one way or the other. Besides, if he knew the boat, he'd probably try calling the owner first to make sure it wasn't a friend or relative.

As they rounded the final curve of the estuary, the deepening shade from the hills and cliffs began to give way to the lighter expanse of sea and sky, where the sun was sinking behind a blazing fringe of cloud, throwing into sharp relief the craggy outline of the Great Mew Stone to the west. He kept to port, clear of the buoys marking the sand bank at the point, and was about to move to free the sails when a black shape travelling fast across the bay towards him caught his eye. It was low in the water but growing larger and more distinct all the time.

He knew the MoD ribs well. There was no hope of outrunning one. Anyway, it might be nothing to do with him. Just act natural. He took out a tin, rolled a thin cigarette and lit it. As he cupped his hands and dipped his head to the flame, he heard the roar of the powerful engine closing. He looked up, letting the smoke sit in his chest and drift slowly out of the side of his mouth.

The engine note softened and the raised bow of the approaching inflatable sank back into the sea. There were three figures on board. He saw one lift a megaphone: "Ariel, kill your engine. We're MoD Police, Marine Unit. We believe this vessel to be stolen and we're coming aboard."

* * * * *

Fran's left hand holding the mobile came to rest against her thigh. "You can slow down," she said; "they've got him."

Lou had turned off the Kingsbridge road just past Kitley Hall and was taking the twists and turns of the narrow shortcut like a rally driver. "Where?" he said, changing down and braking hard for the right-angle turn on to a low stone bridge. He pulled off just before it, next to a couple of other cars already parked there by the side of the stream. He jerked round to face her.

"Mods intercepted him leaving the estuary."

"And Connie?"

"She's safe, Lou." Fran put her hand on his arm. "They have her too. She's okay."

He turned away and got out. She watched him walk away to the stream. He paused at the edge, his back to her, and fumbled in his coat pocket. She saw the white flash of a hanky and his arm moving upwards.

He wasn't long. "Back to the station then," he said, getting in. Later, as they crossed Laira Bridge on the outskirts of town, he said: "I'll see this through and that's it." But he seemed to be talking to himself, so Fran let it go.

Part Three

Monday, 23rd – Wednesday, 25th March, 2015

Chapter 43
Days of despair

"Come and have some scrambled eggs," Lou offered, pausing in the doorway. Connie's upright armchair was facing away from him. She sat gazing out of the window, above the small garden at the rear of her house, at the sky, at its milky, opaque brightness in the grey still of the day. He wanted to switch on the lights but knew she preferred to sit merging with the gloom.

"I'm not hungry," she said.

A divan was pushed against the wall in one corner and opposite was a large table, close to the window. Both were covered in the rubble of the patterns and materials of her abandoned knitting and dressmaking, a piece of scarlet silk still caught in the jaws of the sewing machine.

"You need to eat, Connie," he said gently.

"Later," she said, without stirring. "I'll have something later."

Lou hesitated. If he insisted, she'd get angry; if he left her, she'd stay there for hours. All he could see of her was the top of her head, a dark half-moon above the plain upholstery of her chair. He walked round beside her. She was still in her faded bathrobe, her hands loose in her lap, her elbows resting on the wooden arms.

Her hair had lost its sheen and hung down, unbrushed, one strand caught behind her ear. She looked so flattened, so vulnerable, he wanted to gather her up and squeeze her, hug some expression back into her empty eyes and face. But he knew it wouldn't work, that she would stand unresponsive as before, looking over his shoulder, not resisting, just inert and waiting to sit down again.

"Would you like a cup of tea?"

She looked up at him and noddcd. "Thank you."

"Connie..." he said, imploring her, and he stretched out the palm of his hand towards her. The weekend after next would be Easter and he wanted to suggest a break in the sun somewhere. But she turned away again to the window, and he let his hand fall back by his side.

She heard the creaking of the stairs as he went down to the kitchen. She liked to know he was there. But for now she just wanted to sit by herself. The opaque blankness of the sky was comforting. It asked nothing of her and she could rest there unseen. How could she have allowed it to happen? How could she have been so stupid? The moment Coaker pinned her up against the van replayed again and again in her mind and always it came with the stench of his breath and the coarse rasp of his stubble against her neck, as he fired his ugly words into her ear.

She wanted to be back in the dank, locked room, hidden from the world. She raised her hands in loosely-curled fists, pressing her wrists together, as if they were still bound. "You're no good, never were. Too skinny, too plain, too above yourself. What are you doing here? Why aren't you at home with your parents? You think you're so special. You're not special. Little job in little chemist. Can't even keep yourself safe. Thirty-seven, no children. You've done nothing but bring shame on your family. No good for Lou. You have nothing to give him. He will see this."

She heard him on the stairs again and let her hands fall back into her lap.

"I'll put it here," he said. He pulled a small bamboo table closer to her chair and placed the mug on it, with its handle towards her.

She stayed completely still and he hesitated, searching for words to reach her, soothe her.

"It's only been a couple of months, Connie. It takes time to recover from what you've been through. Don't expect too much of yourself...and it can help to talk about it...you know, when you're ready." He paused, hoping she might say something. But she didn't and his words sounded trite and empty to his own ears. Reassurance didn't help. He knew it.

"What am I trying to say?" he asked himself, struggling to catch hold of something real in himself to tell her. "I just want you to know that I love you," he said. When she made no reply, he added: "I'll be downstairs if you want me."

And he left her so quietly she wasn't sure if he was still there or not. After a while, when she couldn't bear the uncertainty of not knowing any longer, she looked over her shoulder to check, but there was only the open doorway and the dark passage beyond. She let go the effort of holding herself together under his gaze and sank back into the bleakness of her thoughts with a sense of relief.

People's eyes were more than she could bear. When she walked outside, she dreaded bumping into anyone who might recognise her, and she kept her face lowered towards the pavement. She wanted to disappear from view.

A small brown bird swooped on to the neighbour's guttering, its feathers ruffled by the wind. She followed the darting, watchful movement of its head and felt bereft when it flew off again, willing it back where it had been. She wanted life in safe, small pieces; she didn't want people. It would be good to be a small bird, to come and go unnoticed and unjudged.

What did it mean to say he loved her? What did it matter? He was a good man. He would find an English woman, someone with family here, someone who was settled and belonged. They would bed down together and have children...children, who would have aunts and uncles and grandparents close at hand.

She would go back to Hong Kong and get a job – an assistant in a chemist or a bank clerk – something routine and undemanding. She'd live with her parents, serve them and disappear into her own background. She would forget herself. Obscurity, to be invisible and unnoticed, that's what she wanted. And she thought of dying, of taking the path along the cliff edge from Cadgwith Cove to The Devil's Frying Pan and throwing herself in. Lou had taken her there in the autumn and it had thrilled her, scared her too, as she watched the wild sea exploding through the arch of rock, where a cave had collapsed in a hundred metre-deep hole, and sucking back again to reload. She could disappear there easily. It would be quick.

Extinction and the peace of it...the release from self. She longed for blankness, the blankness of the sky.

Chapter 44
Nexus and Nicole

Although it was a Monday, Nexus was already busy when Fran and Debbie Denton got there. It was a gay bar off Sutton Harbour and Fran's local, where she often met up with Kate and Molly and the others. Sometimes, as now, Debbie liked to join her for a drink after work − a chance to slough off the day's cares so that she didn't take them home to her husband and six-year-old daughter. The place was welcoming, with its open fire, soft lighting and comfortable chairs, and reflected the easy-going friendliness of Jay, the barman and owner.

They found a table over towards the bar. "My turn," Debbie said, hanging her coat over the back of the chair. She was soon back with a glass of red wine and a bottle of ginger beer, which she handed to Fran.

"Here's to Lou's return and lightening the load," she said, touching her glass to Fran's bottle.

"It may be a while yet, Debs. I spoke to him earlier and Connie's still very down. Besides, don't forget, five or six weeks and he'll be gone."

Debbie shook her head. "It still hasn't sunk in." She paused. "I don't like change. Lou's one of the good guys. Who knows who we'll get next?"

Fran's head jerked up. "Not all change is bad," she said. Debbie's sharp eyes tightened in a frown.

"Sorry, I didn't mean you." Debbie put her glass back on the table.

Fran shrugged.

"Anyway, how's it going? Better being a woman?"

259

The question took Fran by surprise. It was a stupid question and Debbie wasn't. She was a serious person and someone she respected. She looked away to a group in the corner by the fire, people she knew mostly, although she noted one striking woman she hadn't seen before, taller and older than the rest, with a strong profile and thick white hair layered to the nape of her neck. Sitting next to her was Kate, who saw her and gave her a wave. Fran nodded and turned back.

"I always was a woman," she said.

"Well, your clothes are sure the same, I'll give you that." Debbie looked her up and down. "Leather jacket, jeans, trainers..."

"Clothes are nothing to do with it," Fran interrupted, starting to bounce her heel up and down.

Debbie reached for her glass and took a mouthful, watching her over the rim. She set it down again.

"This isn't idle curiosity, Fran. At work, we're close...you know what I mean. I've always counted on you...absolutely. I want to understand, that's all." Fran felt the intensity of her focus on her, Debbie's eyes glittering with the same resolve as when hunting for answers on the computer. "Is it a physical thing? You know, not being comfortable in your body."

"Body's not the issue," Fran said.

"Isn't it? What about wombs and bleeding and babies. Women have all those. Men don't. You don't."

Fran stopped drumming her foot and leaned forward. "What's going on, Debs? I thought you got it."

"No, I don't get it. If it isn't biological, what is it? What does being a woman mean to you? If it's not about the body, but about...what...a way of being or something, why can't you be that way as a man?"

Fran looked down and circled the wolves on her finger, and when she spoke again, it was with a rigid kind of calm: "My sense of self is female. I never was a man to myself."

"Sounds like nurture to me," Debbie said. "Maybe if you'd been allowed a dustpan and brush from the toy shop instead of a gun, you'd have felt okay." She started to smile, but went on quickly with a new seriousness. "We've been friends from the off and I don't see any difference between you then and now. For heaven's sake, you look the same, you dress the same, you even use the same name. I don't see any change in you at all." The smile came back and spread this time. "'Cept you don't seem to have that fuzz on your chin any more."

Fran ran the backs of her fingers along her jaw. It was smooth. "That's the point," she said. "I've always been the same person."

"Okay, I give up!" Debbie glanced at the clock over the bar and drained her glass. "I've got to go." She stood up and pulled on her squall jacket with its fur-trimmed hood. "Come and have some food. We've got plenty. Put some flesh on those bones."

Fran smiled and shook her head. "No thanks. I'm meeting Molly and Kate. In fact, Kate's already here." She gestured to the group near the fire.

"Well, you're always welcome." Debbie bent down and kissed her on the cheek. "You need to eat, it's good for you." She took a couple of steps away, then turned and came back. "Look, I'm sorry, Fran. I didn't do that right. No offence meant. But this switching's been bothering me. It feels like something's wrong in our culture making people want to do that."

* * * * *

After she had gone, Fran went to the small horseshoe-shaped bar for a refill. There were occupied stools down one side and a crowded table spreading close on the other, so that access to the bar was limited and she had to wait her turn behind a balding man in a waistcoat. She watched the barman filling two glasses with red wine, his sculpted biceps in interesting contrast to his blue eye-shadow. The man in the waistcoat turned and stepped past her, a glass in each hand.

"How's it going, detective?" the barman said. Under his spiky blond hair and dark, curling lashes, his eyes flashed good humour at her.

"Better for seeing you, Jay," she said and meant it. His real name was Jason, but he always said he'd rather be a Gatsby than an Argonaut, although, between them, they knew that what he meant was he'd fallen for Robert Redford in the film version. As he liked to explain: "I can't call myself Daisy, can I?"

"What can I get you?"

She stood her empty bottle on the bar top. She felt winded by Debbie's unexpected attack. "Give me a Rattler. Thanks." It was a local, cloudy cider with a bite to it she liked, and although she seldom drank alcohol she wanted a hit now. "And a packet of peanuts," she added.

"Beware of snakes," Jay said as he flicked off the bottle cap with one hand and tapped the items into the cash register with the other. "They're nothing but trouble!"

Fran raised an eyebrow and smiled. "They don't bother me, Jay."

As she turned, the woman with white hair, whom she'd noted earlier, was waiting behind her and stood aside with a polite smile to let her pass. When Fran got back to her table and settled down again, she watched the woman as she ordered her drink and lingered, talking to Jay. There was an elegance that she couldn't quite fathom. As the woman turned, Fran noted the tapering black jeans and scooped tee under a fitted dove-grey jacket, with slim lapels and its sleeves pushed up. But it was more than just a matter of her clothes, something to do with her physical poise. She was tall and slender and she carried herself well, with her shoulders back and her chin raised, accentuating the strong line of her nose with its high bridge. Clearly, she was over sixty, and yet there was a fluidity and ease to her movements that spoke of someone much younger.

Fran saw her resume her seat with an aside to Kate. For a moment, Kate's laughing profile was caught in the firelight, as she turned to reply, lightly touching the other woman on her arm. Fran felt a stab of jealousy and looked away, taking a long pull from the neck of her bottle. "Stop being stupid," she told herself. Kate had been her best friend since they were eleven. Boyfriends, girlfriends, even a husband and her own switch hadn't changed that. Nor would this elderly bird of paradise, whoever she might be. Anyway, maybe it was more about fear of abandonment than jealousy.

She knew very little about her own parents, except that they had died at Zeebrugge in Belgium when she was a baby, when she had been too young to do anything to save them. But she'd fight for her family now, for Kate and Molly, and Lou too. He'd lost his father before he ever knew him. It was a bond between them.

Her own survival was a miracle. A hundred and ninety-three people, including her parents, died from hypothermia that night in March 1987, trapped inside the roll-on roll-off ferry bound for Dover. The bow loading door was still open as it left port and the sea poured in. Ninety seconds later, it capsized and the lights went out.

Fran twirled the bottle between her fingers, watching the snake coming and going. She was two months old and she'd been rescued.

"Oh, yes? And what schemes are you dreaming up?" Molly's sardonic voice was followed by the thump of a heavy carrier bag being dumped on the table. "People aren't safe when you frown like that."

"Molly!" she said, standing up. "I didn't..."

But before she could finish, she found herself wrapped in a bear hug, with her face buried in the colourful folds of Molly's shawl, which swirled from behind the upturned collar of her royal blue charity shop overcoat. Molly released her and took a step back, appraising her, while uncurling the shawl with one hand and starting to unbutton her coat with the other.

"You look leaner and younger every time I see you. What's your secret?"

Fran laughed. "Food on the run. What can I get you, Molly?"

"A very large gin and tonic. Beefeater's."

* * * * *

By the time she returned with the drink, Molly had already disappeared over to the table in the corner. She was standing behind Kate's chair, with one hand on her shoulder, while chatting to the group and gesticulating with the other. Fran often wondered, as now, where Molly got her energy from. For someone who spent five-and-a-half days a week counselling female victims of domestic abuse, she seemed to have an insatiable appetite for social interaction. Being overweight didn't slow her down in the slightest. Her chins shook as she laughed and chatted, and she constantly pushed her unruly ginger curls back off her forehead and away from her eyes, even though they sprang back there almost at once.

Fran watched Kate leaning to one side to look up at Molly, her lips pursed in amusement. Sometimes, like now, when she looked at Kate she experienced an ache of longing that was bitter-sweet, like grief. She was the sister she had never had. Molly was special, too, but it was different; she was more grown-up. But as a threesome it worked between them. She and Kate were the mischievous twins and Molly was their magnanimous minder. The term they all became friends was the first time she felt like she wasn't alone in the world. The thought took her back to the fire escape at the children's home, the black wrought iron zigzag, with entry platforms you could sit on at every floor. She always sat at the top with a view over the rooftops to the valley below.

The orphanage had been okay, except for the lack of privacy. She'd spent a lot of time up the fire escape on her own. As she brushed some peanut crumbs off the table, she reflected on the irony of needing to be alone to feel less lonely. That was until she changed schools and was befriended by Kate and Molly, who had come up together. They turned her world from monochrome to colour and released some hidden warmth inside her that she'd never known before.

"We've already met." Had she heard that or simply read her lips? The elegant stranger was standing up, her face visible. She was shaking Molly's hand, as Kate introduced them. Well, if Molly already knew her, maybe that explained her presence in the group. Another wave of possessive jealousy rolled through her. She knew she should go over and join them to get rid of this feeling of hostility towards someone she didn't even know. They weren't excluding her; she was doing that to herself.

Kate glanced round, saw her and waved her over. She stood hand on hip, waiting for her. Fran got up, took Molly's glass and walked across. Some of the others seeing her coming shifted closer together to make space, and Kate pulled an extra stool across from the next table.

"Fran, come and meet Nicole," Kate said, coming forward to greet her. She put an arm round her shoulders and steered her in.

"My Saviour!" Molly beamed, taking her drink. "Thank you."

"Nicole, this is my good friend Fran."

"Hello, Fran," Nicole said.

Her handshake was firm and the steady blue eyes held hers a moment longer than was comfortable.

"Hi, Nicole," she said and sat down on the stool. She was glad the introduction was over and she quickly immersed herself in the easy banter of the group, happy to have the excitement of Kate's closeness on her right and the grounded security of Molly on her left.

A little before midnight, Jay came over to them. "Hey, guys, there's a taxi here for Nicole Lanui?"

"Ah, yes, that's me," Nicole said. "Thank you."

Lanui? The name was deeply familiar, but Fran couldn't place it. She watched Nicole as she put on her coat and said her goodbyes, hoping for a clue, but nothing came.

After she'd gone, Fran turned to Molly. "Nicole Lanui, have you met her before?"

"Yes, in Madrid last summer. You know, the Pride festival? Interesting woman. Lives in Spain, somewhere near Barcelona. Can't remember the name now. On the coast anyway. But she's spent a lot of time in India and the States. Used to be a Buddhist. Don't know if she still is."

"Her name, Lanui, I know it from somewhere, but can't think where. What's she doing in Plymouth?"

"Here we go," Kate interrupted, resting her chin on Fran's shoulder. "DCI Jane Tennison back on the case."

"She's a photographer," Molly said. "Over here taking shots for a travel brochure. Maybe you've seen her work somewhere and saw her name."

"No, it's not that." Fran shook her head. The name had a deeper resonance than that.

"Stop thinking about it," she told herself, "and it'll come back to you." Instead, she tried to concentrate on a proposal the others were talking and arguing about for an online local LGBT magazine. But the name kept hovering in her thoughts and she was itching to check her notebook to see if something there might cue her into it.

* * * * *

It was only later, after Molly had dropped her on the corner by her flat, that she was able to do so. She sat on the edge of her bed, flicking through her notebook, while kicking her trainers off and freeing herself from her jacket at the same time. There was nothing there remotely connected. She closed it and chucked it on to the bedside table on her way to the bathroom.

As she cleaned her teeth, watching the white froth gathering at the corners of her mouth and wishing she'd remembered to leave the brush on its charger, she started to think about the next day. Lou was still off because of Connie. The team were pulling together okay and the paperwork for the CPS was pretty much sorted, thanks to Macklin. But things never felt quite so secure as when Lou was there. She spat and rinsed, sticking her mouth under the cold tap.

Leaving on her pants and t-shirt, she slid into bed. She'd shower and change in the morning; she didn't have the energy now. The sheet was cold and turning on to her side she hugged the duvet tight over her shoulders and up to her chin. She thought about Lou and Connie. She understood why Connie was so depressed, but sitting looking out of the window all day long wasn't going to help her get over what she'd been through. She was just sinking deeper and deeper into it. "Doing nothing isn't an option!" She grinned in the dark at her own mantra. No, Connie needed help to get back in the saddle. Isn't that what people said? If you fall off a horse, you need to get straight back on, as soon as you can, or maybe you never will.

Why didn't Lou take her to Hong Kong, back to her roots and family? What an obvious, good idea. She wanted to call Lou and suggest it right away but she'd have to wait. Anyway, he must have leave due. He wouldn't need to wait for his official departure; he could go now. She tried to remember when he was last away. He'd been to Italy with his mother on the trail of his grandfather or great-grandfather, was that it? But that was a couple of years back, surely. No, a trip to Hong Kong would give Connie distance, put Coaker in perspective and...Louis! That was it. Louis Lanui! Of course...the vanishing dad.

She turned on to her back and stretched out her legs. So what? There must be a load of Lanuis in the world. Even so, it wasn't that common. Nicole could be a cousin or something. Besides, she was right here. It must be worth asking the question. She'd tell Lou in the morning, let him decide.

Chapter 45
Lou gets a call

The following morning, Lou carried a tray of fresh coffee and croissants up to the bedroom. The curtains were open, but the room was still dim. He balanced the tray on the edge of the bedside table, pushed the book and box of tissues to the back and slid it further on, until it was properly supported, before switching on the lamp.

Connie was lying with her back to him facing the wall, just the shrouded top of her head showing above the puffy peaks of the duvet. He put a hand near her shoulder. "I've brought you some breakfast." She didn't stir and he wondered if she was still asleep. But as he took his hand away she turned and pushed herself up, stuffing his pillow behind her head on top of her own.

"Thank you." She squinted at the lamp. "Do you mind?" Her breath was warm and fecal and he ducked his head to the side as he lent to switch it off and pass her the tray.

"If you don't need me for anything," he said, "I'm going to go to sort things out at home and maybe see what the surf's like at the same time." The very thought if it seemed to bring his body to life and he felt guilty at the relief he felt to be escaping the pall of her unhappiness.

She pushed the tray off her lap, where he had placed it, down beside her and sank back. "I'm fine," she said. "You go."

"Okay, if you're sure." She nodded without looking at him. "I'll go right now and then I should be back by..." The urgent cry of his mobile sliced into the room. "...lunchtime," he finished, fishing the phone out of his pocket and carrying it into the passage.

"Lou, it's Fran. You got a minute?"

"Sure. What is it?"

"Something's come up. Couple of things in fact. Could I come over, or meet you at the Roses maybe?"

"I'm busy this morning, Fran. What's it about?"

"Personal, not work. I've got an idea for helping Connie and a bit of news for you."

Lou felt curious. Fran was jealous of her time and she sounded excited. "Okay, better make it the Roses. Connie's not up to...you know...seeing people at the minute."

"Right. What time, then?"

"Eight o'clock?"

"Sorry, Lou, I've got training this evening."

"Okay, how about..."He paused. He'd been thinking he would go after supper but maybe before would be better. He'd been doing most of the cooking but Connie wouldn't mind for once. Might be good for her. "How about five?"

"Fine. See you then."

* * * * *

The post-rush-hour traffic was light and Lou made good time to Wembury. As he opened the bungalow's front door, it jammed against the envelopes and catalogues fanned out across the mat. He scooped them up and walked through to the kitchen, flipping quickly through them and leaving them in a pile beside the kettle, as he made a cup of tea. None of it needed his attention now and he had better things to do, but he felt irritated that the letters he was waiting for hadn't come; neither the formal response to his letter of resignation, nor details of the state of his police pension.

He carried his mug through to the living room and was immediately aware of the quality of the light. Connie's house was surrounded by buildings and trees. When he looked out of her windows, the sky was broken up by rooftop chimneys and branches, and the downstairs rooms were gloomy without the lights on, even in the daytime. Whereas here, the wide horizon and uninterrupted expanse of sea and sky flooded the bungalow with light. It was the reason he had bought it. He stood in front of the picture window overlooking the bay and watched the white sails of a yacht disappearing behind the Mewstone. Gauzy, overlapping clouds were sailing past out over the sea, blown by a brisk north-easterly breeze. He followed the dark, moving creases in the water, as the rollers came sweeping in. At the eastern end of the bay, a dozen or so black shapes bobbed in and out of view until he saw the flash of quick hands and a body rise, poised over the creaming edge of a breaker, the board barely visible.

A longing to be in the water broke through his despondency. His board and wetsuit were still in the car; all he needed was a fresh towel.

* * * * *

Later, as he drove back, the traffic was backed up over the Laira Bridge and slow-moving all the way into the city centre. He avoided the police station and paid to park at a meter off Ebrington Street. The Roses was full of end-of-day workers having a 'quick one' before heading home, chatting and laughing loudly, newly energised at their reprieve, together with a few stalwarts he recognised, who seemed permanently moored to their bar stools.

Fran was facing him at a table half-way down. The waves had been good; no breaking up in the middle, just a long, continuous unscrolling. He could feel the new relaxation in his muscles as he moved and his skin was still tingling from the slap and sting of the sea. He didn't want to blunt the sharpness of it with alcohol and collected up a soda water on his way over to her.

"You been in the water?" she said as he sat down. "You've got that glow about you."

"Yeah," he said. "Great out there today. Just what I needed."

She nodded, watching him, taking him in. "How's Connie?"

Her question cast a shadow over him. "She's depressed." That said it all. What was the point of saying more? "It's like she's fallen down a pit. I can see her but I can't reach her."

"I've had an idea about that, Lou. That's why I wanted to see you."

"Go on."

"Why don't you take her to Hong Kong to see her parents? A change of scene, back with her roots, you know, it could drag Coaker out of the foreground and stick him in some kind of perspective."

He nodded and took a drink. Maybe he wouldn't have to serve out his time. He had holidays due. Maybe Maynard would let him go early.

"Might be worth trying," he said, "if she'll go. Trouble is, right now, she hardly leaves the bedroom, let alone the house. I'm sure she'd like to see her family but whether she could face the train journey up, let alone getting on a plane, I don't know."

He couldn't imagine her going willingly into a steel cigar tube that would imprison her thousands of feet off the ground for hours on end. He saw her getting as far as the cabin entry and then bolting down the steps back on to the tarmac and the open air.

"Lying trussed up in a stinking shack, not knowing if you're going to be knifed or raped...or both!" Fran stuck her thumb in the neck of her bottle of ginger beer and flicked it out with a hollow pop, then tried it again.

Lou saw the anger in the gesture as she flicked her thumb a third time.

"But I'll be with her," he said. "Maybe she'll feel safe enough with that. Anyway, I'll talk to her, see what she thinks."

The bottle was empty and Fran pushed it away from her to the edge of the table by the wall.

"There's something else," she said. "It may be a nothing coincidence but it could be significant."

Lou smiled. "Is this the famous Bannerman straight-talk?" he said.

She coloured and he regretted his cheap joke. "Sorry, just joshing" he said. "What is this coincidence?"

Before she could answer, a young woman with earphones and a tray came past, collecting empty glasses, and Fran had to sit back as she leant across her to take the bottle.

"Happy to be here for you," the young woman said, moving away.

"Don't ask," Fran said, as Lou raised an eyebrow. "Where were we?"

"A coincidence."

"That's right...okay...the short cut is I was at Nexus last night and I met this woman Molly knows. She's a photographer from Spain on a job over here. But the point is her name's Nicole Lanui."

"Lanui?" Lou slapped his half-raised glass back on the table.

"Yes, that's what she said. I knew it from somewhere but couldn't place it, and then remembered your dad. He was called Lanui, wasn't he?"

Lou sat staring at her but his thoughts were far away, back in Arcachon, wearing shorts and trailing round dusty streets with his mother. Fran waited, giving him time.

"Do you know where she's staying?" he said at last. "I need to speak to her." His tone was self-possessed but she knew him too well not to register the excitement in his eyes.

"Yes, I checked this morning. She's at the Holiday Inn. Popular place."

Lou checked his watch and stood up.

"Look, this may be nothing, like you said. But I've got to check it out. I need to see Connie first, make sure she's all right, and then I'll go straight round." He shifted his chair back and stood up. "'Nicole' you said, right?"

She nodded.

"Fran, if this leads to Louis Lanui, after all these years..." He trailed off, shaking his head at the enormity of it. "Well..." He dropped his hand and turned to go.

Chapter 46
Lou & Nicole

On his way back to Connie's house, Lou's first impulse was to ring his mother. But he checked himself. There were plenty of Beradinos in the world who had no idea of his existence. Why should the Lanuis be any different? If a Mickey Beradino in the Bronx or a Caterina Beradino in Bergamo had never heard of DCI Lou Beradino in Plymouth, why the hell should a photographer from Spain called Nicole Lanui know anything about an untraceable Louis Lanui from Arcachon?

Even so, he wished he could go straight round to the Holiday Inn and question her. But Connie would have a meal ready and she needed to know, not just in her head, but in her bones, that she could count on him. Besides, although Nicole Lanui was playing havoc with his nervous system, the rational core of him wanted to test Fran's idea for a trip to Hong Kong on Connie. The more he thought about it, the more sense it made.

Nevertheless, when he pulled up outside the house, he sat quietly with the engine running for several minutes before switching off and going in.

He found Connie sitting at the table, their food dished up. From time to time, she made macaroni cheese baked in the oven as a treat, from a recipe his mother had given her. It was the only Italian dish she knew and he never had had the heart to tell her that although it had been a favourite of his as a boy, he wasn't that keen on it any more. But the disappointment he felt was almost instantly replaced by hope at her thoughtfulness. If she was starting to re-engage with him, perhaps her mood was changing.

"What you been doing?" she said as he kissed the top of her head on his way past her to the chair opposite. "I saw you coming five minutes ago. I hurry, get the food ready, but it getting cold by now I think."

"Sorry," he said. He sat down and stretched out his hand across the table to her. But she ignored it, putting a forkful of macaroni in her mouth with one hand and leaving the other resting in her lap. He withdrew his slowly and added: "I was just thinking about what Fran told me, trying to get my thoughts straight."

"You don't want to come in. Had enough of this miserable person." She had stopped eating and was staring at her plate, her fork half-way in the air.

"No, Connie. Absolutely not. It wasn't that. Not at all." He stretched his hand across again and took her loosely by the wrist. "I've had an idea...well, it's Fran's really...and I was just sitting there thinking it through."

"What idea?" she said.

"Why don't we go to Hong Kong and see your parents? See your friends too." She looked up at him but the flat discs of her eyes were unreadable. "We can stay as long as you like. I want to meet your family and you can show me round...show me all the things that were important to you...that are important to you. What do you think?"

He waited. She was looking straight at him but she wasn't seeing him; he knew that. He wanted to start eating. He wanted to check the time. Most of all, he wanted to know her answer. But he didn't dare move, as if she was walking a tightrope and he mustn't do anything to distract her.

Finally, her focus returned. He felt the connection. "Fran clever woman," she said. "You say thank you from me." That must mean yes, he thought, letting go the breath he didn't even know he was holding. "See my parents is a good idea. Be in Hong Kong again, forget all this."

There was even a little of the old sing-song in her voice. It was like watching a film flickering between black-and-white and colour. He gave her wrist a gentle shake and released her. "That's great!" he said, pulling the bowl of salad towards him. "Let's go as soon as we can arrange it."

* * * * *

It was getting on for nine o'clock by the time Lou parked near The Holiday Inn and approached reception. He introduced himself to a jovial man in uniform behind the counter and asked him to let Nicole Lanui know he wished to talk to her.

"No problem, Inspector." The man dialled the room number but there was no reply. "Shall I page her for you? She may be in the bar or the restaurant."

Lou nodded and listened to the announcement: "Please could Ms Lanui come to reception, where a visitor is waiting for her."

"Thank you," he said, looking across the foyer to the bar's comfortable armchairs, hoping to see someone stand up. But no-one did, until two Japanese men in suits rose and turned towards the lifts. Businessmen, he thought, and wondered what had brought them to Plymouth. After they disappeared, the hotel settled back into its late evening hush, barely disturbed by the occasional movements of the barman polishing the surfaces of his domain.

"Must be out savouring Plymouth's wild night life, eh Inspector?" The receptionist smiled broadly, clearly delighted at his own wit. "Would you like to leave a message for her?"

"No, that's okay. I'll wait."

He moved away to a seat on the other side, from where he had an uninterrupted view of the hotel's lobby. A surge of voices and laughter caused him to look across the bar area to his right to the lounge beyond, where a group of four were playing cards. As the deck was shuffled and a new hand dealt, they quietened again, fanning and sorting their cards.

He glanced back at the sliding glass doors midway to reception. 'Tall, elegant, white haired,' according to Fran; he should recognise her easily enough. As he waited, he thought of Fran. She'd make a good DI, if they gave her the chance, and his conscience would be easier if he knew she was leading the team. But it would feel strange not being a policeman after so long. He realised he enjoyed the status of his rank more than he'd thought. Was it really the right move to give it all up? Other people in the force had good marriages. Well, some of them anyway. It depended on their partners. Anyway, tonight, with Ms Lanui, he would be plain Lou Beradino. He was here on his own account.

The inner doors slid open and a draught of cool air delivered two men inside; a young man in a black puffer jacket, closely followed by an older one in jogging pants and a sweat top. The jogger made for the lifts, while the puffer jacket spoke briefly to the receptionist, before leaving again.

He checked his watch; he'd only been there twenty minutes or so. It reminded him of being on stakeout: the crawl of time and the tedium, yet with an underlying tension and sense of anticipation. Maybe Nicole was Louis' ex-wife, or even his sister or a cousin and had known him all her life. Why 'ex' wife? What did he know?

Again, the inner doors glided open, ushering in a smartly-dressed couple, who halted and stood talking four or five yards in front of him. She was medium height. You wouldn't call her tall, he decided. And her hair wasn't exactly white either; it had grey in it. She rested her palm on the man's lapel for a moment and said something that caused him to smile and nod. With a final pat, she moved away towards the lifts, while he ambled into the bar.

It wasn't her. She was smart but not elegant, and there was something unequivocally British and middle-class about her, something that spoke of potted geraniums. Besides, as far as he knew, Nicole was on her own, unless she'd picked up someone. But these two were married, not impatient lovers; long years of acceptance and familiarity were written into their every gesture.

He'd give her until ten o'clock. Connie would be worrying; she didn't like being on her own, especially after dark. If Nicole Lanui wasn't back by then, he'd leave a message and his number. It was just after a quarter to, however, when she walked in; tall, elegant and white-haired, with the poise and self-assurance of a woman used to being admired. He stood up quickly and intercepted her.

"Ms Lanui?" he said.

"Good evening." She lowered her head to look at him.

He thought she was going to continue, but she didn't. He felt wrong-footed and reached for his warrant card.

"Detective Inspector Beradino. I know it's late but I'd like to have a word with you, if I may."

"You may." She gave him a laconic smile and led the way to a secluded corner table.

"So, Inspector Beradino," she said, easing her coat from her shoulders on to the back of her chair, "how can I help you?"

In his experience, few people got his name right after one hearing and those who did were either foreigners or, if home grown, of Italian descent. Nicole had 'continental' stamped all over her, from the relaxed chic of her clothes to the composed modulation of her voice.

"It's quite straightforward," he began, but his throat tightened and he started to choke and cough.

"Are you all right?" she asked, rising. "Can I get you some water?"

He raised his hand to signal for her not to, as the spasm subsided. "No, no. I'm fine, thank you." He cleared his throat and swallowed. "Excuse me."

She sat down again, watching him closely.

He hesitated. His mouth was dry. "Actually, I think you're right." He stood up. "I will get some water."

When he returned, he was carrying two tall glasses and the ice clinked against their sides as he set them down.

"Salud!" she said, picking hers up, and they touched glasses.

"Ms Lanui," he began, "the matter I want to talk to you about is a personal one. It's not a police matter."

"How intriguing!" She looked amused.

He put his glass down. "Let me explain. My colleague, Fran Bannerman, told me she met you the other evening in Nexus."

"Ah, yes. I remember her, of course. She is a friend of Molly Weaver, no?"

"Yes. Yes, she is. And the point is she mentioned your name to me, because she knows I'm interested in tracing someone also called Lanui and thought you might be able to help me."

"Certainly, if I can I will, although my own close family are all dead now. I was the only child of my parents, but I have some cousins anyway."

Lou hesitated. It was the first possible lead to his father in more than thirty years. And when Fran had told him her news, it was as if she had rolled away a rock blocking the sepulchre of all his boyhood hopes and dreams. He swallowed the rest of his water and breathed in deeply.

"The person I'm looking for is a certain Louis Lanui?" He watched her closely as he spoke and saw the momentary start of surprise in her eyes before she looked down at her own glass and took a slow sip. "Originally, he came from Arcachon near Bordeaux," he added, alert now. This woman knew something. He waited.

"What is your interest in this person, Inspector?"

"That's confidential." She looked up sharply. "However, any information you can give me will be much appreciated." His tone had become official. He heard it and regretted it.

"Then I can't help you." She reached behind her, pulling her coat back over her shoulders.

"The name is obviously known to you," Lou said.

"I'm sorry. I have an early start tomorrow. So, if you will excuse me."

As she stood up, he rose too. "One moment. Please. I expressed myself badly." She paused in front of him. "Louis is not in any trouble. As I said earlier, this is not a police matter. It's private, and I think he may well be glad to hear from me, if I can find him."

She stared at him for a long time, before she said finally: "I might be able to put you in touch with Louis, but I need time to think about this, particularly as you will not tell me why you want to find him. You must understand I have his interests to consider, as well. So, allow me to sleep on it and if you give me your number I will ring you in the morning and give you my answer."

He took out his notebook and wrote down both Connie's landline number and the one for his mobile. He tore out the page and handed it to her. "You'll be able to reach me on either of these." She took it and folded it into her pocket. "And thank you."

"Good night, Inspector."

As she walked away towards the lifts, he wondered whether she would speak to Louis first and, if so, what his reaction would be. Would he put two and two together? And again, if so, how would he feel about the possibility of having a middle-aged son he knew nothing about? What if he already had family of his own?

"I would want to know," he said softly, turning to leave. "I would definitely want to know."

Chapter 47
Facing the demons

Earlier that same day, out towards the moors at Yelverton, Rachael Drew had been confronting her own demons. It had been weeks before Oliver's decaying corpse was found snagged on rocks near Pickle-combe Point, half-covered by debris from the crumbling cliff there. At last, the long-delayed funeral was over; and the boys weren't due back at school for another few days, until Sunday afternoon anyway.

She didn't want them to go back at all. As it was, they would only have one more week there before breaking up for the Easter holidays, but the headmaster had been insistent: "At times like these, Mrs Drew, boundaries are more important than ever. While Nicholas and Samuel may be feeling their world is falling apart, it is up to us to show them that it is not." Feeling overwhelmed by the decisions required of her in sorting out Oliver's affairs, she hadn't had the energy or the will to argue with him.

She took her mug of coffee through to the living-room and stood by the patio doors, looking across the garden. It was a fine, bright morning and the sunshine through the glass was warm on her arms and chest. A couple of blackbirds were swooping in and out of the hawthorn near the summerhouse, their beaks as vivid a yellow as the forsythia hedge behind the pond. Clusters of raspberry-coloured flowers were already frothing on the winter currant close by. Why rush? Why not let the boys finish the year and decide what to do then?

"New year, new nest," she murmured. That was another decision waiting to be made. She wanted to move. She wanted to leave Oliver and Yelverton behind and make a fresh start. But she wasn't sure what would be best for Nick and Sam. They'd just lost their father, so was it fair to ask them to give up their home as well?

The phone rang in the hall and she went to answer it.

"Hello, Rachael, it's Polly."

"Polly! What a lovely surprise! How are you?" As she spoke, she carried the receiver back into the other room and sat down in the armchair facing the garden.

"I'm all right, although things have been difficult. Look, is this a good time to talk? I can ring back later if not."

"No, Polly, it's fine. The boys are still in bed and I'm just having a coffee and enjoying the feeling of spring in the air."

"Good. That's good." Polly sounded subdued and Rachael felt an instant stab of regret for not having been in touch with her. "I'm glad you have them home with you; you'll need each other at a time like this. And I'm very sorry, Rachael, that we weren't able to come to the funeral. I wouldn't..."

"No, that's all right, Polly. I understand. I got your message. How is Ron?"

"He's a bloody fool!" Rachael had never heard Polly swear before. The unexpectedness of it, combined with the exasperation in her voice, made her laugh.

"Sorry. I know it's not funny. It's just..."

"Luckily, he's a physically strong fool," Polly carried on, as if she hadn't spoken. "His liver's damaged but it will recover, apparently. I'm picking him up tomorrow."

Rachael was feeling lost. "Picking him up from where? I thought you were talking about...you know...the foreign girls he'd brought over here."

"Well, that too! How could he have been so greedy? We had more than enough. I still don't understand it. But, no, he took an overdose. Paracetamol."

"Oh God, Polly, no! When?"

"Last Thursday? Friday? I don't know, I've lost track. There's been so much going on. They took his passport. It was the last straw." She paused and Rachael heard the pad of footsteps overhead. "Another form of running away, I suppose."

"What do you mean?" Rachael asked, getting up and walking through to the kitchen. The boys would be down soon. She started pulling boxes of cereal out of the cupboard, standing them in a row on the breakfast bar.

"He had flights booked for the Caymans. He hadn't told me. I found them after the ambulance had been. He couldn't face being sent to prison, I knew that, but I didn't think..." Polly's voice wavered. "We've known each other since we were five, Rachael. Our families lived in Looe back then. We were in the same class."

Rachael slid the sugar bowl across from the kettle. "That's almost your whole life. I hadn't realised." The sadness in Polly's voice penetrated her self-preoccupation. "Let's arrange something, Polly. I'd really like to see you and have some proper time together. It's been so long and so much has happened, and right now the boys are about to come down wanting breakfast. Can we meet somewhere...soon? You're welcome to come here if you want."

"All right. What about this afternoon? I won't have much time, once Ron's home." Polly's decisiveness surprised her.

"Okay...yes...that's fine," she said, putting her finger to her lips at Sam as he appeared through the doorway in his dressing gown, with Nick just behind him, already dressed. "The boys are going to the cinema this afternoon." Sam looked round at Nick and punched a triumphant fist in the air, like a tennis player.

"What time shall I come?"

"Oh, I don't know...let's say any time after two. Nick and Sam are taking the bus in." Both boys grimaced and shook their heads.

"Okay. I'll come early. I told Ron I'd visit him about five."

"Great. See you then."

"Rachael?"

"Yes?"

"We'll help each other get through this."

Rachael wasn't sure if it was a statement or a question.

"Yes, Polly, we will...and thanks."

As she slotted the receiver back on its charging cradle, she felt less alone. Polly knew about Roger. There was nothing she had to hide from her and it would be such a relief to be able to talk openly.

She watched Sam stretching for a third teaspoon of sugar to sprinkle over his Weetabix and banana. "Sam, no! You'll rot your teeth."

He grinned at her. "I thought brown was all right."

"It doesn't matter," Nick chipped in. "They're only his milk teeth, anyway."

Sam aimed a punch at his shoulder but Nick swayed to the side and he missed.

"Here," said Rachael, retrieving the local paper from a pile on the unit behind her. She pulled it loose and handed it to Nick. "See what film you both want to go to and what time it starts." She stressed 'both'.

Nick took it and folded it in half when he reached the listings. "Look, *Run All Night*," Nick said, stabbing the listings with his finger. "Meant to be awesome."

"*Theory of Everything* is on as well, though." Sam pointed and looked at Nick hopefully.

Nick glanced at Rachael, then leant close to Sam and whispered in his ear.

"S'pose so," she heard Sam mumble as he went back to eating his cereal.

Nick would get his way, she knew that. Sam was a peacemaker, he didn't like rows, whereas Nick was single-minded and dogged. Resisting the urge to intervene, she went back to the living-room. They would have to sort it out between themselves. More than ever, now that Oliver was gone, she wanted to improve her relationship with Nick. She couldn't always be taking Sam's side. However much he might resist the idea, Nick was going to need her. He'd kick against that and make life difficult, but she'd have to stay calm and rise above it. She was the adult. He needed her to kick against; that's what parents were for.

She looked around the room, realising, as if for the first time, how much it was a reflection of Ollie's tastes and preferences and how little of her there was in it.

"Trust me," he had said. "I think my sense of colour is a wee bit more developed than yours." She snorted at the memory. Wee! He wasn't Scottish; yet he often used it, as if it somehow mollified the put down he was uttering. On the other hand, it seemed to work; and people didn't...she didn't...take offence, until it was too late. The knife went in and out so quickly, you didn't realize you'd been stabbed until the blood started congealing around your savaged self-esteem.

The colours were bold and jarring, and she felt every bit as oppressed by them as she had by him. She hadn't wished him dead; she wanted the boys to have a father. But she had wanted to be free of him and she was glad that she was.

"Mother," a voice said from the door. She turned in time to see Nick advancing towards her, with Sam following a step or two behind, his face still puffy from sleep. "We want to talk to you."

She fought against the instant hostility she felt towards his manner, towards his self-assurance and assertiveness.

"Nick, do you have to call me mother? You know I don't like it."

He sat down in Oliver's armchair and stretched his legs out in front of him, crossing them at the ankles. "Sam," he said, "you take the sofa and mother can have the other chair."

Sam gave her a glance and did as he was bid, while she plonked herself down beside him, stuffed a cushion behind her and settled back. "Right. What's this all about?"

Nick's mouth twisted in irritation, as he was forced to draw in his legs again, in order to shunt the armchair around to face her more comfortably.

"It's to do with Dad's murder," he started, and she felt Sam's involuntary shudder. "We don't understand why that man killed Dad and attacked you, do we Sam?"

"No," Sam said, looking at the carpet, his voice low. "He must be mad or something."

Rachael felt the blood burning her cheeks and saw the glitter in her elder son's eyes. She would not lie, but she would choose how much to reveal.

"Roger Millman was my lecturer at Tamar College. It seems he became obsessed with me, and he was stalking me the night he attacked us." In spite of her resolve, she dipped her head, suddenly dizzy and nauseous as the violence and horror of the night came back at her.

"But why would he want to kill you?" Sam asked, twisting towards her, his voice anxious.

"Yes, it doesn't seem to make sense, does it? But I think it's a form of possession, in a way." She looked back at Nick and softened towards him. He always attacked, when he was hurt. "You know, sort of 'if I can't have you, then no-one will'."

"But that's crazy!" Sam objected. "Then he loses you altogether."

"No," said Nick. "I get it. I take your life, your life is mine." His eyes swivelled back to her. "That's it, isn't it?"

"Yes, Nick; I think that is it."

"So, Dad died because of you." His voice was thin and sharp. "Because Millman wanted you, wanted to..."

"Enough, Nick!" she shouted, leaping up and standing as a shield, between his words and Sam. She felt unnerved. What did he know? How could he know? "That will do."

"No, it won't!" He thrust himself up out of the armchair. He was taller than her and he stood bending over her, his face red and tight with anger. "Dad's dead, because you gave some fucking pervert the come-on!"

"Stop it, Nick!" Sam was up and pulling at his brother's arm. "You can't say things like that. He tried to kill Mum, too."

"Get off me!" Nick hissed, whirling round. He shoved Sam hard in the chest with both hands, sending him stumbling and falling backwards.

When he looked back at his mother, his face was creased with fury, tears running in the reddened rims of his eyes. His chest was heaving and Rachael's hand flew to protect her throat, but he turned away, swinging his arm and sweeping the onyx lamp off the side table on to the carpet. It landed on its side, undamaged.

He raised his foot. "Don't!" Sam yelled. But Nick stamped down hard, crushing the lampshade and exploding the bulb inside it. Without moving, they watched him march out of the room and waited in silence until they heard the slam of a door upstairs.

"What's his problem?" Sam said, accepting her hand to help him up.

"He's hurting, Sam," she said. "We get angry when we're hurt. Are you okay?"

"Not really," he said, retying his dressing-gown. "Everything seems a bit crap."

She sighed, gave him a wan smile and tapped his shoulder. "Come on, help me pick this lot up."

After they had cleared up, Sam sat straddling the arm of the sofa, watching her pushing the vacuum cleaner backwards and forwards, sucking up the remaining fine particles of glass caught in the carpet's weave. Its roaring whine hurt his ears and he waited until she switched it off and pulled out the plug.

"What's happened to that man, the one who killed Dad? Where is he?"

She finished coiling the lead into place, then stood up and faced him, pushing her hair back out of her face.

"Roger Millman, you mean? He's in prison, in Exeter. They'll keep him there until the trial."

"When will that be?"

"Nobody seems to know. Some time in the summer or even the autumn is all they'll tell me."

Sam slid off the arm on to the sofa. "He won't get off, will he? I mean he won't get out and come after you again, will he?"

"No, he won't, Sam." She sat down next to him and rested her hand on his arm. "They've got loads of evidence against him. He'll be in prison for years, believe me." She gave his arm a squeeze. "You mustn't worry about it."

He sat quietly, looking down at the floor, so that his hair fell forward, screening his face from her. "Mum, I'm glad they found Dad's body," he said at last, and she saw his shoulders starting to shake. "I didn't like to think of him alone out there in the cold."

She put her arm around him, pulling him close, and held him tight.

Chapter 48
In Yelverton

That afternoon, the shadows from the larch trees were already beginning their slow push across the grass towards the driveway as Rachael watched the boys hurrying away to catch the bus. At the gate, Sam half-turned to give her a wave, but by the time she responded, they had both disappeared behind the tall cedar hedge.

She turned her face to the sun and closed her eyes, feeling the brightness on her lids and the soft moth of its warmth resting there. And, for a long while, she stood with her arms folded against her stomach, feeling their rise and fall to the steady rhythm of her own breathing and losing her thoughts in the garden's gentle rustling and the soft breeze against her skin.

When she heard the crunch of tyres on the gravel, even though she knew it would be Polly, she resented the tear in the web of her oneness with the world. As she forced her eyes open, it was as if she had stepped back into her own skin and became separated by it.

Polly got out of her car and walked towards her. "You look so peaceful standing there, I'm sorry to disturb you." The warm burr of her voice and the familiar solidity of her made Rachael realise how much she'd been missing her, without even knowing it.

"It's so lovely to see you," she said, opening her arms to embrace her. She sensed Polly's hesitation as she returned the hug, giving a quick squeeze, then releasing the pressure, ready to let go. But when Rachael maintained her hold, she felt Polly relax, as the hug became a shared one, their heads resting against each other.

"I feel very welcome," Polly said at last, stepping back to look at her. "You're crying, Rachael. What is it?"

Rachael smiled and wiped her cheeks with her fingertips. "It's nothing. It's been so long and so much has changed, that's all." She put her arm through Polly's and steered her to the front door.

But after she'd taken Polly's coat and led her through to the kitchen to make some tea, she started crying again. She was standing with her back to Polly, staring at the kettle, her palms resting against the edge of the worktop. "I'm sorry," she said, shaking her head. "I keep doing this."

Polly was sitting on a stool by the breakfast bar. "Talk to me, Rachael. Tell me what's been going on."

The kettle accelerated to a crescendo with a blast of steam, and then clicked off. Rachael poured the boiling water into the teapot and, replacing the lid, carried it to the tray, swirling it gently as she did so.

"Let's go through," she said, ushering Polly towards the living-room.

They settled close together, Polly on the sofa and Rachael at right angles in an armchair, the tea tray on the low table in front of them.

"Where to start," Rachael said and took a tissue from her sleeve to blow her nose. "It's seeing you," she went on. "The last time was at the Canteen, when Ollie was still alive, before Roger attacked us, before Ron was..." She hesitated. Was what?

"Found out?" Polly said.

"Yes, yes, before he was found out." She caught Polly's eye. "I'm so sorry about all of that. It must've been such a shock. After so many years, I can't imagine..."

"It's done now," Polly interrupted her. "I knew he was ambitious when I picked him. It was his energy that attracted me. But I didn't think he was dishonest." She looked down into the cup she was holding. "No, I didn't think that."

"He was mad," Rachael said. "Roger, I mean. After he'd smashed Oliver's head in and shoved him into the river, he said we could be together." Her voice came out croaky and she tried to clear it. "It's my fault, Polly. And Nick knows. I don't know how he knows. But he looks at me like...like he hates me. And I don't know what to do to make it right again. It can't ever be right again, can it? They'll never get their father back, will they?"

Her words hung in the air as she waited for Polly to say something. Eventually, Polly raised her eyes and seemed to study her. "You know," she said, "when our John was killed, I thought I'd never get over it." She paused. "But I did. I still think of him every day, but that's the point. I thought I'd lost him, but he's with me all the time."

Rachael stared at her in astonishment. "Polly, you never said..." She felt the blood flame in her cheeks. "I didn't know...I feel so..." She stumbled over the words, flustered and embarrassed, her own suffering somehow diminished by Polly's loss. "I didn't realise...I mean, what happened? No, I'm sorry...Sorry, I shouldn't have asked that."

"It's all right, lovely." The calm brown eyes engaged her steadily. "I don't talk about John much, only with family, and friends who knew him." A wry smile flickered at the corners of her mouth. "Bit of a scamp that one, like his dad at the same age. Was up to all sorts as a boy; but he'd say 'Sorry, Mum' and put his arms round my neck and hug me." She paused, her gaze momentarily veiled in the memory. "And then he'd just burst out laughing and I couldn't stay cross with him for two minutes."

Rachael thought Polly was going to continue but she didn't, settling back and becoming lost in her own thoughts, as the silence grew between them.

"Can I top you up?" Rachael said after a while, lifting the teapot.

"He was only 22, based at Bickleigh. In the Marines...you know. Be 29 now." Polly stopped again, and when she went on her tone was oddly dispassionate, as if reading a newspaper report. "He was on foot patrol...in Helmand..Lashkar Gar. The Taliban ambushed them...'sustained enemy fire'...." She shook her head and her voice softened. "All those young men," she said.

Rachael imagined Polly's son, in combat dress and armed, patrolling in the heat and dust of Afghanistan, but the face under the helmet was Nick's. She put down the pot and stood up. Circling the coffee table, she came round and sat next to Polly. To lose a son so far away from home and not be there to comfort him or to say goodbye, she felt the devastation of such an irredeemable loss. Never to see Sam again, never hear his voice again or feel the touch of him; her heart lurched with a dreadful ache of longing. The day would come. She would die and be lost to them forever, and they to her. In the uncleared ashes of the fireplace opposite, Oliver's seal head rose briefly from the swirling grey of the grate and disappeared again, merging into the dark, as before.

Gone. John and Ollie both gone, like her grandparents. Death had never seemed so real, so curiously dimensional. "Ancestors", she was thinking, "perhaps, they keep watch." She didn't believe in Heaven or God, didn't even know what they meant, not really. But this sense of there being something more to death than blankness comforted her and took the hollowness from the ache she was feeling.

Beside her, Polly stirred, patted her arm and smiled. "I'm all right," she said, and the present reasserted itself.

Rachael wanted to tell her what she'd just been thinking but a rational voice inside her put her off: "Our children can't become our ancestors, can they?" Some moment of communion, both within her and between them, seemed to have passed, and she felt awkward continuing to sit side-by-side, as if in a car together. "Life's cruel sometimes," she said, not knowing where the words had come from, and moved back to the armchair.

She saw Polly check her watch and she felt a momentary panic at the thought of her leaving, wondering how long they'd been sitting together in silence.

"Have you got to go?" she said.

"No, not yet. We're fine for another forty minutes or so. Ron's not expecting me till five."

"Oh, good!" said Rachael, relieved. She'd wanted to talk about her own troubles and to ask for advice but, aware now of the uncertainties facing Polly, of Ron's attempted suicide and the police proceedings against him, she felt the pain and pity of it. After all, she had wanted to be free of Oliver, whereas Polly loved Ron.

"I am glad he's okay," she said. "But what will you do if he goes...if he goes to prison?"

"It's not really a question of 'if', love, more of how long for. And the answer is: I'll wait for him. What else can I do? 'For better, for worse'; when I said it, I meant it."

Polly's calmness steadied her. If she was going to be okay in spite of everything, then so could she. Except that was about her spirit; what about the practical things, financial things?

"How will you manage?" she said.

"Pretty well, it seems."

Rachael was surprised and laughed in spite of herself. Ron was such a dominating presence, she had imagined Polly would be lost without him, and yet she seemed more solid than ever.

As if reading her thoughts, Polly said: "We don't need men as much as they like to think we do." She smiled and nodded, then added: "As much as we think we do."

Rachael thought of the ebb and flow of her own feelings, of the mornings when she woke and realised the day and her future were her own to shape as she pleased, when she felt optimistic and courageous and capable. But she also remembered the wakeful nights when her doubts pressed in around her, leaving her feeling weak and afraid, as if, like some towering wave, the weight of the world would crash over her, knock her down, suck her away and throw her back again, beaten and broken.

"But what will you do, Polly?" she said.

"I'll carry on. I've already started and it's not as difficult as I thought it would be." Polly put her cup back on the tray. "What I've discovered is I just need to trust my own judgment and act on it ..."

Trust my own judgment! Rachael's thoughts flew first to Roger, until a deeper memory erased him, one she had long prohibited in herself. Her stomach contracted and a burning rose in her throat. Oliver was waiting near the altar, his face turned towards her. She saw the sleek smugness of his smile over his carnation, of his hair combed back, and she knew she did not want to tie herself to him. But, as she faltered, her father's arm maintained its steady pressure, guiding her on up the aisle, past the smiling, approving faces turning to her row by row. No time to think. No time to say, 'Wait! I don't want this!" The vicar's eyes finding her, nodding, smiling, drawing her in like a magnet. She closed her eyes against her moment of capitulation, until Polly's voice drew her back to the fading shafts of light across the carpet.

"... when I first went into Jellop's to see what needed to be done, I felt overwhelmed. There seemed so much of it, so many people all asking questions or giving advice..."

Rachael poured some milk into her cup and took a swallow. She was nodding at Polly but her thoughts slid away again. If only she'd had the courage then to say, 'No!' Such a little word, but so powerful. How different...

"...right-hand man, Joe Pengelly, more or less patted me on the head..." Polly's rising indignation caught her attention again. "...told me to go home and not to worry my pretty little head; he'd take care of everything."

"He didn't!" Rachael found it hard to imagine anyone having the temerity to try to pat Polly on the head.

"Well, no, not literally. But that was his attitude."

"What did you do?"

"That's the point, Rachael. At first, I doubted myself, thought he was probably right, that I should just leave well alone. But once I got home, I thought, 'Come on, Ron's no genius, he just has ideas and sees them through. His authority comes from being decisive'. So, I decided that's what..."

But there would have been no Nick. Rachael leant forward, lowering the cup on to its saucer. No Sam.

"...by actually taking charge. And, besides, with Ron about to go to jail, what am I going to do, if I don't run the business? Don't you find that?"

She looked at Rachael, waiting for an answer.

"Sorry? Find what?"

"Now Oliver's not here to look after...you know, cooking, washing, being there, all the stuff we do...haven't you got empty days? Days with nothing in them?"

Rachael knew what she meant but she didn't want to admit to her lack of direction. It made her feel ashamed. Instead she said: "Oh, no! What with the boys being home and the funeral and everything, I've been up to my eyes in it." The lie made her feel worse and she looked away, wanting an escape from her discomfort. "So, have you started running the business?" She forced herself to look back.

"Yes. I go in every day at the moment, although once I feel everything's the way it should be, I'm going to cut back. I've got some other ideas I want to follow up."

"Have you?" Rachael said, shrinking inside. Beyond taking her A-level and moving, she had no idea what she was going to do. She couldn't tell anyone, not even Polly. She must be strong for the boys, protect them. "And how...how has Joe Pengelly and everyone reacted to your being there?"

"It's been a revelation," Polly said, sitting forward and resting her hand on Rachael's arm. The warmth of her touch was comforting. It seemed to break through her isolation and reconnect her. And the enthusiasm in Polly's expression was infectious; she found herself responding, wanting to know what had happened and feeling as if through Polly's story she might find her own way forward. "I went back the next morning and told Joe I'd be in Ron's office."

"What did he say?"

"Nothing. So that's what I did. I went through and sat behind his desk and realised that, as his wife and a director of the company, I was the boss; and that all I needed to do was to act like it."

"But how did people react to you telling them what to do?"

"I didn't. I don't. Not really. I'm more like a kind of co-ordinator. What I mean is everyone knows what their job is; the business has been going for years. All I have to do is make sure they have what they need."

"You make it sound so simple."

"Yes, well maybe I'm glossing over things a bit." Polly grimaced and settled back among the cushions. "Without going into all the details, I soon realised Joe was more of a hindrance than a help. Rather full of himself, lording it over the others, putting their backs up. So, I asked him to leave."

"Polly! You didn't! What happened?" Rachael was excited. "Surely you have to have a reason."

"I had a reason. Ron's an ideas man and he likes people. He likes talking and doing, and he's good at it. But he doesn't like paperwork, whereas I do. Well, to cut a long story short, I found Joe had been siphoning off building materials for his own use. So I pointed this out and he agreed to the terms I offered him."

"You mean he'd been stealing from the company?"

"Yes, in a word. Not a huge amount, not enough to be noticed anyway, but a regular little sideline."

"But wasn't he the foreman? I mean, supervising everyone and everything?" Rachael felt stunned. "God, Polly, to have the confidence, the courage, the...I don't know...the balls to do that!" And she sat staring at her friend, giving her head an occasional shake.

Polly laughed. "Turns out you don't need balls, actually," she said, "just determination and a clear idea of how you want things to be."

"And is everything going okay since you got rid of him?"

"Yes, fine. In fact, everyone seems happier. There used to be a sort of tension in the yard but that's gone. After Joe left, I made young Paul Davey foreman. He has an easy way with him and the others seem to respect him. And I've put Margaret, our bookkeeper, in charge of orders and deliveries. She's much better organised than Joe ever was. So, touch wood..." She tapped the table. "...everything seems to be running smoothly."

"And you? What do you do?"

"I just talk to people: clients, planning officers, the bank." She waved her hand in the air. "All that kind of stuff, you know."

"And you can deal with those kinds of people?" Rachael was intimidated by professionals, not as individuals but, in general, as superior intellects dealing with matters beyond her grasp. Polly's ability confused her. She had always felt comfortable with her, equal, as if they were on the same level, despite their age difference. "How do you manage? I wouldn't know what to do?"

"Yes you would. You'd be surprised. Besides, Ron's picked good advisers. Our solicitor, Emma Lemon, is very sharp and helpful. She's been absolutely brilliant. And so has Patrick, the accountant. They guide me along, stop me making a fool of myself." She paused and glanced at her watch. "But that's more than enough about me. I want to know how you are."

"Oh, I'm all right," Rachael said, unwilling now to reveal her own qualms and indecisiveness, her feebleness.

Polly raised an eyebrow and Rachael stared back, trying to brazen it out, her face growing hot. Oliver's trick of backing his lies with an affirmative nod, while looking you in the eye, came back to her. She could feel the stammer rising in her own throat, flooding her with a perverse affection.

"If there's anything I can do to help, you only have to ask, my love. You know that, don't you?" Polly covered her hand with her own. "We have to look out for one another now."

The warmth and tenderness were more than she could bear. Rachael squeezed her eyes tight against the tears but they escaped through her lashes and she swept at them angrily. She jumped up and strode to the far end of the room, looking out at the drive. She didn't want to talk about herself. She didn't want to think. She wanted Polly to put her arms around her and hold her and absolve her of the responsibility for herself. But it was impossible, she wasn't a child.

Eventually, she went back and sat down again. "Sorry," she said. She tried to smile, to feign composure. But, most of all, she wanted to push the spotlight away. "Do tell me about your other plans."

Polly's eyes searched hers, silently. Finally, she said: "When the boys have gone back, why don't you come over, spend some time with me? Stay for a little while, if you like."

Rachael nodded once and then a second time. "Yes. That'd be good." And, after a pause, she added: "Thank you, I'd like that."

After Polly had gone, she cleared away the tea things into the kitchen and started slicing onions, peppers and left-over bits for a stir fry to give the boys when they got back. The familiar rhythm of the task settled her and, as she curled her fingers over the vegetables and rocked the sharp little knife up and down, Polly's words floated in her mind and she spoke them aloud: "I just need to trust my own judgment and act accordingly." It wasn't quite right but it was something like that. By the time Nick and Sam returned, she had shaped the words into a mantra of her own: "Trust yourself; be decisive." Over and over she chanted it as she chopped the vegetables and prepared a salad.

Chapter 49
The next day

They were having breakfast when the phone rang. "I'll get it," Lou said and picked up the handset. "Lou Beradino."

Connie had stopped eating and was watching him.

"'Morning, Lou. Have you a moment?" He shook his head slowly at her and turned away.

"Yes, sir."

"Sorry to disturb you while you're on leave." There was a pause. Lou waited. He wanted Maynard off the line as quickly as possible. "Roger Millman hanged himself last night. I thought you should know."

He hadn't anticipated that but as Maynard told him the details the immediate compassion he felt was for the woman Millman had tried to kill.

"Has Rachael Drew been told?"

"Not yet. Fran's on her way in to see me but, apart from Macklin, you're the first to know."

"I'd like to be the one to break the news to her." He was thinking the shock of it might bring back the memories of both Millman's attacks on her full-force. "Reactions can be unpredictable."

"Very well, Lou. I understand. Liaise with Fran will you?"

"Of course. Is that all?"

"Yes, and quite enough. Nasty business, start to finish. At least the scoundrel did the decent thing in the end. Certainly saves us time and money." As Maynard went on speaking, Lou thought of the night of Oliver Drew's murder in Royal

William Yard and how close Millman had come to killing Rachael Drew. Twice! "You're back next week, aren't you?"

"Yes, I am; but I'd like to talk to you about holiday time I'm owed."

"I see. Better come and see me first thing. There's a lot to sort out."

They said their goodbyes and Lou went back to the table.

"She will be relieved now," Connie said after he'd told her what had happened. "She know he not coming after her any more." He took her hand and her cool fingers curled into his. She was quiet for a moment, then added: "But in her dreams, maybe he still there."

"Yes," he said and gave her hand a squeeze. He knew he couldn't protect her against Coaker, when he came for her in the night, but he hoped the trip home to her family might break the grip of her terror.

In the meantime, he needed to talk to Fran and Rachael Drew, but he also needed to keep the lines clear. He glanced at the clock on the mantelpiece. Connie extricated herself and began to clear the table. It was almost nine already. If Nicole Lanui had an early start, as she'd put it, perhaps he should call her, catch her before she went out.

He went back to the shelves where the phone was and fished a directory out from underneath but just as he flipped it open, the phone rang. He knew it would be her this time and he stood looking at the handset without picking it up, as its sharp demand repeatedly shattered the silence, until Connie's arm slid past him.

"Yes...yes, he is. Who is speaking, please?"

"Nicole Lanui," Connie said quietly, handing Lou the receiver.

"Hello. Ms Lanui?"

"Good morning, Inspector." Without the distraction of the sight of her, the foreign intonation of her voice was more apparent. He waited. "The light is bad at the moment, too much cloud. So I have postponed my appointment and, if you are free, we can have a coffee together and I will tell you what I know about Louis."

Excitement and dread rose in him together. "Thank you," he said and paused. He wanted to delay, to arrange to go to see Rachael Drew first, to hold himself apart from this woman, even though she might know where his father was. But he forced himself forward. "I'll be with you in fifteen minutes."

* * * * *

He was thinking of his mother as he walked into the hotel. It was more than forty-five years since that night at Woburn. She was married now, settled. Why stir things up again? Nicole's white hair stood out immediately. She was sitting where the card players had been. She saw him and waved, her silver bangle catching the light. He would hear what she had to say first. He could decide what to do about it afterwards.

"Inspector," she said. "I'm glad you could come." She stood to greet him and offered her hand. He took it; her grip was firm.

"Lou," he said. "I'm not here as a policeman. Please call me Lou."

"Nicole." She smiled, and he relaxed.

A waitress came and took their order.

"Well, Lou, I have a surprising story to tell you, perhaps, and I do so in confidence." Lou nodded. "Last night you were not willing to tell me why you are looking for Louis. I wonder if you could tell me now."

"It's a family matter, Nicole." She waited, expecting him to continue, but he decided not to say more.

"I see." She pursed her lips and studied him. "A family matter." The words hung in the air.

"What can you tell me about Louis Lanui?"

"Very well," she said, taking a deep breath and drawing herself up straighter in her chair. "I was born in Arcachon and grew up there. My mother died while I was at university and, afterwards, you could say I was a little lost, a little uncertain of who I was, if you like." She paused while the waitress served their coffees.

Lou was wondering if she could be Louis' sister, but there hadn't been a sister, had there?

"No problem," the waitress said in response to their thanks and turned away with her tray.

"Yes, it's true," Nicole continued, slowly stirring half a spoonful of sugar into her coffee. "Home, school, all that; it's your whole world. Then, suddenly, you are on your own and having to find your life. Many young people feel lost, I think, no?"

Lou nodded. "I felt like I'd walked off a cliff after university. I didn't know what I wanted to do...or be," he said.

"There you are. Exactly." She raised her hand in a gesture of acknowledgement. "I went from one thing to another; three months here, three months there. Even so, remember Paris in 1968?" She smiled. "Forgive me; you are too young, of course. '*Soyez réalistes, demandez l'impossible!*' and '*Sous les pavés, la plage!*' Ah! W*e* thought we could change the world!" She gave a short laugh and fell silent.

She was back among the barricades, he could see, back on the streets of the capital among the hundreds of thousands of students and workers threatening revolution. He had grown up with his mother's stories of the better world her generation had tried to create, determined amid the apocalyptic images from Vietnam to 'make love, not war'. How naive that all seemed now. Yet she still held firm to the values she had committed herself to then, still believed common humanity would prevail over...how did she put it?...'the rich and the greedy'...something like that.

"In the end, I went to India." Nicole's voice cut through his reverie. "From all over the world, young people followed 'the hippy trail' through Afghanistan to India. You have heard of this?" He nodded. "From everywhere, France, Germany, Sweden, America, Britain, all those hopeful young men and women looking for a better way...for something to make sense of their lives...looking for a spiritual connection, if you will. Australians, South Americans, Canadians." She seemed to run out of breath and shook her head. "So many people."

"And did you find what you were looking for?" He wanted to bring her back to Louis.

She looked up sharply. "Oh, yes. You see, what was missing in me was what was missing in the West. How shall I explain this? In India, in the East, there was a different culture. Despite the dreadful poverty...and I saw things there I had never imagined possible..." She paused, frowning at the memory of them, before continuing. "Even so, there was this shared belief in...how shall I put it?...the connectedness of all life, one could say...and in the moral order of 'karma'. You know what this is?" He nodded. "In some ways, it felt like coming home to me."

Lou shuffled his feet uneasily. "I don't want to seem rude, Nicole, but what has this got to do with Louis?"

"Everything!" she said.

It made no sense to him but it was clear she would tell it her way, or not at all.

"Okay. I don't understand but please go on."

"The way I think of it is a kind of shorthand..." She paused. "You know the Yin and the Yang, the feminine and masculine principles in Chinese philosophy?" Again, he nodded. "They are two equal parts of a circle, one dark, one light, and each contains the seed of the other. For me, the West was yang and the East yin. Both were out of balance and needed the other. When I saw that, I realised the same was true for me. That was why I had felt so...so..." She clapped her hands together, rocking forward. "So like an outsider in my own country. Yes, that's it. An outsider, you see. Someone who did not belong."

She was speaking more loudly and Lou could see her neck flushing. Wherever she was taking him, she was becoming more passionate about it, and he decided he would just let her continue without interruption. Something important was coming, it was obvious. Important to her, anyway.

"But not only on the outside, in my society; but also, inside myself I was not happy. I did not feel...right." She stressed the last word. "And then, in India, I understood. It was the same thing. To the world, I was yang with a yin seed. But to myself, I was yin with a yang seed."

She paused, as if for some signal that he was following her. But the implication of what she was saying had just detonated in his mind and stunned him.

"Bloody hell!" he said at last, as his thoughts reassembled. "You're Louis! That's what you're telling me, isn't it?"

His sudden leap disconcerted her and a flame of fear flared in her eyes, but was doused almost immediately by an icy defiance. "Yes, it is true. I realised I would be much more comfortable as a woman, that that was who I was, truly. So, after a while, I moved to a different ashram, changed my name to Nicole and started my life as a woman. But I needed a cover to fit the book, you understand?" She paused, watching him closely.

"Surgery," he said, needing the stark reality of the word to ground him.

She looked uncomfortable and her face reddened. "In effect, yes. But I could not get this in India and so, eventually, I went to California and found it there. That is my story. Now you know."

She picked up her cup and drank her coffee slowly. He watched her regaining her composure, fascination and revulsion churning inside him. This woman was his father. This woman was the man his mother had yearned for; the man he had spent his boyhood dreaming of finding for her, imagining her joy at being reunited with him. Him! But there hadn't been a 'him' to find. He was a 'she'. What would he tell her? Should he tell her anything at all?

"You seem shocked, Lou," she said. "It is not so uncommon these days, you know."

He thought of Fran. He had accepted her wish to change without question. Why should this be any different? Well, Fran wasn't his fucking father!

"You'll have to excuse me," he said. "You've taken me by surprise. I wasn't expecting this."

"Yes, I see it, and I am asking myself why my story has had such..."

But he wasn't listening. His mind was overwhelmed with its own torment. Christ, her genes were in him. Was that why he was throwing up his career? Did a part of him want to change, too? Bollocks! His line of work yes, not his gender. He wanted Connie and children. It wasn't the same thing.

"Lou?" Her fingers were resting on his arm. "Did you hear me?"

He flinched and regretted it. "Sorry, Nicole, I lost track. Please, what were you saying?"

She took her hand away. "I have told you about Louis. Now I need to know why you are looking for him."

He looked around, playing for time. Several tables were occupied and he hadn't even noticed the people coming in. He could make up a reason. She wouldn't need to know she had a son and that he was sitting opposite her right now. He could leave soon, say nothing to his mother or anyone else and go on as before. He needed time to think, to clear his head.

"Excuse me, Nicole." He stood up. "I need the bathroom. I'll be back in a moment." And he walked away, feeling an instant relief at being alone with his own thoughts.

Chapter 50
Nicole's surprise

By the time he got back to the table, their cups had been cleared and replaced by a bottle of sparkling water and two tumblers with ice and a slice of lemon in them. Nicole's was two-thirds full and his own, as yet, untouched.

He sat down and leaned forward to fill his glass. As he took a sip and settled back, he intended to conceal that he was her son by telling her the half-truth that he had been looking for 'Louis' on behalf of a relative. But, when their eyes met, he knew he wouldn't be able deceive her, even if he wanted to.

"You were right just now," he said, clearing his throat. "I was...I still am...shocked; and I think what I am going to tell you may shock you, too." An urge to protect her feelings swept through him; something instinctive, born of his own hurt. She had abandoned a mother and child without knowing it. She had missed so much; she would feel guilty for so much.

When he continued, Lou spoke slowly, searching for gentle words to break his news. "I wonder if you remember coming over here to the Woburn musical festival in 1968, in the summer."

Nicole brightened and there was new energy in her voice. "Ah, yes. It was exciting for me. It was my first time away from home." She was smiling but as she spoke he saw her smile eclipsed by the shadow of a frown. "But why are you asking me this?"

"Perhaps you can remember a young woman you met there. She was called Pru. No more than a girl really. Long dark hair, ninet..."

"Pru. Ah, yes, I remember her, of course. She was petite, but full of la joie de vivre. You understand? Full of the joy of being alive."

"Was she?" He thought back to his earliest memory of his mother and what he saw again was the sadness in her eyes and his longing for her happiness.

Maybe it was something in his tone, or simply her own delayed intuition, but he saw the light of understanding dawning in her eyes and the anger boiled up inside him again.

"It can't be true," she whispered, her mouth staying a little open, as her eyes searched his.

"Full of the joy of being alive!" he said. "Well, not afterwards, I can tell you! Heartbroken, more like! And it went on, L..o..u..i..s!" He lingered on the name. "It went on year after year. I was ten when she took me trudging the streets of Arcachon, looking for you! And it didn't stop there." The rage from bearing all those years of his mother's hurt and devotion overwhelmed him. "You screwed her and disappeared. No goodbye. No explanation. Nothing, apart from a meaningless note!"

The room was still. His words rang through the silence. People were staring, either at him or into their laps. He didn't care.

"Well, no, not nothing. You left her with something all right."

Despite the venom of his outburst, Nicole remained calm, with a quiet dignity, as if the mantle of compassion had been passed between them. "You are my son, Lou...Louis?" She said his full name softly as its significance hit her. "This is what you are telling me, no?"

He wanted to hit her. He wanted to hug her. He bit down hard.

"Yes. And you're my father — only you're not. You're my mother and I've already got one."

He wanted to hurt her. He wanted to disturb her self-possession, to tear her clothes, mess up her hair, smear her make-up, knock her off her high horse.

"I did wrong," she said, nodding her head. "Yes, yes. But I was young. I panicked. I had to go home the next day, you see. It was my mother's birthday and she was ill. My ticket...everything... was already arranged. When I woke up, Pru...your mother...she was still sleeping. I didn't have the courage to tell her. I...." She stopped speaking but did not look away from him. "I ran away, c'est ca."

"It's good to hear you admit it," he said, feeling angry still but no longer overcome by it.

She nodded but her eyes were slipping away from connection with him to some inner dialogue. Whether she was thinking about the revelation of her parenthood, or was lost among the memories of the music and tents of that long ago July, he didn't know. Probably it was a mixture of both. That information in the present could so alter one's perception of the past was alarming. It was as if the ground he had stood on had lost its solidity and become unstable; and how much more so must this be true for Nicole. He had known he had a missing parent, even if the genders had got mixed-up, whereas she'd had no inkling of being one.

When she spoke again, it was clear she'd been thinking of his outburst and of how her disappearance that day had affected his mother, and then him.

"I am very sorry, Lou, for the pain I caused your mother...and you." She was speaking slowly, as if weighing every word. "What a terrible father for you to have...or, not to have. I was so stupid." She paused. "But I have lost too, that is sure."

Lou looked past her to the bar. He wanted to leave. He wanted to get away from her.

"There's a lot to take in," he said at last. "I need some time to process all of this. Maybe you do too."

She nodded. "We both need a little space, I think. Nothing now is as it was. But Lou," she raised a finger in the air to emphasise her point, "I am very content to know the truth finally, in spite of everything. I want you to know this."

As he followed her towards the lobby, he heard her saying to herself, as if in disbelief: "I have a son. He is a police inspector. This is extraordinary."

She went out through the sliding doors and stood with him at the top of the short run of steps to the path. After a moment's awkward uncertainty, he held out his hand. She took it with a smile and, resting her free hand on his shoulder, she leant forward and kissed him lightly on both cheeks. He hadn't expected it.

"Let's meet again before you leave," he said, "to see...well, to see how we both feel about all of this."

"I take the ferry on Saturday morning. Perhaps we could have dinner together the night before. What do you think?"

"Friday? All right." He wondered about inviting her to Connie's. It would be easier, less intense, with someone-else there. But he'd have to check first. "I'll call you tomorrow evening, if that's okay, and fix a time then."

They agreed he would ring before seven o'clock, as she was meeting Molly and others for a meal after that. Walking away towards his car, he glanced back but the steps were empty. He turned his collar up; the morning air was sharp, even though the sky was clear. He wasn't sure if the hollowness he was feeling was due to having to leave his father so soon after finding him, or to the reality of her being so far removed from the picture he had carried of him in his imagination all his life. She wasn't a father, was she? Both his parents were women now. What did it matter? Mum would still be 'Mum'. Nicole would simply be 'Nicole'. Yes, but he'd always wanted a 'Dad'; and she was never going to be that.

He felt somehow wounded and in need of solace. He wanted to tell Connie what had happened and his mother too, although it might be better to leave her until after Friday. After all, what was the point of unsettling her if he and Nicole decided not to pursue their relationship? But most of all, he realised, he wanted to talk to Fran. Even thinking about doing so seemed to ease some of the tension he was feeling and make everything more normal again. This was her world; she'd help him get a grip on it.

Back in the comfort of his car, however, he knew his first responsibility was to contact Rachael Drew. He rang her. She would be home all morning, she told him, and he said he would come straight over. Twenty minutes later, he was turning off the Yelverton roundabout towards her house and dragging his thoughts back to the news he had to break to her. Surely, like Connie had suggested, she would be relieved to know she was safe from Millman, not only now but forever. "Even so," he grunted, turning in at the gates, "a shock can throw you."

Chapter 51
The forgiving

"He wasn't a bad man, Inspector," Rachael said, when Lou told her of Roger's suicide. It wasn't the reaction he'd anticipated. They were in the boys' 'den', as she had called it, a cosy room with two deep-cushioned sofas at right angles to one another, a wide flat-screen TV opposite and a couple of floor cushions in between, brightly coloured against the dark carpet. Just in front of the window, with its view out over the garden and driveway, were a square table and a couple of straight-back chairs at either end, where they were sitting. A shaft of sunlight cut a swathe across the oak top, casting its grain in amber.

"You're more forgiving than I would be," Lou said. He was struck by the change in her since the last time they had met. Always a striking woman, with her mane of honey-gold hair and hazel eyes, she seemed less uncertain than before and more substantial. Her figure was the same but the way she carried herself was different, somehow more solid and self-assured.

"Death gives a different perspective, I suppose," she said, looking out at the upper branches of the corner beech swaying against the pale sky. Roger had set her free in many ways. He had opened her mind to the prison she was trapped in; a jail not only of her father and Oliver's making and, beyond them, of society's too, but also a prison of her own acceptance of their patriarchal values. He had introduced her to writers whose stories and ideas had given her a different view, like a traveller abroad seeing their own country in a new light. He had helped her to see herself in relationship from without, rather than in isolation from within. And, not least, he had released her sexuality through his passionate tenderness and concern for her pleasure, giving her the sense of the joy her own body and fire could bring another. "It's not simple."

A blackbird swooped on to the lawn, its startling flash of yellow beak and eye grabbing her attention. Are you a messenger, she wondered, remembering Roger's own dark feathers and the silky feel of his chest. What did it mean to die? Where was he? Where was Ollie? Were they watching her even now? The blackbird hopped, stabbed at the grass, looked about, stabbed again and then, without warning, spread its wings and vanished.

Lou felt he had left enough time for her to absorb the news. He tried to gauge her reaction and thought she seemed calm. "Is there anything I can do for you, Mrs Drew?" he asked. She shook her head. "A friend or relative I could ring for you to come over?"

"No, I'm okay," she said, turning back to him. "But thank you." His concern seemed genuine and it was good of him to come out to give her the news personally. She didn't want to seem unappreciative. "I'm going to see Polly Jellop later on." He thought she had finished speaking but she added, as if to herself: "She's a good friend." She'd been looking forward to seeing Polly, only now she felt more like going for a walk on her own up on the moors. In spite of all that had happened, when she thought of Roger or Ollie it was with affection and a sense of sorrow at the waste of them.

Ollie had bullied her but she'd allowed it, hadn't she? She had abdicated responsibility for herself in exchange for his protection, she could see that now; and he was just a failed little boy, who wanted to impress and try to be Mr Big. Instead of standing up to him, she'd taken refuge in Roger's flattery and desire for her, when she had nothing to offer him, not just because she wasn't free, but also because she wasn't formed yet...not really...not on the inside. Going to college had been the first step towards herself, towards finding her own inner ground on which to stand. But she had fallen at the first hurdle, hadn't she? Repeating her pattern, she'd looked for validation of her *self* outside in the arms of another. And Roger was far worse than her in that respect. The hole inside him was so great he had needed total possession of her to fill it. She wasn't angry any more. What she felt towards them was sadness, not bitterness. She wouldn't let it happen again. She'd buy her own house, a safe home for the boys, and earn her own living. She'd establish her own independent life and think about any future relationships after that, not out of need but from a wish to share. "It's better to be two wholes than two halves," she said, "particularly when the two halves are missing the same bit."

Lou felt disconcerted. Rachael Drew was there in front of him and having...all right, a slow, but a meaningful conversation with him, nevertheless. And yet it felt like they were on two different trajectories and would never quite meet, like parallel lines. Perhaps she needed time alone. For all her apparent calm, his news must have had an impact.

"Good," he said and started to ease his chair back from the table. "If you're sure you're okay, I'll leave you in peace." He started to rise and then sat back down again. "There's one more thing I need to mention while I'm here. The criminal investigation into Roger Millman and the death of your husband will now be adjourned 'sine die', meaning without any date being set for its resumption."

"There'll be no trial you mean?" It hadn't occurred to her until this moment. Maybe the truth of her affair would not be made public after all and Nick and Sam would be saved from all that...she would be saved from all that.

"There'll be no trial, but there will still be the coroner's inquest to determine the cause of your husband's death."

The giddy lightness of relief that had flooded her gave way to a returning sense of foreboding. She wanted to ask him if the coroner would want to know about her affair with Roger.

As if reading her mind, Lou added: "The inquest's concern will be to establish whether there was a natural or an unlawful death. The factual evidence will show he was killed by Roger Millman."

"Does that mean the motive for his murder will not be part of it?"

He had been wrong; their parallel lines had met. She was fully focused on him now and waiting for his answer. He decided it would be no kindness to try to sugar-coat the pill.

"Mrs Drew, I am aware of your affair with Roger Millman. If you're asking me whether or not this will come out during the inquest, I'm afraid my answer is that it almost certainly will."

She breathed in deeply and tried to ride the wave of disappointment sweeping through her. But the weight of the anxiety she felt at the thought of Nick and Sam finding out the truth of their father's death was heavier now, for its having been lifted only a moment ago. She would have to tell them, and soon, before the inquest, before they read or heard about it somewhere else. She closed her eyes. Her head was hot and her stomach was churning. She tried to concentrate on her breathing. What was it...in to the count of four, out to the count of eight? She pursed her lips, breathing out.

Lou saw the distress in her. He thought of the inquest and the ordeal she would face, the exposure and the humiliation. But he knew her feelings of guilt would be the worst of it. The papers would play up the salacious details and there would be no protection for her sons. They would blame her, even despise her. They were too close to the fire and would be scorched by it. All they would see was the match in their mother's hand; they would have no sight of where the tinder had come from or who had placed it there.

Rachael opened her eyes again and the anguish he saw in them was the same as he had seen in Nicole's, the moment she had registered who he was and what that meant. Children couldn't see the context, only the close-up. By the time her sons understood and forgave her, the damage done might be irreparable. Was that true for him too? Now that he had a better understanding of his father's abandonment of him...and of his mother...could there be a future for his relationship with Nicole, even at this late stage? An image he'd long forgotten rose in his mind, like a fish being reeled in and up out of the water. He was standing in the dark passage of his grandparents' house, peering through the hinged crack of the door into the kitchen. His mother was sobbing into the shoulder of his grandmother, who had her arms around her. "Let go of him, my treasure, let him go..." she was saying, when he heard his grandfather's key in the door and scampered upstairs before Fabio came in. He couldn't have been more than five or six. He hadn't known who 'him' was, only that whoever it was had done something terrible to his mother. It was a picture that had haunted his childhood nights long afterwards. The injuries he was going to do that man! Better she was a woman...

"Are those tears?" Rachael wondered, struggling to contain her own. He must be more sensitive than she'd imagined. Well, she didn't want to deal with that now. "I'll be all right," she said, standing up.

At the front door, she held out her hand. "Thank you for coming..." She meant to add "and for your kindness" but, with the warmth of his hand in hers, she felt inhibited by the intimacy of it. Yet as she watched him turn and leave, she regretted not having said it and wished she had.

Part Four

Saturday, 2nd – Sunday, 10th May, 2015

Chapter 52
May morning

The sea and sky was a bowl of blue, with white sails scattered like paper litter across the bay in front of them. Sitting in the morning sunshine on the cafe's terrace, with the rocks below and the citadel rising behind them, Lou and Fran angled their chairs towards the water. Either side of the table between them stood bottles of pilsner and ginger beer, beads of condensation sparkling on their glass shoulders.

"When do you go?" Fran asked.

"A week tomorrow."

"Excited?"

There was a pause.

"Nervous, I think," said Lou.

She glanced at him and took a pull on her beer.

"Her parents, you mean?"

He nodded. "Silly, isn't it?"

The easy silence from before washed over them again. It was strange to think they weren't colleagues any more and he felt an unexpected urge to be back on a case with her. The door had been left open for him; but he knew it was just the appeal of the familiar. It would be easier once they were in Hong Kong and what came next had started.

"What about you?" he said. "Doesn't make any sense. You should've got it."

It did make sense and he knew perfectly well why; Maynard wasn't having a 'tranny' in charge of serious crime investigations on his patch. Female and black officers had been forced on him, but he wasn't about to promote sexual 'deviants'. He'd never admit it, of course, but if Fran hadn't

321

changed gender 'he' would be a DI by now. Instead, Maynard had made an external appointment: white, male.

"Let down," Fran said, "but not surprised." Hearing the weariness in her voice, he felt a sudden guilt at leaving.

"How do you cope with it?" he asked.

"I don't. Not really." She looked at him. "I get angry, but what's the use? I wasn't allowed to compete in Kazan at the Europeans last month. That hurt more than not making DI."

"Didn't I read somewhere that transgender athletes have been okayed for the Olympics?"

Fran snorted. "We're talking BJC, not IOC. They'll catch up. Just hope I'm still up to it when they do."

It didn't matter what gender she was, there was a resilience and determination about her that had appealed to him from the start. He was fond of her and he was going to miss her.

"Makes everything twice as hard for you, doesn't it?"

"Three times! One extra for changing and one more for being a woman."

A young couple at the table next to them pushed back their chairs, the metal feet scraping on the stone slabs. Lou watched them move off towards the steps, the mother carrying the toddler, the father following and towing a collapsed stroller behind him. He was wondering if this was a snapshot of his future when a squall of small birds blew in around the deserted plates, their pneumatic beaks claiming every crumb, and drew him back into the moment. At the approach of a waitress, the birds rose as one and vanished on the air like sea spray.

"Makes me realise how tough things may have been for Nicole," he said.

"You letting her into your life?" Fran's small, dark eyes were fixed on him.

Lou picked up his bottle and took a couple of swigs. There was a time when personal questions would have been out of bounds; just some kind of tacitly acknowledged boundary they didn't cross. Where did he want to go with this? He wasn't sure. Who do you hold on to? Who do you let go? He lowered the bottle, bouncing it on his thigh and feeling the chill of it through his jeans.

"Yes, I am." You too, he thought.

"Great," she said and a transforming smile flashed across her face and was gone.

"No choice, really. 'Nessuna scelta', as Fabio used to say." Lou gave a little laugh and added, "Usually when my grandmother asked him to do something he wasn't keen on."

She raised an eyebrow, waiting.

"Mum and Don invited Nicole to Leicester and..."

"Hey! How did that go?" Using her feet, Fran shunted her chair round to face him more directly.

"Okay, as far as I can tell. That is, they've arranged a return visit to her place. Don seems to have taken to her; he's into photography and she's going..."

"Yeah, but what about your mother? I mean, how did she deal with it?"

He put his beer back on the table and followed a pair of kayaks snaking their way past the bulge of the lido. He'd broken the news to his mother over the telephone. There'd been a long silence, which had left him feeling he should have followed his first impulse to drive up and tell her face-to-face. But eventually she'd said, "I have to see him" and then corrected herself; "I have to see her." She'd asked him for Nicole's number and that had been that.

After the visit, she called him. He expected her to be upset but she wasn't. "It's resolved," was what she said. "After forty-seven years, it's resolved; and now you have both your parents." Her voice wavered then but her relief and happiness were plain to him.

"Mum's okay," Lou said and half-stood to turn his chair in towards Fran. "After all those years of not knowing and wondering, she has the answers at last. And it has..." He searched for the right word. "Settled her. Yes, at some deep level she's calmer than I've ever seen her. Most of my life, she was like a boat riding a rough sea, struggling to stay afloat. After she married Don, it was much better, but still choppy at times. Whereas now it feels quite different; like one of those yachts." He pointed out into the bay, where several sailing boats were slipping easily through the water, sails filled and the sea placid. "She's not struggling any more."

"That's great, Lou!" Fran said. "It must be such a weight off your mind." And something in the warmth of her tone and understanding caught him unawares so that he had to swallow hard to maintain his composure. "Guess it makes things easier for you with Nicole too, right?"

He cleared his throat. "Yes it does, although since that first meal together, before she went home, we've got along okay. It'll take time though; we've no history together yet. Even so, I think we all feel naturally tied in now." After a pause, he added: "Funny how quickly wounds start to heal once they're clean."

"Yeah. And talking of tied-in, did you hear Molly's going over to France, too? She and Nicole are cooking something up for the gay pride event in Sitges, near where she lives. Kate and I got an invite as well."

"You going?"

Fran coloured. "We'll see."

Lou knew Kate and Fran were old friends but he'd never thought of it being more than that. Maybe the feelings were one-way. What did he know? Fran's love life wasn't something he'd thought about. She'd always seemed so self-contained; he couldn't imagine her as part of a couple. But, then, what about himself? A year ago, he was a career bachelor. How quickly meeting Connie had changed all of that.

It seemed strange that he knew Fran so little in some ways and so well in others. It was as if rank had divided the professional from the private. There were times they had depended on each other for their lives, and yet here they were, with this unspoken awkwardness between them. If they weren't colleagues any more, what were they? Now, facing each other so directly, the longer the silence lasted, the more uncomfortable it was becoming. Fran had finished her drink and was twiddling the bottle, resting her eyes on it, as he was. They glanced up together and their eyes met. He must say something.

"I'm glad you suggested this." He didn't know how to continue. Was this their own goodbye? Or were they just going to leave things hanging, with a 'see you' and a handshake? He didn't want that. He felt like saying, "I'm going to miss you," and giving her a hug. Why did that seem so impossible? Besides, it would mean he was saying goodbye to her. He saw she was waiting for him to go on. "I was thinking," he said, hoping the words would come, "maybe..."

She interrupted him. "Are we going to go on being friends, Lou? I need to know. You've always backed me and I trust you, but there's a hole now you've gone."

Her gaze was unflinching and he felt embarrassed by her declaration. "Sure," he laughed. "Of course." He picked up his bottle and raised it towards her, before finishing it off. "Just one thing, though," he said, putting it down again.

"What's that?"

"Whatever comes next, no notebook, okay?"

A faint smile creased the corners of her mouth but something in her eyes withdrew from him. His joke was a defensive parry, warding off emotional contact. He hadn't met her, hadn't risked anything of himself, and she knew it.

"I'm sorry, Fran, that was stupid," he said. "I'm going to miss working with you, too." He let the words hang in the air for a moment before adding: "But look, like Connie says, rivers bend, so let's just change course and carry on. Tell you what, when we get back from Hong Kong, come round for a meal. We can catch up and take it from there."

"That'd be good," she said. She held up her bottle. "Your round."

Chapter 53
Oliver's affairs

Rachael followed the traffic down Outland Road towards the city centre. She glanced at the dashboard. It was 9.47am and her appointment was for ten. The 30mph flow came to a dead stop at four different sets of lights before she was able to turn off just before the football stadium, home to Plymouth Argyle, and wind her way round the back to the offices of Neville & Brewster Solicitors.

Even so, she still had two minutes to spare as she pushed through the front door of the converted semi-detached house and checked in at reception. Taking off her jacket, no sooner had she sat down in the waiting area than a door to her left opened and a lean, middle-aged man advanced towards her.

"Mrs Drew, good morning." He held out his hand and she rose to shake it. It was warm and firm. "Gordon Brewster. Please, follow me. We're on the first floor."

The passage and staircase were thickly carpeted, and a window halfway up, where the stairs turned back on themselves, flooded the space with light. The building felt comfortable and well-maintained. It reassured her.

"Here we are," he said, ushering her into a spacious room with a generous bay window overlooking the garden. He guided her to a chair in front of his desk and sat facing her on the other side, with the window behind him. "Would you like some tea or coffee?"

"No thank you," she said. She was anxious to find out about the state of Oliver's affairs and didn't want the awkwardness of cups and drinking while talking. "The truth is, Mr Brewster, I need to know what my position is financially, and I'm hoping you may be able to tell me."

"Yes, of course. But first I would like you to know how very sorry I am that your husband has died so tragically. It must be a hard blow indeed for you and your boys to recover from."

"Thank you," she said. "I appreciate that. Everything is quite confusing at the moment and it's difficult for me to plan ahead when I don't know exactly what our situation is."

"Very well, let me tell you what I can." He opened the manila file in front of him and spread the two top sheets side by side. He scanned them briefly and sat back. "At this stage, I can only give you a preliminary outline of your husband's estate and, to be frank, Oliver's business arrangements are more complex than I had anticipated. There are business interests in France and holding companies with off-shore bank accounts, in which I was not involved. Obtaining the release of the relevant information from such banks is often a lengthy process. They are fiercely protective of the confidentiality of any data relating to their clients' accounts, which is as it should be. Also, French commercial law differs from ours. All of which means that probate will not be straightforward, I'm afraid, and will take some time to complete."

There was something in the sincerity of Gordon Brewster's steady eye-contact and tone of voice that settled Rachael's anxiety, even though she realised she was not going to get the clear picture she had hoped for.

"I see. I knew about the chateau in France but not about the off-shore accounts. Trust Ollie to make things complicated. Well, I won't pretend I'm not disappointed. There's very little money left in our joint account and I'm going to have to rely on the life insurance money coming through to survive. That doesn't have to wait for probate, does it?"

"No, it doesn't. Happily, as long as you are clearly established as the beneficiary of that policy and there is no suspicion of Oliver being complicit in his own murder, if you will forgive me for putting it so baldly, you should receive payment without any delay. Have you notified them and submitted your claim?"

"Yes, I have."

"Good, good. And you enclosed the death certificate?

"Yes."

"Then you should receive settlement almost by return." He smiled and she felt lighter. "About £115,000, I calculate, according to the policy's terms."

"That's a great relief," she said. "I wasn't sure how we would cope otherwise."

"This must be a most disorienting time for you," he said, "with so much to absorb and sort out. If I may presume to offer some advice, I would like to urge you take things as slowly as you can afford to until things are clearer." He tapped the papers in front of him with his forefinger. "And not to take any major decisions for the time being, such as selling your house or moving your sons from the school they presently go to."

Rachael felt irritated; she didn't want to be told what to do. At the same time, she was surprised by his mentioning exactly the two steps she was planning to take.

"Unfortunately, Mr Brewster, decisions have to be made sooner, rather than later. Until I know my position with regard to what I will or will not receive from Oliver's estate, I do not know whether we must downsize and live more carefully or not. What I do know is that the boys' school fees are huge and I may not be able to afford to go on sending even one of them there. That's why I've asked to see you. Can you give me some idea of what I may expect once probate is finished?"

"I understand your concern, believe me, and I will tell you what I can." He moved forward in his chair to look again at the details in front of him. She saw the little shake of his head and grimace of concern just before he looked back at her again. "Looking at the information we have so far, the situation does not seem promising."

Rachael felt it like a punch. The pit of her stomach contracted, as if winded, and she couldn't breathe. She had always known Oliver was a wheeler-dealer, operating close to the line, but with all the properties he had in Plymouth and his various business interests, she had been sure there would be a significant sum left once everything had been wound up. She didn't want it for herself; she wanted it for the boys, for their security and futures.

"I don't understand," she said. "Our house in Yelverton is worth well over a half-a-million pounds, according to our local estate agent, and there are the other commercial properties here in Plymouth, as well as the chateau. They must be worth a considerable amount, surely?"

"This is a shock for you and I'm sorry to be the bearer of bad news," Gordon Brewster said. "The truth is that it seems Oliver financed his various ventures by borrowing heavily against existing assets, the banks concerned taking second and third charges on the freehold properties, including your house."

"No!" she shouted in alarm. "He can't have done that, surely? He never told me. You must be wrong. You must be." She glared at him, her face aflame and her eyes wide in desperation.

He nodded gently, his eyes never leaving hers.

"He can't have." She faltered, bowing her head.

He lifted the receiver to his right and spoke quietly. "Please could you bring us some tea? Thank you."

Rachael's thoughts were whirling, like leaves in a gale, and she struggled to get hold of them. Nick would be destroyed if he had to change school...she'd have to sell the house and buy another...but she'd never get a mortgage, she had no job yet...maybe, Ollie's parents would pay for

Nick...maybe, Polly could give her a job, if she asked her...but how was she going to go to university now?...Thank God that Sam was already in a local school, as he'd wanted...Would her parents help her? She'd never asked them for anything before...perhaps things would turn out to be better than it seemed...this was only a rough outline, wasn't it?...Wasn't that what he'd said?...But Nick would be so angry...how would she ever get close to him again?...And what about the off-shore bank accounts?...He might have thousands stashed there...hundreds of thousands maybe...But what if the debts to the banks come to more?...What if they want to take the house?

"Thank you, Heather," she heard him say and looked up to find a stout woman setting a tray down on the desk. Her glasses on a lanyard swung out as she bent forward.

"There you are," she said with a warm smile towards Rachael, who flickered one of her own in return.

Rachael, taking a tissue from her pocket, heard the door close softly behind her. As she wiped her eyes and blew her nose, she realized these were no longer tears of self-pity or despair, but of exasperation at the stupidity of Oliver's game of Russian roulette with all of their futures. She watched Gordon Brewster pour two cups from the pot, leaving her to add the milk and sugar as she wanted. She was grateful to him for his thoughtfulness and for the time he was allowing her to recover, in the comforting space of his silence. But she didn't need it. She was feeling energized by her anger, knowing that whatever came next was down to her and that she could and would make a life for herself and the boys, a life of her own choosing.

"I hadn't expected things to be so bad," she said, adding, as the resolve hardened in her: "But we will survive."

"The final picture isn't clear yet," he responded. "Until it is, at the risk of repeating myself, I advise you to take no irrevocable decisions yet. The life insurance payment will cover your expenses during probate and for some time after, no doubt. By that time, matters may well have taken on a more manageable and hopeful appearance."

The reasonable tone and message of his words affirmed the growing sense of her own capability; and Polly's words came back to her: "We don't need men as much as we think we do."

"Thank you," she said. "I'm very grateful to you for being so kind and...well, understanding. And you're right, I don't need to panic yet, I can see that. We still have the house and now that my younger son, Sam, has chosen to go to school locally, the fees will be half what they were."

"Ah," Gordon Brewster said. "I hadn't realised that. You say 'chose'. Was he unhappy where he was?"

"Always. He always hated boarding school. He's a very different sort of character from Nick, who absolutely loves it there. But Oliver insisted. 'Give him some steel', he used to say. But I always thought it was doing more harm than good, and he's so much happier being at home and going where he is now."

"I see. Well, that sounds like one irrevocable decision that was well worth making." He laughed, clearly happy to mock himself, and she liked him all the better for it.

When they parted down in the waiting area, from where he had first collected her, they shook hands warmly.

"Thank you very much, Mr Brewster," she started but he interrupted her. "Gordon, please."

"Thank you very much, Gordon, then." She felt oddly embarrassed and wondered whether she should tell him to call her Rachael. Instead she said, "I am glad it's you who's sorting these things out." She gave a little laugh. "Ollie made one good decision, at least."

He didn't smile back but nodded at her with a gravity that acknowledged the seriousness of what she had just said. "As soon as I have more certain news for you, I will be in touch.

In the meantime, if you have any questions or need to discuss any of these matters further, please let me know."

As she drove back to Yelverton, even though the news of Oliver's affairs had turned out to be so dire, at a deep level she realised she was feeling calmer about the future than she had been. There was something staunch about Gordon Brewster that inspired confidence and she was already thinking of him as her ally. She was not alone; she had Polly and she had him. She and Sam would be all right. As for Nick, she'd just have to give him time.

Chapter 54
Hong Kong

It was a little after midday, local time, when Cathay Pacific flight CX238 landed at Hong Kong Airport. Immigration and baggage reclaim went smoothly and as they emerged into the arrivals hall, Lou was relieved to see a sign with his name on it. He raised his hand in acknowledgment and a round-faced man, who was holding it, moved towards them.

Once relieved of their cases and installed in the back of the Marco Polo Hotel limousine, Lou sat back, letting go of the tensions of the flight and listening to Connie answering the driver's questions in Cantonese. He had never heard her in full flow before and he enjoyed the musicality of it: the alien rhythm of her intonation, with a note held somewhere in the back of her throat before the release of the next flurry of dipping and flying birdwords. He took her hand and held it. This was her home, this was where she had grown up. He stared out of the window at the unfamiliar landscape, eager to establish a sense of the place, but the multiple road signs and lanes of traffic were the same as from a dozen other airports he'd been through. Only the place names, repeated in Chinese characters, marked a difference as they flashed by...Lantau...Kowloon...W Hong Kong.

"My parents lived there," Connie said, leaning across him and pointing out of his window, "when I was little, till four or five maybe." They were passing what looked like a major container terminal, with giant cranes and looming gantries blocking out the hills behind. For a moment he was confused and then he saw the narrow channels of high-rise apartment blocks at the far end, dark and cheerless. "Public housing," she said.

* * * * *

After a shower, Lou lay on the bed in one of the hotel's white bathrobes, watching Connie unpack. She seemed okay. She had handled the flight much more calmly than he'd expected. After her experience with Coaker, he'd worried about how she might react to being confined in a small space for twelve hours, much of it in the dark. But once she had finished the meal provided after take-off, she had tipped her seat back and slept most of the rest of the way.

As she dipped towards the drawer again with a small pile of clothing, her dark hair fell forward, masking her profile. When she straightened and turned back for more clothes, her eyes caught his.

"What?" she asked. "Why you looking at me?"

"I like looking at you," he laughed, and held out his hand. She moved round the end of the bed to take it and sat down on the edge beside him. "What's it like to be home?" he asked.

"This isn't home," she said, with a sweep of her arm. "This is luxury hotel room. Bigger than my parents' whole apartment probably. Yes, I think so."

He gave her hand a squeeze. "You know what I mean."

She looked down at him and became thoughtful. After a pause, she said: "I'm happy I see my parents now. I thought I might not see them again. But I worry a little bit too."

"What about?"

"I want you all like each other, like I do."

"Why wouldn't we? We all love you."

She took her hand away and looked down at her lap. "It's not so simple, Lou. My parents always are hoping I get married here. Grandchildren very important for them. I marry you, we live in England and they are far away, live a different life. Maybe they not want me to marry you."

He heard the sadness in her voice and recognised the reality of what she was saying. Closing his eyes for a moment, he felt the loose swaying of his body, as if he was still flying and not yet landed. What answer could he give? Everything was so uncertain. All the pieces in the frame of his life had been altered. And yet, at the core of him, he felt more settled, more solid, than he could remember.

He stretched up and pulled her down towards him, rolling her carefully over on to the bed beside him, so that her head was on the pillow next to his and their faces close together. He leant forward and kissed the lids of her eyes.

"We'll make it work somehow," he said. "We'll come here to see them and they can stay with us whenever they want to."

* * * * *

It was late afternoon by the time they left the hotel and as they walked towards the mall with the underground, Lou found himself constantly stepping off the kerb on to the street to avoid the weight of people streaming against him. He wasn't sure if they were shoppers or commuters. At home, he could read a crowd, but not here. Instinctively he moved his wallet from his hip pocket to one at the front, where it would be less vulnerable, and tapped the cargo pocket by his thigh. The answering stiffness of his passport reassured him. He smiled at his own uncertainty and gladly followed Connie as she negotiated the ticket dispenser and led him on to the train.

During the journey, he thought about their plans and how best to present them to her parents. According to Connie, they had been shocked and confused when she told them he was resigning and why. "They don't understand why you want to give up your job to be a father. They say good father need good job to take care of family." Of course, they were right, but it was more complicated than that, not only because Connie had a 'good job' herself but also because the quality of all their lives would be better, assuming the Centre proved successful. They'd live near the beach and he'd be working normal hours. There'd be no more callouts in the middle of the night, no more weekends lost chasing crooks like Jellop and Coaker.

There were risks attached and certainly a DI's salary was a lot more dependable than a self-employed one, but he'd known Ralph Tanner since the summer he'd bought the bungalow, and he'd seen Ralph prosper since then, as the Wembury Surf & Sailing Centre established itself. That's why Ralph had offered him the partnership. He needed an injection of capital to improve the facilities and upgrade the equipment. But, more than that, he needed another pair of hands he could trust to help with the social programmes he was running. There was no reason why the Centre shouldn't continue to flourish.

"What you thinking about, Lou?" Connie's hand was on his arm and her shoulder bumped against him as the train stopped. The doors were opening, with people jostling to get out.

"Is this us?" he said, shifting his weight forward, ready to stand up.

"No, not this one." She held on to his arm. "Next one, Kwai Hing."

He settled back again. "I was just wondering how best to explain to your mum and dad about the Centre...how best to convince them what a good, healthy life we're going to have there."

"Dad okay maybe; he's not so serious as my mum. You will see. She thinks being a policeman is being a good person, like being a teacher or doctor. You make valuable contribution to society." Connie laughed. "Sailing and surfing she thinks just having good time, like dancing, not proper work."

"Does she know about the youth work Ralph's involved in there? It's not just holidaymakers and weekenders, you know. He's changing some of those kids' lives around."

336

"I told her this, but she say..."

"Those Hawkins twins, for example," he interrupted her, incensed at her mother's criticism. "Remember them? They were a two-man...well, a two-boy crime wave around Stoke: truanting, vandalism, burglary, you name it. But now all their energy's going into surfing and competing. Do you know that police call-outs to Stoke went down by something like sixty per cent after they started at Ralph's? If that's not a valuable sociable contribution, I don't know what is! Tell your mum about that."

"You can," Connie said, pulling away from him. "No good shouting at me."

"I'm not shouting," he said, struggling to stifle his anger. It wasn't her fault, he knew that.

"Come on, Connie," he said, wanting to put things right between them, but before he could continue the train shot into the bright blur of the station and she stood up.

"We get off here," she said, already moving away from him.

As they emerged from the underground, he was struck by how much darker the day had gown. Heavy cloud now covered all but a low wedge of sky and he could smell the rain in the air. Connie was hurrying across the plaza towards a minibus on the far side and he quickened his pace to catch up with her.

"I'm sorry," he said as he reached her. She was waiting to board behind an elderly man, whose head was so bowed it was invisible above his narrow, stooped shoulders. "I didn't mean to take it out on you."

Supporting the man's elbow, Connie helped him on to the bus, then paid the driver and found them the last two seats together towards the back.

"Long journey, we both tired," she said, holding on to the seat in front of her as the minibus pulled away. "When we eat, we feel better." She smiled at him. "My mother very good cook, you see."

The tension in him eased and he sat quietly, looking out of the window. He was hungry, he realised, but for the moment he felt content to be sitting comfortably with nothing asked of him. At one point, between the distant screen of hills, he thought he glimpsed the silver metal of the sea and a dark armada of other islands massing further out. But they were instantly replaced by a copse of high-rise apartments, growing larger and more defined as the bus wound its way towards them, the towers of glass and concrete gradually extinguishing the dark green shawl of vegetation behind.

* * * * *

As they took the lift thirty-nine floors up, his earlier sense of anxiety returned. Meeting her parents for the first time was going to be awkward. It wasn't just that they spoke little English, while he understood no Chinese at all, but more that, without the title and prestige of being a senior detective, how could he reassure them he would be a good husband for Connie and a good father for their grandchildren?

The lift opened on to an empty corridor. Faded green doors with black numerals stretched away on either side. Connie paused in front of number 16 and shifted the strap of her bag higher up her shoulder. She rang the bell.

A woman, taller than he had expected, lean and wearing glasses, opened the door and beckoned them in. He recognised her from the photograph on Connie's bedside table, as he did the pot-bellied man with broad shoulders who rose to greet them from a small sofa by the window behind her.

There were smiles, handshakes and a rapid crossfire of excited Chinese as Lou was swept into the small living room and Connie was embraced first by her father and then by her mother: "Ah Ba!" she cried; "Ah Ma!". "Meilin!" her father said, holding her close, before releasing her to her mother, who clung to her. It was the first time he had heard her called by her birth name.

Here she was with her family, Meilin Wu, the Chinese woman he was going to marry, when she would become Connie Beradino. He didn't want that; he didn't want that at all. He wanted her to go on being Meilin Wu forever and to go on being rare and exotic. And he realised this foreignness and unknownness in her was what had drawn him to her, as if she called out to some unrecognised part of him that wanted to come into being. This was why he was here.

"Ah Ba, Ah Ma," Connie said, linking her arm through theirs on either side of her, so that all three were facing him. "This is Lou..."

THE END

About the author

Charles Becker has worked as a wine merchant, English teacher and university student counsellor. He has three children and four grandchildren and lives with his partner in Plymouth, Devon. This is his first novel.

Acknowledgements

I want to thank my treasured partner, Jenny Strang, for all her encouragement and patient feedback, draft after draft; and, so too, the members of the Plymouth Writers Group for their support. Also, I want to thank Jim Bruce of *www.ebooklover.co.uk* for his professional and invaluable help in preparing this manuscript for publication. And, finally, I want to acknowledge the inspirational setting of Royal William Yard and the Ocean City of Plymouth, without which this book would not exist.

Special mention

There is no fruit without first a plant, its roots and the seed it came from. Without the love of my children, Keats, Mo and Lucy, their mother, Suzy, and their own children, Reece, Oscar, Noah & Hannah, my wish to write might have withered along the way.

Printed in Great Britain
by Amazon